SPACE FORCE

ALSO BY JEREMY ROBINSON

Standalone Novels
The Didymus Contingency
Raising The Past
Beneath
Antarktos Rising
Kronos
Refuge
Xom-B
Flood Rising
MirrorWorld
Apocalypse Machine
Unity
The Distance
Infinite
Forbidden Island
The Divide
The Others
Space Force
Alter (coming soon)
Flux (coming soon)

Post-Apocalyptic Sci-Fi
Hunger
Feast
Viking Tomorrow

Horror Novels
(written as Jeremy Bishop)
Torment
The Sentinel
The Raven

Nemesis Saga Novels
Island 731
Project Nemesis
Project Maigo
Project 731
Project Hyperion
Project Legion

The Antarktos Saga
The Last Hunter – Descent
The Last Hunter – Pursuit
The Last Hunter – Ascent
The Last Hunter – Lament
The Last Hunter – Onslaught
The Last Hunter – Collected
Edition
The Last Valkyrie

SecondWorld Novels
SecondWorld
Nazi Hunter: Atlantis
(aka: *I Am Cowboy*)

Short Story Collection
Insomnia

Comic Books
Project Nemesis
Island 731
Godzilla: Rage Across Time

ALSO BY JEREMY ROBINSON

The Jack Sigler/Chess Team Thrillers
Prime
Pulse
Instinct
Threshold
Ragnarok
Omega
Savage
Cannibal
Empire
Kingdom (coming soon)

Chesspocalypse Novellas
Callsign: King
Callsign: Queen
Callsign: Rook
Callsign: King 2 – Underworld
Callsign: Bishop
Callsign: Knight
Callsign: Deep Blue
Callsign: King 3 – Blackout

Chesspocalypse Collections
Callsign: King – The Brainstorm Trilogy
Callsign – Doubleshot
Callsign – Tripleshot

Jack Sigler/Chess Team Universe Guidebook
Endgame

Cerberus Group Novels
Herculean
Helios

Jack Sigler Continuum Novels
Guardian
Patriot
Centurion

Humor Books
The Ninja's Path: Inspirational Sayings for the Silent Assassin (by Kutyuso Deep)
The Zombie's Way: Words of Wisdom for the Recently Undead (by Ike Onsoomyu)

Non-Fiction
The Screenplay Workbook: The Writing Before the Writing

Anthologies with Robinson Stories
Kaiju Rising: Age of Monsters
V-Wars: Night Terrors
SNAFU: Survival of the Fittest
MECH: Age of Steel
Fearful Fathoms II
Predator: If It Bleeds
Joe Ledger: Unstoppable
Kaiju Rising II (coming soon)

SPACE FORCE

JEREMY ROBINSON

BREAKNECK MEDIA

For Neil 'DatAss' Tyson.
(Loretta insisted.)

1

STONE

"If you're going to ruin someone's life, do it on a Wednesday. The difference from other days of the week is subtle, like real maple syrup from a tree and Aunt Jemima. Both are sweet, improving the flavor of a warmed-up circle of batter, but one is corn-syrupy swamp mud and the other tastes like the transmogrified body of Jesus probably should.

"There are three things you should know about me, all of which could have been inferred from the previous, but I'm not sure you're intelligent, so here's the breakdown. I'm Canadian, I'm no longer Catholic, and you don't want to cross my path on a Wednesday.

"Because you've 'survived' the first two days of the week pushing papers or data from one place to another. You're cradling the fledgling hope that comes from Thursday, nursing it into a robust Friday that delivers a more mature expectation for the coming weekend and the fleeting taste of freedom it brings.

"But me, on a Wednesday, I will abort your zygote hope with a single sentence. Or a word.

"Because I know you. And there is nothing—not even Aunt Jemima's unholy liquid horseshit—worse than being exposed for who and what you really are: a..."

"A what?" Hale asks.

"That's all I got." I say. "Wasn't sure how nasty I wanted to get."

Hale stares at me. "I'm pretty sure whatever name you decide to call them won't be as harsh as aborting zygote hope. Bonus points for the vivid imagery, though."

I shrug. "I got 'A's in English."

Hale adjusts our pitch, bringing us closer to the docking bay of Alpha Station, AKA the International Space Station. "Teacher wasn't big on subtlety?"

I check my Rapid Fire Taser's charge, ensuring the weapon is ready to go. Our little how-do-you-do at the ISS isn't scheduled, and might not be welcome. Since projectile weapons in space are a big freakin' no-no, the RFT—capable of dropping a dozen enemy combatants in seconds—gets the job done. With enough juice, a single target could be cooked from the inside out, but the kill setting is reserved for war time...which this is not...and never has been.

Because space is *not* a war fighting domain.

"You think it's over the top," I say.

"The word 'overkill' comes to mind," Hale says.

"Everything about us is overkill. It's how I think now. It's in my damn blood."

"It was a robo-call." Hale smiles, adjusting the controls, preparing to dock. "Thirty seconds."

I unbuckle and head for the rear hatch, which will open like a giant sphincter and drop the human deuce that is me into the shitter that is Alpha Station. I suppose that's harsh, too. The ISS has been a beacon of international cooperation and scientific research, even while the rest of the world bitches about who won the Eurovision competition and Americans say, 'What the fuck is Eurovision?' But after twenty-five years without fresh air or a can of Febreze, I can't imagine it smells any better than King Kong's dingleberries. "They called at *three in the morning*. Every day this week."

"Do you even know where to send your e-mail?" Hale asks.

"Not yet."

"So it's just catharsis."

"First of all, my therapist calls it 'therapeutic verbal cleansing.' Second, I'm going to use my Dick to hunt them down, knock on their door, and verbally cleanse all over their faces."

My Dick isn't my actual dick...or a person. The D.I.C. (Defense Initiative Computer) was named by a gray-haired conservative who I suppose didn't bother saying the acronym aloud. Each member of Space Force has their very own Dick. Even the ladies. And most of us have etched a K into the Comic Sans logo emblazoned on the keyboards. Seriously. Comic-freaking-Sans. When the higher-ups discovered the team's graffiti, we claimed the K was for 'keyboard' and feigned ignorance about what it spelled. Maybe the guy who named the computers actually had a good sense of humor?

Hadn't considered that before...

"Ten seconds," Hale says. "Sounds like your therapist has her hands full."

"Had. It was a long time ago. And she *definitely* had her hands full."

Hale glances at me through her helmet visor. "You didn't?"

"How do you think I landed this shit post?" I stand by the door, weapon shouldered. For a moment, I'm transported to a time when I was the best at what I did. Seal Team Six. A real badass mo-fo, especially for a maple tree-humping Cannuck...at heart. I was raised in Vancouver, but I was born in the United States. So while I identify as a Canadian, I'm legally a 'Murican citizen. After a drawn out fire-fight in Syria left two men dead and me a little shaken, General McNasty—can't remember his real name—required me to attend three therapy sessions. What he didn't tell me was that my therapist would be smoking hot—and his daughter. If I'd bothered to remember the general's last name, I probably wouldn't be here now.

Probably.

Maybe.

It wasn't until after our third session ended atop her desk, theatrically cleared off—because who hasn't wanted to do that?—that we learned our sessions were being recorded for evaluation...

And now I have two great regrets: the end of my Seal Team career... and not getting a copy of that video.

Upon being reassigned to Space Force, I was given a commission and found my responsibilities growing—much to McNasty's chagrin, I'm sure. Nearly everyone else was discharged for a variety of reasons that never seemed to land a reticle on me. So now I'm Mission Commander at a Captain's rank, which is fun to say, but doesn't really mean much when there are no missions to command.

The *Rex*, officially named the *T-1-Rex*, the United States' first and only space fighter, bumps to a stop and is followed by the repetitive thump of seals engaging and the hiss of the airlock pressurizing. When I first heard the fighter's name, I asked, 'Do you need small hands to fly this thing?' No one laughed. It was awkward.

"Let's make it official," I say, chuckling to myself about the seals engaging, their flippers bitch-slapping each other into submission.

"Space Force Command, this is Strike Team Zed. We are in position and ready to breach. Stone is requesting green light for go. Over."

Hale gets a reply a moment later. "Strike Team *Alpha*, please use your official designation, and repeat request. Over."

"Are you serious?" Hale asks. While technically, we *are* Strike Team Alpha, we prefer to use Strike Team Zed, as in Zero, because we're the *only* strike team in Space Force. There's just the two of us, and Hale is a woman.

"No offense," I say.

"What?"

"Never mind."

She's a top-notch pilot, and unlike the majority of Space Force, she actually requested her transfer from the Air Force, and turned down an offer from NASA. While she takes her job a bit more seriously than I do, I find her wit amusing, except when it's turned toward me. She can whittle a person down to a stub like a verbal Jeffrey Dahmer. Her native Hawaiian looks distract from the emotional pain she's capable of inflicting, but I'd never tell her that, lest I be subjected to physical pain.

"Follow protocol or be grounded. Over." The voice on the other end of this conversation belongs to Billy. That's right, he's a grown man who demands to be called 'Billy,' despite having the perfectly respectable name of William Forte. Turns out he'd rather have a dumb sounding name than share a moniker with an actor who tends to play unintelligent characters...despite *The Last Man on Earth* being one of the best shows ever made. Billy could use a callsign, or just go by just his last name, but nope. Billy.

He's on the team because the bug that crawled up his ass gave birth to a xenomorph that's been dancing a jig on his colon since before he was born. His anal-retentive tendencies rub a lot of people the wrong way, including Hale.

Hale sighs. "Space Command, this is Strike Team Eat a Dick, requesting permission to get all up in this biznatch." She gives me a wink. "Over."

The line goes silent.

I smile, picturing Billy's red face. He's probably broken out in a sweat and is now tugging at his Ron Swanson 'stache like he does when people vex him. My smile fades in a flash of compassion. Billy's a good guy. He's loyal to the team no matter what, despite his threat to have us grounded. He's just wired differently.

Billy comes back on the line. "Hale..."

"For the last time, it's pronounced Ha-lay." She toggles off the mic. "Stupid mainlander."

"Hey," I protest.

"Stay out of it."

I raise my hands in submission.

"Apologies for misspeaking," Billy says. "Again. But my request stands, and time is running out."

She rolls her eyes. "Fine... Space Command, this is Strike Team *Alpha*, requesting permission to breach Alpha Station." She toggles the mic off again. "Ugh, you see what he does to me? Alpha twice in one sentence."

"That's bad writing," I say. "Mrs. Decker would not approve."

"Who?"

"English professor."

Hale stares at me for a moment, and then switches on the mic. "Over."

After a brief delay, Billy's voice returns. "Copy that, Strike Team Alpha. You are green for breach. I repeat, green for breach. Mission is a go. Over."

"Hard copy, Space Command, over and out." She turns to me. "You want company on this one?"

"Why not," I say. "You're just my pilot. Won't matter if you get killed."

She pushes up from her seat and joins me by the airlock hatch. I look at her empty hands. "You gonna just point your fingers and say 'pew, pew, pew?'"

"You know I don't like guns," she says, which is Hale's way of reminding me that she's an ace in space, but also skilled in hand-to-hand combat. I want to point out that all the kung-fu in the world won't help her against a ranged weapon, but she'd probably just kick me in the nuts and finish the breach solo.

Instead, I say, "It's not a gun. It's a taser."

"It has a trigger and shoots stuff."

"Stuff? They're *electrodes*."

She launches a raised eyebrow into the orbit of her forehead. "You want to find out what it feels like to be shot by that thing?"

I say nothing. To do so would be to invite a wrath that makes Khan's look downright tame.

She yanks the lever to open the airlock. Eight segments separate, sliding away—it really does look like a robot's asshole—revealing an empty airlock, which was expected.

It's always empty.

"Ladies first?" I ask.

"I'm not being your human shield."

"Yeah, they might flick paperclips at us. I hear they can be dangerous in Zero-Gs." I step ahead and clutch the lever to open the second hatch, giving us access to Alpha Station.

"Why would they have paperclips on the ISS?"

"For paper," I say. "Duh."

"Why would they have *paper* on the ISS?"

"Paper airplanes, obviously." I pull the lever. "For fun." I mimic throwing an imaginary plane, whistling as I point out its path through the airlock.

"Uh, Stone?"

The plane's whistling path fizzles out. "What?"

She points into the ISS. "That."

When I look forward, all of my good-natured fun disappears faster than the airplane's flight came to an end. Two men dressed in Chinese battle gear have their weapons leveled at us. I can't ID the rifles, but I have no doubt they fire projectiles, which again—big no-no in space.

I slowly wrap my finger around the RFT's trigger, hoping no one will notice. I lowered it during our conversation, but I'm a quick draw. A full spray from the hip will take care of these bozos. I just need to keep them distracted long enough.

"Seriously?" I ask. "If you fire those things up here, you'll kill us all. This is hardly realistic."

In reply, the two men pull their triggers.

The last thing I see before falling back are explosions of red covering Hale's body, and then my own.

2

HALE

I was a late bloomer. Didn't grow boobs until age sixteen, but when I did, they were hard not to notice. That changed when I discovered sports bras—thank you, oh wise creator of spandex—but I suffered a few years of gawking from the opposite sex. I don't blame guys. They're hard-wired to drool at curvy objects, and, well, let's be honest, I have nice boobs. But this one dude, Bret Brigham, got his mental wires crossed and assumed that because he was infatuated with my chest, that I wouldn't mind his fingers on my body.

One day, at lunch, he feigned tripping into me. Got his grope on, and a swift punch to the chin for it. He retaliated by weaponizing a bottle of ketchup, firing beams of red on my chest with laser-like accuracy. The kids watching stopped laughing when I flipped Bret over my back and stomped on—and broke—his bottle-wielding fingers.

That was nearly twenty years ago. I'm far more stable now.

Mostly. Sort of.

"You've got to be kidding," I say, sitting up after being driven to the floor like a one-legged flamingo, who's just had his leg swept by Johnny from Cobra Kai. My irritation is fueled, in part, by embarrassment. At having been ambushed and not seeing it coming. But I'm also pissed about being a giant freaking mess. "Paint balls? Each of these suits costs a half million to produce. More if you include the cost of R&D."

Stone sits up beside me, smearing his hand across his facemask to clear the paint. He looks down at his space suit—officially called 'cosmic armor.' I shit you not. We just call them space suits, but that doesn't change the price tag.

"Ugh..." Stone raises his red arms. "I look like a tampon."

I backhand his shoulder, glad that my visor is still partially obscured by paint. If he sees my smile, he'll just be encouraged...as will the two buffoons standing over us with the paintball guns. While they've all resigned themselves to our crumbling situation, and the likely end of their careers, I'm still hoping my track record will let me move onward and upward at NASA. Getting reprimanded for a space suit that looks like a...a tampon...isn't going to help.

"Gotta have a little fun on the sinking ship, right?" The deep voice belongs to Frank Taylor. He's a former Army Ranger and Stone's BFF. When they're not beefing up their arms or at the shooting range, they're playing multi-player video games and shouting at strangers around the world. On the surface, they're very different. Stone is an athletic, trim white man. Taylor is black, a foot taller, with muscles the size of Stone's head, and his job is less glamorous—security. Like everyone here but me, he was sent to Space Force for upsetting some-one somewhere. In Taylor's case, he disobeyed a direct order, saved a bunch of lives, and rather than getting a medal, he got swept under the rug. His lax behavior stems from disenchantment more than actual douchebagery, so I'll forgive him this trespass.

His partner on the other hand... Nick Quaid. He's an engineer, and I suppose he's a good one, but his personality prevents me from clicking 'Like.' He's got a thin, blond mustache to boot, and that's just creepy, like the kind of guy you wouldn't want your daughter hanging around in the 1970s. A less handsome Matthew McConaughey from *Dazed and Confused.* The southern accent doesn't help any...though I suppose on a kind and handsome man it might be charming. God damn, why couldn't Quaid be Matthew McConaughey?

The worst part about Quaid's 'stache is that it inspired Billy's. Billy looked almost innocent before, and now he looks like a young Wilford Brimley who's seen some shit. Honestly, what's the deal with mustaches? The only thing 'Movember' does for me is make me want to hide in a closet full of stuffed animals and flowers. All to raise awareness for men's health, or something. Like women don't hear the moaning and groaning of every man suffering from a cold or an ingrown nail. Poor babies. I'm not unsympathetic to sick people—men, women, or whatever else people identify as these days—but a mustache is more likely to make me reach for my mace than to ask why a man decided it would be cool to look like a child abductor for a month.

I might have issues.

Let's pretend I don't.

"Ya'll look like dipshits," Quaid says. "That's what you look like."

"So much more descriptive," I grumble, climbing to my feet and removing my soiled helmet.

"I know, right?" Stone says. "It's like he doesn't even try. Use a metaphor every now and again. Sheesh."

Quaid waves us off. He's not big on words.

Taylor offers his meaty, gloved hand to Stone and pulls him up.

"Chivalry *isn't* dead," I comment.

"Bros before—"

I point a finger at Taylor. "Don't finish that sentence."

I put up with a lot, but I'm not going to be relegated to the 'hos' category, when I am capable of kicking just about any ass on base. I didn't fight my way out of Hawaiian poverty—sometimes with my knuckles, becoming a fifth-degree black belt in Shaolin Kung-Fu, and rising through the Air Force ranks—to be disrespected. Only Stone can get away with speaking to me like that, and that's only because I give it to him worse.

"Sorry," Taylor says, but then he shrugs. "You would have called me sexist for offering."

I meet his earnest eyes with a squinty glare. Then I let him off the hook with a grin. "You're right. You passed the test."

"That was a test?" Taylor asks.

"Every time one of you opens your mouth around me, it's a test."

"Speaking of tests," Quaid says. "Ya'll failed big time."

"Like it matters," Stone says, helmet under his arm. He pushes past Quaid, out of the very *still-on-Earth* simulator, and onto the ramp leading down to the training center's floor. His feet echo in the vast space designed to train hundreds of men and women, but which currently contains just the four of us. "No one is keeping track. No one cares. Not anymore."

"Pretty sure they never did," I say.

Taylor tilts his head in agreement. "You did."

"Pretty sure Billy is keeping track," Quaid says.

"Affirmative," Billy's voice says from the intercom system. "That was one of your more spectacular failures, Stone, but far worse is the breach of protocol carried out by Quaid and Taylor. Where did you get those weapons?"

"They ain't weapons," Quaid says. "Not really."

"'Not really,' is hardly a defense," Billy says. "Did you kill that man? No...well, not really. Pff."

"Just having a little fun while we can, Billy," Taylor says. "Nothing wrong with that."

"There's a *lot* wrong with that," Billy says. "But this is all beside the point. Our current interaction is not social. I simply wanted to inform you that Colonel Lauren Jones was on her way down."

Stone and I look at each other, eyes going wide as we look at the state of our space suits.

"You've got to be shitting me." Despite Stone's lax behavior, he's a soldier at heart, and getting caught red-suited by the Colonel is not something he will enjoy. For me, it's worse. He has a future in the private sector, while my experience as a fighter jet pilot, and *Rex* pilot, over-qualifies me for most jobs. There's no way I'm spending six hours at a time cooped up in the cockpit of a civilian airline with some weird co-pilot who bites his nails, smells of Jōvan Musk, and is named Steve. Or Mike, or Dan, or some other piloty sounding name.

"Go!" I say, motioning him toward the locker room. "Hurry!"

In general, space suits are not made for running. But our cosmic armor is fairly form-fitting and flexible. Exposed to the vacuum of space, it will pressurize and expand. Under normal circumstances, it fits more like body armor, hence the embarrassing name.

We blaze a trail past rows of lockers that had once been filled. Men and women shared the space for one year, and then most of them were gone, along with the president who funded all this. Turns out his vision wasn't exactly shared by the Pentagon, and the moment they had the freedom to act, they carved down our budget and transferred most everyone away. Space Force shrank as fast as it grew, like a geriatric erection.

I inwardly cringe at the image.

"She's coming!" Taylor whispers from the door.

I shove Stone into the nearest shower stall, follow him in, and yank the curtain shut behind us.

"There're easier ways to get me in the show—"

"I'm looking for Captain Stone." It's the Colonel.

I twist on the water, dousing us in a frigid stream.

Stone does a little jig, mouthing, "Cold! Cold! Cold!" But he doesn't blow our cover by jumping out. As a Seal, he endured far worse, including cold water training. He can handle a cold shower, and probably needs one.

He settles down when the water warms. "In here, Colonel. You don't mind if I salute behind the curtain, do you?"

His humor is lost on her, but I can't help but smile. For a moment, we stare into each other's eyes, water dripping over our heads, streams of red flowing down the drain.

Before it gets weird, the Colonel says, "Please don't. Is First Lieutenant Hale available?"

I cringe when even my superior mispronounces my last name. How many times have I corrected her? Apparently not enough. When I tense up, Stone puts a hand on my shoulder to keep me quiet.

"It's Hale," he says, pronouncing it correctly, "and I haven't seen her recently. I think she said something about waxing her—"

I stomp on his foot, silencing his comment and forcing him to clench his teeth.

"Are you all right, Captain?"

"Dropped the soap," he says. "Keep Quaid away from the stall while I retrieve it."

"Hey," Quaid says. "I ain't no—"

Stone clears his throat. "Colonel, to what do we owe the honor of your presence in the locker room?"

"I would prefer to deliver this news in a more formal manner, but in my experience, expediency is preferable to formality. I trust you will update Hale and Forte—"

"He prefers Billy," Quaid says.

"Dude," Taylor says. "Shut-up."

The seriousness in the big man's voice is disconcerting. The Colonel is hard to read, so the news must be bad enough for Taylor to sense.

"I will make this short and as painless as possible. Then I will retire to my quarters, where I will not be disturbed for the remainder of our time here."

"Remainder of our time?" Stone asks.

"Congress just voted," she says. "Space Force has been defunded and disbanded. To recover some of the nation's financial losses, Space Force assets will be divided between the Air Force and NASA. Starting tomorrow."

Anger wells up in my chest. My fists clench with enough force to split an atom. I left the Air Force for this. I gave up NASA. I believed in Space Force, gave everything to my country, and now they just swoop in and take it all away, dooming me to a life with Steve the pilot?

"Sonuvabitch!"

My eyes widen in shock.

And then the curtain is yanked open, exposing Stone and me, holding on to each other, dressed in space suits, soaking wet. At least the paint is gone...

The Colonel eyes us up and down. Her blue uniform and bunned hair are impeccable as always. But a frown and a furrowed brow mar her normally calm face. She takes a deep breath and sighs, letting it out slowly. Then she looks at Stone, and says, "Be sure to wear your helmet," and yanks the curtain shut.

3

STONE

The mix of emotions churning through me is confusing, mostly because they have nothing to do with me, and everything to do with Hale. I've long since resigned myself to the inevitability of this moment. I have a plan in place. Already have a position with a reputable merc outfit lined up. But Hale's desire to leave Earth's orbit has not yet been satiated, and until it is, she's not going to be happy. And strangely enough, for all our ribbing and antagonizing, that matters to me. A lot.

When she leans back against the shower wall, expression numb with shock, I'm propelled into action. When I shove and stumble through the curtain in a wet space suit, I'm propelled to the floor. "Colonel," I call out, but she's already gone. I peel the wet space suit off in pieces, helped by a silent Taylor.

"Damnit," I grumble, sluicing out of the suit like a cold, rotten banana squeezed from the bottom. "Damnit."

I kick out of the pant legs, my ass cold on the floor. Still dressed in a wet one-piece flight suit emblazoned with the Space Force logo, I lunge to pursue the Colonel, but I slip and fall again. I peel off my damp socks, find traction on the floor, and shove off.

By the time I reach the locker room exit, the door at the far side of the training center is already swinging shut. I sprint the distance, moving faster than I have in a long time. The doors open outward, spilling into a long hallway, a second set of doors, and then the circular parking lot around which the Space Force buildings were constructed in record time. From above, the base vaguely resembles a power switch, with the lone entry road extending out over a long bridge connecting us to North Carolina's mainland. The whole base was built on Portsmouth Island, filled in and expanded to fit Space Force's sudden and 'yuge' needs. I heard once that it was supposed to resemble Atlantis, which it does.

When the parking lot is full, the rings of cars form the city's inner circles. But now, with the lot mostly empty, it just looks like a round hand extending a middle finger toward the solar system.

If I plow through the double doors, I should be able to catch the Colonel in the parking lot, before she has a chance to retreat to her quarters and lock the door. I extend my hands slightly, bracing for the impact.

A second before impact, I spot a shadow through the door's small window. Realizing what's about to happen, I attempt to put on the brakes, but it's impossible. All I can do is mentally groan at what might be one of the worst mistakes of my life.

I see it play out in my mind's eye. The door slamming open, propelled by my weight and speed. The Colonel's five-foot-tall, lithe frame, being catapulted into the wall. Maybe *through* the wall. If I don't spend time in Leavenworth it will be a miracle.

My hands hit first, but instead of the door giving way, my arms do, folding inward. I barely have time to register the oddity when my face collides head-on with solid metal. All of the force I feared would turn the Colonel into a projectile is reflected by the unmoving door, knocking me back like a young Mike Tyson caught me with an uppercut.

Laid out on my back, I stare at the ceiling, fifty feet overhead. *How much money did they put into this place?* I wonder, while my senses slowly return. *Too much,* I decide, and I push myself up. I blink my eyes and freeze when I see the disappointed gaze of the Colonel watching me through the window.

When she slides away, I get to my feet, stagger a few steps, and then more carefully push through the door. "Colonel."

The hallway on the far side is empty.

How the hell did she do that? It's a good twenty-five feet to the next doors, and another twenty-five to the exit. "She's a damn cheetah..."

"Ahem." I turn and flinch when I find her standing beside me. "Good to see getting knocked on your ass hasn't affected your situational awareness."

Her sarcasm is odd, like a stranger has just walked up and started tickling my ass cheeks. Unwelcome and unnatural. In all the time I've known her, she's been a straight-laced professional.

"Colonel," I say again, pushing past her out-of-character behavior. "What's going to happen?"

"I'm assuming you'll take a high-paying, private-sector job," she says. "Congrats."

"Not me," I say. "Hale."

She eyes me for a moment, reevaluating. "You care about her."

It wasn't a question, but I say, "Uh, I suppose..."

She rolls her eyes, very un-Colonel-like. "Grow a pair, will you?" She leans against the wall, digs into her pocket, and retrieves a pack of cigarettes and a lighter. When I flinch at the sight of them, she says, "Fuck you," and lights up.

A long cloud of smoke flows from her nostrils, making her look more like a dragon than I ever imagined possible. "Like the rest of us, she's going to be discharged."

When I start to object, she holds up her hand. "Unlike the rest of us, who will be generally discharged, she will be *honorably* discharged. It's the best I could manage for the only person here who actually gave a damn."

While I'm tempted to keep my attention on Hale, a detail from her statement jumps out at me. "The rest of *us?*"

"We're all here for a reason," she says. "Stepped on someone's toes, slept with someone's daughter, disobeyed an order. To the former president, Space Force was a gleaming beacon of superiority and a distraction from the shitstorm surrounding him. To the rest of the military, it was a laughable joke. And then it became a kind of purgatory for the problematic deplorables. That's you. And that's me."

I don't bother arguing. Her past is a mystery to me, but I can't deny being steeped in shit. "She deserves better."

"Hale is tainted goods," she says. "From hanging around with the likes of you. No offense."

She takes a long drag from her cigarette, flicks it to the floor, and crushes it underfoot. "But mostly it's because she makes poor choices."

"I get it," I say. "I suck balls."

"You might suck balls. I'm not privy to your private affairs. But what I meant is this: she *chose* to be the butt of a joke, and all this time she was unaware of it. Her naïveté to the reality of Space Force isn't commendable, and it's not something anyone wants on their team. She sealed her fate the moment she jumped on a sinking ship while singing Kumbaya and drinking the Kool-Aid labeled 'End of Career-Aid'...or something."

I'm staggered by her lack of decorum. I'm not offended by it, just caught off guard. She's been putting on an act this whole time. Had she been herself, I might have actually liked her.

"Colonel—"

"Lauren," she says. "Or Jones, if you must. My duties finished the moment I informed you all of your fate. This time tomorrow, we'll both be civilians."

I fall into a trance-like silence. This is the most real any higher officer has acted in my presence. It's unnerving and refreshing.

"Look," Jones says. "You're not a bad guy. She could do worse. But you're not doing her any favors."

"To be clear, we're talking about Hale, right?"

"Who else would we be talking about?"

I make an executive decision to not tell her about my Amazon Echo with a cutout of Olivia Munn dressed as Psylocke taped to it. I've never been more interested in hearing the weather. "Right. Sorry."

"The point is, the best thing you can do for her, is to stop being her friend, or whatever it is you two think you are."

"Friends," I say, eyes on the floor. "Still."

"Good. Then maybe she'll be able to dig herself out of this hole." She looks around her like she can see the whole 300-acre base. "She'll smell like shit, but if she starts making good choices, she might clean up well enough."

"Well enough for what?" I ask.

She shrugs. "UPS? Fed-Ex? It's a living, isn't it?"

Not for Hale it isn't.

Anything short of her dreams is defeat.

"I suggest you spend the rest of your day packing," she says.

"And then?"

"Carpe diem," she says, "for tomorrow we leave."

With that, she plants her foot against the door and gives me a smile. "We really are a bunch of fuck-ups, aren't we?"

I hear footfalls approaching on the far side of the door, and I manage to look through the glass in time to see Quaid charging toward it like a freight train, which he's prone to do thanks to an excess of energy—or energy drinks. One of the two. He does pee a lot, though.

The door shakes from an impact, Jones's wedged foot enough to keep it closed.

"You're lucky that wasn't Taylor," I tell her, and I look through the window, smiling when I see Quaid laid out, possibly unconscious. In the background, Taylor watches, chuckling. Behind him, Hale walks toward the exit on the training center's far side, head down.

Just let her go, I tell myself, trying to heed Jones's advice.

"Have a nice life, soldier," Jones says, already halfway to the exit. "Try not to get anyone killed." She pushes the door open and exits in the glowing white light of day. I turn back to the training center in time to see the door close behind Hale, maybe for the last time.

4

HALE

The women's barracks was never overpopulated. It was built to house two hundred women, but Space Force, at its short-lived pinnacle, only employed fifty women. That's been whittled down to two, not including the Colonel, who resides in a separate building, on her own, like she's Quasimodo sans the bell-tower and the hunchback. I know she's just being anti-social on account of not wanting to be here, like everyone else on this damn base. Had even a handful of them seen the real potential Space Force presented, we might still be funded, might still be pushing the envelope of what is and isn't possible.

Instead, we'll go our separate ways and live mediocre lives.

While my mind and language are often filthy, I believe in a higher power, and I don't think She'd want us to accept mediocrity. I don't mean that everyone needs to dream of space, or scientific breakthroughs, or changing the whole world. Just that everyone should do what they love and do it as best they can. Whether you're surfing, teaching, or collecting trash—and want to be—hold your head high and kick ass.

Despite this positive outlook, I've yet to consider what I would do if my dreams were suddenly unattainable. The reality of this situation has left me shaken.

I sit on my perfectly made bed, looking at the room's meager décor. I've got a photo of my parents on the desk, but the walls are free of art—or any kind of personal self-expression. The closest thing I have to decoration is an American flag pen resting on my desk, beside a pad of paper and a tablet, laid out in neat order like I'm Billy. Really, I just wanted to impress anyone who might inspect the barracks.

Now I know that there was nothing I could do to avoid this fate. You can't organize shit nuggets and make people want to step in them.

The worst part is that while everyone else saw and smelled steaming feces, I saw a deep-fried Snickers bar covered in hot fudge—the chance of a lifetime.

The ever-present voice of positivity inside me says to buck up, that employers will clamor to hire someone with a track record like mine. I was the *only* female pilot in Space Force. Within a year, I would have piloted the *Rex* into orbit.

Freaking orbit.

"Goddamnit!" I shout, and then I perform a perfect spinning hook kick that decimates my wooden desk chair, embedding the top half in the wall. Chest heaving with anger, I stare at the chair and reel in the raw power that broke its body...and will, seeing it as a metaphor for myself.

Feeling meta, I sit on my bed, cross my legs in a lotus position, and close my eyes. After several deep belly breaths, I start to relax. My mind moves to the past, to simpler times studying Shaolin techniques. I would wake early, join my class on Kalihiwai's Anini beach, and then spend an hour surfing. Despite having been based on Portsmouth Island for three years, surrounded by sandy beaches, I have yet to repeat that morning ritual.

Have I lost myself? I wonder. *Am I blinded by ambition?*

These questions, and all my anger, begin to drift away as I visualize negative energy flowing out of my body. Shaolin Kung-Fu is often about controlling emotions, about releasing or repurposing that energy. Recently, I've dealt with stress by adopting Stone's sarcasm, which is admittedly fun, and a more aggressive outlook on physical confrontation. My sensei would not approve. Then again, if the entire Kung-Fu world saw him as the butt of a joke, he might be a little pissy, too.

The others think I'm naïve. That I don't see it. But I watch the news. I know what people think. I follow poll results. I see the Daily Show jokes. Trevor Noah is a bitch-ass punk, but he's not wrong. And...fine, I watch every day, but I stream that shit online and skip the commercials.

Deep breaths, I think, trying to let my anger drift away, but it just keeps on coming, bubbling to the surface like the perpetually erupting volcano expanding the borders of my home state. I count to ten as I breathe in, and then ten again as I breathe out. Focused on the numbers, my anxious thoughts drift away. Tension melts from my muscles.

This is what I need, I decide in a moment of clarity.

Kung-fu is my future. I can go home. Open a dojo. Be Mr. Miyagi to someone too young to recognize my face from Trevor Noah's damn Space Force parody, where I was played by Ronny freaking Chieng, who is both a man and Malaysian, which is insulting on so many levels. The man thinks he can say anything because he has pinchable cheeks and an adorable accent. It's infuriating. I'm at *least* an Olivia Munn...if she'd stuck around for more than a few episodes. We have vaguely similar features. My forehead scrunches as I remember how Stone decorated his Echo...

Breathe, damn you.

In for ten seconds, out for ten seconds.

In for ten seconds, out for ten seconds.

In for ten seconds...

A gentle knock on the door is followed by a subtle pressure shift as someone opens it uninvited.

"WHAT?" I shout.

I open my eyes to find a stunned Maggie Chieng, wide-eyed and biting her lower lip. I suppose we're friends. Being the only two women left on the team, we kind of have to be, but I can tell she's perpetually afraid I'm going to vent my frustration on her. Which I would never do. That's what Quaid is for.

"Sorry," she says, I thought I heard you say my name.

Damn. I must have been mumbling my thoughts aloud.

I shake my head. "I don't think so."

"You definitely said 'Chieng.'" She steps further inside the room, spots the ruined chair, and stops. "I think, maybe, given our new circumstances, you're remembering certain...events from the past year? Maybe someone who shares my name and poked fun at you?"

I let out a sigh and scooch over on the bed. "I promise not to kung fu you."

She sits down beside me, and after a moment of silence, I ask. "You're Chinese—"

"My *parents* were Chinese," she says. "I'm an American."

"I mean...racially."

"Racially, I'm a human being. Homo sapiens if you want to get—"

"I don't." I take another calming breath, which helps put me at ease and lets Chieng know she's not helping. "Why don't you study kung fu?"

"Ummm," she says, mulling over how to answer, not because she doesn't have one, but because she doesn't want to set me off. In the end, she opts for the truth, which she always does. It's why I like her. "Because I'm not a stereotype."

"FYI, your *species* is homo sapiens. Your race is frikken' Chinese."

"Chinese is a *nationality*, and like I said, I'm an *American*. I was born in Boston. If you want to get old-school scientifically racial, I'm technically Mongoloid."

"Isn't...isn't that an insult?"

"If you're not a Mongoloid, and a racist, maybe. And FYI, you're a Mongoloid, too."

"Hey..."

"You see? Racist, right? You're a member of the human race. That's the only race that matters."

"Ugh, I just got mentally kung-fued." I've picked a senseless argument with a superior mind. Chieng holds three doctorates, despite being only thirty-five. Astrophysics, astrobiology, and art therapy. Why art therapy? Who the hell knows. She likes to paint, I guess. Then again, maybe it's just to keep her from being a different kind of Asian stereotype...of course, the slight Boston accent does that all on its own. I swear, her PhDs are really just making up for the occasional 'pahk the cah' slip-up. She's done a good job hiding the accent, but it comes out when she's stressed.

Which...strangely enough...she's not.

"Why aren't you upset?" I ask. "We just got canned."

"M.I.T. offered me a position. With tenure. Unlike most of the country, they were excited about what we were doing here...well some of it. They want to continue it for non-military applications."

"Of course, they do." The news simultaneously depresses and pleases me. Chieng works as hard as I do. At least one of us will be rewarded for our efforts. I pat her knee. "You deserve it."

"And if we ever need a test pilot," she says. "I know who to call."

Her pixie dust of hope flitters over me and then falls right past. "Pretty sure my career is over. I'm headed home."

"Then...what are you doing here? By yourself? There's no reason to stay under the radar. We've got the place to ourselves. Why not get wild?"

I raise an index finger. "You...aren't coming on to me, right?"

"Get me drunk enough, and I might," she says with a smile. She tugs my arm. "Everyone else is in the Fishbowl. We should go, too. Say goodbye."

The Fishbowl is our recreational lounge. Big-screen TV. Foosball. Ping Pong. All the traditional stuff bought by and for the brosefs of the world. But, she's right, and thanks to her social anxiety, she won't go without me. I allow her to pull me out of bed and to the door. I look back at my room, still feeling like I should pack, but knowing I have so few material objects that it will take just minutes.

I can do it in the morning, I think, and then I follow Chieng toward the exit, and the man I really don't want to say goodbye to. "I just need to make one stop on the way."

5

STONE

"Whiskey, tango, bravo, this is StoneCastle. I have deployed in the AO and am en route to the LZ, requesting a sitrep, ASAP. BolognaCojones, do you copy, over? Ksssh."

"Uhh, what? Bruh, this guy is whack."

"This *guy*," Taylor says into his headset, "is your commanding officer, maggot. You will respond to him with all the deference he is deserved. Kssssh."

"Yo, these guys are straight-up nuts." BolognaCojones sounds like he's a white suburban teenager gaming from his bedroom. That he has yet to use a racial slur is something of a small miracle. He's probably a nice kid in person, but the anonymity of online gaming loosens people's tongues.

Unfazed, I address the other member of our four-man virtual unit. "SecondWind, can I get a sitrep, and a hard copy? Over. Ksssh."

"Uhh, it's SecondWorld."

"What?" I say, scanning the list of screen-names on the bottom left of my PC's monitor. I see myself—StoneCastle—Taylor, aka PlayerWe2, a callsign I still don't really understand, and SecondWorld. "Copy that, SecondWorld, apologies for the verbal transgression. What does that mean? SecondWorld?"

"It's a novel I wrote. Google it."

"Who hasn't written a novel these days?" I ask Taylor with a roll of my eyes, and then I toggle my mic. "Copy that, SecondWorld. Now, can I get a sitrep, ASAP? Over. Ksssh."

"Hard copy," SecondWorld says. "Contact, southeast. Three hundred meters. Four tangos moving hard on our position. Another three have reached the LZ and have taken cover. They have eyes on. Ambush is likely. Recommend a flanking maneuver to secure the LZ, and then deal with the second team. Kill zone is fifty meters out. Ten seconds until it shrinks. Over." There's a pause, and then a "Ksssh."

"Good man," I say, smiling. SecondWorld might be a writing hack, but he gets my brand of gaming. "Bologna, take notes. You could learn a lot from a soldier like this."

"Eat my ball sweat."

"Stow that shit, soldier!" I shout. "Hump it to the LZ, flanking maneuver. SecondWorld, you take point. Bologna, if you go AWOL or FUBAR this mission I will personally ensure you are KIA IRL."

"What the fuck?" BolognaCojones says with a nervous chuckle. He's young and is now confused, unsure about whether or not to be amused or intimidated, which is gold for my gaming stream. Despite having a million plus subscribers, no one knows who I really am or even what I look like. But I enjoy jumping into multi-player games with Taylor and making people uncomfortable whilst delivering the win for Team StoneCastle.

"Abbreviate that shit, soldier," I shout, crouching down beside my teammates on screen. We're all dressed in the ragtag gear of men and women dropped onto a battlefield, forced to scrounge for weapons, armor, and mini-skirts. "Over! Ksssh."

"W...TF?" Bologna says. "Over...ksssh."

"Well, well, well, look at that. You *can* teach processed pig balls new tri—"

A loud *chick-eww* report is followed by a string of pubescent cursing that makes it hard to track where the shot came from. BolognaCojones was just taken out by a sniper...which is odd because we're currently crouch-walking through a small gulley. I can't see any other players ahead or behind, and there is no line of sight on us from the sides.

"Stone..." Taylor says, leaning closer to his monitor, squinting at distant pixels.

"I know," I tell him. We suspect the same thing, and it's bad news for Team StoneCastle, though it could make for big video view numbers, especially if we come out on top of this.

"Pick me up!" Bologna says, as he crawls toward us on his hands and knees, health slowly draining away. Saving him would mean remaining stationary for eight seconds, and this will likely be over in the same amount of time, for better or worse.

"Negatory," I say. "No time. SecondWorld, flank right with PlayerWe2. Try to draw their fire while I—"

Chick-eww...

Taylor yanks his headset off as his on screen-self drops to his hands and knees, helmet destroyed by a magical bullet capable of cutting through the hillside. "Damn Chinese hackers!"

When playing on a public server, a good twenty-five percent of our games end like this—death at the hands of Chinese hackers who can see through walls, auto-aim, run super-fast, turn invisible, no-clip through terrain, and take a shit ton of damage without flinching. They're easy to identify as Chinese because the Internet cafes preferred by the country's gamers auto-assign random, unpronounceable names like XXiiizpixxZZ123. Always a prolific number of Xs. No idea why they bother tacking on the number. Like there are 122 other XXiiizpixxZZ players who came before.

"Flanking!" SecondWorld says, already halfway up the jungle hill, despite the odds being stacked against us by software designed to alter the gaming experience. "Ksssh."

"I respect your aplomb, soldier!" I strike out to the left. Even if I can drop just one of them, it will be a victory.

Chick-eww!

"I'm hit!" SecondWorld says. "Man down! Over. Ksssh."

Unlike Taylor, this SecondWorld guy is staying positive despite being unfairly butchered. I make a mental note to friend him in-game and then lean out from my hiding spot behind a palm tree. I scan left to right and see nothing but digital jungle.

"Uhh, Stone..." It's Taylor, beside me rather than in my headset. I glance at his screen and see the enemy, crouching and standing, again and again, over his body, rubbing his virtual nether region in my compadre's face.

"No one tea-bags my friend!"

On my screen, I turn and open fire, full spray. Bullets strike and kill BolognaCajones and PlayerWe2. While Friendly Fire warnings flash on my screen, the enemy—xxxSRIzzXXXin34—fires a single shot...not even looking at me.

Chick-eww.

I fall to the ground, dead along with my teammates.

Captain tea-bag wastes no time rushing over and granting me a POV display of his ass, crouching over my head. "China numbah one!" he shouts. "China numbah one!"

"Uhh, Stone..." It's Taylor again. This time I look at him, rather than at the screen. He's not looking at the game. He's looking behind me. He points over my shoulder with a look of 'ohmygodyouaresoscrewed' in his eyes.

Assuming there is some kind of general standing behind me, I swivel around in my chair prepared to tell them to sit and spin on something uncomfortable. I'm being discharged. I'm not a soldier anymore. I don't take orders, and I sure as shit don't care what anyone in uniform thinks of me. Not anymore. At least, that's what the four beers in me have to say about it.

My bravado disappears the moment I look up into Hale's shrunken paper eyes, and then I scan downward to the scantily clad body of Olivia Munn in full Psylocke regalia. Hale finally noticed that the head of my Alexa cutout was hers, rather than Munn's. My heart pounds. I try to hide it. But I'm mortified when I look up into Hale's intensely dark-brown-eyed stare.

"I can explain," I say, wondering how I'm going to spin it. Probably doesn't matter, of course.

Hale has become one of my closest friends and confidants, like we're two of the Golden Girls. Obviously, she's Blanche Devereaux, and I'm that saucy tart, Sophia Petrillo...and I guess, we're elderly lesbians in this fantasy... Whatever. The point is, we're close, but not quite close enough, and we'll never get the chance. Come tomorrow, we will go our separate ways, and all I will have to remember her by is a cut-out of her head on Olivia Munn's body, whispering sweet nothings about the weather and my grocery list. "But first, can I have that back?"

I reach my hand out. She looks down with a raised eyebrow that says, 'Eat shit and die of bubonic plague.'

I withdraw my hand and sink into my chair, unaware of the continuing stream behind me, broadcasting the Chinese hacker humiliating me, and my current conversation to fifteen hundred stream-gazers.

"I can see that you're angry..."

"You taped my head on Olivia Munn's body," she says. "You're damn straight I'm angry."

She lets me stew in buzzed nervousness for a good five seconds. Then she motions to her body and says, "I'm at least a Tia Carrere."

When she smiles, my nervousness bubbles out as ridiculous-sounding laughter. "Ohh. Oh man. You got me. But really? Tia Carrere? You're dating yourself."

She shrugs. "Wayne's World was my favorite movie when I was a kid."

"Tia Carrere is also the logical choice," Chieng says, stepping out from behind Hale clutching a 12 pack. "She *is* native Hawaiian."

"Thank you, Sergeant Smartypants," I say, pointing to the brews. "That for sharing, or are you going to drink them all, lose your mind, and go streaking through the parking lot? Because I'm not sure which I'd prefer."

"Sharing," she says, looking stern, but then she gets a gleam in her eye, the likes of which I've never seen in a person with an IQ over 120. "But the streaking is still on the table." She heads for the couches where Billy and Quaid are watching *MegaForce*—a classic, and we think, the partial inspiration for Space Force.

Hale hands the paper doll to me. "We came here to party. Try to keep up."

With that, Taylor turns on some Childish Gambino, and starts grooving in his seat. "They can take Space Force from me, but they can't take my groove!"

The grand finale Space Force bash has officially begun.

Only Jones is missing, but I doubt she would join us, even if we promised a somber mood and to pretend we enjoyed her presence. I rise from my chair doing a white man's jig, still blissfully unaware that the stream is still live and the number of people tuning in to listen is ticking higher by the second.

6

"Good Lord, I think my eyes are melting," Taylor says. We've just finished watching *MegaForce* for the second time. I've never liked the movie. It was too far before my time to enjoy for nostalgic reasons. It's like a dose of the 80s mixed with 'shrooms and speed. But alcohol makes it better.

We're seated on the array of couches, lounging back, enjoying each other's presence, fully. Perhaps for the first time. With the pressure of active duty removed, we've relaxed and really let our true selves show. Billy is actually funny, capable of quoting any movie ever made. Even Quaid has some redeeming qualities—including more compassion for marginalized people than I would have thought possible. Appalachia, where he grew up, is near and dear to his heart.

It's unfortunate that we couldn't have done this before. The camaraderie of the night would have gone a long way to forming a more cohesive unit. But not even that could have saved us. We've been walking around with toilet paper stuck to our feet for years, while the rest of the military branches have been laughing at us, and the world at large has parodied us. Not even a string of movie nights could have overcome that kind of negative energy.

I lean back into Stone, his arm casually around me like we've been a couple for years. He hasn't made any overt advances. All I've really been feeling from him is affection, which is welcome, and again, probably too late. In 24 hours, we'll be half the world apart, me returning to Hawaii and him staying on the East Coast.

"We're out of brews," Quaid complains, checking all the empties on the kitchenette table, and then the small fridge. "We are well and truly lacking in alcoholic beverages."

Stone raises his hand. "That's a problem I can solve."

"What's a problem you can't solve?" Billy asks.

Stone snaps and points at him. "Exactly, you mustached wonder."

"You're sauced," I tell him.

He smiles at me, but it's more earnest than drunk. "Just having a good time." He motions with his head for me to stand. "Join me?"

In response, I smile and stand, waiting for him to lead the way.

"We will return, post haste, with liquid brain melt," Stone declares.

"Take your time," Taylor says with a sly grin directed at me.

I roll my eyes. This wasn't my idea. In fact, letting Stone lead me out of the room in front of all to see, after being all cozy on the couch, feels like a high-school level of cheesy, blatant showmanship. Like when Jake Panela led Lucy Bresnahan beneath the bleachers during a varsity basketball game. For weeks, it was a joke that the buzzer sounded like Lucy moaning. Wasn't so funny a few months later when her baby bump began to show.

I'm no Lucy Bresnahan, I tell myself.

Then again, I *am* following him out of the room, so I suppose we're equally guilty of generating high-school-drama giggle-time. And honestly, I don't care. For the first time in a long time, I really don't give a tumbling turd what other people think of me.

As soon as we're out of the lounge and in the silent hall, we've got nothing to say. We walk, side by side, like we have a hundred times before. But this time, we're silent. Conversation has never been hard for us. We kind of just flow. But the tension between us, positive as it might be, is generating enough mental feedback that I can't think of a damn thing.

Our hands bump into each other as we walk.

When it happens again, I flinch, and laugh. "This is so totally high school."

"It's fucking ridiculous," he says, smiling. Then he reaches out, offering his hand.

I take it.

Silence descends again, but this time it's not awkward. It's content.

We need to have a conversation. That's clear now. But it's not going to happen tonight.

We arrive at his quarters five minutes later.

"Just a sec," he says, letting himself in.

"You're not going to invite me in?"

"You've already seen the place," he says. "I mean, you broke in earlier to abscond with my sex doll."

I step inside, uninvited, while Stone digs through his closet. He's not the neatest man in the world, but it's been a while since he felt the need to impress anyone. Despite being one of the best operators in the military, his fate has been on the fast track to nowhere, and now I know why.

Am I jealous of the General's daughter? Sure. But that was in the past, and from what I've heard, not even a casual fling. What we've got...it's been a slow brew.

It could last, I tell myself, but I have no idea how. One of us would have to give up something, even after losing everything.

Then again, maybe we'd be horrible together in real life, outside the weird bubble that is Space Force. At first, we rubbed each other the wrong way, but time has worn away the rough edges of our relationship that began professionally, morphed into a friendship, and now, because time is fleeting, is being shunted into something more.

But is it something good?

When Stone emerges victorious, a bottle of Maker's Mark 46 bourbon whiskey in hand, I give him a smile that says a bit more than, 'I'm happy.'

He holds the bottle high. "Our champion emerges from the slough of despond, trophy clutched in..." He sees the look in my eyes. The bottle lowers and then drops to the bed. He steps closer, our faces inches apart.

"I'm not sure this is a great idea," I manage to whisper.

"I'm not sure I care."

"Neither do I." I take a step back. He steps forward.

"We're drunk," I say.

"Are we?" He glances at the liquor. "I mean, yet? You've never thought about this when completely sober?"

I take another step back and he closes the distance again.

"Are you talking about screwing, or something more?" I ask.

He smiles. "Are those things mutually exclusive?"

"They are not," I say, stepping back again, this time being stopped by his dresser. "In fact, I would say they are inherently connected."

His advance stops short. My last words have sobered him a bit. He clears his throat. "So this is big, then? Like game-changer big?"

"Like we'll need to have a long talk in the morning big," I say. "Yeah."

Some guys would bullshit their way through this moment, just to get in a lady's pants, but Stone is not one of those men. For all his bluster and sarcasm, he's a noble man at heart.

I trace an invisible line with my index finger, an inch away from my smiling lips. "Move past here, and you're in it to win it, soldier."

He glances down at my chest. "Just to be clear, there *are* parts of you already crossing that line. If they're fair game, maybe I'll just—

"Ethan," I say, using his first name and smiling wider at his nervousness. His deflective humor is a miserable attempt at hiding his—

I'm caught off guard when his lips press against mine. We both tense up for a moment, and then relax, lingering in a slow embrace, lip-locked and unmoving.

After a moment, we separate slowly.

When a tendril of spit connects our lips, Stone wipes it away and offers a gentle, "Gross."

Our laughter is interrupted by the sound of a blaring horn. In the city, we might not have noticed the sound, but on Portsmouth Island, where the population is under ten, the honk is out of place and unwelcome. Stone splits his blinds and looks out into the circular parking lot.

"The hell is this?" he asks.

Outside, a fleet of 18-wheelers is arriving from across the long bridge connecting us to the mainland.

"They said we had until tomorrow," he grumbles, and then he looks down at his watch. "Assholes."

He holds his wrist up, so I can see the time. It's 12:30am. Tomorrow has officially arrived, but them coming to evict us in the early morning hours is a dick move of unparalleled proportions. "Who would do this?"

"*McNasty,*" he says.

"You think he's *still* carrying a grudge?"

"Honestly, I think he was jealous, either of me, or his daughter. I'm not sure which. The man's a pariah. The kind of limp-dicked asshole people only follow because he's in a position of power, not because he's an inspirational, or even competent leader. He's what you'd expect if Satan dropped a deuce, a Rabbi took that excrement and fashioned a shit-golem, and then named him McNasty."

"McNally," says a deep, aged voice from the doorway. "And while people in low positions of power might think those unsavory things about me, others, who have core values of common sense and decency, understand that I am a fair and balanced man beyond reproach."

I lean to the side, looking around Stone, who has closed his eyes and kept his back turned to the door. A short man wearing spectacles and a general's four-star uniform stands in the doorway, hat tucked under his arm.

I snap a salute, and it is not returned.

"No longer necessary. As of twenty-four hundred, you are no longer a member of the United States armed forces. And as such, I must ask that you remove yourself from the—"

"Horse and shit," Stone says.

"You could at least face me while you disrespect me," McNally says.

"I can't..." Stone says. "I'm...waiting."

"For?" the General asks.

"If you must know, I'm still sporting a partial. You kind of interrupted a moment, here."

"Another conquest?"

"Jasmine wasn't a con—"

"If you're referring to my daughter, her name was Sarah."

"Not even close," I grumble, nudging Stone with my elbow.

Stone adjusts his pants and turns around, standing awkwardly. "I might not know her name, but there are a few things I do know about your daughter, which you, good sir, do not..."

My eyes widen as the General's words sink in and are digested by my inhibited mind.

"The first is that she's a certifiable freak in the—" My elbow slams into Stone's ribs, replacing his diatribe with a sharp, "Oww!"

I lean in close and whisper, "He said 'was'! Her name *was* Sarah."

Stone swallows, purses his lips, and furrows his brow. "Uhh, sir...is..."

"Sarah," I say.

"Sarah...is she...okay? I mean, is she...alive?"

McNally shakes his head. "She's married with three kids. Idiots. All of you. You have thirty minutes to collect your belongings and get off my base."

"What?" Stone says, his dander rising again. "You can't just—"

"Your other option is the brig." Two MPs step into view behind him. "Thirty minutes. A bus is waiting to take you all to the mainland."

I glance out the window and spot a big, yellow school bus waiting down in the parking lot.

"If you need to tell your tales of woe, there's plenty of press waiting for you on the far side."

"Press? Are you trying to humiliate us?" Stone asks. "I mean, I know why you don't like *me*, but the rest of these people haven't done anything to you."

"My presence here, at this ungodly hour, and the press's, has nothing to do with me, and everything to do with *you*. The moment you decided it was a good idea to broadcast your drunken party to the Internet, you sealed your fate, and forever tainted people's view of Space Force."

"What are you talking about?" I ask, and then I turn to Stone. "What is he talking about?"

But Stone is just as dumbfounded as me.

"Maybe it was Billy?" Stone asks.

The General grunt-sighs, takes out his phone, switches it on, and turns it around. We're shown the static view of a video game. On screen, StoneCastle lies dead on a grassy hillside—the final scene from Stone's earlier game. McNally taps his volume button. As the sound grows louder we can hear *MegaForce* in the background, coupled with Taylor and Quaid singing the *Captain Planet* theme song.

My mind races in reverse, playing back the night's conversations. I clutch my eyes and force myself to stop thinking. If I remember too much, I'll end up on the floor, drooling in a brain-dead fetal position.

Stone looks pale and mortified, but then he cracks a slight smile and leans in a little closer. "Huh."

"What?" I ask, hoping he'll tell me that the feed is only available locally.

He points at the phone. "Two million viewers. That's..."

When I shrink in on myself, his voice trails off.

"Thirty minutes," McNally says, his voice followed by the sound of his feet stomping away.

"I'm sorry," Stone whispers. "I didn't know."

When he puts his hand on my wrist, I pull it away.

After a moment, he says, "I'll let you pack; I'll go tell the others." He stands and backs away toward the door. "See you on the bus?"

When he starts to close the door behind him, I say, "Stone."

"Yeah?" he says, sounding hopeful.

"I'm in *your* room."

"Right," he says, eyes flitting about. I've never seen him so undone and miserable, but he deserves everything he's feeling and then some. My self-destruction has been live-streamed to the world because of him. No one will hire me now, for anything. Who's going to want a joke for a sensei?

He leaves the door open and then pushes his way past the two MPs, who have stayed behind to gawk. Despite what I've just said, I close the door behind Stone, lock it, and melt into his bed, hiding from the world and wondering if that kiss still holds any meaning.

7

STONE

I'm trying to get a grip on my anger, but it's either righteous as fuck, or the alcohol in my blood is keeping me on the straight and narrow of Rage Street. The squeaky small voice of my logical mind reminds me that I wronged McNasty, that my actions were inappropriate. That I really did deserve this shit assignment, and I was lucky to have not been dishonorably discharged on the spot. He could have made things worse for me.

But punishing the rest of Space Force for my transgressions...

Is that what he's doing? Squeak, squeak.

Damnit. Even Jones said they were all here for a reason. Aside from Hale, every last member of Space Force is a screw-up in some form or fashion. That we're still here, while everyone else was shipped off or discharged in the past few years either means we're the best the USSF has to offer...or the worst.

But that doesn't justify treating Hale poorly. She's done nothing but serve with distinction, right up until the end. Whatever might have been transmitted out to the world was after she'd been kicked in the imaginary nuts.

You're just upset because the man gave you blue balls. Squeak.

Okay, that's at least partially true, but despite never taking Space Force seriously, I've grown to like these people. They're my friends. And when someone disrespects my friends, even if they're deserving, I rise to their defense.

By the time I reach the Fishbowl, the rest of the team has noticed the commotion outside. They're gathered by the windows, looking out at the parking lot.

"The hell is going on?" Taylor asks, when I enter the room. "Where's Hale?"

"Packing, I'd guess," I say, heading for the computer station.

"Failed to seal the deal?" Quaid asks.

"We were interrupted," I grumble.

"Oh dang," Quaid punches his open palm. "Who cock-blocked you?"

"McNasty."

"General McNally is *here?*" Chieng asks, standing from the couch and straightening her clothing. "*Now?*"

"Why would he be here now?" Billy asks, wringing his hands together. While some members of the USSF respect McNasty's authority, no one likes him. He was involved in most of our cases to one degree or another. I wonder how Colonel Jones crossed him, and then I decide it doesn't matter.

"We're being evicted," I say. "Better pack your shit. We have thirty minutes to GTFO."

Billy's eyes widen. "Gerty... Oh *no.* Gerty!" He scrambles from the couch and makes a beeline for the door, slamming into it, tumbling to the floor, and rolling back to his feet with all the grace of a limbless ferret.

The room is locked in time for a moment. I raise a hand, about to question who Gerty is, when Taylor says, "No idea."

Quaid shrugs. "Hell, if I know."

"I'm sorry," Chieng says, hurrying toward the door, growing more sober with each step. "I'm...I'm going to gather my things."

"What are you doing?" Taylor asks, when I resume my course for the computer station.

I pick up my headset and turn the monitor toward him and Quaid. When Taylor sees my still-dead on-screen body, he understands. He says nothing, but points toward the headset, shaking his head. The man has read my mind, but there's nothing he can do to change it.

"Hoss," Quaid warns. It's the first time I've seen genuine concern in his eyes. He pantomimes taking a drink and stumbling around, trying to tell me that I'm drunk.

I shake my head, despite knowing he's probably right. "To the..." I look at the stream counter. "...holy shit, three point two million people watching—"

Taylor starts choking on nothing.

"—this is Captain Ethan Stone, aka StoneCastle, coming to you live from Space Force Command. In the following days, it's likely that Congress and the President are going to try painting everyone involved with the program as colossal fuck-ups. And I know, *I know*, talking to you now, via a video game live-stream, is probably not the best venue—I probably said some embarrassing things earlier. But this might be my one and only chance to set the record straight.

I take a deep breath. "Before being assigned to Space Force, I was a Navy SEAL. Best of the best. Good people are alive because I killed bad people. I was sent to Space Force to be the butt of a joke the previous administration wanted to tell. We've been mocked and humiliated by comedians, pundits, and our nation's leaders. I should be ashamed of my time here, training to fight a war that will never happen. Instead, I'm proud of what we have accomplished. If there ever was a war in space, we'd fucking crush it. The only real thing wrong with Space Force is that the people in charge are colossal dick-holes, and well, there's no one to fight. So instead of taking one up the ass for the world's amusement, I say..."

Don't do it. Squeek!

"Thank you...for allowing us to serve you, even though we weren't needed. If you want to have at us for blowing off a little steam tonight, go right ahead. We are tougher than anything the universe can throw at us. That includes you, Anderson Cooper, with your angelic white hair and your 'take-me-now' eyes.

"I was sent here for a single mistake...made three times...once on camera...to be mentally and emotionally castrated by an asshole with four stars on his shoulders. I should be angry at him, and when I started this rant, I was. But now, General McNasty... Thank you for sending me here. Without you, I would have never met the people I now consider family..."

Taylor and Quaid are on board now, nodding their approval.

I glance at the stream counter and note that we're approaching four million.

I swallow and continue. "...or the woman I—"

The power goes out.

"Quasimodo's soiled taint," I say in the darkness that follows. "What the hell?"

Emergency lighting snaps on.

McNasty's voice booms from the intercom. "You have twenty minutes to pack your belongings and vacate the premises. Or don't. Watching you all be dragged out would be...amusing."

"Ain't nothing to be done about it," Quaid says, putting his hand on my arm. "Better to do what the man says than cause a ruckus. After a speech like that, last thing you want is to be thrown out like a dog. Keep your head up and hang on to what pride you got left."

My wang-jangled nerves calm a bit. "That might be the wisest thing you've ever said."

"Probably the last time, too, so take what you can git."

Taylor towers over us. "You lead, I'll follow."

We've both been accepted to the same private contractor company. I'm not sure if my little rant has put that in jeopardy, but he's telling me if it did, he'll stand by my side.

I wipe a faux tear from my eye. "Don't you dare 'oh captain, my captain' me."

"Seriously," he says. Offering his hand, arm flexed, in a tribute to one of our all-time favorite movies.

I take his hand like we're about to arm wrestle, and quote, "'Dylan, you son of a bitch.'"

We have a good chuckle and then the reality of our situation sets in. The clock is ticking. "Time to pack."

We leave the Fishbowl for the last time. I take a glance back and remember all the good times had here, especially as the base's personnel was whittled down to the point where we had to make our own meals in the mess, and empty the trash ourselves. It was kind of a summer camp experience, but with guns and training simulators, and our very own satellite—dubbed 'Peeping Tom' after Billy showed us what it could do.

Nineteen minutes later, I'm standing in the parking lot watching a frenzy of worker ants loading our gear and tech into a small fleet of 18-wheeler trucks. The men are tired and humorless, until they see me, then I'm greeted, universally, by snickers. I don't know if it's simply because we're Space Force, or they heard my dramatic diatribe, but it's starting to get on my nerves. I have half a mind to show these muffin-topped movers how much ass Space Force can kick, but I decide to let my cut-short words be my final goodbye.

I stand stoic by the yellow humiliation bus, waiting for the doors to open, and my team to arrive. Taylor arrives first, standing beside me without a word. Then Chieng and Quaid, falling in line and observing our silent vigil without being instructed to.

When the bus doors open, I allow the others to enter first. Chieng sits in the front and Quaid joins her, no doubt to make one last attempt at pouring on his Southern lack of charm. She sighs, but says nothing.

I continue to the back of the bus with Taylor. We take seats across from each other. "You know you don't need to sit back here anymore, right?"

He smiles. "I like to say, 'wee' when we go over the bumps."

Billy enters next, followed by a woman. I stand, expecting it to be Hale, but the hair is wrong. Instead of straight and black, it's straight and blonde...which means it's not Jones either...

Billy sits near the middle of the bus, managing to avoid making eye contact with anyone, despite all eyes being on him, and on his lady friend, who is a knockout. In some ways, she looks like a super model, but the image is thrown off by the gray Space Force flight suit she's wear-ing. When she sits down beside him, Taylor and I look at each other, dumbfounded. Has Billy had a mistress hidden on base this whole time? Did he hire a stripper for our final night, and then forget about her?

"Is that Gerty?" Taylor asks.

I'm about to shrug when Hale steps on board. She makes eye contact with me, doesn't smile, and sits across from Quaid and Chieng.

Way too much like summer camp, I think. Every year of that humid, puberty-ridden drama-fest ended with my heart being broken by a girl who suddenly couldn't stand the sight of me.

Not this time, I think, and I stand, ready to pour my heart out.

McNasty cockblocks me again, stepping into the bus with a broad smile. "Enjoy civilian life," he says, and then to the driver, a sleepy-eyed black woman who looks like she was dragged from bed for this, he says, "Drop them off at the far side of the bridge."

With that, he leaves and watches the bus pull away. We sit in silence as the bus rounds the parking lot. I can sense the stares of the men outside, but I don't bother looking. No reason to heap hot coals on my own head.

Halfway across the bridge, our driver perks up. "Don't worry, ya'll. I don't work for that asshat. I'll take you where you want to go."

I'm about to thank her when a shrill screech fills the air, knocking me to the floor in pain, clutching my ears. I don't hear the bus tires lock, but I feel it when I'm sprawled forward. When we crash into the bridge's side wall, I'm tossed down the aisle, stopping in the center of the bus.

When the shriek stops, I push myself up, groggy and disoriented. "What was that?"

"Look!" Billy says, pointing out the window.

A line of orange energy descends from the sky. It's a translucent wall, plunging toward the ocean. I follow its track around and realize it's surrounding all of Portsmouth Island.

Billy cranes his head up. "It's coming down above us!"

When the top of the bus sparks and is carved in half, I scream more in regret than fear, and close my eyes.

My holler is cut short when a strong hand grasps the back of my shirt and yanks me back.

The orange energy slices through the bus, and then the bridge below. Everything jolts downward as concrete and steel are severed like they're made from Jell-O. But the modern construction holds.

Through a wall of translucent orange, I see Hale stand and face me, all of her disappointment replaced by concern. Instead of any number of expletives, all I can think is, *she still cares about me.* But when I smile, she frowns and points behind me. The mystery wall has come down around the island, separating us from the rest of the world. I look out the window and up. It stretches up into the night sky, farther than I can see.

Before I can react, my cell phone comes to life. As I pull the device from my pocket, I see everyone else aboard the bus do the same.

"Well," I say. "This can't be good."

8

HALE

The wall of orange energy cracking the bus in two like a bright yellow, well-cooked crustacean in the hands of an aging and famished Martha's Vineyard yuppie, also cleaves away my anger. Toward the politicians who sent us packing. Toward the people who have mocked us, and will continue to do so. And toward Stone, who thought he could make up for embarrassing me before the world, by embarrassing me a second time.

What the hell was he thinking he'd accomplish with that speech?

And what was he about to say when the power went out?

I look at him through a shimmering wall of energy. He's looking back, but the connection I usually feel with him is missing, not because our fledgling relationship is irreparably broken, but because his features are distorted.

When my phone comes to life in my pocket, I wonder if it might be my parents. With the press on the far side of the bridge, this is likely going out live, and if the world knew we were on this bus, they're probably wondering if we're alive.

I pull the phone out and look at the screen.

"Well, this can't be good," Stone says, but his voice is muffled, like he's talking through a thick window. I glance up and notice that he's looking at his phone, too. As is every other passenger, save for Billy's strange companion, who's even less recognizable on the far side of the energy wall. I don't know who she is, or how Billy snuck her onto the base, but she did save Stone from being carved in half. I'm grateful for her impressive show of strength. Saving Stone's life means I get to kick his ass when this wall comes down.

I return my attention to my phone screen, where a white symbol slowly rotates over a black screen. It's like a backward P, with two bumps instead of one. Like if a P and a B had a love child.

My first thought is that I'm looking at an alien language. I mean, that's the only thing this can be, right? Russia can't shoot force fields from space. China sure as shit can't. Hell, maybe it's Canada. They haven't exactly been happy with us since the trade wars. They might have motive, but not the capability. Space Force had access to some of the most advanced tech in the world, and the orange wall descending from orbit is beyond the capabilities of any nation on Earth.

As the symbol rotates clockwise, my brow furrows.

"Is...that a—?" our driver asks, wide-eyes staring at her phone. "Lord have mercy, it *is!*"

If not for the force field separating us from our friends, I might have laughed. Our first contact with a superior intelligence is being misinterpreted as an interstellar dick pic. I'm sure it means something in their language—hopefully a message of peace, but that seems unlikely. If it's like Japanese kanji—characters with meaning beyond consonants and vowels—the meaning could be nuanced and intricate. It could take months to decipher the true meaning.

The spinning phallus fades to black.

8-bit text scrolls across the screen.

`Human race. We are Xxxinquixxx.`

Through the force field I see Taylor and Stone look at each other like they know something I don't.

`All your base are belong to us.`

"What the hell?" I say.

"Are they trying to communicate with memes?" Chieng asks.

I hold the phone up. "This is a meme?"

"In 1989," Quaid says. "Based on the 'Engrish' translations in Zero Wing. That's a video game. It was pretty awesome. You should look it up."

"Yeah, that's at the top of my to do list, right after Survive the Apocalypse and Rebuild My Life." My eyes linger on the force field, following the broad arc as it wraps around Space Force. "It might be a meme, but they also mean it." I point across the hazy orange bridge. "Our base *does* belong to them."

"All our base," Taylor says. I can barely hear him, but the field's distortion only adds to the grim sound of his voice.

"You don't think they've captured every military installation in the world?" Billy asks.

`Make your time. We are coming.`

"We have to assume so," Stone says. "And we need to get ahead of this before—"

"Get *ahead* of it?" I say. "We don't even know what *it* is."

"Doesn't matter what it is." He points toward the ceiling. "It's coming from up there."

"We got some shit on the roof?" the frantic bus driver asks, sinking down, large eyes staring upward.

"In space," Stone says. "And that's *our* domain. This is our fight. It's what we've been training for."

It's not much of a speech, and no one is very moved by it.

"I'm as surprised as anyone else, but...space *is* a warfighting domain," he says.

Billy raises his hand, objecting. "We're no longer enlisted and commissioned members of—"

"Horse and shit," Stone says. "McNasty might have evicted us, but I'd bet my left—hell, I'd bet both my nugs—that the paperwork hasn't gone through yet, and probably won't as long as *this* is happening. And if that's true..." He looks me in the eyes. "...if our country...if our world is in danger from *space?* It is our duty to fight for—"

The bridge lurches down a foot, nearly knocking me into the force field. There's a moment of silence while everyone clutches seatbacks.

"Uhh-uh. Nope, nope, nope," the bus driver says. "I'm out. Ya'll have fun saving the universe."

She opens the side door, hobbles down the steps, and does a funny kind of penguin speed-walk, following the bridge toward the mainland.

In the distance, I can see the lights of countless media cameras pointed in our direction. But I doubt they're pointed at us anymore.

The bus shudders again, sliding downward. Orange sparks topple from the roof as it tilts into, and is eaten by, the force field. The severed vehicle stops at an angle, the middle ends lying on the pavement. Molten metal oozes from the edge, sizzling against the force field, kicking up a noxious smoke.

We can't stay here much longer...and we definitely can't touch the energy field.

"Something new is coming through," Quaid says, phone in hand.

```
Rules of engagement:
Battle to the death.
No holds barred.
Last man standing wins…
```

"Wins?" I ask. "Wins what?"

The moment I speak the question, I realize the answer.

Billy's mystery friend states the obvious for me. "Earth."

To make this even more bluntly clear and melodramatic, an image of earth from space fills the screen. But it's not just the blue planet we're used to seeing. There are hundreds of orange spines jutting up into orbit, ending at large black circles, big enough to see despite the small image. The image is a real-time view of the planet from space, and each one of those lines represents a spacecraft.

But only one of them matters now. The one above us. Winner takes all.

"These are gaming rules." Stone holds up his phone. "For a battle royale." He eyes the force field, following its path around the base. "They've turned Portsmouth Island into a death zone."

"I think it's safe to say they've done the same to other military bases around the world," Taylor says. "Does that mean we're all playing? How does that work? Do all Earth forces have to—"

The phone updates.

```
Who will fight?
```

A long list of military forces from around the world appears in abbreviated form. It's a long, scrollable column with more acronyms than I can decipher. I stop scrolling when I start recognizing United States forces.

USAF
USMC
USN
USSF
USSS

"Look," Quaid says, "there we are!" He taps his finger on the screen, and the USSF is highlighted on all our phones. The rest of the abbreviations fade away and the USSF logo fills the screen. "Did I just...? Fiery cotton-candy shit sticks, I did."

The question of whether or not fending off an alien invasion was Space Force's duty is no longer up for debate. Quaid has just volunteered us for the job...all *seven* of us, only four of which are actually inside the base's perimeter.

The bridge jolts downward again. As well as it was designed, it can't hold itself up indefinitely while severed in two.

A timer appears on our phones, counting down from 30 minutes.

"Hale," Stone says, inching closer to the force field. He holds up his phone, manages to minimize the alien counter, and dials a number. I flinch when my phone rings.

When I answer it, he says my name again. This time his voice comes through clear. "Jen." He sounds nervous, and sad. "I'm sorry. For—"

"Stone," I say. "Aliens have invaded."

"It could still be the Chinese," he says. "It's the name. Zinquix." His pronunciation of Xxxinquixxx is about what I imagined, too. "All the Chinese hackers use names like that. It can't be a coincidence."

"How could the Chinese do all this?" I ask.

"Just...get to the launchpad and work that angle, okay? Cell signals can get through, so call me when you find something."

When I detect trace amounts of regret still lingering in his eyes, I take the burden from his shoulders by saying, "I forgive you."

The bridge lurches downward. Something somewhere snaps, sending a vibration through the floor. When Stone's side of the bus starts rolling into the force field, he scrambles away, shouting, "Out the back! Go! Go! Go!"

While Taylor leads Billy and the mystery woman out the back door, Stone lingers.

"You can finish your live-stream speech when I see you again," I tell him. "In private."

He smiles, and it's the last thing I see before nearly falling from the bus's open end. Quaid has thrown the front half of the bus, which must be front- or four-wheel drive, into gear and hit the gas. A trail of sparks chases us across the bridge, which is now wobbling side to side.

"Go, Stone," I whisper. "Move your ass."

9

STONE

The theme song to *Chariots of Fire* rears its ugly head from the abyss of my childhood, playing in my head during our trans-bridge run. I refrain from humming that shit aloud, because if we survive what comes next, I'm sure as hell selling my story to Hollywood. Who knows how much those song rights cost? Also, I kind of want the world to think I'm the kind of guy whose go-to inspirational running song is something by DMX. At the very least, *Eye of the Tiger*. I mean, I don't really remember much about *Chariots of Fire*. Just an image of someone running on a sandy beach, and the theme song playing. I think it was the movie's final scene, and might have been inspirational at the time, but I want to be relevant, man, not some geriatric jogger in 70's-style tight shorts.

I try to shift gears into another song and end up with fucking *Footloose*.

Screw it, Kevin Bacon is still the best man to be six degrees from.

As the lyrics flow through my thoughts, I cut loose across the bridge, which has begun to sway in a stiff breeze. The air inside the massive force field is being disturbed from above, swirling into a column of air that's not quite a hurricane, but not exactly gentle on the wounded structure.

"What theme song are you running to?" I ask Taylor. He's chugging along beside me, a little sweat on his brow, but still hauling ass. We go for a run every morning, so this is nothing new. Neither of us like earbuds, so we end up running in silence, listening to the music in our heads.

"Spider-man," he says.

"Like the movie soundtrack?"

"Naw, man, the original cartoon."

The soundtrack in my mind flips to the iconic music. "Muuuch better. Muchos gracias."

"De nada," he says, and glances back.

The bridge groans behind us, close to giving out. Taylor and I have reached the safety of the massive pylons holding aloft the island portion of the suspension bridge. If the dangling portion goes, the part beneath us will remain standing.

I think.

But Billy and the woman I'm assuming is the mysterious Gerty, are still a hundred feet back and in danger of being dropped into the ocean.

"Should we go back for them?" Taylor asks.

When Billy sees us stop, he does the same. He waves us onward, while bending over to catch his breath. Unlike Taylor and me, Billy is not big on exercising...or standing. This is more moving than he's done in years, and it's already taking a toll. As exhausted as he looks, he doesn't look worried. He either has more faith in the bridge's stability than I do, or he has suddenly developed a penchant for self-sacrifice.

As impressive as that would be, Billy is more useful alive than as a martyr. Taylor and I aren't dolts, but Billy's mind is a unique resource. Whoever is attacking us is using tech beyond our current experience, and we're going to need his brain to find workarounds.

"Dude," I say.

"I got this," he shouts back.

"Seriously?" Taylor starts back down the bridge.

"Seriously," Billy says, standing up straight and then saying something to Gerty, who has stopped beside him and hasn't even broken a sweat. She nods, steps in front of him and then crouches down in a butt-out position that is both awkward and somehow erotic. A flamingo presenting itself to its mate.

Definitely a stripper.

"Whoa," I say, flinching back when Billy puts his hands on her shoulders. While I might normally find all this amusing in a way I'd never want my parents to know about, this is neither the time nor the place for a shag.

Then he hops up, planting his full—and not insubstantial—weight on Gerty's back.

"Ohh!" Taylor and I shout in unison.

I'm expecting the woman to faceplant with enough force to scrape her nose off, but she holds his girth like he's nothing more than a plucky homunculus.

Then...she starts running.

Fast.

Taylor and I kind of stand there in a stunned silence. The giant force field of doom was less of a surprise. When that lady in *The Crying Game* had a Johnson? *That* was less shocking. This is like Moses-parting-the-Red-Sea level of insanity. I feel like I'm looking at a mythical beast, like if a pug and a unicorn had an in vitro baby in the womb of a velociraptor, and a squash-faced, curly-tailed, winged dog just hatched from its egg. It's both horrifying and magical.

As Gerty runs between us with all the speed and vigor of Sea Biscuit, the bouncing Billy shouts, "T-t-try to k-ke-ep up, bitch-es-es-es!"

And then they're past, cruising toward the temporary safety of Portsmouth Island.

"What the fuck?" I ask.

"Hell, if I know."

"Can't be a stripper, right?"

"Maybe a yoga instructor?" Taylor offers. "They have core strength, right?"

"*You* couldn't have pulled that off," I say, watching them shrink into the distance. "Look at them go!"

Taylor's eyes turn up to the sky. "We really should try to keep up."

We break into a run again. At our current pace, it will take a good ten minutes to clear the bridge, which is important. Not only are we exposed, and unarmed, we're also in what resembles a battle royale scenario. That means a few things.

1) We have a small window of time to arm ourselves.

2) At some point, we're going to have company, most likely descending from above.

3) The glowing wall of orange death is going to eventually close in, consuming the bridge and anything else it touches. Including us.

"What are you thinking?" Taylor asks a few minutes into our run.

Billy and Gerty are now out of sight, having run down the road, past the entry gate, and back into the base.

"That this can't be the Chinese," I say, "Hacker name or not. It's just too much. Too big. I mean, hell, they've only just launched their first aircraft carrier. How the hell could they have launched a network of satellites capable of beaming energy walls back down to Earth?"

"They couldn't," he says. "So, aliens, then?"

"Has to be."

"But why the gamer shit? All Your Base. Battle royale. Aliens are gamers?"

Despite our love for gaming, and our defense of games as a legit form of storytelling, we both know they're not exactly the preferred format for Earth's intelligentsia.

But we're not dealing with Earth's intelligentsia.

"Must be like an Explorers situation," I say.

"Huh?"

"*The Explorers*? 80's movie? Ethan Hawke. River Phoenix."

I'm astounded by his blank stare. Taylor is a little younger than me, but aside from Millennials, who hasn't seen *The Explorers*? "Ugh. There're these kids, and they—you know what? That doesn't matter. They encounter aliens whose sole experience with Earth has been television broadcasts. So they're expecting something a bit different than what they find. If these..." I point to the sky. "...guys experience Earth through video games, then maybe—"

"They think this is normal for us," Taylor says. "That this is how we battle."

"And that we do it, twenty-four seven, around the world."

"Well, I guess that's nice of them, then," he says.

"What's nice?"

"Waging battle in a way they think we'll understand, even if they're wrong...though I guess *we* understand it well enough."

"Well enough to win?" My question is punctuated by the fact that we've been pushing ourselves, and I'm starting to get winded. I look at the countdown on my phone. Twenty-one minutes left. I'm going to need a nap by the time this counter hits zero, and I'm still partially buzzed. If

I don't get a good long drink of water soon, I'm going to get a hangover without ever drinking too much, which is just no fun at all.

"What's our win ratio?" Taylor asks.

"In game? Two percent?"

"That ain't good."

"Most people never win," I point out. "And the hackers almost always win."

"What about real life?"

"We're both alive, so, better," I say.

He nods. "Much better...before we wound up here." He looks ahead. "Damn, this is a long bridge."

Before I can chime in with bitching of my own, the sound of a revving engine pricks my ears. I stumble to a stop, unsure if we're going to be run down by an alien in a car. Hands on my knees, sucking in air, I watch a Humvee smash through the base's gate and charge across the bridge, heading straight for us.

I look over the bridge's side-rail. The ocean churns far below, waves kicked up by the swirling wind. We'd probably survive the drop, but the swim wouldn't be easy, and we're in North Carolina— so there are sharks...but I guess Jaws should be low on my list of things over which to shit myself.

I relax a bit when the vehicle swerves into the next lane. The vehicle's headlights force me to squint until it pulls up beside us. The window slides down to reveal Gerty sitting behind the driver's wheel, looking like Jennifer Lawrence in a Vidal Sassoon commercial as she looks over, hair swooshing into perfect position. "Billy sent me back for you."

I head for the driver's side and wait for her to get out.

The window drops down so Gerty can address me again. "What are you doing?"

"Driving," I say.

"I'm perfectly capable of—"

"I'm totally not a sexist," I say, which makes me totally sound like a sexist, "but you're not trained to handle a vehicle like this, and you're not a member of Space Force, so—"

"You're wrong," she says. "On both counts."

Taylor climbs into the passenger's seat. "Who are you, then?"

She grasps her flight suit in a 'I'm about to dazzle you with my supple bust' kind of way. Before I can protest, she yanks. The zipper gives way to her impressive strength, revealing her torso, which is far more impressive than I was expecting.

"Wow..." It's all I can manage for a few seconds. Then I reach out for a feel.

She swats my hand. "No touching."

"But," I say. "You're not...human, right?"

She looks down at her brushed metal body, built like something out of a Terminator movie. Clothed, she looks as human as anyone else. "Doesn't mean you can get all handsy. Now, get in before I leave your soft ass on the bridge."

10

STONE

"Sooo," I say, looking Gerty up and down like a lecherous pig, sans the dirty thoughts. "Billy *built* you?"

She nods.

"On his own?"

Another nod.

"How?" I ask.

That Billy put something like Gerty together without any of us knowing is a bit mind-boggling. "Where did he get the funding?"

"I was a special directive," she says.

"From *who?*" A special directive implies a person of power set up a black fund for Billy with the express purpose of creating a super-hot, AI-driven robot, though I suppose the super-hot bit could have just been Billy's fantasies playing out in his work.

"The former president."

"For what purpose?" Taylor asks. "You don't look like you were made for combat."

"The true purpose for my creation was shrouded in secrecy, but it doesn't take much imagination to figure out." Gerty looks at me, holding my gaze while having no trouble staying on the road. When she offers a faux smile, I see who she really looks like.

"Oh, that's..." My face scrunches in disgust.

"Billy gave me the tools to defend myself, should the need arise," she says, "and the free will to determine my own fate."

"Then you and Billy haven't..." Taylor lets the question hang in the air for a moment. "I mean, obviously. You're unfinished, right?"

"I can't believe you'd ask that question," I say with mock disgust, as the vehicle pulls past the shattered, now guardless gate. "Buuuut?" I raise an eyebrow at Gerty.

She grins, revealing her AI is not only very intelligent, but also somewhat witty. She seems to have no trouble picking up on the subtleties of our attempts at humor, and also isn't offended by them. Billy somehow descended into the uncanny valley and came out the other side with a humanoid robot who looks and feels human...until you see her without clothes on.

Gerty slows the Humvee as we approach the parking lot, still full of moving trucks, their personnel, a handful of MPs, and General McNasty himself. They're all kind of bumbling around, looking up, somewhat mystified. I can't fault them for it. I'm sure the rest of the world is doing something similar. But it means the General, and all the men here under his command, have no concept of what's going to happen when the timer hits zero.

I glance at my phone. Eighteen minutes to go.

When McNasty sees us coming, his body language says he's furious. The MPs react to his tirade by raising their M16s toward the Humvee and spreading out to cover us from all angles.

Gerty brings the vehicle to a slow stop. "You want me to handle them?"

"Handle them?" I ask.

"I don't need to kill them, if that's what you're worried about." She zips up her flight suit, hiding her metal body.

"I suppose you could distract them. Maybe give us a chance to slip away." The maze of parked trucks should be easy to get lost in. If we can make it inside, we'll be impossible to find before the timer is up. And then I won't have to try reasoning with McNasty. When the space shit hits the fan, he'll have to listen to me. "But don't make them shoot you."

"Would take more than a few bullets to—"

"Step out of the vehicle with your hands up," McNasty shouts through a megaphone. *Of course, he's got a megaphone.* It's like a pre-requisite for power hungry d-bags, because eventually people tune out a grating jabber-jaw.

"You sure about this?" I ask Gerty.

"You're the boss," she says.

"Say what, now?"

"I told you, I'm a member of Space Force. You're my commanding officer."

"Technically..." I point at McNasty. "He's your commanding officer."

"He's my commanding popped-ass implant."

I snort. "You definitely belong here with the rest of us."

"That's how I was made," she says with a wicked grin. "Now, be ready. You'll know when it's time."

Gerty pops open the door and slides out with a smile plastered on her face. When all eyes turn toward her, I think whatever she's got planned might work. We're just ten feet from the nearest tractor trailer. If she can keep the attention off of us, for just a few seconds...

"You ready?" I ask Taylor.

"You sure about this?"

I tilt my head toward the force field, which is casting everything in a kind of calm, sunset-like orange glow. It's the middle of the night, but it feels like dusk. "Ready or not, they're coming in seventeen minutes."

Gerty looks back and winks, which I think is our signal to start moving. I open the door. When I step out behind the broad door, I note the MPs' trance-like attention, locked on Gerty. I can't help but look for myself...and I get equally lost in the sight.

Every time I think she is going to pull out the sexy, she goes in the other direction. Instead of batting her eyes and asking the group of men what all the fussy-wussy is about, she starts humming *Take On Me* by A-ha and doing the 'best mates' meme dance—jogging in place, bringing her knees up high, with her upper arms jutting out and her dangling forearms swinging back and forth in time to her steps.

Taylor stops, too. "What in the name of all that is holy?"

McNasty snaps out of his confused state, locks eyes with me, and flares his nostrils like Smaug about to roast him some Bilbo. He stabs a meaty finger toward us. "Arrest them!"

As soon as the M16s swivel toward us, our options are limited to just one: give up. The MPs have likely never seen action, and as well trained as they might be, there is a chance one of them will flinch if we bolt. Fending off an alien invasion with a bullet hole in my back might be tricky.

Gerty stops her dance and scoffs at us. "How did you *not* get away?"

"Gerty..."

"You told me to distract them, and I did," she says, stepping toward the front of the Humvee while three MPs track her with their weapons.

"Not helping," I tell her.

"I was helping, but—"

"Not another word!" McNasty bellows. "Not. One. More."

He glares at Gerty until she sighs, rolls her eyes, and gently thumps her head in frustration against the Humvee's hood. "Ugh."

Then he turns his fire and fury on me, face red with anger. "This was your doing, wasn't it?"

"This?" I say. "You're going to have to be more specific."

"This!" he says, motioning to the force field with both hands raised.

"Are you implying I created a force field and am leading an alien invasion?"

He looks ready to implode. I know this is the wrong time to push the General's buttons, but it's hard-wired. The man destroyed my career. He's like a sandpaper thong up my ass crack during a run.

Irritating...is what I'm trying to say.

He takes out his phone, showing me the fifteen-minute timer still counting down. "This... Who's to say how long we might have had to respond? To pick the best possible option? Was it you?"

"If you're asking if it was Space Force...maybe. Yes. But it wasn't me...and it was kind of an accident."

McNasty looks a bit peaked. "Accident? Accident! You have committed this base to fight in some kind of arena combat with the fate of the world at stake, and you're telling me it was an accident?"

"Look at it this way, it could have been the ABDF who tapped their name acronym first."

"What...is the ABDF?" McNasty says, grinding his teeth, trying to control his nerves.

"Antigua and Barbuda Defense Force," Taylor says. "They only have a hundred fifty active duty personnel."

"Oh my god," I whisper to Taylor. "You so complete me."

"You know it," he says before we fist bump.

"And how many active personnel does *Space Force* have?" McNasty asks.

"On base?" I say.

"Three," Taylor says.

"Four," Gerty corrects.

"Okay," I say. "I kind of see your point, but look at all these strapping young men." I motion to the MPs around us, who now just look confused. They have no idea what's happening. "With a little help and guidance, they could—"

"Help and guidance from who?" the General asks.

"*Whom*," Gerty says.

The General's IBS must be acting up, because he convulses for a moment before reining himself in.

"From me," I say, "sir. Like it or not, we are now your—and this world's—best chance of surviving what's about to come."

These are the most earnest words I've spoken to the man since he had me removed from the SEALs. His reaction to them is nauseating despair. He takes a step and pitches forward.

When I take a step back, an eager, young MP raises his rifle a bit higher. "Just trying to get out of the line of fire," I say, as the General puts his hands on his knees and dry heaves a bit. After three empty regurgitations that sound like one of those Made-in-Taiwan, kids-toy groan sticks, McNasty wipes the drool from his mouth and attempts to compose himself.

But he can't.

Because he's terrified.

That's the real problem here. But I can't call him out on it. Not here. Not now. Because people who can't handle the stress of impending combat tend to make horrible choices. So I decide to implant one into his mind.

"I can explain everything," I say. "Just don't throw us in the brig."

"Do it," he says, snapping his fingers at the MPs. "To the brig. Now."

When the young MP says, "Move it. Now," I motion my head for Taylor and Gerty to obey, and they do. With the young guard in front of us, and three behind, we're led away through the parking lot. When we're out of sight and earshot of the General, the young MP turns around, looking a little sheepish—like an attractive Ryan Gosling. Yeah, I fuckin' said it, Gosling is a funny-looking S.O.B. The MP asks, "You mind telling me where the brig is at?"

11

HALE

There's nothing like pulling up to a wall of press in a school bus that's been severed in half by a blazing wall of light from space. Kind of like stepping out of a high school bathroom after having violent diarrhea to discover the snickering boys' basketball team standing outside the door. Not that anything like that ever happened. I mean, it's oddly specific, sure, but...ugh.

Overwhelming. It's overwhelming.

The blazing lights. The commingling voices. It's an assault on the senses that leaves me speechless and dumbfounded, until the wall of reporters crowding in realize I'm numb to them, or maybe having a stroke.

A strange silence settles over the throng surrounding the disemboweled bus. I spot Quaid and an apologetic-looking Chieng sneaking out the back. As they round the crowd, Chieng mouths, "Sorry," and then pantomimes a steering wheel in her hands. They're looking for a ride... which is a good idea, so I decide to not mentally flagellate them for abandoning me.

When all I can hear is the gentle crackling of the orange force field, I start to relax and manage to look into the eyes of the nearest reporter, a blonde woman who looks like a Barbie doll—fake boobs, fake nose, and a plastic complexion. She flashes an expensive smile and says, "Do you know what he was planning to tell you? I mean, he *was* talking about you, right?"

"Huh?" is the most articulate response I can come up with? "Who?"

"Captain Stone," she says, like I'm insane for not knowing what she's talking about. "Because it sounded to me like he was about to—"

"Lady," I say, and thrust my hand back toward the wall of orange energy rising into the sky.

"So you're not going to say?" she asks, and then lowers her mic. "Brilliant. That's going to play so well for ratings. Build suspense and your audience will grow. You're doing great."

She raises the mic again, but she's cut off by a man with a serious mustache and a matching unibrow. He strikes me as a serious newsman, who might focus on the fact that Earth has likely been invaded by aliens, and not on the love life of a disgraced Space Force pilot. "Kurt Chazman, Channel Seven News. Our polls show that forty-seven percent of people are more interested in the impending attack. That's a big number..."

"Is it?" I insert. "Seems like that should be a solid one hundred percent."

The reporter's chuckle is so grating that I'm sure it's the reason he hasn't risen above the echelon of local news reporter. It occurs to me that the people gathered here aren't the best and brightest journalists the world news has to offer. These are the gossip hounds, come to gawk at the demise of Space Force. Stone's public speech whipped them into such a frenzy that they haven't stopped to consider that standing just outside ground zero of Earth's first hostile contact with extraterrestrials might not be a great idea. Of course, the collective IQ of these people might be equal to that of a dandelion. Sooo...

"That's right," he continues. "Fifty-two percent are more concerned with Captain Stone's potential proposal."

"Proposal?" I'm aghast at the notion, and my reaction draws the reporters in even closer, a zombie horde out to eat my brain and offer it up to the media-numbed masses.

"That sounds like a no!" Barbie says.

"There are literally aliens, in space, soon to be down here, and you are more concerned with my love life?" I'm addressing the reporters and whatever buffoons took their poll at one in the morning. "Wait, what is the other one percent concerned about?"

"President West announced tariffs on..." Chazman looks at a notebook. "...on Jesus. Because 'There can be only one savior for humanity and it be [him].'"

I close my eyes and lower my head. Our new president isn't much of an improvement over the last, but he's mostly a figurehead, happy to let Congress govern the nation. That led to Space Force's demise, but I can't say I blame them. Until fifteen minutes ago, Space Force was really just a big playset for a man-child. I can see that now, but that man-child was also right...somehow.

"If you ever want to find out what's going on between Stone and me, you need to get the word out that people should evacuate the area surrounding the force fields," I say. "Do that, and I'll be the first to tell you what he was going to say, when he says it."

If we live.

The reporters go silent for a moment, and then, as though controlled by a hive mind, they turn to their individual cameras and all say basically the same thing in unison, "You heard it here first, Lieutenant Hale will dish on her steamy relationship with the hunky Captain Stone, but to make that happen, you folks need to get..."

I slink away, stepping up into the bus, and then out through the back. No one sees me or even notices I've gone until Chazman turns around to ask another question, lets out a squeal, and says, "She's gone, like a ninja!"

A second squeal makes me jump. A Dodge Charger stops in front of me. The passenger's side opens from the inside and a familiar voice says, "Get in, honey!"

Leaning over, I can see Quaid and Chieng in the backseat, and our bus driver in the front seat, behind the wheel. "Well, come on now, child. We gots to go!"

I climb in, slam the door shut, and I'm pinned to my chairback as the tires catch on the pavement and propel us forward. Reporters dive out of the way as our driver shouts, "Move your pale asses!"

When we're clear of the scene and free of the reporters, Quaid pipes up from the back.

"Pale asses?"

"They was all white folks," our driver says. "Ain't no black folks got time for this shit."

"You don't think that's racist?"

She glances over her shoulder at Quaid. "You sure that's a rabbit hole you want to climb down into, Mr. Blond Mustache?"

"Now you're insulting a man's facial hair?" Quaid's getting a little worked up.

"Well, it does looks like a cute little caterpillar crawled up on your—"

"I'm getting a little fucking tired of having to remind everyone that a disaster of cosmic proportions is about to break out."

The car goes silent.

"Apologies," our driver says, and then she offers a consolatory smile. "Name's Loretta. Sorry I left ya'll on the bridge, but I knew we needed some faster wheels."

"This is your car?" I ask.

She forces a smile. "Let's just say Space Force commandeered it from a midlife crisis with legs."

"You're...not with Space Force."

"Well, no. I'm with Schuber."

"Schuber?" Chieng asks, leaning forward between the seats.

"Like Uber, but for school buses."

"Well," I tell her. "We definitely owe you."

"About fifteen grand," she says. "School buses ain't cheap, and I got bills to pay. You know? It's not like I do this because it's fun, or because I like talking to people."

I want to tell her to send her bill to the aliens, but I don't want to risk her ire. She strikes me as a good woman, but also as someone who's endured a lot and who's not about to put up with anyone's shit. "I'm sure," I say, about to tell her where to go, when I note that we're already en route. Chieng must have told her.

Loretta is used to commanding a lot of power on the road and drives the Charger with all the authority a several-ton bus grants. Cars honk as we force them into right lanes, or off the road. Drivers and pedestrians, whose eyes are mostly turned up toward the sky despite the results of Chazman's poll, cuss us out as we roar past. That we don't kill anyone on our way to the Space Force launchpad is a small miracle.

Maybe the Holy West is looking out for us?

I'm expecting to be greeted at the gate by a guard, or maybe by some more of McNally's MPs, locking down Space Force's sister site. But the small base, which consists of a single building, like a squat control tower, a lone hangar bay, and a patch of concrete, is devoid of life, and power.

The car slows as we approach the locked chain-link fence. "This is where you all want to go?"

It doesn't look like much. Aside from a generic, 'Keep Out – U.S. Government Property' sign, there are no indications about what might lurk inside. I glance to the north. The orange spire jutting up into the air has shrunk, but it's still easy to spot. I look west to see even thinner lines stretching up from Camp Lejeune and Cherry Point. Fort Bragg and Pope Air Force Base are even further in that direction, home to the U.S. Special Forces. They're too far away to see, but I'm guessing they're cloaked in orange light beamed down from the night sky, too. If any base stood a chance of fending off an alien invasion, it was them. Instead... it's us.

The invaders have covered all the major bases, but smaller sites like the launchpad have either been overlooked, or not deemed a threat...which is probably true. Hurray...

"I think it's locked," Chieng says.

"Doesn't look locked to me," Loretta says, and then she stomps on the gas. The car lives up to its namesake, charging into and through the fence. We race down the long drive, coming to a screeching, spinning stop in front of the control tower.

Loretta does a little shimmy in her seat like she's got the chills. "Ohh, that felt good."

When she notices all of us staring at her, she adds, "I drive a bus... every day. Zero to sixty in minutes, not seconds. A girl needs to cut loose every now and again."

I don't bother pointing out that Loretta is far from being a girl, and old enough to be Chieng's mother. She got us here, though, and for that, I'm grateful. And then, when Loretta climbs out of the car, I'm confused.

When no one follows her, she says, "What are ya'll waiting for? Ain't we got the world to save?"

Quaid leans forward. "Is she serious?"

"As sweet tea," Loretta says, demonstrating that she can drive *and* has keen hearing.

"Sweet tea is serious?" Chieng asks, getting a scoff out of Quaid.

"You Yankees," he says, shaking his head as he exits the vehicle. "Is sweet tea serious..."

I step outside, look over at the launch pad I've never actually used, pluck my smartphone from my pocket, and dial Stone.

He answers with, "Hola." In the background, I hear someone complaining about him using the phone.

"Who is that?" I ask.

"MPs," he says. "We're being taken to the brig."

"Space Force doesn't have a brig," I point out.

"Well, no duh," he says, but offers nothing more. *Ahh*, I realize, *the MPs don't know that.*

"Don't suppose you have a plan yet," I say.

"I was kind of hoping you'd take care of the smart bit," he says to me, and then, "Seriously, if you try to touch me again, I will bitch-slap you back into your mamma's womb, and she's not going to be happy about having to pop you out again. I am *on* the phone." He clears his throat. "MPs have no manners. Anywho, we're going to try to stay alive in here... call me back when you have a plan. Okay?"

Great...

"Sure," I say, deadpan.

"And Hale?"

"What?"

"Kisses." When he starts making kissing sounds in the phone, I hang up. Across the tarmac, the hangar bay both beckons to, and intimidates me. I glance at the countdown on my phone.

Ten minutes...

12

STONE

"That's not going to win you any brownie points," Taylor says when I hang up the phone.

I stopped to take the call from Hale in a random, beige hallway inside Space Command. We're in the base's central building, which houses officer's quarters, operations, administration offices, and an armory. The latter being my destination.

"She loves it."

"Famous last words of a soon-to-be emasculated man."

"Umm, hello?" The young MP is aghast that I have totally disrespected his 'authority' and taken a phone call despite his demand that I don't. He's baffled as to why I'm not intimidated by him, not because his presence is commanding, but because he believes the weapon he holds speaks louder than his voice—which probably only stopped cracking in the past few weeks.

I give the kid a once-over. He's clean cut, healthy, and out of his element. Probably pictured a military police assignment on U.S. soil being a clean and easy ride to a G.I. Bill education, and now he's knee-deep in oily stank.

"Captain Suburbia," I say to him, and am appalled that he gives me his full attention. "What's your name?"

"T-Toby."

"Course it is," I say with a sigh. "Here's the situation. We're about to get bitch-slapped by a bunch of who-knows-whats from who-knows-where, and you're kind of putting a monkey wrench in the plans of the few people who might be able to keep you alive."

"The General gave me an order. It is my duty to follow it." The young men with Captain Suburbia buck up, showing their comradery via raised chins and smug looks. They're pushing it...

"Toby..." I pocket my phone. "I'm going to forgive you for being a dick, and for your name. You can't pick your commanding officer any more than you can pick the people who name you."

"I changed my name."

"Goddamnit," I whisper, pinching my nose. "Okay, here's the deal. The General is sending me to the brig because he doesn't like me."

"You're kind of a prick," says one of the other men, a skinny dude trying to hide the fact that he's getting off on his little power trip. But his Nick Nolte smile is hard to disguise.

"Actually," I say, "it's because I slept with his daughter."

The stunned silence and raised eyebrows say I've struck a chord. The slowly spreading smiles say they've at least seen his daughter, and despite being at least ten years younger, they are impressed.

"Three times," I say, and the MPs start giggling.

"Holy shit," Toby says. "That's awesome."

"I faked PTSD after arresting a drunk Marine just to lay on her couch," the tall fellow admits.

And just like that, I've broken through the mental and emotional defenses of four young men. "So, as you can imagine, when it comes to me, the General isn't exactly thinking clearly. And right now, we need some really clear thinking."

"Do you know what's happening?" Toby asks.

"You serious?" Taylor asks.

The lack of 'holy shit, aliens are invading,' in the kid's eyes says he's clueless. Of course he is. The MPs don't carry phones, and McNasty didn't tell them anything. How can I best explain this to a bunch of young men?

"You all gamers?" I ask.

"Who isn't?" says the tall guy.

I decide not to answer that question, because to these young men, everyone is a gamer to some extent or another. And he's right. There aren't many people who don't game these days, on PCs, consoles, or handheld devices, but that doesn't mean they're gamers.

"Battle Royale?" I ask. "PUBG? Fortnite? Ring of Elysium? Mavericks?"

"Yeah, of course. What's your—" Toby's eyes widen.

He's getting the picture.

"That's what's happening here? That orange wall thing? It's a dead zone?"

"Holy shit," says the shortest of the bunch, whose uniform looks a little too big. "This is awesome."

While the young man in me agrees—this is totally fucking awesome—the adult version of me, who is the actual me and knows countless lives are at stake says, "Not awesome. We have..." I pull out my phone again and reveal the countdown on screen. "Six minutes before the drop starts. That's a very small head start to get the weapons and gear we need to fend off a large-scale assault on this base from an unknown enemy."

"And if we don't," Gerty says, "every man, woman, and child on this planet will likely die. Horribly."

"What?" Toby says, voice quivering.

"What are you doing?" I grumble at Gerty.

"Motivating them," she says.

"They *were* motivated," I whisper. "Now they're pissing themselves."

She glances at their pants. "I don't see any moisture leakage." Then to the MPs. "Are you all wearing diapers?"

"Look," I say loud enough to reassert myself as the captain of this sinking vessel of a conversation. "Do any of you know who I am?"

"Captain Stone?" Toby guesses. "That's what the General called you...among other things."

"Weren't you a SEAL?" asks the fourth man of team MP. He's a bit squirrelly looking, with big bulging eyes constantly wary for something that hasn't shown up yet. Kind of like a less handsome Michael Cena. "I saw your profile on the Daily Show."

"Ohh, they did you on SNL," the tall one says. "That's chote."

"That's what now?"

"Chote." the tall MP says. "Means it's good."

"Since when?"

"Some weird science fiction novel a few years ago," Taylor says.

"You're aware of this?" I ask.

He shrugs. "Aware, but in denial. The novel became a bestseller, but it's true lasting legacy was...chote."

"You know a chote is a penis that is wider than it is long," I say.

Taylor scratches his head. "Is that even possible?"

"How is that a good thing?" Gerty asks.

"It's like saying something is bad, when it's good," Toby says. The off-topic conversation is putting him at ease.

"Who says that?" Gerty asks.

"People in the early nineties," I explain. "The eighties kind of left everyone in a neon stupor. It was a confusing time. No one says it anymore."

"So bad means bad again and chote means good?" Gerty ponders this for a moment, grows serious, and says, "This is a slippery slope of a discussion. We have just five minutes remaining."

"Right," I say. Back to the pep-talk that will hopefully result in our movement being unhindered from here on out.

"Recognize me now?" I ask and then, in the more energetic voice of my in-game persona, I say, "I want you maggots to hit the LZ, ASAP. Tangos at my six are lit up, soldier!"

Eyes widen with recognition. "Captain Stone...Castle?" Toby says.

"In the flesh," I say, a trace of my online voice remaining. "And if anyone can handle an IRL battle royale situation, it's me."

Toby and his MP mates have a debate with their eyes, all of them unsure, but ultimately deferring to Toby, their de facto leader. "What should we do?"

"You know how this works." I mentally guestimate the number of human beings now on base being around fifty. "Fifty V fifty. Winner take all. We're in it to win it, boys. In a battle royale, that means staying alive. Nothing else matters. Don't keep track of your kills. Don't get competitive."

"Right," Toby says. "Last man standing."

"Last race standing," Gerty adds. "These *are* aliens we're facing."

Her words pale the young men once more.

"Look." I place a hand on Toby's shoulder. "Spread the word. Squad up. Find a defensible position. We'll handle the rest."

My plan doesn't exactly put him at ease, but he nods like a toy woodpecker sliding down a pole.

"Now, move it, soldier!" All four MPs flinch and strike out back the way we came, weapons raised, moving in formation like they're a bona fide SEAL team.

"We'll handle the rest?" Taylor asks, when they take a left turn where they shouldn't have.

I shrug. "You know, I put on this optimism for you, and you can't even say it looks good on me?"

"Wait," Gerty says. I've baffled the robot. Shocker. "You're wearing optimism?"

"It's a metaphor," I say.

"Ohh, I see." Gerty rubs her hands over her thighs like she's proud of her wardrobe. "Well, I'm wearing 'You're all going to die.'" She smiles. "Like that?"

When Taylor and I stare at her, wearing Grumpy Cat frowns, she holds up an index finger and waggles it back and forth. "Tick tock."

Running away from Gerty's discouragement and toward the armory, Taylor and I find our stride again.

"Don't listen to her," I tell him. "This is what we do. This is what we've always done. Find the enemy and shoot them dead."

"Actually, I mostly made friends with local people, recruiting and training them to defend themselves, but sure, death and destruction. Let's do it."

We arrive at the armory a moment later, only to find the door locked. Of course, it's locked. It's an armory.

"Maybe we can pick the lock?" Taylor asks.

"Look out," Gerty says, grasping the door handle, which dents under her fingers. With a quick yank, the door is torn open, giving us access to the weaponry within. It's not quite Neo's fantasy armory from The Matrix, but there are more guns and ammo than a brouhaha in Alaska, the most rootin' and tootin'est state in the union, despite what Texas would have you believe.

With just minutes to spare, we make short work of armoring up, snagging some high-tech gear, and gathering a small arsenal.

Gerty does the same, sans the armor, which I suppose she doesn't need, and then she fills a backpack with enough spare ammo magazines to gun down an army of Smurfs. I mean, the imaginary army in this scenario could be any army, but I just really hate Smurfs. I mean, Papa Smurf is okay, but fucking Brainy? He tilts the scales of imaginary justice toward making blue-smeared genocide not just palatable, but intoxicating.

"One minute," Gerty declares, standing by the door, HK416 assault rifle in hand, heavy backpack over her shoulders.

"Good to go?" I ask Taylor.

He thumps a fist against his armored chest. "Level three everything, baby."

I nod my approval. "I want to see this." I head for the door with Taylor on my heels. We move to the rear entrance, which is much closer, and barrel out into the orange glow of a force-field illuminated night.

The back of the building is a manicured garden of concrete walkways, staircases, and planters full of lush plants from around the world. It's a relaxing place to hang out, but it does nothing to ease my tension in regard to the impending alien invasion.

"Ten seconds," Gerty says, and we look skyward.

When my mental countdown hits zero, I say, "I don't see anythi—"

The shrill scream of a thousand babies mixed with the wail of David Lee Roth having his nuts clenched in a hippo's jaws fills the air like a klaxon. It drops me to my knees, hands over my ears, grunting for no one to hear, "No...fair..."

13

HALE

"You ever wish you could 80s montage your way through a problem?" Quaid asks. He's on a knee, attempting to pick the door's lock. Once the door is open, we'll have a short amount of time to disable the alarm system, but our keycards should still be active, and *should* do the job. I'm not a fan of double-should-ing something, but there aren't many other options.

"That doesn't even make sense," Chieng complains, nervously bouncing from one foot to the other. She's afraid we'll get caught, despite my assurances that we are the last thing on anyone's mind at the moment.

"Like, if you could mentally leap forward in time? Your body would be business as usual, but your consciousness—your inner narrator—would be immune to time moving forward." When Chieng just looks baffled by the assertion, he adds, "C'mon Chieng, don't be a dotard."

Challenging Chieng's intellect is never a good idea. Despite appearances, Quaid can hold his own, but Chieng operates at a higher level. Not quite a Billy-level of super-human intellect, but she's about as smart as you can get without being too socially awkward.

She must really be shaken, because she doesn't rise to the challenge with a quip or a mental wrestling reversal.

"Ya'll are gonna save the world?" Loretta says, leaning against the building's walls, arms crossed, looking on while projecting disapproval and doubt.

"Feel free to vacate the premises, civvie," Quaid says. "I'm montaging."

He starts humming 'Maniac' from *Flashdance*, and I can't help but mentally join in.

Quaid focuses on the lock, biting his lower lip as he works paper clips into the deadbolt.

I crouch down to help, but my hair hangs in the way.

I tie it back with a bandana from my pocket.

Chieng's nervous bob becomes a quick-step run in place to the *Maniac* beat.

The lock begins to turn.

I tense up, looking closer.

"All right, that's enough of this shit," Loretta blurts out.

The music in my head stops. I snap out of my laser-like concentration.

"We almost had it!" Quaid complains.

"Ya'll have been montaging for *five minutes* and aren't any closer to opening that door. Plus, you're doing a shit job with the song I first broke the lawn chair to."

"Broke the lawn chair?" Quaid asks, turning to Loretta, who is sitting behind the wheel in the Charger.

"Dropped the Skittle?" she says. "Opened the Pringles?"

"Pringles?" Quaid is baffled, as am I.

"Once you pop..." Loretta says.

"Ohh," Quaid says, but I still don't understand until he translates. "You got deflowered to 'Maniac?'"

She shrugs. "Was that or bowling. Now..." The Charger roars to life. "Get out the damn way."

The *tap, tap, tap* of Chieng's feet still running to the tune catches my attention. "Chieng." Nothing. "Chieng!"

She flinches to a stop, touching down hard after being lost in the montage. I help her out of the way, as Loretta revs the engine. The car sounds like it could plow through one end of the building and out the other.

Tires spin.

The car lurches forward.

The door folds inward...a few inches, as Loretta gently nudges it with the car's front end. When she pulls back, puts the car in park, and sets the safety brake, the door swings open.

"Well, that was anti-climactic," Quaid says.

"It's open, ain't it!" Loretta says.

Ignoring the argument, I step inside, locate the beeping security panel, and swipe my card. The red light turns green, and the hallway lights blink to life. I've only been to the launchpad twice before. Once for a tour, and then again for an orientation, which was brief. After that, it became apparent that I'd never really have a chance to fly the experimental craft hidden within the facility's lone hangar.

I head up the stairs feeling like a student who has returned to school during the summer to find the place eerily haunted and devoid of what made it feel alive—people. When Space Force started losing funding, the T-1-Rex was the first program to be scrapped, despite billions being spent on research and prototype construction. The first-and-only space fighter developed on Earth has been collecting dust since. I've logged hundreds of hours in the flight sim, but I've never set foot in the real thing.

I step into the control tower, looking over the high-tech consoles where twenty people should be seated, ready to provide support to Space Force's one-and-only space fighter pilot—me. But the screens are powered down and blank. And the seats are empty.

"Kind of creepy," Chieng says. I think she's talking about the base's empty-dead vibe, but then she runs a finger over a desktop. "Place hasn't been dusted in years."

"Right..."

"You think all of this works?" Chieng asks.

The computers snap on to a Space Force boot screen. I'm not sure how much money was put into the little rocket ship-shaped 'A' in 'Space,' but I have to admit, I like the way it slowly spins around, especially on my Dick. The systems here should be identical to those on our Defense Initiative Computers, and in the simulator, so we should be able to get up and running by the time the timer runs out. Speaking of...

I look at my phone. Three minutes. Loretta was right, we did spend too much time montaging.

I turn to find Quaid at the back of the room, beside a wall-mounted control panel. He pushes buttons, one by one, bringing the Launch Pad to life.

Chieng sits at one of the consoles, waiting for the system to finish booting. Loretta takes a seat next to her, says "Comfy," and then leans back. "How many millions of my taxpayer dollars did each of these— yeargh!" The chair's front wheels lift off the ground and the rear set rolls forward, as though the furniture took offense to her criticism and decided to suplex her.

Loretta rolls off the chair all in a fluster, waving her hand at her face like she's overheated. "Oh Lawd, I done been attacked!"

She calms down when we have a laugh at her expense.

"Watch out for them rolling chairs," Quaid says, "Or you might not live long enough to be killed by aliens."

I have mercy on Loretta as she rolls over onto her belly like a cooked sausage and struggles to push herself up. I reach down a hand and have no trouble pulling her up, despite her plump rolls.

She eyes me suspiciously and pinches my biceps. "You a man?"

I nearly drop her back on the floor. "I look like a man to you?"

"To be fair," Quaid says, "ain't the first time you been asked."

If I had a projectile to throw, I would have aimed low and center mass. Short of tossing Loretta, which *is* tempting, I'm unarmed.

"Coming up on the one-minute mark," Chieng says, fingers working the keyboard. "Hangar is still powered down."

"I'm on it," Quaid says, pushing a button on the control panel.

Outside the large windows overlooking the concrete launch pad, the hangar's external lights blaze to life. I step toward the glass to watch the hangar doors open, revealing the *T-1-Rex*, the world's most technologically advanced...

"What the fuck?!"

Twelve men locked in 'oh shit' stillness, and dressed in scary-as-hell black ops uniforms stand in front of the hangar in two lines.

"Holy shit," Quaid says, sliding to a stop beside me. "Those are our guys."

On the ground, the men clump into tight clusters, weapons raised, ready for action. They're heavily armed and well trained. I've seen Stone and Taylor move with the same kind of disciplined fluidity, but there is something more ominous about these men.

And then Chieng reveals why. "No. Spetsnaz."

When I was a teenager, I liked this guy named Todd Richard. In hindsight, he was strange, and hairy, but he played the drums like a magician, so I crushed hard. I wasn't big on parties then—it was awkward being taller than boys my age—but Todd was the host, and he had invited me personally.

That was going to be the night, I believed. Todd was going to...break my lawn chair. Only it wasn't, and he didn't. I walked in on Todd with two of my friends. It was a sucker punch to the taint that left me staggered and winded. Hearing that the men outside are from Russia's most elite fighting force—like fucking grizzly bears with guns and vodka for blood— has a similar effect.

I lean forward, hands on the console, to catch my breath while trying to make out their uniforms and any identifiable insignias, but their black gear and armor is featureless. "Are you sure?"

She turns her monitor toward me, revealing a security feed zoomed in on the men. "Don't look at what they're wearing. Look at what they're holding."

Their weapons, I realize, and I scan the men. I see an AKM, which is a modernized AK-47, an OSV-96 sniper rifle, and a VSS Vintorez, which I once heard Stone call the 'limp dick of the Russian military.' The sound-suppressed rifle fires fast and accurate at range, but it uses 9mm ammo, a relatively small caliber compared to the heavy hitting 7.62 used in most Russian weapons. That said, it works just fine against adversaries without body armor...which we are.

It's at that moment that one of the men stands up straight and levels an index finger at us. Quaid, Loretta, and I drop down like a bunch of kids caught playing ding-dong ditch, but it's too little, too late.

"They're coming," Chieng says.

On screen, the two lines of Spetsnaz charge toward the control tower. They make it just ten steps before a high-pitched scream, like that of a tortured leprechaun whose pot of gold was shit in by Richard Simmons, blares from everywhere and nowhere and knocks us all to the ground, hands clutched over our ears. It's from this lowly position that I look up through the big windows and see the silhouettes of parachutes sail past overhead.

The cavalry has arrived, I think, but then I notice that all the parachutes are red, with a bold yellow #1 stenciled in the middle. *Number one? Who the hell is number one?* When the sound comes to an abrupt stop and my thoughts clear, I remember Stone and Taylor's rants about gaming cheaters.

China...

China is number one.

14

STONE

The blaring sound comes to a sudden stop, but it leaves a ringing in my ears. It's not uncommon to announce a change in a battle royale game with a sound, but making it loud enough to give the dead hearing damage is a serious dick move. I suppose that should be expected from assholes who invade planets.

A flash of blue light draws my eyes back up. A beam of light snaps down to the ground, its destination hidden by the base's structures. Within the beam, a dark blur slides down to the ground.

"Is that it?" Taylor asks. "Did they just send one fighter?"

"Perhaps their prowess in battle makes anything more an unfair battle?" Gerty says.

With most of the base's occupants being glorified movers and inexperienced military police, just about anything an advanced alien civilization sent to fight would be unfair. But having to only keep track of, and defeat, a single adversary, would simplify the situation.

And then a wet blanket descends from the sky in the form of forty-nine more lines of light, each of them shuttling something large toward the surface. Some of them are larger than others, but none of them are what I'd call small.

I stagger back when a beam of blue energy strikes the ground just a few feet away. A static charge raises the hairs on my arms, and tugs on my non-regulation beard, but it doesn't feel dangerous...until a hulking heap of armor lands atop a concrete planter, decimating the large leafy plant within, and shattering the pot's sides open like flower petals.

Taylor and I snap our weapons up, but we don't open fire. I'm looking for a chink in its maroon-colored armor plating, but I don't see any.

"Don't let them be robots," Taylor says. "Please, not robots."

Gunfire erupts from different parts of the base. It's followed by the sounds of screaming. The force field surrounding the base flashes with three bands of red, shooting up toward the sky.

The hell was that?

Gerty approaches the enemy, which currently looks like a crumpled up chunk of red aluminum foil.

"I don't think that's a good—"

An appendage snaps out, catching Gerty in the torso. She's launched into the air, as though the Jolly Green Giant had reached down and flicked her. She sails a hundred feet before crashing into, and through, the wall of a maintenance shed.

"Well," Taylor says, backing away, "At least I can say I knew a robot."

I back away at an opposite angle, which will allow us to fire from different sides without having to worry about shooting each other... unless the bullets ricochet.

"Dibs on not telling Billy," I say.

"Damnit," Taylor says.

A gurgling roar rises from the unfurling alien. It's wet and viscous. Definitely something fleshy under all that armor. The plates twist and fall into place, forming something like a cross between a gorilla in the back and a giant tiger in the front. Its long neck tapers to a smooth domed head that sports a sinister grin of triangular teeth. The red and black exoskeleton is stylish and intimidating, but the underlying shape is hard to ignore.

"If you ignore the arms and legs..." I say, noting the claws at the end of each.

"I see it," Taylor says with a bit of a chuckle. We're probably about to die. Why not have some fun before the end? "Like a short dick."

"A chote," I say, with a grin, aiming for the joint of its shoulder.

"'Chote' it is," Taylor says. "On three?"

The Chote spins toward Taylor, its jaws opening wide. The gurgling roar that emanates from its mouth sounds like an elephant placed its puckered sphincter against a trombone and let loose a moist fart.

"Three!" Taylor says, opening fire.

I adjust my aim to compensate for the creature's movements, and then pull the trigger, unloading a full spray of 5.56 caliber ammo. I feel like Rambo, my muscles flexed and my veins popping as they pump all-American blood into my white knuckled grip, holding the bucking weapon as it unloads a fusillade of lead fury. My confidence is short-lived. Sparks fly from the armor, but I can't tell if any penetrate. The thing bucks and thrashes under the assault, its movements more confused than in pain.

With a leap it closes the distance between itself and Taylor. The Chote lowers its head and then snaps it up. Had Taylor not rolled back out of the way, he'd have been struck with the same force that sent Gerty flying. His body, being made of flesh, blood, and bone, rather than whatever metal Gerty's body was built from, would have popped like a water-balloon full of ground beef and strawberry syrup.

The Chote unleashes another roar, and I can tell from Taylor's twisted up face, that it smells as gnarly as it sounds.

"Oh," Taylor says, scrambling back while raking his teeth over his tongue and spitting. "Oh, God."

Rather than finishing him off, the tip of the phallic head, upon which I see no eyes, turns skyward.

It's waiting for something...

A series of blue beams descend from above, much smaller than the first bunch, and more numerous. When the Chote sees a beam strike the concrete a hundred feet away, it snorts and gallops toward it. Gallop is a generous word. The thing's movements are awkward, its back end pushing too hard, the legs kicking out like a bucking horse, while its slender arms reach out and pull it forward. There's nothing graceful about the Chote, almost like the thing is still getting accustomed to its armor—which would be good—but it manages to cover the ground in seconds, despite looking ridiculous.

As I reload my SCAR-L's magazine, knowing its bullets are useless against the armored behemoth, I realize the truth about what has just descended from above.

The weapons have spawned.

I turn south and spot a glowing beam of energy before it flicks out. I have no idea what's been dropped over there, but if I'm right, it might be our only hope of inflicting damage on the armored alien.

"Keep it busy," I say and sprint away.

"Keep it what?" Taylor's voice fades behind me as I run. "Suck my ba—"

A whoosh of energy cuts through the air. It's followed by a Doppler effect of Taylor's voice gaining on me and then passing me. "—aaaaaaalllllllssss. Oof!" He pinwheels past me and lands in a fortuitously placed bush, the layers of small branches breaking his fall.

"That's not what I had in mind," I say, running past him again.

"Fuck and you," he grumbles, pushing himself up from the foliage and leveling his weapon back the way he came. "It's some kind of anti-gravity weapon. Picked me up gently enough, but the landing..."

As he unloads his assault rifle at the Chote, who is now charging, I race onward, in pursuit of whatever spawned a short distance away. I vault over the short wall marking the boundary between the manicured garden and the relatively barren natural landscape of Portsmouth Island.

I flinch when two more red bands of light surge up through the force field. I have no idea what they mean, but they can't be good.

Beyond the wall is a sloping hill covered by grass that's been shorn like a college bro's back—smooth. It's like stepping on a water bed full of mud. Water oozes up through the grass, reminding me that before a bazillion tons of concrete and sand were poured, the island was mostly tidal swamp.

The barrage of bullets behind me falls silent as Taylor tears through all forty rounds. In the silence that follows, his voice is easy to hear. "Oh, shit. Oh, shit! Oh—"

A crackling whoosh punches through the air, and I feel just a trace of the anti-gravity weapon's effect slap into my back. Taylor's voice dopplers toward me again. "I haaaatteee yoooouuuu."

He flies past overhead, abandoning his weapon midair. Landing on it would not only hurt like hell, but it would probably break some bones, if not his back.

He falls out of view on the far side of the rise.

I'm struck with intense fear, knowing my friend could be dead, and that I'll likely be next, but then I hear him cursing, and I know he's okay. Men who are hurt, curse. Men who are dying, scream.

I scoop up his weapon as I pass it.

I crest the hill to find a muddy path the size of Taylor's fifty-pound ass carved into the hillside from where he landed all the way to the bottom. He pushes his soiled body up from the dirt, looking equal parts pissed, humiliated, and relieved.

"I'm not doing that again!" he shouts.

I toss him his rifle. "Just run!"

He's up and moving just after I pass.

Our target is just fifty feet ahead, the blue glow of whatever techno-logy beamed it down to Earth just now fading. To find the other spawned weapons, we're just going to have to stumble across them.

Maybe one will be enough, I dare to hope.

And then I see it—a neat square of yellow about the size of a napkin. *What...*

I slide to a stop and immediately recognize the green, white, red, and yellow pattern as a tartan. I pick it up and the fabric unfurls to reveal what is either a colorful Catholic schoolgirl skirt, or Willow Ufgood's kilt.

"We got skirted!" I shout, holding it up for Taylor to see. He's already at full stride and pounds right on past, eyes wide with disbelief. While battle royale games are rife with weapon pickups, they're also ridden with swag you can pick up along the way to make yourself look cool, sexy, or silly before being dropped by a sniper's bullet. That aliens invading Earth thought to include the annoying detail vexes me to no end.

A hooting, like a wet laugh, draws my eyes to the top of the hill Taylor slid down. The Chote stands on it, victoriously pumping its head and neck in and out... "Ohh," I say, unable to verbalize how deeply my eyes have just been violated. "Ugh."

I unpin a grenade, cock it back, and chuck it toward the air-humping alien.

I stumble back before running again. With the base at our back and the ocean ahead, and the force field a few hundred feet beyond that, there is only one place we can go. "Get to the church!"

Glancing back to observe the grenade's effect, I watch the hand-thrown projectile drop toward the Chote's domed head. The alien points its weapon—which looks like a futuristic rifle with a bowl on the front—at the grenade. Then it pulls the trigger.

The frag is launched away, faster than I can see, heading toward the church, which is a quarter mile away, near the coast. The grenade hits the steeple's side, punches straight through, and explodes.

15

HALE

"What in the name of Daniel Day-Lewis was that?" Loretta says from the floor, rubbing her ears.

"Time's up," Chieng says, moving to the north side of the O-shaped tower. The orange force field surrounding Portsmouth Island is just over the horizon, stretching up into the night. Inside it, streaks of light flash toward the ground and then fade. I can't see what's happening, but I've watched enough battle royale games to guess.

The invaders have arrived.

The game has begun.

In some ways, I envy Stone. His enemy is uncomplicated. He'll have no regret over killing something that's not human and wants to take our planet. Me, on the other hand...

The Spetsnaz have recovered from the blaring sound and are approaching again, this time a little more cautiously. That they're still out in the open means they know we're unarmed, and that they didn't see the Chinese infiltrators when they floated past.

How the hell are we going to open the hangar doors and get there without being intercepted by Ivan?

We're not.

Our best and only option is to reason with them. I mean, Earth has been invaded. All of us, and our countries, are at risk. If they want to kick some alien ass, fine by me. I'll fly 'em where they need to go.

So how do I make contact without getting a bullet in the face? Bang on the glass? Attempt sign language? There're no intercoms. I doubt we could find the frequency of their comms in time. Wave a white flag like we're in a frikken' Warner Bros. cartoon?

"You all need to hide," I tell the others, and when I turn to face them, everyone is already gone. "Seriously? You guys already—"

"Ahem," a deep voice rumbles from around the corner. A man dressed in all black steps into view from the stairwell at the tower's core. He's got one hand on Chieng's shoulder and holds a weapon against her side. As far as hostage takers go, he's pretty gentle. She doesn't even look frightened, or in pain.

I focus on the weapon and understand why. The weapon is a non-lethal taser.

What kind of Nancy horseshit is this? I mean, Ricky Mazoni was more intimidating, and he was a ten-year-old with short-man syndrome. Liked to beat up my friends until I put my foot in his conveniently placed face. This guy might be holding a painful weapon, but he lacks little Ricky's menace, even with the black mask concealing his identity.

"Sorry about this," the man says, "but I'm going to need access to the T-1."

"Seriously? Canada?"

The man's head snaps back like he's been slapped. "What? Canada? Pfft."

"You just said, 'soory boot this'." His accent wasn't quite so clear, but there was enough of it to ID his nation of origin. "Okay, eh? Bunch of hosers."

"We don't say that," a second man says, exiting the stairwell in a huff. He's sporting a middle-aged ponch and the slight hunch of someone who spends too much time behind a computer screen. "*Strange Brew* wasn't the only movie made about Canadians."

The lead man lowers and shakes his head. He wasn't hard to read, but he also wasn't blatantly confirming my suspicions. His partner, Poncharello, seems like the kind of guy who took a few too many hits on the ice.

They're not Canadian Special Forces, which wouldn't be too surprising. Our two nations haven't been BFFs since the trade wars and the annexation of Montreal. Sure, President West returned the territory, but lives were lost, families were displaced, and trust was broken. So why send these knuckleheads instead of Joint Task Force 2—the Delta operators of the great white north?

And how the hell did everyone get here so fast?

Below us, someone slams into the hangar's side door, ignorant to the fact that the door on the far side was ruined by Loretta's driving.

"Hey, eh," says a third man, exiting the stairwell. He's almost portly, squeezed into his uniform. "I think someone is comin' in doon there. They're working that door like a bull moose wit a hard on."

The lead man sighs and lowers his weapon, letting Chieng go. "Again, soory 'boot this." He pulls off his mask to reveal a kind-looking face and a bald head. He gives me an earnest smile. "I'm Captain Bruce Klark. We're what you'd call your Canadian counterparts."

"Canada has a Space Force?" Chieng asks, even though the question on the tip of my tongue is, *are you named after the true identities of Bruce Wayne and Clark Kent?*

"CC1. We're a small division within the Royal Canadian Air Force. Anything more than that seemed..."

"Excessive," I say.

Klark looks out the window at the distant orange glow. "But now..."

"They caught us all with our pants down," I say.

"Well..." The way he says it, like I might have missed a memo about the impending alien invasion, sends roots of tension down my back.

Another thump below captures Klark's attention. "Is that one of your people?"

"Spetsnaz," Quaid says, stepping out from the tower's south side and making all three Canadians jump in surprise. Non-lethal and jumpy. I'm thinking these men didn't even attend Basic. Turns out Quaid wasn't hiding. He was just keeping an eye on our company. "Two squads. One keeping watch, one infiltrating."

"Spetsnaz," says the chubbiest Canadian. "Oh...oh, no."

"'Oh no' is putting it lightly," Quaid says. "They're Spetsgruppa Alfa." When no one reacts, he says, "Alpha Squad. Not only are they the very best Russian Spec Ops has to offer, they also have a reputation for being somewhat-to-completely psychotic."

Psychotic sounds bad...when it's coming your way. "What if we could talk to them? Join forces?"

Quaid shakes his head. "If they're here, they know what they want, they know how to get it, how to use it, and what to use it for.

The moment they see us, they'll rain down metal..." His eyes flare. He raises a finger, says, "Be right back," and then disappears back to the far side of the control tower.

"They must be here for the T-1," Klark says. "Same as us."

"What were you going to do with it?" I ask.

"Pick up our go-team and then..." He turns his head upward. "Probably too little, too late, honestly, but here's the hard truth: as bad as the odds might be against us succeeding, they're much worse for you."

"Really," I say, clenching my fists. Assuming he's read my file, he knows I can kick his ass.

"I mean..."

"Can't we just give it to them?" the portly Canuck asks. "Open the hangar and just stay out of their way?"

It's not the worst idea in the world. It might even keep us alive. But there is no way in hell any psycho Russkie jarhead who's had his humanity electro-ball-shocked away can pilot the *Rex* like I can—if at all. It's not remotely like handling a jet, especially when zero-Gs are involved. Plus, I kind of feel like I've been waiting all fucking day in the hot sun for my chance to ride Space Mountain, and now I'm getting kicked out of line. "Not going to happen."

"Why the hell not?" Loretta asks, making all three Canadians jump. They had no idea she was hiding under the console behind them.

"Just stay under the desk, Loretta." I head for the stairwell door, where the Canadians keep watch. "I will try to reason with them, but the moment someone pulls a trigger, I'm going *La Femme Nikita* on their asses."

It's big talk, and it sounds good, but I have no illusions about taking out twelve Alpha Squad members with Quaid, Chieng, and Team Maple watching my back. When Poncharello blocks my path and says, "I'll do it," I'm somewhat relieved.

Telling the feminist in me to shut the hell up, that I don't need to measure dicks with the poor man's Space Force, I motion to the stairs. "Have at it."

He stands up a bit straighter, sucks in the ponch, and says, "Back in a jiff."

When the sound of his footsteps fades, Loretta pipes up from her hiding spot. "Uh-uh, ya'll know he ain't comin' back."

Below us, the door crashes open.

"Hold your fire!" Poncharello shouts. "We're here to he—"

A quick three round burst rips through the air.

Silence follows.

And then, footsteps.

I back away from the stairwell beside the Canadians and Chieng. Loretta pushes herself further under the desk, but there is no hiding from whoever is coming up the stairs.

I snap at Klark. "Weapon."

He searches his belt, draws a weapon, and tosses it to me. I catch the small canister in one hand and give it a look. "Pepper spray? *Pepper spray?* These assholes probably flavor their borscht with this!"

Chieng accepts a canister of pepper spray from the chubby soldier and backs further away. She might be a member of the U.S. military, but she wasn't recruited for her fighting ability. Like these three men, she's here because of her mind.

I glance back at the orange force field to the north, wishing Stone were here, but knowing whatever he's up against is probably worse. I mean, if we all die horribly, maybe the Spetsnaz will still somehow manage to save the world, which kind of feels like putting hope in crocodiles putting out a fire—they'd be intimidating as hell, but probably eat everyone running away from the flames.

I jump when a black-gloved hand wraps around the door frame.

Pepper spray aimed, I wait to see a set of eyes, and I hope they're not masked.

When Poncharello steps into the room, I nearly douse him with liquified agony, but I manage to hold my fire. He's not a threat to anyone, and never will be. His black uniform glistens with blood. He stumbles into Chubs. "Soory." Then he staggers over to Klark. "Soory. Then turns to me. "Soory."

It's like an invisible lumberjack runs through the room and chops out his legs. Poncharello hits the floor hard enough to make me wince, despite the fact that he is undoubtably dead before he lands.

Before I can even think about what to do next, Quaid runs into the room, dives beneath a console and shouts, "Take cover!"

16

STONE

"Dear Lord Jesus," I pray to the sky as I run toward the church, the remnants of its steeple still fluttering down to the ground. "Please smite our enemies. Is that something you do? Smite?" I don't think so, so I shift gears. "Dear Jesus's dad, please smite these assholes, or at least give us a way to smite them on thy behalf."

As usual, the higher power I'm trying to make sense to ignores my pleas. I consider using logic with God, but if God is real, then he also made the platypus, and where is the logic in that? They sweat anti-bacterial milk, they lay eggs, and they have duck-bills. And a venomous spur on their leg. Seriously? If God is real, He also made the Chote, and who's to say which side of this conflict He's on. Maybe the phallic assholes are the ones doing the smiting on the Big Man's behalf?

"I mean...this can't be something you'd condone, right?" I shift my attention back to the son. "Love your neighbor and all that."

"You might be talking to the wrong person," Taylor says. He's got a good second lead on me, but he can still hear my one-sided conversation. "He also said to turn the other cheek."

"But he was talking about people, yeah? I mean, if it's not a person, he pretty much gave us permission to eat them, right?"

Taylor manages to smile back at me despite the fact that we're running away from an alien with a hard-on head and an anti-gravity weapon.

"Didn't realize you were so churched," he says.

Taylor grew up in the Baptist church. He's fully indoctrinated and probably qualifies as a believer despite his questionable hobbies, his ability to consume copious amounts of booze, and killing being part of his job.

"Sunday school," I say. "The teacher had legs like..."

I turn my eyes skyward again.

"Sorry..." I continue, "but really. You made her. You know what I'm talking about."

Taylor laughs, but it's kind of a 'you're so screwed' chuckle, like I'm the only one being chased down by an alien.

"Okay, so, I'm not winning myself any brownie points with God," I say, heading for the church's red front door. The solid oak would stop bullets, but once we're inside the building, we might find ourselves in a Three Little Pigs scenario. "I should probably stop talking, and start thinking. Short of converting and becoming a celibate monk, I'm pretty sure there's nothing I can do to win the Good Lord's favor."

"Lucky for you," Taylor says, shouldering through the door. "That's not how it works." He slams the door shut behind us and locks the deadbolt. The door is never locked, in part because there is nothing to steal, aside from some old Bibles and hymnals that look like they haven't been used in a hundred years. Also because the building has been unused since Space Force set up camp.

Shouldering our weapons and aiming them at the door, we back away down the opposite sides of the sanctuary, rows of pews separating us.

Outside, the Chote roars, either in excitement that his prey is trapped, or in frustration that it can no longer see us. I probably shouldn't try to guess at the emotional state of an alien being, though its earlier thrusting seemed pretty straight forward. Maybe a solid 'fuck you' air hump is as universal throughout the galaxy as a smile is here on Earth?

I crouch down behind the front pew. It's solid and bolted to the floor. Old-school churches were built to last.

Outside, the Chote stalks. Its silhouette, cast in the dull orange glow of the force field's light, shifts past the stained-glass windows framing the doorway. And then, inexplicably, it backs away.

When a huffing sound fills the air outside the building, I'm instantly annoyed. "Is it laughing at us?"

"Sounds like it," Taylor says.

"I ain't no little pig!" I shout, standing and aiming at the window.

I'm about to unload my magazine into the glass, knowing that, even if I manage to hit the Chote, it wouldn't do any good. For the first time in my career, my weaponry is infertile. I might as well be firing blanks.

When the Chote goes still, and I zero in on its body, Taylor shouts, "Down!" and he tackles me to the side.

There's a loud *whump*, followed by an explosion of shattering wood, ancient nails, and glass. Above us, the front half of the church peels off into the sky. Orange light flows into the shadowy building, and twinkles off something round resting atop the pragmatic looking podium, behind which a cross manages to stand defiant.

I focus on the spherical object. It's black and sleek. Definitely out of place.

A weapon spawn.

The beams of light didn't just teleport items to the ground; it also sent them *inside* structures. It's super cool and *Star Trek* sexy, but it kind of punctuates just how technically advanced the Chote are, and how FUBAR our situation is. Despite all that, I push myself up.

The front of the church is missing.

Outside, the Chote is pumping its body again, and I have no doubt it's just enjoying the mayhem, believing it has nothing to fear.

"This asshole thinks we're a couple of AFKs," I grumble, using slang for Away From Keyboard, which Taylor has no trouble understanding. We've played many a game where we've found ourselves in the Chote's shoes, shotgunning a handful of AFK players and padding our kill-death ratios.

"Well..." Taylor says, and that's all he needs to say to make his point. We might be mobile, but we're essentially at this thing's mercy. The alien's armor is impenetrable to conventional weaponry. It's freakishly awkward, but it's strong, fast, and armed with a weapon that can toss us through the air and level even the third little piggy's brick house.

But Taylor hasn't seen the weapon spawn.

"Cover me," I say.

"Cover you?" He sounds like I've just farted into his mouth after eating a week old chimichanga from Taco Bell.

"Just do it!"

Without another word, he rises from behind the pew and opens fire. Bullets ping off the Chote's head armor, filling the air with sparks and what sounds like a rapid-fire drum beat mixed with high-pitched church bells.

I dive-roll onto the platform, realizing it might have been a little overkill showy, but shit, if you're going to fight and be killed by aliens, you might as well look cool while doing it. I dive behind the podium, reach up, and snag the baseball-sized device. It's solid black, like a sphere of obsidian. For a moment, I worry that I've grabbed someone's paper-weight, but then I notice it has been resting on a flat circle the size of a quarter.

"Down!" Taylor shouts.

I duck behind the podium and brace for oblivion.

Behind and above me, the back half of the church blows apart and scatters across the land between us and the coast. My arms are struck by the force, and I feel like they're about to be ripped from my body, but the podium bolted to the floor takes the brunt of the impact and holds its ground.

I place my thumb atop the smooth circle, searching for a button. As soon as I touch it, the device's interior flashes red. A beep sounds with each flash, building in speed as my eyebrows rise.

"Fire in the hole!" I shout, standing and chucking the device, which lands at the Chote's feet. There's a moment of confusion as the alien looks down. Then its armored jaw drops, and it lets out a kind of whine.

Then the device explodes...or rather, implodes, sucking in every-thing within a ten-foot radius. The Chote, several pews, the foundation and the soil beneath are compressed into a sphere just slightly larger than the device. It falls to the ground at the center of a newly formed crater that is already starting to fill with water oozing out of the wounded earth.

Above us, the force field pulses white, the shimmer rising up from the ground and heading skyward for all to see. *It's announcing deaths,* I realize. The white pulses are for the Chote, which means the red ones... *We're getting our asses kicked.*

As the dust settles, I'm relieved to see Taylor, still in one piece, rising up from his hiding place behind the front row. The back of the church isn't as lucky, but we're alive, and we've just ticked off our first kill.

I kiss my fingers and place them on the cross that is miraculously still standing. "Thanks, big guy. Owe you a conversation when this is wrapped up, but just...look the other way when Hale and I get together, okay? Cause that's going to be all kinds of freaky you're probably not down with. Cool?" When all I hear is the still swirling wind flowing through the church's wreckage, I say, "Cool," and climb down from the stage.

Taylor and I approach the crater, our useless weapons raised, as if the ball of wood, earth, and alien flesh could pitch itself out of the hole and into our nards. Seeing the oozing sphere at the bottom of the crater, my fears are arrested. I lower my gun and eye the one lying beside what I'm pretty sure was some kind of mini-black hole grenade.

The Chote's anti-gravity rifle survived the blast. Again, just like in the games we play, the spawned weapons are immune to the effects of other weapons, remaining intact for the victors to loot.

"Nice," I say, stepping into the crater.

"You sure you want to do that?" Taylor asks, and then he very quickly changes his tune. "Hurry!"

When I look up at him, he's got his back to me, aiming his weapon toward where the back of the church used to be. I snag the anti-grav rifle, which is lighter than it looks, and hustle back up.

An unarmed Chote is charging at us from the coast. It must have dropped in the water and is a little late to the game. "Now who's the AFK?" I say, stepping through the rubble.

"You don't even know how that thing works," Taylor warns, but I was watching. All the Chote did was pull the trigger. It waited a bit between each shot, suggesting there's a charge time, but I don't think there is anything more to it.

When the Chote is close enough to see what I've got in my hands, its strange, jutting run comes to an abrupt stop. It slides through the mud, carried by momentum, and then scrambles to reverse course. "Too late, biotch," I shout and pull the trigger. The weapon whumps and nearly snaps from my hands, but the effect on the Chote is far more dramatic. The creature is launched skyward, out over the water. For a moment, I think it's going to splash down and maybe survive to fight again, but then it strikes the force field.

Orange sparks and tendrils of red, white, and green erupt from the point of impact like a festive fireworks display. "Note to self," I say, flipping open an imaginary notebook, and jotting in it with an invisible pen. "Do not hit force field."

"Because, gross," Taylor adds.

"I love this gun," I say.

"You're enjoying this too much," he says.

"Maybe," I say. "A skosh."

The force field pulses white again announcing another Chote death. *That's two,* I think. *Forty-eight to go.*

My internal celebration is cut short when the force field pulses red three more times.

My phone pings from my pocket. It's not a chime I've heard before, so I pluck it from my pocket and have a look. A counter is ticking down from five seconds, pinging with each new digit. I clamp my hands over my ears just before the air fills with the ear-splitting sound of Alvin and the Chipmunks being slowly murdered by a howler monkey.

When I recover from the fresh audio assault, I'm struck by a wave of disorientation. Looking toward the coast, I feel like I'm moving, like I'm floating closer to the force field.

But that's not what's happening.

The force field is shrinking.

17

HALE

After lying under a desk for ten seconds, hands clasped over my head, I start to feel a kind of grating suspense, like the proctologist is keeping me waiting before shoving her finger up my butt. "Quaid..."

"It should have happened by now," he says. "I don't know what's wrong."

"What's wrong is that we're about to get prostate exams from a bunch of Russians with thick fingers!" I shout.

"Umm," Loretta says, still in hiding. "Ain't nobody putting their finger near my puckery bits."

"It's a figure of speech, Loretta!" I shout.

"Well, it's not a figure of speech I've he—"

"I made it up!" I shout. "What I mean is, they are going to *kill* us. Is that better? Are you happy now, Loretta?"

"Well, why not just use figures of speech people know?" she shouts.

"That's called a cliché," I say, "And Mrs. Decker would not approve."

"Who?" Chieng asks.

"Godamnit," I mutter. Banter is so much easier with Stone. It's hard to train with someone for years and then, when the shit finally hits the fan, find yourselves separated. And now look, my inner monologue is using shit-hitting-fan clichés. Deck *and* Stone would be ashamed.

"I'm soory," Klark says, ducking behind a chair that's going to do little to protect him from anything more than bad posture. "Is this how Space Force normally conducts itself?"

"*Excuse* me, Judgey McMoose-Fucker," I say, glaring and ready to savage the lot of them. "You guys just—"

A sound like weird, clanging thunder pounds through the air, drowning out my voice and shaking the whole world.

Have the aliens discovered us? Are we under attack?

A moment later—silence.

And then shouting. In Russian. I hear two voices, but I can't tell if they're angry or horrified.

Quaid slides himself out from hiding. "It worked. Holy shit, ya'll, I think it worked!"

He rushes to the hangar side of the control tower, and I hurry after him. "Quaid, what did you..." The tarmac outside comes into view. Starting a hundred feet out, the pavement has been reduced to steaming slag, glistening with shards of shiny metal. I'm about to finish my question when I see one of the Russian teams.

They've been reduced to sludge.

Quaid must see them at the same time, because he pitches forward, clutching his mouth and his stomach. "Oh..."

I lean forward, looking down to find four more Alpha Squad soldiers lying below, torn to shreds, and very, very dead. Despite the fact that these men clearly died quickly, I feel bad for them.

"Celine Dion on a pogo-stick," Klark mutters, looking out over the mess, gripping a chair-back for support. "What did you do to them?"

"Well," Quaid says, straightening himself up and pursing his lips. "As I'm sure ya'll know, the Outer Space Treaty forbids the deployment of WMDs in orbit, on the moon, or just floating around. That includes nukes, chemical, and biological warfare elements. What it does *not* include is kinetic weapons."

"So you just dumped a bunch of metal on them? From orbit?" I ask. I've heard about kinetic weapons, and I knew they fell under Space Force's purview, but I had no idea they'd been deployed. The program I'd heard about was dubbed Project Thor. The plain and simple of it is that super dense and heavy tungsten rods could be dropped from orbit and accelerated by gravity. They'd hit the surface with the force of a nuke, but with none of the radiation. They were supposed to be bunker-busting, city-destroying ordinance clean enough to allow ground troops to follow. I never imagined they could be used as an anti-personnel weapon.

"Tungsten pellets," Quaid says, and then with a bit of a flourish, he continues, "Project Metal Storm. You have to adjust for atmospheric density and wind, but..." He motions to the gore outside without looking at it. "As you can see, accuracy is achievable."

"You say that like you weren't sure before," Chieng says, staying back from the window. She knows what's out there, and doesn't want to see it.

"You say that like you're proud," Klark says.

"Well, I did design it..."

"You *what?*" I say.

Quaid's eyes widen. "Which is totally top secret. You can't tell anyone."

I knew Quaid was an engineer, but I was under the impression that he'd been working on the *Rex*, which honestly made me a bit hesitant about flying the thing. That he'd been working on ways to brutally kill people makes a little more sense, but it's no less disconcerting.

Before the debate over who signed an NDA and whether or not they're still enforceable with Space Force being dissolved begins, the Russian shouting below shifts from maybe angry and maybe horrified, to *definitely* angry. I creep back toward the stairwell doorway. "They sound bull-with-an-elastic-band-around-his-nuts angry."

"Nobody does that anymore," Quaid says. "They use flank straps to—"

I shoot him a look, and whisper, "I. Don't. Care." Then I hold a finger to my lips.

The men below are rushing us, their boots heavy on the floor and then up the stairs. While our odds of surviving have improved, even Captain Hockey Puck isn't rushing over to help me, so we're likely all going to die anyway...

Unless I can summon my inner grizzly and out-psycho them.

When the black mask of the first man emerges from the stairwell, I kick hard, aiming for his chin. The plan is to knock him senseless, break his jaw, and take the fight right out of him.

That's not even close to what happens.

The man catches my leg in one meaty Ivan Drago arm, lifts me off the floor, and tosses me to the side like I'm made of fucking balsa wood. It's like I've got little fucking wings on me and a wind up, elastic powered propeller. I crash into and over a console, taking the monitor with me.

I'm as embarrassed as a great tit at a penguin party...not because the smaller bird has made a *faux pas* by not being dressed in a penguin tux, but because those well-dressed, flightless shitheads are going to make hella tons of 'hey, great tits' jokes. Fucking penguins.

I'm also damn lucky the soldier decided to chuck me instead of putting a line of bullets into me. I'm guessing my proximity, and the fact that I'm a woman, are what saved my life. Neither will protect Klark or Chubs, who are both dressed like the men Spetsnaz are trained to kill.

I cringe at the sound of men screaming in pain, but I'm confused since I haven't heard gunshots yet. I shove myself up to find both Russians clutching their eyes as they're doused by a stream of Chieng's mace.

"Eat my shit, mother bitches!" Chieng screams, slathering the men with a kind of manic frenzy. The small canister fizzles out of ammo, the stream of spray reduced to a sputtering shart.

As I climb back over the desk, the men wipe their eyes and start laughing.

Laughing.

While tendrils of drool and snot ooze from their various orifices, the men shake off the assault and raise their weapons toward the control tower's far side.

Taser prongs snap against their armor, crackling with electricity, but they fail to reach human flesh, their painful potential wasted.

The Spetsnaz open fire, each man unleashing a spray of rounds.

"No!" I shout, charging the men.

As the nearest spins around to face me, I slide across the floor like I'm stealing second, and I deliver a nut-shot so hard I'm pretty sure I feel his balls unravel around my knuckles. As tough as these two might be, a punch in the jimmy will shrink even the most hardened man into a fetal position. He collapses in on himself and does nothing to stop me from drawing the knife from his belt.

I rise behind his partner and things start moving in slow motion. Bullets chug from the man's AKM, casting sparks, shattering glass, and shredding workstations as people dive for cover. Klark and Chubs spiral toward the ground, both of them trailing jets of blood, their deaths synchronized.

I hesitate for a moment.

This is a threshold I haven't crossed before. I'm not like Stone and Taylor. I've been trained to drop bombs, fire missiles, and pilot aircraft—and spacecraft—so far from the enemy that I'd never have to witness the damage done. A knife is a different scenario.

As the soldier's aim angles toward Chieng, my arm moves on its own volition, stabbing the large blade into the Spetsnaz's back.

He shouts in pain while throwing a wild elbow that catches me in the forehead. His rifle rises toward me as I fall backward. He's not about to make the same mistake twice. But in turning to fight the lion in front of him, he's ignored the rhinoceros behind him.

"Oh, I don't think so!" Loretta collides with the man as though possessed by Refrigerator Perry himself. The soldier is launched to the floor. Instinct guides him around to fire at Loretta, but he'd forgotten the knife in his back. He lands hard, weight, gravity, and momentum con-spiring to shove the knife, and its hilt, deeper into his back. He goes rigid with a not-so-manly shriek and then falls still.

After liberating the Russians—one dead and one emasculated—of their weapons, I scan the control tower's far side, expecting to see every-one, aside from Loretta, dead. What I find is Chieng behind cover. Quaid is standing frozen, a miraculous outline of bullet holes in the wall around him. The Canadians are lying down on the job, which is totally insensitive, because they're both bleeding out.

"Soory," Chubs says.

Klark follows with his own, "Soory." And then they both die.

"What...the...shit?" Quaid says, snapping out of his frozen state to check each man's pulse. "I mean, it's like they were here just to show us how dangerous and bloody things could get. Like we needed a tangible example of how high the stakes are."

A silence settles over us as our eyes meet. For a moment, I feel like someone is watching me from beyond the invisible wall of a dimension I can't quite see or address directly. *Hope you're enjoying the show, ass-holes*, I think, but I'm snapped out of my fourth-wall ruminations by the sound of hushed Chinese voices sifting through the control tower's shattered windows.

18

STONE

"ZOD is closing in," Taylor says, and I catch a trace of awe in his voice. We've been playing battle royale games since they got big a few years back. We're fans of the genre. Seeing it in real life is equal parts 'Holy shit, this is horrible' and 'I've got a raging geek boner.'

All battle royale scenarios have a collapsing outer wall that kills players trapped outside it. The blue line. The zone. The wall of doom. Each game has its own take. Since we play a lot of these games, Taylor and I use the same name for it across the board. ZOD. Zone of Death. And the association with Superman's Kryptonian nemesis, General Zod, doesn't hurt, because, you know, he kills people.

Most ZODs kill slowly, giving players a chance to escape their cold embrace, but in some hardcore modes, getting hit by the zone means instant death. The Chote have clearly borrowed from those more nefarious scenarios. There are no second chances in this game for the planet. No magic health kits. No speed-boosting energy drinks. A headshot won't knock us to our knees to wait for revival. It will kill us. Because as much as the Chote have tailored this to feel like a game, it is real.

And that's not all bad, because as good as Taylor and I are at fighting in the virtual world, we are better in the real...despite what our current assignment suggests.

In both the virtual and real worlds, situational awareness is key. If you don't know where the enemy is, or might be, it's a helluva lot easier for them to put a bullet in you...or launch you into the force field blender. Ducked down behind the church's ruins, we watch and listen.

The occasional gunshot rings out, often followed by a scream and a pulse of red light moving up the force field.

I flinch when a chorus of voices rise up from the distance, followed by a strobe of red. *They found the movers,* I think, *huddled in hiding and defenseless.*

It's hard to say what's happening and where, other than people are dying and everywhere. But there is one thing that is clear: we can't help anyone from where we are now, and if we don't bother trying...if the representatives of the human race are only concerned about themselves, what does that say about all of us? Maybe we're not worth saving?

To hell with that, I think, rising from my hiding spot and preparing to be selfless as fuck.

Taylor follows without complaint. We crouch-run across the open field, as if ducking a foot lower will help keep us off the enemy's radar.

"What's the plan?" Taylor asks, when I stop at the manicured garden wall.

"Way I see it, we have two options. First, we try to win. Kill all the mofos and end the game."

He nods, but doesn't look convinced, probably for the same reason I'm not. If we were the architects of this scenario, you better believe we'd stack the odds in our favor and have some kind of contingency plan that ensures we win, no matter how well our opponents played. If we'd be dicks like that, you better believe that aliens—who are basically dick-shaped—would be, too.

"Option two, we work our way through the barracks, training center, and then get to Ops...and Billy, if he's still alive. If anyone can figure out a plan, it's him."

"Wait," Taylor says. "Your plan is to find Billy and have *him* make a plan?"

"I know, it's a good plan, right?"

"Freaking genius," he says with a smirk. We both know the score. Neither of us have exceptional IQs. When it comes to strategy...to winning a fight...that's us. But we're not the guys who come up with the big ideas that win wars. We're not solving peace in the Middle East or directing military campaigns. We're hauling and kicking ass on the ground.

And while McNasty technically has experience with waging war, I'd rather serve under an old, crusty diaper worn by our former president.

Seriously, I'd wear that dung-helmet with pride before taking another order from my aging, cock-blocking superior. And I fully admit that I'm being a little bitch about it. If I had a daughter, I'd probably have kicked my ass.

It's not his ire, or even his discipline choices that irk me. It's his holier-than-thou attitude and lack of respect for the men who do the killing on his behalf. I've seen his record. He moved up the ranks without ever once facing combat. Going to war is easy when it's other people's lives on the line. While he sat in an office, the men beneath him—men like me—risked their lives.

If we're going to come up with a grand plan, it's going to be with someone whose opinion I value. And despite being an occasional deep-fried turd, that's Billy.

"So," Taylor says, peeking up over the concrete wall and parting the shrubbery above us. He points toward the nearest building. "Barracks..." His finger shifts to the building to our right. "Training..." He motions to the building beyond, which we can't see, but we both know is there. "Ops." The big building at the base of the circular layout, directly opposite the bridge, is where we'll find Billy and his big, beautiful brain.

"Sure you don't want to run it?" Taylor asks, but then he parts the shrubs again, giving us a southward view. A few hundred feet away are four Chote, all of them armed with weapons I don't recognize. They're clueless we're here, but they're also heading in our direction.

"They're squading up," I say. "They *do* squad up."

Taylor gently hums the *Jurassic Park* theme, revealing he's understood my incredibly vague and butchered reference like only a true BFF can. Then he looks back, his face glowing orange in the force field's light. "What about that?"

I look at the massive, curved field closing in on the island, destroying everything it touches with a hiss. In a game, we'd have a map that showed us where the circle would close, giving us an idea of where we need to...

Hold the phone. Literally.

I turn on my phone and smile when I see an overhead view of the island displayed. A wall of orange closes in around the island, chewing through the bridge. A second circle, just a black line, shows where it will stop. "Looks like the whole base is inside the first circle," I say, showing Taylor the phone. The Chote might have stacked things in their favor, but they're being faithful to the genre. I mean, if they hadn't come here to kill us all, I probably would have enjoyed gaming with them.

Oh damn, I think. *Maybe I already have?*

Xxxinquixxx...what if the hackers Taylor and I have been complaining about all this time weren't actually Chinese? What if I've been a racist asshole without ever realizing it?

Not wanting to dwell on my own shortcomings, of which there are many, I push this train of thought from my mind and focus on the here and now. "Time to get sneaky," I say, crouching low and following the wall to the garden entrance. Lying on the concrete, I snake my way past delicate topiaries, metal benches, and concrete tables. Pollen-collecting bees, hard at work, buzz overhead, ignorant to the threat posed to their planet.

"I hate bees," Taylor grumbles.

"You're not allergic?" I ask.

"They're just little stinging bitches," he says, shuffling behind me.

I glance back, spotting a sizable hive in a potted tree. "Well, try not to piss them off."

We continue on our way, reaching the barracks back door without being spotted. I pull myself up into a crouch and tug on the all-glass door. Locked. Unfazed, I dig out my ID and swipe it against the keycard reader. A light flickers green. A loud *buzz* sounds as the door unlocks with a *thunk.*

I freeze, eyes wide. It might have been quieter if I'd broken the damn glass. I tug the door open just wide enough to squeeze through. Without standing, I slide inside while Taylor urges me to move faster. The Chote Squad heard us and are closing the distance.

When Taylor is inside the door, I pull my foot back and let it gently slide closed. The hallway is dark. The tinted glass of the door and the surrounding windows dull the orange glow outside and no doubt reflect it back. The Chote arrive a moment later, two of them looking right at the door, but not seeing us on the other side.

I point the anti-grav gun at them, but don't pull the trigger. Blowing the back of the building off and launching four Chote isn't exactly the definition of a covert op, and I'm pretty sure that's what's called for here. Stealthing your way to a target is always easier than shooting your way. At the same time, it *would* be amusing.

"I think we're good," Taylor says, as we scoot away from the door.

"Let's wait for them to—"

A thud echoes out of the hallway we passed whilst scooting.

"Did you check the hall?" I ask.

"Thought you did," Taylor says.

A large Chote emerges from the hallway, the squad outside still oblivious to our, or his presence. And yeah, I called it a him. For all I know, we're fighting a bunch of extraterrestrial chicks, but I have a hard time thinking of these giant phalluses as being female.

The domed metal head faces me, and then Taylor. A chuckle rattles out of its chest, as its arm rises, melee weapon in hand.

"Hold on," Taylor says, looking at the weapon. "This asshole's going to frying pan us?"

"Not on my watch," I say, raising the anti-grav weapon up. Stealthing is good until a plan goes FUBAR. Then it's time to blow shit up.

The Chote's blank gaze snaps toward the weapon, and in a flash of recognition, it yelps, digs its claws into the floor, and holds the pan in front of its face. "Oh man, this is going to be funny," I say, and pull the trigger.

19

"Hey!" I shout through the control tower's shattered window. Outside, the sounds of approaching boots and whispering Chinese go silent. "Nǐ hǎo. Uhh, China number one!"

And that is the extent of my Chinese. Hello, and an English phrase that's become popular in China since online gaming connected an entire generation with the outside world. Hearing those words irks Stone and Taylor, but maybe they will provide a cultural bridge here? If we can just dialogue with these guys, maybe they'll realize that we all want the same damn thing. The Russians came in guns-a-blazin', but maybe the Chinese are smarter?

"China numbah wun," a solitary voice replies, and I feel a smattering of hope until he speaks again. "You sound old. Can I call you aunt? You can teach me English?"

"Oh," Loretta says, "that boy is full of sass."

"Your English sounds just fine," I say, dander rising. "Take a look around you. See that mess? That's what happened to the ten Russian Spetsnaz who pissed us off. Unless you want to wind up looking like them, you'll hold your ground and have a conversation."

I whisper to Quaid, "Can we use the metal storm again?" The idea of raining down metal from space to gooify several more men makes me queasy. Granted, they might be here to kill us all, but it's like we needed to slaughter a cow and we used a bulldozer to do it. But we might not have much of a choice.

"It costs twenty million to get one payload into space," he says.

"Meaning?"

"I used our only shot," he says, "unless you want to use the big guns. They're the size of a telephone pole, weigh 24,000 pounds, and hit at ten times the speed of sound. Buuut that would kill the Chinese, us, and a few thousand more as the shockwave obliterated everything for a few miles in every direction."

"Oookay," I say. "Any other ideas?"

"Do not trust Chinese," a deep Russian voice says. The Spetsnaz who will never have children is sitting up, hands still clasped on his balls.

"Tie him up," I tell Quaid and Chieng. They set to work, binding him with power cords, while I keep his AKM trained on his head. The other Russian weapon we recovered, an OSV-96 sniper rifle, is a one-hit-kill weapon—against people and vehicles—firing .50 caliber rounds. But it won't do a ton of good indoors, or even be helpful against the Chinese, who are just outside. It's not a bolt action rifle, but the 8X scope mounted atop it, and its long-ass barrel would make using it at close range impossible.

"They are, how you say, wolf in sheep's clothing," the Russian says, as his wrists are cinched together.

"Pretty sure they're dressed like you," I tell him.

"Is metaphor."

"What?" I say, baffled by his train of thought.

"A phrase applied to object or action that is not literally—"

"I know what a freaking metaphor is," I snap.

"They are...honey lips," he says, mulling over his choice of words and then adding, "Sweet talkers."

"Old lady," the Chinese man calls from outside, proving the Russian wrong. "You teach me Ingrish now? I want to learn how to pick up chicks in California."

Assuming we're just bumping up against some cultural differences, I turn to Chieng. "A little help?"

She steps closer to the broken window, wisely staying crouched down and out of sight. She spits off a string of Chinese that sounds almost terse.

Whatever she said is greeted by silence.

"What the hell did you say?" I ask.

"I told him we would like to have a civil conversation and to cut the 'old lady' bullshit, which was definitely meant to antagonize you, by the way." She tilts her head toward the Russian. "I'm with him. Well, not actually. I mean, not like we're on the same side."

"Chieng."

"What I mean," she says, "is that I think he's right. They're bullshitting, which means they're up to something."

"Well, I ain't poking my head out to see what it is," Quaid says.

The Russian chuckles. "American Space Force only recruits little girls."

"In case you haven't noticed," Loretta says. "Three out of four of us got the ta-tas. I'm not even *with* Space Force, and the only male here, aside from your Neanderthal ass, looks like a wispy tart with a rapey mustache."

Quaid looks wounded as he strokes the sides of his mustache. "You think so?"

"Honey, I wouldn't bend over to pick up a thousand dollars if you were standing behind me."

I'm not sure Loretta's outburst did anything to improve the Russian's opinion of women, and I don't really care. "In case you forgot, I'm the woman who relocated your nuts to your throat."

"You're not brave enough to—"

"Don't need to be brave," I say, yanking the Russian up. I poke the AKM into his back and shove him toward the window. "Just smart."

He grunts in pain, as he shuffles the distance. I'm sure he's fairly well petrified. If we were taking bets, my money would be on him getting a bullet in the head. But his pride keeps him upright and moving. He's Alpha Squad, after all. He's not going to let me, or Chinese Special Forces, intimidate him.

The Chinese man outside finally speaks, again in Chinese.

Chieng's reply is terse and short. "He asked if he could show me something, which sounds a little pervy, so I told him I wasn't interested in seeing anything that small."

"Mmm-hmm," Loretta says. "Now that's how it's done, honey."

After a moment of silence, the Chinese man says, "Old lady, you come back. You are nice. New lady is not nice. We're friends now. Come outside...come here...I show you...come now..."

"Is pushy little bastard, no?" the Russian says, as we inch closer to the window.

"Why didn't you kill us?" I ask him.

When he says nothing, I push the AKM against him a little harder. "Your team is dead, and the longer you act like a little, ball-less bitch, the closer we get to being evicted from our planet."

He grins. "You were my target...to capture. The rest..." He shrugs. "Lucky."

"You need me to fly the *Rex*?"

He nods toward the window. "As do they. Is only reason they have not blown up tower."

I pull him back, short of the window.

"What are you doing?" Quaid asks, "Let him have a gander."

"They might kill him," I say.

"Well, yeah...and?"

"And he's talking," I say, pulling the Russian back a little further.

The big man gives me a nod, "Thank y—"

I drive the AKM's butt into his stomach, dropping him to the floor. He lands on his knees, pitched forward and gasping. Then I approach the window myself.

"The hell is she doin'?" Loretta asks, aghast.

"Testing a theory," I say, and I step into view.

Below me is a mash of pavement and crushed corpses. Standing at the gore's far side is a lone Chinese soldier dressed in all black, except for a red patch with a yellow #1 on it.

What is it with Chinese and being number one? I wonder.

Then I notice a line of shed clothing stretching from the man's position outside the gore to the base of our building.

"Oh," the lone soldier says. "Ahh...Hello. Old lady? You don't look too old. Uhh..."

He was clearly not expecting me to look out the window. All of his pushiness was intended to make me wary. Now that I've shown myself and seen what's going on, the jig is up.

He raises his weapon at me. It's some kind of modified bullpup rifle, capable of unleashing a shit ton of bullets, but not great at range. I roll my eyes, knowing this information is in my brain only because I've watched Stone and Taylor play one too many games. If I'm honest,

I sometimes watch their streams. I'd never admit it, but they're pretty entertaining.

"You're not going to use that," I say, taking a step back. When the soldier sags a bit, I know it's true, and I turn my back on him. I hurry toward the stairwell. "We have incoming!"

When I reach the stairs, I turn the AKM downward, flinch at the sight of five soldiers wearing helmets, facemasks, boxers, and nothing else, and then dive to the side as they fire upward. As the only pilot capable of flying the *Rex*, they might not want me dead, but I've caught them off guard and pointed an AKM in their direction. The gunfire is a knee-jerk reaction.

A barrage of bullets chews up the ceiling where I had just stood. The patter of bare feet on stairs follows.

"Oh, hell naw," Loretta says, picking up the big sniper rifle, stepping in front of the stairs and pulling the trigger. The kickback snaps the rifle out of her hands and up over her shoulder, but the bullet makes its way down the stairwell. Judging by the chorus of pain-filled screams, the massive, armor-piercing round has punched its way through all five men.

I pick myself up, look down the stairs, and see it for myself. The back wall is a Jackson Pollock painting of human insides. The five soldiers lie atop each other on the stairwell, all of them dead.

I squint at the five bodies, unconvinced there are only six of them total. Then I hear the pitter-patter of feet on the roof, like Santa has come to throw down and try to steal the *Rex*, because Rudolph is sick of his shit. "Windows!" I shout, just as six scantily clad soldiers swing down toward the glass on either side of the building.

20

STONE

The anti-grav gun whumps through the air, striking the Chote with its church-shattering force. In an impressive show of strength, the alien holds its position, the strength of its claws and body proving too much for the weapon. But its armor...

I don't know if it's got a loose button or a faulty seal, but a single chunk of plating snaps off, and then the rest follows, exposing the Chote's true form.

As the monster's armor flies back along with the wall, windows, and door at the end of the hall, Taylor and I scream in horror.

"My eyes!" Taylor says.

"It's worse than I imagined!" I shout.

With the anti-grav blast complete, the Chote turns toward us, extends its face from the folds of its neck, and roars.

While the creature's shape hasn't changed all that much, its appearance has gone from a sleek killing-machine to a naked, fleshy, embarrassing mass. Its skin is a mottled gray, like a zombie with extreme varicose veins. The bulbous backside is a wrinkled, flaccid mass from which its strong legs emerge. I can't even guess at the evolutionary purpose of a body like this, but I'm sure, where they come from, it's an advantage. Here, it's just...

"Gross," Taylor says. "Look at its face."

The Chote's face, taken on its own, isn't quite as ugly as an H.R. Giger alien. Its skin is smooth. The mouth is broad and filled with oversized molars. Unlike its armor, there's not a canine in sight. Four large, human-looking brown eyes, two on either side of a single flaring nostril, stare at us.

"Ugh," I say, taking a step back, out of disgust rather than fear.

The Chote flinches at our reaction and turns its head down to look at itself. It lets out a weird, warbling squeal upon seeing its own nakedness.

When the creature looks up again, its pupils have dilated into comical black circles glistening with what might be tears of embarrassment.

The Chote's head shrinks back inside its neck as the alien spins around and runs for the non-existent back wall. It lunges outside, careening past its four somewhat dumbfounded comrades, who watch him blaze a trail through the gardens, and then across the open land.

Taylor and I could make our escape. It would be easy. But the scene is absolutely gripping. Even the other Chote can't turn away, as the naked alien plows across the land, lets out a wail, and then throws itself into the force field with explosive effect.

They're morbidly terrified of being seen naked, I realize, and I wonder if they know what their bodies resemble.

As fleshy confetti spirals out to be consumed by the encroaching barrier, and a white pulse races into the sky, Chote Squad bursts into what must be laughter.

Not only are the Chote giant dicks, they're also assholes. Even to their own kind...like if college bros evolved into a species of their own.

"I'm thinking we should go now," Taylor says.

In response, I start to back away, but I'm stopped by the sound of large approaching feet behind us. A quick glance back confirms it. A Chote has emerged from the intersection at our backs, just thirty feet away. With a roar, it charges, forcing Taylor and me to run toward the squad outside, who have also snapped to attention and now wait for us with open arms and jaws.

With each step, I run through my limited options. I could blast the squad and hope the shot takes out all four Chote. I could fire behind me, knocking back the lone alien. Both choices are not without their risks. If I miss any of the four, our situation won't be improved much. If I fire inside the building, I could bring part of it down on top of us.

Maybe the best choice is to make like Monty Python's King Arthur when facing the mind-numbing menace of a catapulted cow—run away. *It wouldn't be a retreat,* I tell myself, *but a strategic restructuring of the battleground.*

The question is, where to go?

There's one hallway branching to the right.

It could work, but then we'll have five Chote chasing us and no way to know if any lie ahead.

And then it hits me. Taylor sees my grin and asks, "What are you going to do?"

"Evasive maneuvers," I say, pulling him to a stop beside me. "Hold on!"

Taylor knows I'm about to try something a smidge loco, but we've been a team long enough for him to trust me. Granted, the life he's usually putting on the line with my antics is a digital one, but trust is trust.

He wraps his arms around my shoulders and holds on tight. When he sees me point the anti-grav gun at the floor, he shouts, "Oh shit!" and leaps up, wrapping his legs around my waist. For a moment, I feel his full two-hundred-pound weight pulling me toward the floor. Then I pull the trigger and become weightless.

We surge upward as the lone Chote dives beneath us, sliding across the barren linoleum, its armor squeaking until it grinds to a halt.

Taylor and I collide with, and crash through, the second floor's hung ceiling. We're then dropped to the floor.

"Whoa!" Taylor says, as he clings to the floor, his lower half dangling. I push myself up, grasp his wrist and pull, as the Chote beneath him writhes around, trying to right itself. The alien destroys the walls around it, snapping and clawing in a frenzy. If Taylor fell right now, it would be like dropping him into a blender.

And then I nearly fall, when three, pink balls of light snap past my head and disintegrate the wall behind me. Chote Squad is closing in. If the lead alien, who fired the weapon, hadn't been running, I'm pretty sure I would have ceased to exist.

"Pull!" Taylor says, his voice rising an octave. "Pull! Pull! Pull!"

The lead Chote slides to a stop and takes aim, straight at my face. Knowing I'm about to die, my life passes before my eyes. Sunny the goldfish. Hamper the hamster. Pugsly the pug. And then I'm back in the present, and baffled. The Chote is struck from behind by his still charging counterparts. He pulls the trigger again, but his aim is thrown off.

"I...*am!*" With a heave, Taylor rises to the second floor and we spill back, him landing atop me.

Above us, the ceiling is vaporized.

"If it were raining, this would be how our romantic comedy movie ends," Taylor says, calm again, now that he's slightly removed from mortal danger.

"I was really bad at naming pets," I say.

"Say what, now?"

"I saw my life flash before my eyes, but all I saw were my pets."

"Maybe because they're the only things you've ever really loved?" Taylor asks, and I can't tell if he's being serious or yanking my chain.

He rolls off me just as the frenzied Chote leaps up onto the second floor, demonstrating again just how outmatched we are. I scoop up the anti-grav gun I'd dropped to help Taylor, level it at the thing and pull the trigger. A rapid fire clicking sounds from the weapon. I turn the weapon over, glaring at it like it has betrayed me. I spot an illuminated gauge that's now blinking red. "Out of ammo," I guess.

The Chote I now think of as 'Frenzy' pitches forward, roaring in excitement, its jaw hanging open.

Taylor shouts back at it and then unloads his assault rifle into its mouth. It doesn't do any real damage. The sharp fangs aren't even part of its real mouth, but the alien flinches back under the barrage, giving me time to charge. A split second after Taylor's rounds run dry, I do my best impression of Babe Ruth and swing the anti-grav gun like a bat.

The collision rattles my arm, prying the weapon free and carrying through the wrecked floor. Frenzy's head snaps to the side, staggering it into a single step back. Then it laughs at us, mocking us, until the floor beneath its rear-most foot crumbles.

Claws dig divots into the wall as Frenzy tries to arrest his backward momentum, but his talons are too sharp and his weight too much for the drywall to resist. When he sees the wall will be no help, he pinwheels his arms in the air, trying to maintain his balance. But he loses his fight against gravity and spills back, landing atop the squad, who roar in frustration.

Never ones to look a gift alien in the mouth, we make a break for it. Our boots squeak on the floor as we round a corner and keep putting distance between us and the Chote. We're not headed in the right direction, but right now, anyplace that puts us farther away from the Chote Squad is the right direction.

"Look!" Taylor says, pointing ahead. A subtly glowing weapon spawn lies on the hallway floor ahead of us, and it is distinctly weapon-shaped and not a mini-skirt, or a hat, or socks—like it's Easter morning back in the Stone household.

Thinking about childhood reminds me of my flashback and Taylor's observation. Could that be true? Have I never really loved someone before? I mean, I love Taylor. We're tight. I'd trust him with my life, and my pog collection. But maybe I haven't given anyone my unconditional love like my child-self did with those pets?

Before I follow the tangential rabbit-hole any deeper, the floor in front of us wells up, as a Chote crashes up through the floor, separating us from the weapon.

They could hear us running, I think.

I spin around as a sound, like a car accident mixed with Barney the Purple Dinosaur getting kicked in the Django, fills the hallway behind us. While Frenzy has cut us off, Chote Squad followed our trail.

I take a deep breath and let out a sigh. I'm going to die in an empty hallway, murdered by dong-shaped aliens, having only really loved a goldfish, a hamster, and a pug.

I flinch when a *ding* sounds out behind me, and I shout as I'm grasped by something impossibly strong and yanked backward.

21

On the hangar-side of the building, where the glass has been chewed up by metal storm fragments, the three Chinese infiltrators hit like wrecking balls. Thousands of tiny squares of tempered glass burst into the room. Dressed only in black boxer-briefs and harnesses, the Chinese trio look like strippers at the weirdest bachelorette party ever. The weapons over their shoulders are a stark reminder that they're killers and will attempt to slaughter everyone in the control tower aside from me.

Behind me, the other three soldiers swing out wide, careen toward the glass, and strike with enough force to stun all three when they fail to shatter the unmarred glass. Their naked skin squeaks against the smooth panes as they bounce and roll.

I'd snicker if the men didn't quickly recover, plant their feet against the glass, and point their weapons at it. They're going to shoot their way through, reunite with the stripper squad, and commence with the blood-letting.

"Not going to happen," I say, raising the AKM and unleashing three five-round bursts. As the Chinese soldiers' bullets shatter the windows, mine exit via the newly formed gaps and strike each man in his mostly naked core.

The hell were they thinking? I wonder, as the three soldiers fall two stories to the ground.

Attacking without clothing and armor strikes me as profoundly foolish. Then again, it allowed them to sneak up on us, unheard—no clunking boots, no swishing fabrics, no clinking metal or plastic—and the Chinese military is known for being creative to make up for their lack of technological superiority. What they tried was the last thing I would have expected, and it would have worked, if I hadn't realized my worth and taken a peek out the window.

Shouting spins me around, AKM ready to fire. But finding a target is impossible. Each of the Chinese soldiers is being engaged by unlikely attackers. The man closest to me has been beset by Chieng and Loretta.

Our bus driver-turned-Ronda-Rousey clings to the man's weapon, forcing the barrel toward the floor. She bites his bare arm hard enough to draw blood. It prevents the man from wrapping his finger around the trigger. Even if he did, the only thing he'd hit is linoleum.

Chieng is no less effective, her hands and supremely manicured nails, layered with enough gloss to make them adamantium-strong, gouges, slices, and scratches the man's skin.

Their target is bloodied, in pain, and distracted, but he's not quite out of the fight. I take aim at him, trying to track his movement with the rifle's attached red-dot sight. My finger wraps around the trigger as I exhale, and—

Chieng's head snaps into view. I nearly put a bullet in it.

I'm going to have to do this the way I know best, I think, lowering the weapon and clenching my fists.

As I move in, I glance at the Russian as he engages the second soldier. He lunges up, snapping the back of his head under the Chinese soldier's chin. The impact stuns the man, knocking him back. But he's far from out of the fight. As the Chinese soldier's bullpup comes up, the Russian, whose hands and feet are still bound, springs into the air like a Bushido inch-worm. Both legs snap out, knocking the weapon from the Chinese soldier's grasp.

When the Russian hits the floor, he brings his legs back with a double-sweep kick that knocks his target to the floor. The last I see of him, he's steam-rolling toward an absolutely confounded Chinese man.

Beyond them, I see Quaid riding a third soldier like a rodeo clown on a bull. He's got a power cord wrapped around the man's neck and his legs around the man's waist, holding tight as the soldier slams him into the wall over and over.

"Keep him still," I shout at Chieng and Loretta, as I charge into the fray.

Chieng latches on to his free arm, locking him in place, but freeing him from the barrage of claws long enough for him to see me coming.

The man pivots while carrying the burden of both women and manages to snap out a kick that connects with my side and proves that the Chinese, while unconventional, aren't entirely ineffectual.

I wince and clutch my side, glaring at the man. He sneers back at me, taunting me to approach again...and I do, pretending to have fallen for his bait. He kicks out hard again and connects with my side, but this time I move with the kick, minimizing its impact and latching on to his leg.

His eyes go wide for a moment, and then I deliver a trifecta of pain.

My elbow inverts his knee with a crack that is followed by both Loretta and Chieng shouting, "Ohh!" in sympathetic agony.

I then deliver a merciless kick to the man's groin, which folds him inward and draws another shout of sympathy from the Russian, whose memory of that kind of pain is still fresh. I glance at him just long enough to watch him resume his attack, headbutting his adversary into submission.

I'm about to finish off my target with a throat strike that has about a 50/50 chance of knocking the man down for the count, or sending him to the Pearly Gates...or wherever Chinese people prefer to go. But Quaid's voice stops and drops me with, "Look out!"

The rapid-fire spray of a bullpup fills the air, chewing up anything taller than four feet, which at the moment is the man I had set to work on. His body twitches as bullets punch holes in him, ending his agony. With the strings of life snipped, he falls atop Loretta, who assails him with a flurry of punches and derogatory statements.

At the far side of the tower, Quaid releases the soldier he'd strangled and lets him fall to the floor next to the smoking bullpup. The fusillade was the man's last-ditch effort at either fending off Quaid or taking some of us with him. All he managed to do was put his partner out of his misery and increase the stank of death already filling the control tower. When the Russians died and the men voided themselves, their thick armor and clothing mitigated the true pungency of their passing. But these Chinese dudes' thin boxer-briefs aren't exactly filtering out the sushi shit particles. The smell of blood is revolting on its own, but the true scent of death is so much worse.

It leaves those of us still living reeling in disgust. Even the Russian, who's groaning and wincing as he earthworms away from the man he's bludgeoned to death with his own forehead, complains, "Is gross. Moy nos tayet!"

I move to the back wall, which is free of the growing puddle of death-ooze, and I regroup with Quaid, Chieng, Loretta, and the Russian, who leans back against my legs, like we've known each other for a long time and seen some shit together. Like I'm fucking Grizzly Adams and he's Ben the Brown Bear.

As irritated as I am by his presence, when he lets out a deep, resonating chuckle, I can't help but smile. Not because I find him amusing or I'm feeling some sort of kinship over the fact that he helped us fend off the Chinese attack, but because I'm pretty damn happy to be alive. We've survived the Canadians' apologies, the Russians' Alpha Squad, and whoever these freakin' nutjob Chinese soldiers were supposed to be. That my people are still standing, including our bus driver, is something of a miracle.

"Had I known Space Force pilot was tiger," the Russian says, "I would have approached with more caution, yeah?"

"Yeah," I say, trying to exude more toughness than I feel.

He holds up his bound hands. "We are friends, now, no? I will not try to harm you."

I crouch down and yank off his black mask. The man underneath has no hair atop his head and a thick, gray beard on the bottom, like Stone in fifteen years, if he went bald and put on a few pounds. The man's forehead is red and swollen from using it as a battering ram against another man's skull.

"Name?" I ask, knowing that he, like all special forces, will have been trained to give only his name and serial number, if he gives anything at all.

He catches me off guard by saying, "Ivan Petrovitch."

"For real?" I say, remembering how I'd called him Ivan in my head. "That's a little cliché, don't you think?"

"Clichés exist for reason," he says. "Ivan is popular name in Russia."

"Okay, Ivan," I say. "Why are you suddenly being friendly? And don't give me any tiger bullshit."

"Canadians are dead," he says. "Alpha is dead. Siberian Tiger is—"

"Siberian who-what?" Loretta asks.

"Chinese Special Forces," Ivan says. "They are...crazy."

"Says the Spetsnaz," Quaid says.

Ivan growls at him and says, "Spetsnaz are disciplined aggression, fearless precision."

"Honey," Loretta says, "You all is a lot of things, but mostly dead." When he diverts his cold gaze toward her, she raises her arms and says, "I'm just pointing out the obvious. Your men are deader than Judas."

"Siberian Tiger are deadly because they are...unbalanced," Ivan says, motioning toward the closest, mostly unclothed dead man. "I...am not. My men are dead, but my mission remains same."

"To kill us all?" Chieng says through her hands as she covers her mouth.

"Nyet," he says. "To kill all of them." He motions toward the ceiling, but clearly means the aliens.

"You didn't think to *ask* if we wanted help?" I say, irritated. "All of this could have been avoided with just a bit of civility. I would have gladly flown an international mission into space to fuck these guys up. Instead, just about all of you are dead and we're still stuck with an engineer, a physicist, and a bus driver!"

No one on my team complains about what I've said, because despite my demeaning tone, it's all 100% accurate.

"Is not our fault Space Force claimed right to combat aliens," Ivan complains.

"How were we supposed to know what would happen?" Quaid grumbles, knowing he made that particular mistake.

Ivan chuckles again, this time in a way that makes me frown, because it's condescending. He's shaking his head. "You Americans. There was time when Russians respected you. Like you, not so much. But respect? Da. Now you elect showmen and hate each other more than enemies."

"Watch it," I say, making a fist.

"You? You are different, but your President West received same intel as all first world nations around globe. Warning from aliens, four weeks ago. Along with simulation. While rest of militaries prepared for battle royale, West has been playing like video game in Oval Office. Supreme Commander Putin tells him is *not* game. Is warning. Is incoming real-world scenario. West replied, 'I am genius president. Biblical, like George Washington. Ain't nobody going around doing this thang like me. You don't think when we write the next Bible, I won't be up in that shit? Naw, I own this right here. Level thirty-five.' No joke. Not even paraphrase."

Loretta breaks the silence that follows by saying what we're all thinking. "Mmm-hmm, that sounds like him."

"So, Ivan, what exactly are you proposing?" I ask.

"Set me free," he says. "I fight with you. Save world."

Before I can answer, a voice calls to me from the night. "Harooooh? Auntie? You okay? You alive? I come in now?"

22

I hit the elevator's back wall hard enough to think I'm being attacked, to believe that the end is once again upon me. And this time, nothing flashes before my eyes.

What the hell? Do you only get one life-flashing event? Is it a one-time deal? Or do I no longer love my childhood pets? Does anyone know how these things work? I'm not sure why I want to revisit the experience. Maybe I think someone else will be there. Maybe I think someone else *should* be there?

Seeds of doubt never grow into anything useful.

When Taylor coughs and says, "Not that I don't appreciate the save, but maybe a little gentler next time?" I lift my head and find Gerty standing above us, elevator doors closing behind her.

"A little gentler," she counters, "and you'd be dead. Or missing a limb."

To punctuate her point, Frenzy's hand snaps through the closing gap, reaching and swiping. Gerty catches hold of the arm and pulls. The alien's face collides with the door, eliciting a grunt. While it's held in place, Gerty winds up and clocks the domed metal head, denting the armor and spilling the much larger Chote back into the hallway. She calmly presses the door-close button, and smiles as we're sealed inside.

"Going up," she says, pressing the button for the roof. I might have gone back down, but who am I to argue with an AI that I'm sure is smarter and crazy-stronger than me? Her flight suit is a smidge shredded and dirty, but she looks no worse for wear after being launched through a building.

New plan: where Gerty goes, we go.

"I have to admit," she says, leaning against the wall like this is just a casual elevator ride to a hotel room, "I wasn't expecting to see you two meat sacks alive again. I was disappointed I'd missed your dismemberment, but maybe there's still a chance?"

When my eyebrows turn up in concern, she grins. "You don't like my killer-robot humor?"

She crouches down. "Relax. I like Sarah Connor more than the Terminator. And I did just save you. Again." Then she reaches out, presses her index finger against my nose and says, "Boop."

Taylor chuckles. "You got booped."

Gerty twists around, and faster than Taylor can react, she taps his nose, too. "Boop."

Taylor's smile fades, as he bathes in humiliation alongside me.

"Ain't nobody fast enough to get off the boop train once it gets moving," Gerty says, leaving Taylor and me to just stare at her for a moment. She stands again. "Got a plan?"

"Work our way through the barracks, training center, and back to Ops."

She nods like all that makes sense, but then says, "What then?"

"We were kind of hoping Billy would handle the 'what then.'"

"Really?" she says. "I mean, the endgame is pretty obvious here, right?"

"Uhh, yeah?"

"You, better than anyone, know what comes next," she says, and then she states the obvious with bitter disappointment in her voice. "Kill all sons a bitches."

"Did you just quote *Left 4 Dead*?" Taylor asks.

"Left 4 Dead 2," she says. "Yeah. I'm trying to communicate in terminology that will make sense to you both. This...all of this...is a game to these things, and the only way to achieve what we want is to go for that tasty chicken dinner."

Taylor and I both grin. She is speaking our language.

"And how do you propose we kill fifty Chote?" I ask.

"Forty-three," she says. "I killed four. I'm assuming you two killed the other three?"

"Well, we definitely killed two," I say. "The other one we kind of just embarrassed into suicide."

"Ooh," she says. "That's not cool. No one likes a bully."

"It wasn't on purpose," Taylor says.

"Still..."

"Well, I don't know about you," I say, "but we find killing the Chote kind of difficult."

She nods, and I realize I have no idea how hard her journey has been. She's a robot, but it's hard to not think of her as sentient. If I hadn't seen her metal chest, I'd have never guessed she wasn't human. "It is an uphill battle."

"Then you don't have any ideas about how to get the job done?" I ask. "Aside from a mass booping."

She smiles. "I was going to ask Billy." She points two fingers at Taylor and me. "You guys aren't the fastest cockroaches in the kitchen."

"I'll keep that in mind." I push myself up, as the elevator slows to a stop, dings, and opens its doors.

"Now we're cockroaches," Taylor complains.

"Cockroaches I like," she says, stepping out onto the orange-lit roof.

"Because Billy programed you to like us, right?" Taylor says. "I mean you barely know us."

"Good point," she says, and she tweaks her head to the side.

"Wait, did you just edit your code?" Taylor says. "Can you *do* that? How do you feel about us now?"

I bump into Gerty when I spot the thing at the building's far side. For me, it's like hitting a brick wall. For her, a minor annoyance. She glances back, glaring. "TBD."

I barely notice the subtle threat that a future, unfriendly Gerty might pose, because the current, very real threat, is like the kick of a colossal brain fart that reduces my thought process to something like, "Oooooooh shit. OOOOOOH shit."

The Chote at the end of the roof, between us and where we want to be, is a good fifteen feet tall and even more heavily armored. If it is a Chote. Its phallic shape has been concealed by what looks like a mech. The robotic legs are short, but powerful, supporting a broad body with arms that hang nearly to the ground and are tipped not with hands, but with futuristic looking cannons.

"Ugh," I say. "It's not just a battle royale. It's class based."

"Meaning?" Gerty asked.

"Meaning the Chote we encounter could be like the normal grunts we've already met, which, honestly, are frikken bad enough. But they could also be like this." I motion toward the giant Chote. "Or anything in between. Or worse. And if their class is powerful enough, which I think this is, they don't need to worry about weapon pick-ups."

"It's like some kind of Wunderchote," Taylor says.

Gerty rolls her eyes.

"Wait, you're not going to hold that against me?" Taylor says.

"Well, it ain't helping," she says, and holds a hand out to him. "Gun."

Taylor slides his SCAR off his shoulder, but thinks twice before handing it over.

"Really not helping," Gerty says, and Taylor acquiesces. "And you know how the saying goes. If I wanted you dead..."

"You'd buy us chocolate pudding?" I say.

"Are you allergic to chocolate pudding?" she asks. "That seems unlikely."

"Totes allergic," I say. "Both of us."

"Mmm," she says, taking the assault rifle.

The Wunderchote begins hooting a laugh. Then it opens fire with both arms. Spheres of green, crackling light pound toward the ground.

Taylor and I look at each other, eyes wide, and we speak in unison. "BFG 10k"

"That's not from a battle royale game," he complains.

"Not sure it matters," I tell him. The classic weapon first appeared in the first-person shooter game, *Quake 2,* and it quickly became a legend because of its over-powered ability to turn any noob into a killing machine. This thing has *two* of them. If those Big Fucking Guns have the same kick, whoever it shot at down there is about to become a puddle. A flash of red rising into the sky confirms it.

"How many is that?" I ask, as the Wunderchote starts doing the running-man dance, shaking the rooftop.

"Twenty-seven," Gerty says, feeling the rifle's heft in her hand.

More than half of the people on base have already been killed, and the first circle hasn't even finished closing yet. Not a good sign.

"You know," I tell her, "bullets don't do a whole lot to—"

She silences me by holding the rifle like a football and throwing a spiral that would make Tom Brady squee. The eight-pound rifle-turned-projectile slams into Wunderchote, shattering on impact, but with enough force to launch the thing off the building's side. There's a moment of silence and then a slam after it falls all ten stories to the concrete below.

I look to the orange force field, but there's no surge of white.

The Chote inside the mech must have survived the drop, I think, *but at least it's out of commis—*

A mechanical and angry roar sounds out from far below, growing louder as it rises toward us. The Wunderchote surges up over the building's roof and then crashes back down with surprising grace.

"Well," Gerty says. "Fuck."

23

"Come on up, real slow," I say down the stairwell. Our lone Chinese infiltrator has volunteered to surrender himself.

"Dead people are hard to walk on," he complains, strangely detached from the fact that he's stepping on the pulped remains of his compatriots. He thumps into the stairwell wall as a body rolls under his foot. It's a brutal walk of shame to put anyone through, but I think of it like a birth for the man: he'll be covered in blood and shit when he reaches the top, but he'll also be a new man, reborn to the concept of not being a #1 douche.

I cover him with the AKM as he reaches the top and quickly scan him for weapons. He left the bullpup and a handgun outside, but that doesn't mean he's not some kind of ninja. Wait, no, ninjas were Japanese. *Is it racist to mix them up?* And here I am, a black belt in Shaolin kung-fu. The difference between Chinese and Japanese martial arts should be at the forefront of my mind. I blame Stone. Sarcasm rarely takes time to evaluate the accuracy of what's being said.

Ah well, at least no one can hear my thoughts and will think less of me, unless there is something to that fourth-wall crap.

And if there is, *Get the frick out of my head.*

"In there," I motion to the hangar-side of the control tower with my head. The bodies have been cleared out, dragged to the structure's far side, and the doors closed to help staunch the stink.

When Ivan sees the small Chinese man slink in, he bursts out laughing, deep and hearty, like a Tolkien dwarf. "This is soldier in China? This is wheat before thresher."

No shit, I think.

Actually, I'm not sure what that means, but it sounds right. I look the man over. Up close and without a weapon in his hands, I'm seeing his size and slightly hunched posture for the first time. He probably spends more time in front of a computer than at a shooting range. I doubt he can run to the bathroom without getting winded or tripping over himself.

I direct him to a chair and shove him into it. When I plant my hand against his chest, which lacks any kind of armor, I feel ribs and little else. I lower the AKM, drag a chair over, and sit across from the man.

Ivan chuckles. "You don't even tie him up. Poor, small man."

"Don't make me gag you," I say. The big Russian makes an effort to clamp his lips shut, but fails to hide his smirk.

I turn to the Chinese man, whose posture hasn't been improved by sitting down. "Name?"

"Wang Jianguo," he says.

"So good that Stone's not here," Chieng says.

I smile, imagining all the wang jokes that would just roll off his tongue without a thought. That is, if he was gaming. I know he can be a professional when he needs to be. "I know, right?"

"Sooo," Quaid says, and I stop him from continuing with a raised hand. Whatever filter Stone would be able to employ in this situation, Quaid lacks it, and whatever joke he's about to tell isn't going to be funny.

"Ya'll trying to not make fun of his name?" Loretta says.

"What is wrong with my name?" Jianguo says, eyes squinting.

"The next person to speak that isn't me or our new friend here, is going to find out what it feels like to have a bullet in their foot."

"Is not good," Ivan says, and when I glare at him, he adds, "Bullet in foot. It hurts for year, at least, longer with sepsis."

"You speaking from experience?" Quaid asks, chuckling at the ridiculousness of the possibility.

"Da," Ivan says. "I have been shot in foot three times."

"In combat?" Quaid asks. "That seems like a lot."

"By parents," Ivan says. "Was punishment."

"For what?" Loretta asks, following this tangent to whatever dark corner of Ivan's past it will take us.

"Stealing," he says. "Cookies."

When all of our jaws collectively drop, he shrugs. "Were difficult times. Made me man I am today." His good humor melts away as his eyes and lips turn downward. The man who laughed despite the deaths of his entire team descends into an uncomfortable malaise.

"Oookay," I say, swiveling back to Jianguo, whose upturned eyebrows show concern for the Russian's well-being. "Can I call you Jian?" Abbreviating his first name, rather than using his last name, is an act of mercy. Just about everyone here, including myself, will not be able to hold back a barrage of wang jokes. It will be funny at first, but at some point I will look into Jian's sad eyes and realize I'm a monster. God forbid Stone ever meets him. Calling him Jian will be good for everyone.

And now I've got *Everybody Have Fun Tonight* by Wang Chung stuck in my head. Ugh.

He nods in a way that suggests he understands and appreciates my reasoning.

"So, Jian, who are you?"

"Not a soldier," he says, and I just nod. "I am a hacker. Number one, best."

"In China?" I ask.

"In the world," he says.

"*You* are DigiDragon?" Ivan asks, perking up, the look of a killer back in his eyes.

Jian's eyes light up. "You know me?"

"You are on short list of targets to kill."

Jian shrinks back in his chair. I haven't heard of him, and I don't know what he's done to the Russians, but it was apparently bad enough to put him on Alpha Squad's radar, and he didn't even try to wiggle his way out of it. He knows what he did, and that people might want to kill him for it. So he might not be a bad guy with a gun, but he's definitely not a good guy, either. His weapons are his brain and his wiry, little fingers.

"I will not kill you." Ivan forces a smile. "Alien invasion has way of changing perspectives, no?"

"You literally just tried to kill us," I point out, annoyed. "And you did kill the Canadians, who were really nice, by the way."

"Was mistake," he says, like that makes everything better. "And not any more. Old ways of doing things need to change. Now, we work together, no?"

"No more shooting people?" I ask.

"In head," he says, "or in foot."

Somehow the Russian killing machine has managed to have his own personal character arc while I'm trying to interrogate the newcomer. I'm not sure how that happened, but Ivan is a bit of an attention hog. Back to the matter at hand...

"Jian," I say. "Why are you here?"

He rolls his eyes. "Siberian Tiger planned to fly me up to aliens in your *Rex*. Infiltrate the ship. Install a computer virus."

"C'mon, ya'll, that's the plot of *Independence Day*," Loretta says. "The movie. I mean, don't get me wrong, Will Smith is a piece of ass I wouldn't mind tapping, and that Jeff Goldblum, his voice is like sugar, but that's the dumbest thing I've ever heard, and I'm just a bus driver."

"I feel like you're not using the 'piece of ass' phrasing right," Chieng says, looking uncomfortable.

"Well, you know what I mean. That's what's important."

"It's not important," Jian says, losing his patience. "It's dumb. Like the plan. Like I told them. A computer virus made for any operating system on Earth will not work on alien technology. Their computers could look like slugs for all we know!"

"First, I doubt it," I say. "Second, if the plan wasn't going to work, why did you come with them?"

"No choice," he says, despondent. "I die at home, or I die in the alien ship. One is at least interesting...and if I am lucky, maybe I can learn how to stop them. Because I'm smart."

"Number one, smart," I say, and he nods with ferocious abandon.

The Russian chuckles. He can't help himself.

"And what was *your* plan?" I ask the Russian.

"Find mothership. Infiltrate. Blow it up."

"Blow it up?" Quaid says, skipping right past how hard it will be to locate and reach a mothership while there are hundreds of alien craft in orbit. "With *what?*"

Ivan shrivels up a little bit.

"Did it just get cold in here?" I quip, and he seems to understand the jab.

He sits up straight, sticking out his neck. "Portable nuke. Is outside." When we all stare at him in abject horror, he says, "What? Is hidden."

I clear my throat, but find myself still unable to think straight, let alone speak.

"What was your grand plan?" Ivan asks. "The great and noble U.S. Space Force, home for derelict personnel, who was to be no more in morning. How were *you* planning to respond to threat you did not know existed until now? Hmm?"

"We were going to do what we do best," I tell him, filling myself with false confidence.

"Play video games?" Quaid says.

"Get drunk?" Chieng adds.

And I can't snap at either of them, because we actually do those things quite well, too. But it's not like we had anything more to do when not training.

"Drive buses?" Loretta says.

"You know," I tell her. "You *can* go home."

She shrugs. "I'm with Jian. If we're all gonna die tonight, I'd prefer a front-row seat, and maybe I'll find a way to help."

I nearly douse her fire with a bucket of 'I doubt it,' but she already has helped. She might not have meant to gun down five men with one bullet, but when the shit hit the fan, she wasn't afraid to get in front of it and take a full load in the face while firing back. So, instead, I say, "Yeah, you will," and I offer a fist bump, which she taps like Will Smith's ass...or something.

"What is plan, then?" Ivan asks. "What is it Space Force does that no one else can?"

I crouch down, draw a knife taken from one of the dead, and hold it against his bonds. "Improvise," I say, and I yank the knife up. The blade cuts through the rubber coating, but grinds against the metal wire.

I look at the blade in sour disappointment. "That was supposed to be more dramatic." I saw at the cables, working my way through the metal fibers. It's a full minute of hard work until the wire gives way and Ivan is able to work his hands free. "Improvise," I say again, and I get a laugh out of the big man.

He holds his freed hands out, requesting the knife, and I decide to trust him. I spin the blade around and hand it to him. He cuts through the cable binding his feet with one mighty tug, and then offers the knife back.

"Keep it," I say, and he nods in thanks before pushing himself up.

"Now," I say, "About that nuke?"

24

STONE

"Stay in a tight group," I say, facing down the massive Wunderchote.

"That so we can die together?" Taylor says. "How romantic."

"Condenses its spread. When it fires, scatter. We need at least twenty-five feet between us and the BFG spheres." It's ridiculous that I know the range, in feet, of a weapon that until this moment only existed in a video game where feet are measured in game units—256 to be exact. For all I know, they've increased the range. If they have, well, I'll probably cease to exist before I realize I was wrong, so that's something.

"How come it hasn't fired yet?" Taylor asks. "BFG recharge time is two seconds."

As technologically advanced and dedicated to recreating gaming experiences in real life as the Chote might be, faithfully recreating something like the BFG might have been a stretch. With a two second recharge time, the rooftop would already be a technicolor kaleidoscope of glowing green death beams.

How long has it been since it fired?

Forty-five seconds? A minute?

"And then what?" Taylor asks.

"And then what-what?" I say.

"After we dodge the BFG!" he says. "Then. What?"

"Umm." I don't get to finish revealing my non-existent strategy. Two balls of explosive green energy launch and converge on our position. Long laser beams stretch out, searching for flesh to sear. "Go!"

I break right, while Taylor heads left. Gerty remains rooted in place.

"Gerty, move!" I shout. "The beams affect everything they touch!"

I know she's heard my warning, and the lines being carved into the rooftop are impossible to miss, but she waits, crouching slowly.

She's waiting, I realize, *but for what?*

I don't stop my outward arching sprint until I'm running along the building's edge, a good forty feet beyond the BFG's estimated range. That's the good news. The bad news is that I'm running closer to the Wunderchote. The next time it fires, I won't have nearly as much time to react.

The roof's short safety wall shatters as it's struck by some kind of projectile weapon. I glance down and see Chote Squad matching my pace, scrambling through the manicured garden behind the building. I duck away from the edge, making myself a much smaller target to the one taking aim with an alien rifle he must have picked up inside the building.

Where's Frenzy? I wonder, and I get my answer a moment later. The elevator doors burst open and the nutjob alien spills out onto the roof. His roar is drowned out by the crackling of BFG spheres passing by, the green beams of energy falling ten feet short of hitting me—but close enough for me to feel the intense heat emanating from them.

I glance back, thinking I'm going to watch Gerty melt to slag. Instead, I find her crouched down and calm as the two spheres race toward her. Just as an outstretched beam of laser light is about to strike her, she springs from the roof, like fucking Tigger on crack, rising high above the BFGs' range and sailing toward the Wunderchote.

After finishing a savage roar and arm flail, Frenzy, who is enjoying the game far too much, opens his alien eyes and looks forward. The roar becomes a high-pitched squeal. The BFG lasers strike first, locking Frenzy in place as his body shakes and quivers, his scream reaching impressive decibels.

Then the two balls of light strike and burst with explosive force, eradicating Frenzy, a thirty-foot patch of roof, and the three floors beneath it.

Wunderchote's head snaps back in surprise. Then it looks left and right, no doubt hoping it's not being watched. But if this is a true battle royale situation, it's being broadcast to all the Chote...and maybe even to the world at large. If he doesn't manage to kill us here, he's going to spend the rest of his alien life being ridiculed. Then again, the Chote don't seem to cope with shame very well. He might throw his gargantuan self into the force field.

But he might not get the chance. Gerty descends from her arc like a mortar shell, arms reaching for the Wunderchote's head. He sees her at the last moment, raising up a defensive arm. She impacts with an armor-denting force and tears into the BFG, ripping out components and no doubt disabling one of the two cannons.

The whump of an anti-grav gun pulls my attention back over the building's side. A single member of Chote Squad launches up toward me.

As I scramble back, the rising Chote slams into the side of the roof, turning its graceful rise into a sprawl of limbs. But it doesn't forget why it's there. As the Chote's body spins, the metal domed head tracks me, and the anti-grav gun swivels toward me.

But the pinwheel proves too chaotic for the creature. When it pulls the trigger, the invisible force throws me back, but it's nothing a quick roll can't correct. The effect on the Chote is far more dramatic. While the roof is slammed downward, the alien is launched another hundred feet in the air. As it catapults away, the Chote loses his grip on the anti-grav weapon and plummets to the ground.

I take a moment to watch him slam into the concrete with a crunch. The armor's joints crack and separate, allowing a thick ooze to seep out. A moment later, a bright white flash rises into the sky. It's followed by two red flashes, as somewhere else on the base, more human beings are cut down.

Behind me, the Wunderchote lifts his big arm up and slams it down, crushing Gerty beneath its weight and dragging her across the rough tar. She doesn't flinch. Doesn't scream. Her only reaction is to hold on and glare up at the alien.

She's lifted and slammed down two more times until her hands come away with fistfuls of metal. It wasn't Gerty who gave way, it was the Wunderchote's armor.

When she lies still, I fear the worst, and the Chote assumes victory.

Both of us are wrong.

Gerty shoves off the roof, launching herself up under the mech's chin and delivering a savage kick that snaps its faux-head back. She then grasps hold of its jaw and pulls as she descends. Her tattered jumpsuit peels away, revealing a shapely, but very robotic body. With her feet planted, Gerty pulls, and then flings the Wunderchote. It's not quite a throw—the mech never really leaves the roof, but it does stumble forward and faceplant.

"Yes!" Taylor shouts from the roof's far side, thrusting his fists in the air. But his victory dance is premature. The Wunderchote is already righting itself.

Instead of pressing the attack, Gerty leaps across the roof, landing beside Taylor. She grasps hold of his armor, spins, and chucks him from the barracks to the training center's roof. Then she leaps again, landing beside me.

"I was wrong about you," I say with a smile. "You are Space Force."

She flashes a smile, still pretty, despite the Terminator body, and says, "Stay alive. Find Billy." She sticks out her tongue and plucks a small, metal, solid-state drive from it. "When I see you next, let me know if this works."

I'm about to ask what the hell she's talking about when I suddenly find myself airborne. I hit the deck hard, but manage to mitigate the impact by rolling...and rolling...and rolling. I slide to a stop beside Taylor and lift my head to watch what happens next.

Gerty faces off with the rising Wunderchote, allowing it to stand tall once again.

How much time has passed? I wonder. How many seconds until the BFG is fully charged?

What the hell is she waiting for?

The Wunderchote lifts its one working cannon.

Gerty charges, her powerful footfalls denting the rooftop beneath her. A crackling green sphere of destructive energy launches toward Gerty. She *dives* at it.

"What the fuck..." Taylor whispers.

As the green beams of energy sizzle across her body, she spins around and holds her hands out toward us, offering two Arnold Schwarzenegger thumbs up. Then she enters the sphere of energy, forcing it to burst against her body.

The closeness of the explosive blowback of energy staggers the Wunderchote. It doesn't destroy the mech, or kill the alien inside, but it does prevent him from seeing what is left of Billy's creation pass through the billowing green light. The remaining football-sized projectile, that was Gerty, punches into the mech's armor, embedding itself in the thing's chest.

Eyes wide, I manage to shout, "Down!" before what must have been Gerty's power source explodes.

Heat scours my back as the explosion's force slaps the air from my lungs. When it's over, I lift my head to cough and suck in a breath. But I freeze when I see what looks like a small mushroom cloud rising from what remains of the barracks. Behind it, a white flash rises up into the sky. As the building crumbles inward, three more flashes shoot up. Not only did her sacrificial act kill the Wunderchote, but it killed three other aliens inside the building.

When there is no red flash, I realize that the Chote never saw Gerty as alive, and therefore as a member of the human race. Their mistake, I think, and I push myself up. After a victory like that, my instinct is to offer some kind of 80's action-movie pithy remark. Out of respect for Gerty, though, I stay silent.

Taylor puts his hand on my shoulder. "We need to move."

I break for the stairs beside the elevator structure. Without Gerty backing us up, I don't want to get caught in the confines of a metal box.

Two flights down, Taylor comes to a sudden stop, a look of panic in his eyes.

"What is it?" I whisper, crouching beside him and drawing my completely ineffectual sidearm.

He hesitates like he doesn't want to answer, but then says, "We have a code SS situation."

I look at him in horror for a moment and ask. "Are you sure?"

Eyes widening, he nods.

I look toward the stairwell door, wondering how best to handle this and say, "On three. Ready?"

"More than," he says with a grunt.

"One...two..."

25

HALE

"Really?" I say, looking down at a metal suitcase resting on the tarmac.

"Is hiding in plain sight," Ivan says.

"I'm not sure you understand the concept," I say. "A suitcase lying where a suitcase shouldn't be—especially a fancy metal one—draws attention."

"Is still here, no?"

"Because everyone who could have found it is dead," I grumble.

"Meh," he says with a shrug. "Win, win."

"Pretty sure you're not using that correctly, either."

"You Americans, always right. Is why no one likes you anymore."

"Pretty sure I know why no one likes us, and it's not because we're always right."

"Always *think* you're right," he corrects.

"That was just one man," I complain.

"Who spoke for you all."

"Not for me," I say.

"Ahh," he says with a chuckle. "You were pussy-hat wearer? Marching in vagina parade?"

I've taken part in a few marches during my lifetime, but while other people were wearing knit pink hats that somehow resembled lady bits, I was wearing a helmet and pulling Mach 2. That's how this chick made a difference for women—by doing my job better than the men, and aiming higher. Turns out, my fatal flaw was aiming too high. Had I kept my sights on the clear blue skies patrolled by the U.S. Air Force instead of the sparkling void of space, I'd still be flying. Then again, if I wasn't here, who would help Stone kick some alien ass?

I smile with the realization that I'm exactly where I am meant to be. The Island of Misfit Toys isn't all bad. Screw Santa Claus.

"Well, you can carry it," I say.

Ivan shoulders the sniper rifle I've allowed him to carry and picks up the suitcase nuke. He gives it a vigorous shake. "Nuclear bomb cannot detonate by accident. You could shoot, or blow up, and it will not explode."

"Yeah, well, you can test that theory on your own time." I tilt my head back toward the open hangar, where the others are busy, prepping the *Rex*. "Our chariot awaits."

"Is space chariot," Ivan says with a smile.

"Have you been in space?" I ask.

The big man purses his lips and shakes his head. "Have you?"

"Simulated space," I admit. "Lots of time in the vomit comet."

It's not a lot, but it's the best prep available for zero gravity, short of actually going to space. Funding was reduced when congressional seats shifted before any training missions could extend to space. The *Rex* was grounded a short time later, primarily because of fuel costs. Overnight, Space Force became the most high-tech and poorest military branch. It was the beginning of the end. But the vomit comet—officially called a reduced-gravity aircraft—gave me enough zero-G experience that I'm not concerned about that aspect of our impending journey. The plane follows a parabolic flight path, shooting high into the sky, and then diving back down, giving those on board a simulated zero-G experience for thirty seconds. The maneuver is repeated sixty times per flight, providing a half hour of float time, and about an equal amount of puke time for newcomers—hence the nickname. I never lost my lunch on the flights, and honestly looked forward to each and every one.

I wish I could say the same now, but this flight could determine the planet's fate, and will very likely end in my death. So, for the first time, my stomach churns as I head for my ride.

I glance at Ivan beside me, a nuke in hand. Despite never feeling the nauseating effect of zero gravity and facing the same slim odds of survival, he's calm and collected.

"How do you do it?" I ask.

"Is personal subject," he says. "But I prefer missionary to—"

"Not *it*," I say. "This." I mimic his stoic face and wave my hand around in front of it.

He laughs, deep and hearty. "I know what you mean. I am, how you say, joshing you."

It's my turn to laugh. "No one says, 'joshing,' unless it's the 80s."

"1880s?"

"What? No. *1980s.*"

"Term comes from late 1800s," he says. "A man named Josh Tatum."

"You say Tatum, I hear Channing."

"Ugh," Ivan says. "Is hairless man-woman who gyrates and bad acts?"

"That's the one." I lick my lips and add, "Mmm-mm."

Ivan squints down at me. "Now you are one who is joshing?"

"I'm joshing the shit out of you," I say, and we share a good laugh. If Ivan hadn't tried to kill my people, I could see us being friends. That he doesn't hold a grudge after his men were turned to puddles says more about his professionalism and less about his character. Despite his Mr. Rogers act, I need to remember that he's a killing machine. As long as he's my killing machine, we're all good.

If that changes...well, let's hope it doesn't.

As we approach the hangar, I get a good look at the *T-1-Rex* and have no trouble ignoring the mash of human flesh spread out before the ruined control tower. The stink of death warmed by the summer air and kicked up by an ocean breeze is nearly enough to garner my attention, but the *Rex* overpowers it all.

The spacecraft is sleek and dangerous looking, designed for the dual role of space fighter and transport. Visually, it's similar to an F-117 Nighthawk, but closer in size to a B-2 bomber. In the air, it's fast, but not exactly maneuverable. In space, it will handle like a dream. Its only real limitations are those of the people inside it.

Unlike stealth aircraft, the *Rex*'s black paint job is offset by an orange cylinder running down the center of the ship. In a worst-case scenario, this hardened tube can be ejected from the ship in four stages, carrying crew and passengers through the atmosphere and back to the ground.

I've never understood the orange streak. Had they painted the whole thing black, it would be all but invisible against the backdrop of space. But someone in the chain of command liked things to look sexy...and orange. So that's what we have. The aliens are definitely going to see us coming. The question is, will they be prepared to defend against an assault on *them?*

"Prepped and ready," Quaid shouts down to me from the *Rex's* side hatch. "Fuel is at full. Weapons systems green. She's just been sitting here, waiting for a chance to prove herself."

"Well," I say, starting up the mobile boarding stairs, "she's about to get her chance." It feels more like boarding a commercial flight than a military aircraft, once again reflecting the odd choices of whoever helped shape the craft's broad design.

"*Rex* is she?" Ivan asks from behind me.

"Aren't most vehicles referred to in the feminine?" I ask.

"Is *Rex*. Is boy's name."

"First, anyone who names their kid 'Rex' shouldn't be allowed to have kids. Second, it's named for the *Tyrannosaurus Rex*, of which there were plenty of females."

"Reminds me of mother," he says, as I step aboard the *Rex* and forget all about our conversation. I've been in the simulated version of this more times than I can count. To be here, in the flesh... Goosebumps rise on my arms, and a shiver runs through my body.

"Should have named ship Channing," Ivan quips, noting my reaction.

"Funny," I say, and I step up next to Quaid. "Stow the nuke someplace safe, yeah?" He gives a tentative nod and steps out of the cockpit. I flinch when I find Jian sitting in the co-pilot's seat.

"Hallo!" he says, giving me a big grin while his fingers fly over the controls and code scrolls across the screen. "I make the ship better, okay? You see?"

"Whatever you're doing," I growl. "Stop now, or I'll feed you to Ivan."

He stops typing, but his index finger slowly glides over to a final key. He hovers for a moment, and then taps the key. The code disappears from the screen.

"He insisted," Chieng says, from behind. "He seemed to know what he was talking about. Knew all about the *Rex*. How it worked. What it could do."

"I downloaded the plans years ago," Jian confesses. "I know the computer system like the back of grandmother's hand."

"You mean your own hand?" I ask, taking the seat next to him and running through a pre-flight check to make sure he didn't screw anything up.

Jian becomes sullen. "Grandmother used to hit me. I see her hand approaching my face. A lot."

I stare at him for a moment. "Good talk." Then I turn my attention back to the pre-flight check, which the *Rex* passes with flying colors. "Everyone find a flight suit that fits, and get in it. We're launching in ten minutes."

While they set to work getting dressed—something I still need to do as well—I pull out my cellphone, think twice about making the call, and then tap Stone's number. There are four rings, and then Stone's panicked voice, saying, "Shit! Shit! Shit!"

26

STONE

"That was crazy," Taylor whispers. Cloaked in darkness we sit side by side, our conversation hushed. "Do you think she meant to do that?"

Remembering the way Gerty jumped through the BFG beam and emerged as an explosive powerful enough to drop the Wunderchote and half a building, I nod, forgetting he can't see me. "No doubt. She might not have been human, but she represented the best of us."

"Kind of weird that Billy made something like that, yeah? I mean—" He grunts and sighs. "—that he created an intelligent sexbot without anyone knowing seemed unlikely, but not really surprising. The ladies aren't exactly lining up for a night with stud Billy. The guy wants to be called 'Billy.'"

Another grunt. Another sigh.

"But she was the real deal. A fighter. A sister in arms. Kind of wish I'd known that before."

"I don't think many of the men I've served with would be willing to make that kind of sacrifice." Jumping on grenades to save your compatriots is a Hollywood cliché, but it doesn't happen that often. It's not that soldiers aren't brave enough to sacrifice themselves, it's simply that when things are going sideways, reactions are instinctual, and when a grenade lands nearby, instinct guides everyone away from it. Soldiers aren't trained to dive on grenades. If they were, there would be pig piles of men being blown to smithereens.

What Gerty did was more than jump on a grenade. She threw herself into Mount Doom, knowing her demise would save us.

And now we have to honor that sacrifice...right after we finish up.

"How you doing over there?" I ask.

"I'm at about 75%," Taylor says. "You?"

"Same." I take a deep breath, trying to relax, and gag on the stench. "Holy hell, what did you eat?"

"Don't try to peg your stank on me, man," Taylor says.

A squeak like air being let out of a pinched balloon fills the air. I can't help but chuckle. "Just let loose. You're clenching."

"I'm trying to stay quiet," Taylor complains. "You want speed or stealth? I don't think I can do both."

"Fair enough," I say, still smiling. I have to enjoy the humor of our situation now because once we're out of here, neither of us are going to mention this to anyone. It's bad enough when it happens during an online gaming session, but during combat? It's the kind of situation that can haunt you for the rest of your career.

Between rounds of gaming and copious amounts of Mountain Dew for me, and coffee for him, a run to the bathroom is occasionally required. This can usually be accomplished in the time it takes for match-making to complete and a round to start. But sometimes, upon reaching the bathroom, nerves and biology unite against you. It was these situations that gave birth to the code: SS. Surprise Shit. If the situation arose, we would simply text SS to the other and the team would be informed that the missing man would be AFK (away from keyboard) for a few minutes, but would soon return...a pound or two lighter. SS is a reality of long-term gaming that no one talks about, but the struggle is real.

And the moment we stepped in this darkened bathroom on the eighth floor of the training facility, my bowels awakened with the force of Mount Vesuvius, kicking off the first ever double SS. It's not exactly a proud moment in the history of special forces, but it's giving us a chance to collect ourselves and an odd place to appreciate Gerty's sacrifice.

"So, we hit the ground floor, work our way through the sim and gym, and out the far side to Ops?" Taylor says.

"Sounds simple."

"But it won't be."

"Probably not," I say, and continue the conversation whilst carrying out my cleanup duties. "Maybe we should recon a few floors, check some rooms for spawns, get properly geared up before moving on. We have a destination, but what are the odds that the circle will close on Ops? Slim to none. We should try to be ready for multiple outcomes."

"Makes sense, ungh, almost done."

"Geez. You giving birth?"

"To triplets," he says.

"Sounds like more than that," I say. "You're the octoshitter."

"What?"

"Like the octomom, but for dumps."

"Classy."

"Have you *watched* TV lately?" I ask, flinching at a fresh wave of stench I decide to say nothing about. "That's a fuckin' hit waiting to happen."

The sound of toilet paper being unraveled from the next stall over signifies our side-mission is nearly complete.

"Don't flush," I say, standing and buckling my pants back in place. It feels weird leaving a full load in the toilet, but there's a good chance this whole building and our recently deposited gifts, will be vaporized by the force field as it closes in.

"Copy that," he says, unspooling some more toilet paper.

"Didn't take you for a buncher," I say, waiting outside the stalls.

"I'm not. Folding is obviously superior. But since I can't see what I'm working with, I'm going for maximum surface area and texture. A man needs to be clean. You didn't fold, did you?"

After a moment of concern, I say, "I eat enough fiber that everything comes out clean. Like a rabbit."

"Sounds like too much fiber," Taylor says.

The blaring scream announcing a change in the circle makes me flinch even though it's muffled by the building's walls. I flick on my phone and look at the map. The orange circle has closed in on the island, but has yet to strike any buildings. The preview of the next circle, represented by a small white outline, will change that. It's closing on the southeast end of the island, carving the training facility in half and fully encapsulating Ops and the administrative building, which has been empty for months. We're currently outside the next circle, and we have four minutes before the zone starts shrinking toward us.

"Pucker up and finish wiping," I say. "We need to bug out ASAP. Zone closes on our AO in four mikes."

"I love it when you talk all military," Taylor says. I hear his stall door open, but fail to see him in the dark against the phone's glare. I turn the screen around to light him up, but I see something else.

Something not right.

"What?" Taylor asks, his voice even quieter than before.

"Did you use the handicap stall?"

"I'm not a Philistine," he says. Despite there not being a handi-capped person on base, before or after the invasion, his personal code keeps him from violating social rules, like using a handicap stall. Despite my protests, we walked an extra fifty feet past the women's room, which is bigger and nicer, so he could drop the kids off in the Men's Only pool.

I creep closer to the stall, gun in one hand, phone in the other.

The phone vibrates and I flinch—hard—flinging the phone upward as my thumb somehow swipes to answer the call. I see Hale's name and face displayed on the screen as the phone pirouettes away, filling the room with a dull strobing light. Fearing I might miss an important update, or just a chance to talk to Hale again—and maybe figure out a way to get her in my life-ending montage—I forget all about the handicapped stall and focus on catching the phone.

I reach for the glowing beacon, and connect, but my fingers clench late. Instead of catching it, I knock it higher. "Shit! Shit! Shit!" I reach in the dark, lunging forward, and I career into something solid, while the phone falls toward the floor. I attempt to peel myself away from the toilet stall frame for one last attempt, but it's too late. The phone lands...with a wet slap.

The device's glow illuminates the inside of Taylor's toilet. If the big man's shit were a docking station, the phone would be perfectly placed, embedded vertically in a white and brown untouchable mash. I'm sure there are only seconds before the water and piss seeping into the phone renders it useless, so I shout, "I'll call you back!"

When the screen goes out, I lean back and curse a few more times for good measure. Taylor has remained oddly silent throughout my ordeal.

"Where you at?" I ask.

A moment later, his phone glows to life, illuminating his sober face.

Right. The handicapped stall. I raise my weapon again and freeze at the sound of a long, hitch-pitched fart that someone clearly tried to pinch off, but they failed.

"Who's there?" I ask.

"You better be in a wheelchair," Taylor says. "Or at least have a limp."

With his cover blown, our fellow bathroom occupant unclenches, and a sound like the Kraken coughing up a hairball thunders in the bathroom. It's followed by a rank breeze identifying the true source of what I've been smelling all along. The sheer force of the blast, coupled with the smell, raises the hairs on the back of my scrote...which I didn't know was possible, but there it is.

Weirdest Spidey-Sense ever.

"Check for feet," Taylor whispers.

I crouch down, planting a hand on the bathroom floor, making a mental note to wash it, or at the very least, not rub my eye, or pick a tooth or something, and I lean my head down for a peek. Beside me, Taylor lowers the phone, extending the reach of its glow into the large handicapped stall. A pair of armored feet flinch back, the claws dragging gouges into the floor.

Holy hell, we've been sharing the bathroom with a Chote this whole time!

Stacked up next to the feet is a pile of loose armor, shed, so the thing can drop an alien deuce. I guess Chote get SS, too.

I stand up fast, motion for Taylor's phone, and when he places it in my hand, I switch on the small but bright LED flashlight, quadrupling our visibility. Inside the stall, the Chote lets out another long squeaker. This time it's followed by the bang of me kicking in the stall door. A high pitched, horrified scream comes from the Chote, whose toilet-top naked-ness has just been exposed. A second scream comes from me as I stare into the thick toothed, wide-eyed face emerging from the thick folds of skin. The chorus of horror climaxes with a single gunshot, which punches through the un-armored face and makes Taylor and I both shout in pain. Firing a weapon in an enclosed space, especially one with tile floors and walls, is a very bad idea...unless you're shooting an alien in the face.

The single round does the job. An unarmored Chote is no match for a .45 caliber bullet.

I stumble back as the now-dead alien's sphincter finally relaxes. The Chote unloads the SS it had been attempting to hold in since we entered the bathroom. We hurry out of the bathroom as the toilet overflows. I hold my breath until the door is shut behind us, then I gasp for air.

Before I can remark on what we've just experienced, the sound of heavy feet thunders above us. The screaming and the gunshot have attracted attention. "No time to loot!" I shout, and I race toward the stairwell with Taylor at my heels, and who knows what directly above us.

27

HALE

"Hello? Stone?" There's a loud slap that makes me flinch, and then Stone's muffled voice says something about calling me back. When the phone beeps in my ear, I pull it back and look at the screen. Call disconnected.

Did he hang up, or is something wrong?

Of *course* something is wrong. He's surrounded by a shrinking force field and battling against an alien invasion. When I realize he could have never answered, I feel relief and a bit of pride. That he's alive means he's also fighting...and winning.

Give 'em hell, Stone...and call back soon.

I dock the phone in the *Rex*'s console and move to the back, dressing in cosmic armor, a pair of words I will never say aloud. They're kind of a cross between traditional space suits, motorcycle leathers, and military armor—sleek and sexy, black with racing stripes down the arms, but able to be pressurized. They can stop a bullet and hold back the vacuum of space at the same time. They come in two sizes—men's and women's— which is totally sexist to both sexes. Jian is forced to wear a women's, while Loretta fills hers out a little too much, but manages to squeeze her slightly too-plump self inside, and doesn't mind at all how she looks in it.

"Mmm, honey," she says to me, running her hands over her hips. "Ya'll got a full-length mirror up in here, because I feel like I look good."

"How you feel is all that matters," Quaid says.

She has no trouble hearing the sarcasm in his voice, but is unfazed by it. "Boy, you couldn't handle all of this."

And that's the moment I decide I really like Loretta. Not only will she stand up and fight when need be, but she's also a confident woman, no matter what other people think. I should be more like her.

"Everyone find a seat and buckle up. I want helmets on before we launch, just in case." I pick up a badass-looking black helmet of my own. We don't need them now, but if something goes wrong in orbit, still being able to breathe would be nice.

"I like Space Force suits," Ivan says, flexing inside his. The sleeves hug his big muscles and squeak as he flexes, stretching the fabric. He thumps the armor plating over his chest with his fists. "They fit tight in right places, no?"

When he eyes me up and down, I roll my eyes and head for the cockpit. "Whatever you say, Captain Moose Knuckle."

Loretta and Chieng have a good laugh.

"What is funny?" Ivan says. "What is moose knuckle?"

After Quaid checks his crotch to make sure he's not also the butt of a joke, he joins in laughing.

"Moose is majestic creature, no?"

Tension-reducing laughter builds. Loretta is bent over. Chieng wipes tears.

Ivan's face turns red as his patience wears thin, but I think that has more to do with not understanding than being the butt of a joke, so I fill him in. "Your pants are a little tight, comrade. Your kielbasa is on display."

Ivan leans forward, stares at his bulging crotch, which is pinched down the middle by an unfortunately placed, and too tight seam. As I enter the cockpit and sit down beside Jian, who smiles at me from his too-loose women's space suit, the big Russian bursts out laughing.

"Captain Moose Knuckle. Now I get!" Ivan gives me a thumbs up after taking his seat. "Would prefer armor, but am satisfied with showing off goods, no?" He sits with his legs open wide, his shameless bulge revealed for all the world to see, which right now, is me and Jian.

The little Chinese man mutters something in Mandarin and turns forward. He tugs on his suit, trying to make it tighter, but fails.

"Don't sweat it," I tell Jian, feeling bad for his wounded ego. "When the suits pressurize, he's going to be singing like Mariah Carey."

"He's going to make millions of dollars?" Jian says, his depression deepening.

"What? No. He's going to have a high-pitched voice," I say. "From getting his balls crushed."

"I like what you said. Voice like Mariah Carey. I want a voice like Mariah Carey. I want to know what love is. I want to say something with Snoop Dog."

"Goddamnit..." I pinch my nose. "Fucking language barriers. We don't have time for this shit." I put my helmet on, lock it in place, and toggle my mic. "We are airborne in sixty seconds. Anyone not strapped in and helmetless will become paste or asphyxiate. Stone is counting on me, and I'm not going to let him down."

"Uhh," Ivan says, raising a hand from his seat, where he is already buckled in and helmeted. *"Whole world* is depending on *all* of us."

"Ivan, I swear to Ghandi, I will break my foot off in your colon if you say another word."

After seeing his grin, I focus on the controls, getting the *Rex* ready for its first and likely last official flight.

"All systems go," Jian says from within his helmet. His voice is muffled, so I reach over and toggle his mic. "Sank you," he says with a little bow, and he repeats, "All systems go."

"Thank you... I know." Hands on the controls, I ask, "Everyone ready?"

I receive varying degrees of confirmation from Quaid, Loretta, and Chieng while Ivan says, "To the infinity beyond!"

I want to correct him. Misquoting Buzz Lightyear is an offense to all things American, like vegan bacon and macaroni and cheese without hotdog slices. Instead, I give the throttle a kick and guide us out of the hangar.

"Turn," Jian says, as we nose toward the mash of Russian bodies. "Turn!"

The *Rex* is too large to start turning right away. If I did, we'd collide with the hangar's side and damage the wing, ending our mission, paid for in the blood of idiots, morons, and three apologetic Canadians. Driving over the remains feels like a desecration, like a declaration of not caring about the dead, but, well, they're dead. Between the corpses and the ruined pavement, the front end jounces a bit.

"Just testing the shocks," I say, hoping no one will ask about, or deduce the truth. Jian cringes with every bounce, but says nothing more.

When I put enough distance between the *Rex* and the dead to ensure the vertical take off doesn't fling them about like soupy confetti, I pull to a stop. The most dangerous part of any flight is the take off and landing, and that's especially true in an experimental VTOL space ship you've only flown in a simulator. So I take a moment to center myself.

I open my eyes when I hear fingers tapping buttons.

"Do not touch my controls," I growl. Jian pauses and once again pushes a final button in slow motion.

Then he says, "VTOL ready."

My forehead creases and I inspect what he's done. "What the..." The *Rex* is perfectly prepped for take-off.

"I tell you," Jian says. "I steal schematics. I understand *Rex*. I cannot fly, but I know this." He waves his hands over the console. "Co-pilot," he says with a smile.

I give him a half smile. Better than nothing. "Co-pilot."

"Okay, everyone, cross your fingers and pucker your..." A beam of blue light appears on the tarmac in front of us. "...shit."

"Pucker your shit?" Ivan says. "Is this American expression?"

"Contact!" I say reverting to Stone's in-game lingo. "Twelve o'clock."

An armored thing appears in the center of the light. It's hard to make out as I squint, but once the blue beam is gone and the thing is bathed in the *Rex*'s outer lights I wince. "Ugh."

"Yīnjīng!" Jian shouts.

"What!"

What I took for fear in Jian's voice is actually excitement. "Is penis! Alien penis! Like anime!"

"I don't know what the hell anime you're watching," I say, "but right now, I need you to activate the weapons systems."

"Manual or automated?"

Automated? The hell is he talking about? "Manual."

He snaps out of his delight and his fingers fly over the system. The *Rex* is equipped with an array of kinetic turrets designed to hit targets in zero-gravity, but at this range, they'll work just fine on this thing.

"I want to see it!" Ivan says, unbuckling and stepping into the cockpit. "I want to look our enemy in the ey—ugh. Is gross."

The alien shakes its bulbous backside, opens its sharp-toothed maw, and lets out a roar none of us can hear through the *Rex*'s thick hull.

"Weapons live," Jian says.

I use what looks like a joystick to place the target finder over the alien's body, feeling violated every time I look at it. My thumb hovers over the trigger.

Why is it just standing there?

It's waiting, I realize, *but I don't have to.*

Just as I'm about to pull the trigger, five more blue beams strike the ground in front of us. As more of the dick-things appear, I swat Ivan. "Back in your seat!" Then to Jian. "You play video games?"

He looks at me like I've just asked him if he's had sex with an anime pillow. Of course he has. I shift control of the weapons system to his side of the cockpit. "I'll fly. You shoot."

His eyes light up with child-like excitement, but it fades as an onrush of G-forces crushes him into his seat. The powerful VTOL engines shove us away from the ground. The force pales in comparison to the speed of a traditional launch, but when you're not ready for it...

I'm smiling until I see the creatures below us get struck by fresh beams of light. When the glow fades, their armor has changed.

They have wings...

The six aliens, each the size of a rhino, glow blue and peel away from the ground with an ease that matches the *Rex*.

"Shoot!" I shout at Jian. "Shoot now!"

"Do not shout at me, Auntie!" he blurts out, and then he pulls the trigger, unleashing a fusillade of sharp metal shards designed to shred satellites, a space station, or other orbital crafts. Not a single shard hits its target, but the aliens are forced to peel away, slowing them down and giving us a chance to make a getaway.

When we're five hundred feet up, I punch the front-end thrusters and cut the back, putting us into a somersault. When the nose is facing upward, I slam the throttle as far as it will go and let out a "Woohoo!" that's cut short by a manly scream. I look back to find Ivan clinging to his seatbelt, legs dangling.

If he lets go, he'll die.

If I slow down, we all will.

28

STONE

"Tikki Tembo," Taylor whispers as we creep down the stairwell. So far, we haven't heard any signs of pursuit. Whatever Chote were above us either didn't know we were directly below them, or they didn't know where the stairwell was. "No Sa Rembo..."

I pause on the stairwell below Taylor. "You trying to channel Jackie Chan or something?"

"That's racist," Taylor says.

"Is it Chinese?"

"Well, yeah, but—"

"Not racist. What the hell is it?"

"A kid's book. I sometimes recite it when my nerves are frayed. You never read *Tikki Tikki Tembo*?"

My blank stare is all the answer he's going to get.

"Little dude fell in a well." He shakes his head like he's ashamed of me. "Did your parents even love you, man?"

"You know the answer to that question," I say, my mood truly souring since the aliens arrived. I mean, life and death battles against aliens bent on humanity's destruction ain't great, but they lack the emotional depth of a childhood spent in foster care.

"Dude, I'm sorry," Taylor says, and he means it. "I wasn't thinking."

I give him a smile. "You rarely are." I continue down the stairs. "So, how does it go? The story?"

"Tikki Tikki Tembo-no Sa Rembo-chari Bari Ruchi-pip Peri Pembo—"

"Are you shitting me? That's his *name?*"

"Exactly," Taylor says. "He falls into a well and his brother, who runs for help, is so exhausted from saying that long-ass name that Tikki nearly drowns. That's why the Chinese have little, short names now."

"Wait, isn't *that* racist?"

"It's actual Chinese folklore, man. The racist shit is that joke about the Chinese naming kids after the sound of a falling pan. Pong, Ping, Chung. *That's* racist."

"Chieng told me that joke," I note. "Is it racist if she tells it?"

"No," he says, thinking, "though she doesn't identify as Chinese...so maybe? Did you laugh at it?"

"Well, yeah," I admit. "It's kind of funny. Her name *is* Chieng."

"Then *you're* the racist. You gotta get this PC shit straight, man. Only make and laugh at jokes that are derogatory to white people, unless you're at a comedy show. Then not laughing is more insulting than the joke, unless the comedian uses the N-word. Then you damn well better not laugh."

"So complicated," I complain, standing by the stairwell exit on the bottom floor. "I think I'll stick to fart jokes."

"Good call," Taylor says. "You know, I'm not sure this conversation is getting us anywhere. I mean, shouldn't we be planning things out right now?"

"Like advancing the plot?" I ask, and then I shrug. "I feel like we know each other a little better."

"So, character development, then?"

"Makes sense," I say. "But this is really a debate to have with Hale."

"Right. I forgot that literary banter was kind of your thing. Verbal foreplay."

I give him a wink. "Still can be, baby."

"You couldn't handle all this." He motions to his body. "So what's the deal with you two now? Is it for real?"

"I think so," I say.

"But..."

"I didn't see her when my life flashed before my eyes."

"Hold up, what?"

"I saw my pets, man. They're who I felt connected to when I was a kid. Who I loved unconditionally. But I didn't see Hale...so, I'm not sure."

"Okay, your pets? For real? That's sweet as shit, and a little sad."

"No kidding."

"But have you told Hale yet? I mean, have you laid it all on the line?"

"Not even close," I admit.

"And she hasn't said anything to you?"

"We were working up to it."

"Next time you see her," he says. "Work fast."

A rhythmic thumping vibrates the floor. It's muffled, but definitely coming from somewhere on this floor.

Taylor places his ear against the metal door, and I do the same. The thumping is joined by a wavy bassline, ascending and descending.

"Is that..."

"The Humpty Dance," I say, confirming his suspicion.

"Someone's got a death wish," he says.

"Or the Chote like late 80's rap."

"Don't confine Shock G to the 80's," Taylor grumbles. "He's done a lot since Digital Underground."

"He'll always be Humpty to me," I say and smile. "Pronounced with an 'umpty.'" I nod my head to the door. "Let's see what this is, before the Chote zero in and get another kill."

I push through the door and am assaulted by Humpty Dance lyrics and rhythm. It's hard to not strut to the groove, but my training compensates, resisting the urge to James Brown shuffle my way down the hallway leading to the training center's gym and the sim station.

Before the stairwell door shuts behind us, I hear thumping from far above. The din has summoned the Chote. It won't be long before they reach the first floor.

"Keep your eyes open for loot," I say and hurry down the hall, moving faster than I should, but somehow still not fast enough.

"If we can give feedback when this shit is wrapped up, I'm going to complain about the sparsity and quality of the loot," Taylor says.

"I know, right?" I pause by the door to the gym and peek through the window. It's a vast space, and it looks untouched. If there are any weapons that can help us in there, they'll be hard to find amongst all the weights, training machines, and gear. But there is at least one weapon here I know where to find—the Rapid Fire Taser. In training mode, it's harmless, but with the flick of a switch it carries a punch. At least, against people. Who knows what it will do to a Chote, or if it will do anything at all. But I can aim it and shoot it, and that'll make me feel better.

A wave of sound thumps into my body as I open up the door. The Humpty Dance is in full swing. In response to the cacophony, a chorus of roars rumbles against the stairwell door. *Chote Squad,* I think. Probably still upset about losing one of their own.

I push through the door and the sound, heading into the gym while scanning for weapons. Finding none, I head for the music. It's coming from the simulator...

"I'm gonna do some quick loot recon," Taylor says. I give him a nod and we head in separate directions. It's not always wise to split up, but since this isn't a game and we can't resurrect each other, our best chance at surviving is finding some weapons. Best way to do that, and shut the musical beacon off, is to separate...briefly. If I have to see my life flash before my eyes again, I'll feel better seeing my buddy's face at the end of it.

I creep up to the simulator and find the airlock hatch open.

"Hello?" I shout, but my voice is drowned out by talk of lumpy oatmeal and gangsta mack.

I creep inside, stepping into the cargo hold, which in the real *Rex,* is full of passenger seats, and I freeze in place. There's a woman in the cockpit, her back to me. She's dressed in sweat pants and a bra, dancing to the music and drinking from a bottle of Jack Daniels. She's not Hale, but she's definitely attractive. And she's working her hips like this isn't her first dirty dance. I have no idea who she is, but she's cutting loose and clearly fun at a party. Sadly, her revelry is about to get us killed.

I spot a smartphone on a console, connected to the simulator's Bluetooth entertainment system. Why does the simulator have an entertainment system? Because the real *Rex* does. Why does the *Rex* have one? Because everything about Space Force was done in a gold-plated lavish kind of way. Had it been done right—sleek and refined—and given a name that wasn't the birthchild of some 1980's fantasy, Congress might not have torn us apart.

Not that it will be a problem now. I suspect the gold-plated toilet seats in the officers' quarters will be upgraded to platinum, now that the world knows there are aggressive aliens in the neighborhood. Assuming we survive...assuming I get this music shut down. I pick up the phone and tap the pause button.

The music falls silent, and the woman's voice fills the simulator as she finishes a further two lines of the Humpty Dance before realizing she's singing solo.

Then she turns around. I lock eyes with the woman for a moment, both of us trying to suss out if what we're seeing is real.

Then we both scream.

A moment after our voices fade, Taylor walks in behind me holding a katana pilfered from the martial arts training area. It's mostly for display, but I'm guessing it cuts better than a Ginsu. "Everything okay? I thought I heard—" He spots the woman, gives her a once over, and has a completely different reaction from me.

With a sly smile and an approving nod, he says, "Colonel Jones... I knew you had some curves under those starched uniforms."

And then, outside the gym door, an alien a cappella group lets out a warbling roar, like mutated turkeys in violent heat.

29

The Earth has been invaded by hostile, video-game-loving aliens that look like armored dongs. We're being pursued by six of them after their armor got upgraded for flight. Ivan is still hanging from his seat, trying to not become a human pancake, which I appreciate, because gross. And the man I...have feelings for...is fighting for his life with no way to get help from the outside world, or from me. But I'll be damned if I'm not going to enjoy the rush of flying the *Rex* for the first time.

"Whoooohoooo!" I shout, pushing the *Rex* higher into the sky while my body is plastered against the seatback and my suit compresses to keep me from passing out. We carve through a layer of clouds and explode into the clear night sky. The simulator did a good job of duplicating the ship's controls and how it responds. Flying it is second nature. But what it couldn't do was mimic the G-forces that comes as you accelerate toward Mach 2, and then beyond.

I've missed this. I didn't realize how much until now.

And for the Southerners in my midst, I let out a "Yeehaw!"

I glance over at Jian. His eyes are crushed shut, but he lacks the placid expression of someone who has passed out. Instead, he has the scrunched up, constipated look of someone who *wants* to pass out, but is being kept conscious by his compressing cosmic armor.

"Eyes open, little man," I say. "We need to know if we're being followed."

He opens one eye, peeking at me. "Can we slow down?"

"If a big-ass alien shaped like an armored Yīnjīng was cruising toward your backside, wouldn't you want to know about it?" When his discomfort becomes a sneer, I know he's on board. But can he overcome the physical challenges of rapid acceleration?

With a grunt and grinding teeth, he reaches out, takes hold of the weapons controls and rotates the roof turret to the stern, giving us a clear rear view. Six glowing blue lights are a good five hundred feet back, but they're not just matching our pace, they're closing in.

"You're going to have to engage," I tell Jian.

He moves the target reticle over the nearest invader, but its flight pattern is unpredictable and spastic. "Is too hard!"

A string of Russian curses turns me around. Ivan is slowly pulling himself back toward his seat, aided by Loretta and Quaid, who are clinging to his sleeves. If I slowed down a little, it would take him just seconds to get in the seat and buckle up, but those few seconds would allow the enemy to catch up, and unleash whatever extraterrestrial unholiness they've got planned.

And then, they prove that distance doesn't really matter. An AMRAAM air-to-air missile can track and hit a target a hundred miles away. An advanced alien race shouldn't have too much trouble with a few hundred feet.

Balls of blue light pulse from all six...whatever they're called. *Dongles,* I decide.

"Sorry!" I shout, and then I pull back, increasing the angle of our climb to ninety degrees.

I watch the Dongles zip past below us through the turret cam. Jian tracks them as they gracefully spin around and continue their pursuit, just a little further back than before.

"We're losing him!" Quaid shouts from the back.

Ivan has nearly lost his grip on the seat belt. His arms are slipping out of Quaid and Loretta's grip.

Damnit...

"Time for a vomit comet!" I shout, knowing that Ivan will at least understand the reference. Then I catch everyone off guard, arcing hard through the sky and putting us into a thirty-degree, free fall dive. At our current height we'll smack the ground in just ten seconds. The moment we hit the magic angle, gravity disappears.

Weightless for a moment, Ivan hauls himself back into this seat and yanks his belt into place. The moment I hear it click into place, I shout, "Try not to puke!"

Gravity reasserts its dominance over us as I pull up, put the *Rex* into a spin to avoid another barrage of blue spheres, and then hit the metaphorical afterburners. I don't fully understand the tech behind the *Rex*'s propulsion system, but it's cutting-edge, top-secret stuff that kicks gravity in the nuts and doesn't require gobs of fuel. I think some of it came out of the Aurora program, which officially doesn't exist, but totally does. The rest is above my pay grade and that's fine with me. I just want to fly like a motherfucker.

And I do, much to my passengers' dismay.

Jian's shout comes in waves as we spin toward the atmosphere.

"Keep firing!" I shout.

I watch him struggling to aim. The screen is a blur of blue lights as the six Dongles pursue and fire. Their blue balls fill the sky above as they miss their mark. High above, they burst, dissipating blue energy no doubt powerful enough to disable the *Rex* with a few good whacks.

When Jian doesn't fire, I shout, "Just pray and spray that shit!"

He crushes the trigger with a shout, unleashing a spray of shards that spiral out behind us, covering a large patch of sky. For a moment, I worry that we'll be peppering anyone below, but we're out over the ocean now.

Orange sparks fill the sky behind us as the Dongles get a face full. Four manage to peel away from the barrage while the other two take a full load and explode. Mixed with the balls of orange flames are coils of strewn innards.

Is there anything that's not nasty about these things?

"I did it!" Jian shouts, still holding down the trigger, firing at nothing.

"Ease up!" I tell him. "We're not trying to kill sharks."

"For soup?" he says.

"What? Soup?"

"Shark fin soup?"

"Sonuva... Just track the others and keep them off my back until we reach orbit. Then we're going to have some fun."

"I'm sorry," Loretta says from the back. "Did you say orbit? Like space?"

"This is a spaceship," I tell her.

"How did you miss that detail?" Quaid asks.

"I got caught up in the moment, I suppose." She's looking about, nervous, like she might try to open the door and dive out.

Ivan puts a meaty hand on her knee. "I have you," he says, and sounds oddly compassionate. "You helped me into seat. I will help you not die."

Loretta smiles, slightly relieved.

Then Ivan speaks again. "And if you do anything foolish, I will kill you myself."

As Loretta reels back, Chieng says, "Dude. Not cool!"

"What?" Ivan says. "I make quick. Painless! The abyss of death is free of anxiety, no? I will send. Is no problem."

"Oh, Lord Jesus," Loretta says. "Have mercy, and save me from these evil-ass aliens and this crazy-ass Russian!"

Ivan takes Loretta's hand in his and says, "Amen."

"*Amen,*" she says and squeezes her nervous energy into him.

While Jian sets to work tracking and firing at the enemy with a bit more confidence, I angle us up into the atmosphere, pouring on the speed it will take to break free of the atmosphere and Earth's gravitational pull. This is usually achieved with the assistance of a multistage rocket, but the *Rex* can pull it off solo. The Dongles keep pace while dodging Jian's attempts to shoot them down, but as we continue to accelerate, shredding through the air, they start to fall back.

I'm not sure if we're actually outrunning them, or if they're simply not powerful enough to reach orbit, but I'm not going to complain. When four blue streaks of light strike them, and they're pulled upward as white pulses of energy, I realize they have a shortcut. "Oh, come on."

Free of being shot at for the moment, I focus on the task ahead. We've been accelerating for nearly two minutes, and the next thirty seconds are the moment of truth. Of all the insane things the *Rex* was designed to do, leaving Earth's orbit without an assist is the most dangerous and theoretical.

"Almost there," I shout, trying to reassure myself as much as my passengers. When no one replies, I turn my head to the side and take a peek. Jian is locked in place, gripping his armrests, eyes wide. He's wearing a hint of a smile. He gets it. Despite the agonizing journey, and the potential for a violent death at the end, we're about to enter space, a destination only five hundred and fifty people have been to before. It's an exclusive club I've wanted to join since I was a kid.

Behind us, Ivan looks almost casual now that he's buckled in. He's still holding Loretta's hand, but it's a wasted effort, as she's unconscious. Not even the pressure-regulating cosmic armor can keep someone from passing out in fright. And she's not alone. Quaid is out cold.

And then there is Chieng. Out of everyone, she appears the calmest. She's looking past me, smiling as the field of stars above grows clearer. With the light of civilization far below us and the depths of space ahead, the Milky Way appears the way people on the ground can only see through photos.

I join in her appreciation, marveling at the endless beauty.

I feel hope.

And joy.

It's a sensation of endless possibility.

If everyone on Earth could experience this, the human race would be a unified thing. There'd be no war. No racial hatred. No unwelcome refugees.

And then, as we cruise past 40,000 kilometers per hour, four penis-shaped Dongles flash into being a few miles ahead of us. And they're not alone. A squadron of alien spacecraft awaits the *Rex*, determined to keep us on the ground or in pieces.

"Well," I say to Jian as we cruise toward the wall of heavily armed Dongles. "Any bright ideas?"

30

"What the hell are you two doing here?" Jones says, picking up her discarded Space Force sweatshirt and slipping it on. She's tipsy enough to enjoy belting out a solo, but not enough to feel shameless about it when caught.

Jones closes the mock airlock door behind her, sealing the metal sphincter. The door, modeled after the actual *Rex*'s, will withstand a beating, but if we're lucky, the Chote won't think to open it.

"Why aren't you two with the others, drinking to your hopeless futures?" Jones's practiced sternness is fighting to return, but she's still sporting a half-smile.

"McNasty kicked us out early," I say.

She snickers and stumbles into a seat. "'McNasty.' I've always enjoyed that."

Taylor tugs me aside and whispers. "Sure that's what you want to lead with? We don't have a lot of time, here."

"I can't just go full alien invasion. We need to ease her into that."

"Good luck," he says, glancing at the inebriated Jones before moving back to the door, standing guard with the katana.

Jones squints at him. "What's going on?" She eyes me up and down. "Why are you armed?" Her eyes widen in time with a smile she tries to squelch, but can't. "Is this a mutiny? Are you taking control of Space Force?"

She catches me off guard by standing and offering a salute, which is exactly what I should have done the moment I realized who I was addressing. "I'm with you. Screw McNasty. Viva la revolución. Viva la fuerza especial!" She chuckles. "I can say 'Space Force' en Español."

"I noticed," I say. "Listen... Colonel..."

"Lauren," she says. "I told you."

"Jones," I say.

"Fine."

"How long have you been down here?" I ask.

"How long has it been since you all started your farewell party?"

"Right... Look, we're in a lot of trouble here, and it's not from McNasty."

The disciplined military mind drowning in spirits struggles to surface. She blinks and sits up straighter, but that's all she can manage for now.

"Space Force Command has been invaded by a sizable enemy contingent with advanced weaponry. They've already taken down a large number of our people."

Exaggerated worry stretches across her face. "Not Hale? Because I'm rooting for you two. I mean, your careers are over, but your lives don't need to be. You know? You feel me? Happiness can exist outside the military. Civilians are perfectly happy living their small lives, protected by—"

"Jones," I say, taking her shoulders. "I need you to focus. Hale, Quaid, and Chieng are outside the zone of action. We're here with Taylor and Billy. Other than us, there were about fifty movers and MPs accompanying McNasty. Now, there's maybe twenty left, and forty-something of them. We're outnumbered and outgunned."

"Sounds like a job for John Rambo," she says through a fading grin.

"I'd take a sober Lauren Jones right about now." I crouch down in front of her. "I know you can hear me."

"What I'm hearing is a final prank," she says. "A mouthful of horse-shit that I'm not swallowing no matter how much honey you drizzle on it. A turd is still a turd, even if it tastes like—"

Whump!

Something heavy slams into the airlock door, shaking the simu-lator's insides. Chote Squad has found us, but they haven't figured out how to open the door. With their big, armor-clad hands, the touch-screen granting access won't respond. We know how afraid they are to show some skin, so they're stuck with trying to force their way through.

But they don't really need to. The force field is closing in again. I glance at my phone. The zone closes beyond the simulation. In five minutes, we're going to be exploded into globs and then burned from existence.

"I think the door will hold," Taylor says.

"But if they wreck it..." I say, holding up the phone so he can see the map displaying the shrinking zone's progress. The outer circle has nearly reached the training center's outer wall. The sphincter design is strong, locking into a seamless, airtight lock. But if they manage to bend the metal or dislodge some gears, we're going to be trapped in here.

"What was that?" Jones sounds a bit more like herself. She's attempting to blink her way out of a drunken haze.

"Ma'am, everything I told you is true. We are under attack. We are about to engage with the enemy. And if you're not able to lend a hand, then find someplace to hide and get ready to run. In five minutes, this whole building will be dust. Do *you* understand?"

She's a little bit stunned. It's no doubt been a long time since someone spoke to her like that, and never a subordinate.

"Do you understand?" I shout.

She staggers a bit, like I've just slapped her, but I think I'm seeing what it looks like when a rush of adrenaline kicks inebriation to the curb and says, 'Find some other mind to fuck up, you sorry-ass sonuvabitch.'

Another slam against the door makes us all jump. It helps sober her a bit more.

"How many?" she asks.

"Three," I say, and add, "Heavily armed with high-tech gear. Bullets won't do shit."

She points to the sword in Taylor's hand. "And that will?"

"It's all we have," Taylor says.

She shakes her head, pointing to the sim's weapons compartment. On the *Rex*, it would be full of lethal weapons. In the sim, it holds just one—the Rapid Fire Taser. I rush to the locker, open it, and instead of one weapon, I find three. In addition to the RFT there are the two paintball guns previously wielded by Taylor and Quaid. They're far from lethal, but that doesn't mean they're useless.

After confirming they're loaded, I toss a paintball gun to Taylor and hand the other to Jones.

The door is struck hard, the vibration moving through my feet and up my legs.

"Are they using C4?" Jones asks.

"Just their bodies," I guess. They could be shooting the doors, I suppose, but they're definitely big enough to hit it with that much force.

"What are we supposed to do with these?" Taylor asks.

"Aim for their faces. Try to blind them." I ready the RFT, charging it to full. Against one human being, all twelve charges would be enough to stop a heart. I'll be happy if we're able to stun them, but I'm not even holding out hope for that. The prongs work by anchoring into a conductive material, often skin, but the Chote armor repels bullets. Our best chance of survival is if Taylor and Jones can obscure their vision enough for us to slip past and get the hell out of Dodge before it's erased by a giant wall of energy.

"You might want to tell her where their faces are," Taylor points out and then ducks down as the door is pounded once more.

"What's he talking about?" Jones asks.

"The people outside this door," I say. "They're not exactly people."

She just stares at me.

"They're...drones. Robotic monsters." It's a lie, but it's a version of reality that will be easier to believe than aliens. "Probably made by the Russians or the Chinese," I add.

"Don't forget the Canadians," she says, buying into my story. "They're still pissed at us about Montreal...which is unlike them, right? Shouldn't they have let that go by now?"

"Colonel," I say, focusing her again. "They're going to look like monsters. Arms and legs. Phallic bodies."

"They're totes gross," Taylor says with a chuckle.

Jones rolls her eyes. "When will adult men stop thinking penises are funny?"

Taylor and I stare at her, both of us trying not to say, 'They *are* funny.' We manage to stay silent and the tangent comes to an end as the Chote bash the door again.

"Heads will still be about six feet up. No eyes. Sharp teeth. Just aim for the smooth dome above the jaws. That's your best bet."

Jones nods, steps to the side, and aims the paintball gun like she's a special operator who's been itching for action. I'm sure she'd normally carry herself with a lot less swagger and a lot more reservation if she hadn't been drinking, but right now she feels like one of the team, so I'll take it.

"Open the door in ten seconds," she tells Taylor, and then to me. "Stand clear."

I want to ask her why, but by the time it would take to ask and get her answer, ten seconds would be up. So I step to the side, shoulder my RFT, and take aim, waiting for the seconds to tick by.

My life doesn't flash before my eyes, but my mind does flash back, just a few hours. I see Hale's dark brown eyes staring into mine. I feel the swirl of emotion in my gut again. Jones is right. I don't need to be a fighting man to be happy. I need Hale.

I decide that if she moves back to the islands, I'll go with her. I can give nature tours and take up surfing. As long as I'm with her, it doesn't matter.

The metal sphincter loosens under Taylor's command, spiraling open just in time to let a big alien turd blast through. The Chote had been prepared to slam into the door. When it opens, the thing's momentum carries it into the simulator, through the cargo hold, and into the cockpit—where it strikes and somersaults over the chairs and into the control console.

Jones lets out a surprised chuckle and then faces forward.

Two Chote block our path, armed with weapons they must have recovered while pursuing us. Lucky looting bastards.

"Fire!" Jones shouts with all the testosterone-fueled vigor of a seasoned vet in the midst of battle. Then she and Taylor pull their triggers and unleash an anticlimactic barrage of paint pellets.

31

"Umm, hello?" I say, when Jian remains locked in place, eyes plastered wide. *Is it possible to pass out with your eyes open? Did he have a heart attack?* "Jian!"

He flinches back to reality. "Bùyào nàyàng zuò! Āyí! Dàshēng de shēngyīn xià dàole wǒ!"

"Little man, I have no idea what you just said, but if it was a brilliant idea for how to survive this mess, can you repeat it in English? Hell, I'll take Engrish, if that's all you can manage. And if you *don't* have any bright ideas, the least you can do is *start pulling that damn trigger!*"

Jian seems to fully grasp the futility of our situation for the first time. Instead of taking aim and firing our weapons, he starts tapping keys and buttons.

"What are you doing?"

"Bright idea," he says.

"We need to shoot them," I grumble, watching his fingers become a blur. "Not compose EDM."

He huffs a laugh, and is strangely no longer nervous. I'm not sure if he's just in the zone, or supremely confident in what he's doing, but at least he's doing something.

When the array of enemy ships starts to glow blue with power, I say, "Running out of time."

He stops moving, finger hovering over the keyboard's enter key. "Hold on."

"What are you doing?" I ask, despite time not being on our side.

His next two words fill me with hope and dread.

"Last Stahfightah."

"Everyone hold on!" I shout, before pushing my head back and gripping my armrests with both hands.

A sudden burst of speed pins me to my seat, throwing us into the enemy's midst. For this to work the way it did in the movie, we need to be surrounded, which might also keep them from shooting for fear of friendly fire. I have to give Jian credit; it's a ballsy move.

I wish Stone were here to see this, I think, and I'm then thrown to the side. The *Rex* starts spiraling and tumbling in random directions, propelled by the gas jets covering its exterior, which make it unbelievably maneuverable in space. As the G-forces climb, I glance at the targeting screen and see the reticle snapping from one target to the next. *Automated...* This is what he meant. Jian gave the *Rex* the ability to auto-aim. Stone constantly complains about cheaters, but I think he'd appreciate Jian's modifications. When it comes to actual war, cheating is more than acceptable—it's necessary, especially when your side is losing.

"Ty-ran-o-saurus Rex!" Jian shouts through gritting teeth. It's very dramatic, in an anime kind of way. "Fiiire!"

Shard streams explode from the *Rex*'s cannons, all perfectly aimed at the swarm of enemy vessels. I try to watch through the cockpit viewscreen, but the blur of movement fills me with nausea, so I focus on the targeting screen and don't fare much better. Everything is moving faster than I can track or register.

Bursts of blue light confirm that the attack is having an impact, but it's impossible to tell how much damage is being done. As our rate of spin increases, even I have a hard time not feeling ill. As some of the others shout in distress, I clench my eyes shut and wait for the ride to end, hoping that Jian considered the human limitations of the people inside the *Rex* when he programed this automated attack.

I clench my butt cheeks when we shake from an impact, but it's short-lived. And a moment later, our rate of spin slows. With a few long puffs of gas, the *Rex* comes to a stop in the exact same position we were in at the attack's start. A twinkling debris field—some of it bits and pieces of armor, some of it frozen chunks of alien flesh—orbits our position.

I catch my breath and turn to Jian, intending to say something supportive. Instead, I scream in horror. "Jian!"

His head...has exploded.

The inside of his facemask is a mash of chunky gore.

"I am here!" he shouts back.

I blink at him, trying to make sense of what I'm seeing.

"Auntie," he says, sounding sullen. "I threw up."

"He ain't the only one," Quaid says. When I look back, I see three out of four helmets plastered with puke. The only face looking back at me is Loretta's.

When she sees my astonished look, she smiles. "I once road a Tilt-A-Whirl fifteen times in one day. That wasn't so bad."

"Is new vomit comet, da?" Ivan says, not at all embarrassed.

"Stop!" I shout when he starts to undo his helmet.

"Cannot see," he complains. "And smell is...well, it smells like grandmother's... never mind."

"If you take those helmets off now, you'll coat the *Rex*'s interior with half-digested borsch, and that could fuck up the electronics."

"You can't just leave us in these things," Chieng complains. "My eyes are burning!"

"I can see my supper," Quaid says, sounding like he might hurl again. "Oh, ugh... I need to chew more."

"Everyone sit still. Let me make sure we're not about to be blasted to bits." I put us in a slow turn, watching through the viewscreen, while the automated targeting searches for enemies. It snaps to bits of debris on occasion, but it quickly moves on.

"We're clear," I say. "For now." I unbuckle and float out of my seat. I take just a moment to marvel at my first real zero-G experience, then I slide over to Jian, unbuckle him and pluck him up.

"I'm going to move you all to the airlock—"

"Airlock?" Chieng sounds nervous.

"Seems harsh," Quaid says, but he's more snarky than concerned.

"Just don't take your helmet off, okay?" I push off my seat and glide through the cargo hold, stopping against the airlock door—what Stone calls the sphincter, which I guess I can see...if the Iron Giant had a butthole. I plant Jian on the floor, put his hand on a grab bar and say, "Wait here."

When I turn around to get the others, I find Loretta already guiding the big Russian back. Without gravity, she has no trouble handling him.

"I got you, hon," she says. "Just don't squirm."

I fetch Quaid and Chieng together, shoving them ahead of me.

With everyone gathered by the hatch, I open it and push them inside. I recover a container of wipes from a utility compartment and toss it in with them. Then I close the door and turn to Loretta. "Get in the cockpit. Watch the view screen and targeting system. You see anything, you scream like a mofo, and I'll come to you."

She gives a nod and glides away.

I turn back to the airlock window. "Okay, take off your helmets. Do it slow."

"Like a striptease?" Quaid asks.

I roll my eyes. "Yes, like a strip show. Try to mitigate any spillage. We don't want puke to get on your suits."

When Jian starts wiggling his hips around, I can't help but laugh. I'm tempted to let him continue his sultry helmet removing dance, but he did right by us with his automated weapon-system upgrade. I switch my coms so I'm talking only to him. "Jian. You don't actually need to dance."

He goes rigid.

"Don't worry. No one can see you, and no one else can hear me."

"Thank you, Auntie."

As the helmets come off, globs of barf float out and away, but not too much to avoid.

I switch my comms back to everyone. "Use the wipes to clean away any debris from the neck seal."

The four of them are comrades in arms now, working together to clean and avoid the puke. When they're clean and gathered by the hatch, Quaid says, "Clear. Now what?"

"Clip the helmets," I say, knowing that Quaid is familiar with the wired carabiners meant to be used for hooking in during a spacewalk. He gingerly collects each helmet, spilling a little more of the puke, dodging warbling blobs as he goes. After a minute, all four helmets are clipped in place.

"Do a quick double check," I order.

"Is not hokey pokey," Ivan complains.

"Just do it," I say, and the four comply. My caution is rewarded when Chieng wipes a chunk away from the back of Jian's neck. At this point, I'm not overly concerned about the ship being ruined. I just don't want to smell their stank.

When I open the hatch, all four launch back inside. People have a natural aversion to unsealed airlocks, and for good reason. With all of them clear, I close the door again and then open the outer hatch without pressurizing, just enough to let the vacuum of space super-suck every bit of debris out. The helmets are swept clean, and every bit of barf is sent flying into the depths of space, where their frozen bits will tumble forever until acted upon by an external force.

When all the air and gunk have been removed from the airlock, I close the outer door and start pressurizing.

"Umm," Loretta says. "Umm!"

"Is that you screaming like a mofo?" I shout to her.

She attempts to stand and launches herself into the ceiling. She struggles to crawl out, using handholds on the roof, and then pushes herself back down to the floor, like it matters where we're standing, now that up and down don't exist. She collides with a seat and spins across the cargo hold until she collides with the wall.

"Out there," she manages to say. "Something...I don't know what!"

"You know what to do," I tell Quaid, and I shove off for the cockpit. I reach it in seconds, having no trouble guiding my weightless body back into my seat. I strap myself in and think, I was made for this.

Then I look at the viewscreen, take a deep breath, and let out a long sigh that would have spun me around if I wasn't seated.

"What is it?" Quaid asks, his voice clear through the comms, as he recovers his helmet and clips it back in place. "We in more trouble?"

The only word that comes to mind would normally stir up a political argument on the ground, but up here, facing something so dumb-founding, it's strangely appropriate. "Bigly."

32

STONE

The Chote spasm in confusion as their domed heads are slathered in colorful paint. The sudden shift in perception must have convinced them that the attack was far more devastating than it actually was. They buck, spasm, and roar like a couple of German cyberpunks flailing about to industrial music. It's comical until one of them starts pulling the trigger on its weapon, shooting out a long beam of green energy that singes everything it touches.

I dive to the side, narrowly avoiding being cut down like Obi Wan, and I roll back up, ready to fire. But at what? I see no chinks in the alien's armor.

And then the Chote provides one for me. As the alien on the left side of the door spasms, its hind leg kicks out, smashing into its neighbor's side and dislodging an armored panel. The loose, veiny flesh hidden beneath bulges out like a giant skin tag.

It's a revolting target, but it's also a big one. I take aim, pull the trigger, and hold it down. I don't think I'm going to get another chance at this, so I let all twelve prongs launch.

The blinded Chote snaps rigid when it feels the sharp darts hook into its flesh, but the prick it feels is nothing compared to what it experiences when I turn on the juice, unleashing the full force of the RFT into the creature's loose, fleshy side.

The high-pitched squeal the creature unleashes is enough to freeze the other two Chote in place. The blinded alien leans away from the sound, confused by what's happening.

"That's our way out!" I shout, pointing at the gap between the blind and the convulsing Chote. I leave the RFT on full blast and head for the gap between the pair. "Don't touch its armor!" I add, as I note the electrified Chote is starting to sizzle and smoke. A sound like frying eggs emerges from inside its armor.

We race through the exit, passing between the aliens before the blinded one can clear its vision or think to block the exit. It's tempting to attack the creature while it's disoriented, but attack it how? The RFT is spent, the paintballs don't actually hurt it, and my handgun is useless against its armor.

Outside the sim, I turn around to make sure the others made it out okay. Jones is right behind me, a bit off balance, but keeping up. Taylor, on the other hand, lingers in the doorway. I want to shout at him to quit dicking around, but I'm not sure if the Chote understand English, and I don't want to give away Taylor's position, or ours.

But then the Chote at the front of the simulator, still trying to right itself, shouts out something in an alien language. The blind alien makes a kind of 'Huh?' sound and turns its paint-slathered head toward Taylor. But the motion is too little, too late, and provides my partner with the opening he was looking for. As the alien twists, a gap appears in its armor.

Taylor stabs the sword in. There's a moment of resistance as the blade strikes whatever flexible material holds the plating together, but then it punches through and plunges three feet into the alien's body.

The thing's head arches up as it shrieks. For a moment, the two wounded Chote voices mingle in perfect harmony, like those two little chicks in Godzilla, who sing for Mothra. And then the RFT runs out of juice.

The electrified Chote flops to the floor, twitching for a moment before going motionless and letting out a long stream of flatulence.

"Ohh!" Jones and I say in unanimous revolt.

"These aren't drones at all!" Jones complains, and then she turns to Taylor and says, "That might not be enough to kill it."

Taylor sets to work on the sword, twisting, yanking it up and down— a madman in a rowing contest.

The Chote jolts and spasms as he dices its insides into chunky soup. When the creature falls still, he says, "I think that did the job." Then he withdraws the sword and is doused in thick alien goop, as it sprays from the wound.

"Ohh!" Jones and I shout together.

A stunned Taylor takes a face-load of gore, before being knocked back onto the floor by the force of it. When the stream dwindles down, he shakes his hands out and attempts to wipe his eyes clear. As soon as he does, a gas bubble bursts, sharting a fresh glop of insides onto his cheek. He sits still, too shocked to move.

The dark red organ slides past his mouth and clings to his chin like white spaghetti tendrils, dripping fluid into his lap.

My stomach lurches.

Jones's lets go. She pitches over the side of a weight bench and hurls, which is probably a good thing. The less alcohol in her system, the better.

But all the puke in the world isn't going to help Taylor.

Behind him, inside the simulator, the last Chote is righting itself.

"Taylor, contact on your six!"

It's basic information provided in the simplest way possible, but it sneaks past Taylor's numbed mind and reaches the part of him that is trained to act without thinking.

He rolls away from the gore, runs out of the simulator and dives to the side just as the last member of Chote Squad charges. The alien is incensed by the passing of its compatriots, its attack primal and headstrong.

Jones and I fall back through the maze of exercise equipment and weights, maneuvering through the tight spaces while the Chote slams into them, toppling through the mess and becoming tangled.

"Okay," Jones says, watching the flailing alien. "Come clean. What is really happening?"

"Would you believe an alien invasion?" I ask.

She winces in revolt like I've just pinched her butt. Before she can speak, the training center's far wall is eaten from the outside by a wall of orange light. Sparks, smoke, and dust burst away from the force field as it slides slowly toward us, eating everything it touches.

"Yes," Jones says. "Yes, I would."

"Good," I say, "because these assholes have put a force field around the base and are forcing us into a last-team-standing fight for the fate of the planet."

Jones pukes on her feet, stands again, and wipes her mouth with her sleeve. "Great. We can handle that."

Her false confidence, which is thinner than the Emperor's hosiery— Non-existent. It's non-existent. Like the *Emperor's New Clothes,* but his... Never mind.

She backs her statement up by turning and running. Honestly, it's what I should do, too, but I'm not going to leave Taylor behind. While my partner picks himself up behind the Chote, I keep its attention on me by firing my pistol into its metal-domed face. The bullets pancake and fall to the floor, but the Chote doesn't take its attention off me, or stop fighting against the haphazard barrier of equipment between us.

Weight machines, stationary bikes, treadmills, and Stairmasters fall to its wrathful assaults. But I stay a few feet beyond its grasp, swapping out my last magazine and draining the bullets into the now scuffed armor.

"Get moving!" I shout at Taylor, while pointing at the wall of orange eating its way through the building, just ten feet behind him. The air crackles with energy and the sound of matter being destroyed. Combined with my gun's report, it's a miracle Taylor can hear me at all.

As he works his way around the training center's track, I start to ponder an exfil strategy. All I come up with is, "Run out the doors."

One step at a time, right?

Happily, someone accustomed to working on the long game has my back.

"Stone, lead it to me!" Jones shouts. I turn around to find the woman standing on the far side of a weight bench loaded with enough pounds to flex the metal bar. She's laden the bar with at least a thousand pounds ...and quickly. Jones might be small, but she's no weakling. That was a lot of weight to move, even in fifty-pound increments.

Leading the Chote to her is simple. I just have to keep running away.

A low-lying rack of dumbbells has other plans. I slam into it a moment after Jones shouts, "Behind you!". Then I'm ass-over-tea-kettle to the hard floor. I look up in time to see the Chote above me, tossing aside a rope trainer machine with its jaws.

I get my feet under me and grab the closest thing to me. When the Chote swings its open jaws back toward me, I greet it with a twenty-five-pound kettle-bell, slamming the thing into the side of the head. It reels from the impact, but I know I haven't done any real damage.

When the Chote swipes out with its claws, I've already hurried away and joined Jones on the bench press's far side. She's crouched down behind the bar, just waiting. I'm not sure if her calmness stems from drunkenness or confidence, but I try my best to appear as unruffled as she does. I mean, I'm the hardened special operator. She's been pushing papers and dealing with the brass for years. Then again, maybe that's harder.

The Chote recovers, lowers its head like a stalking predator and lets out a snarl, patience lost.

"Taylor," Jones snaps. "Get your ass over here!"

He looks over at us, covered in gore, and lets out an exasperated sigh. Then he starts trudging toward us.

"Be ready," Jones says to me.

"For what?" I ask, but then I understand her plan. The Chote is going to charge and get stuck between the weight support beams. Then we'll hoist the weights up and let them drop. It's a solid plan except that neither I nor Jones can lift a thousand pounds. Even together. Even with Taylor's help.

I'm about to point that out when Jones shouts, "C'mon you saucy tart! What the hell are you so afraid of?"

The Chote coils to pounce, and in a guttural voice that catches me off guard, says, "I'm going to sit on your face."

Jones and I snap back as though slapped.

"They speak?" she asks.

"Not until now," I say, and then I shout in surprise when the Chote lunges. Exactly as planned, the thing slams into the support beams, which are designed to take a beating and don't give. What they do is shake. A lot.

The Chote's metal jaws snap shut just inches from me. If I hadn't spilled backward, I'd be faceless.

The weights are nearly knocked off the support's back side, but then the bar bounces forward and slips past the lip. All one thousand pounds drops onto the Chote's neck, denting the armor and pinning it down.

The alien struggles against the weight, its limbs pushing hard against the floor. It's going to take a few seconds, but it will definitely recover.

Happily, a few seconds is all Taylor needs. As the Chote struggles to lift the weight, the big man vaults off a bench, lands on the alien's back, and thrusts the blade between a gap in its flexed armor. He repeats his earlier attack, flailing the hilt about, unleashing a blender inside the now quivering alien.

When the Chote lies still, Taylor takes a deep breath, embraces the inevitable, and withdraws the sword. A volcano of gore is expelled from the wound, dousing Taylor. He doesn't try to move. Doesn't flinch. He bathes in the blood of his enemies.

The moment the flow subsides, he climbs down and without a word, heads for the locker rooms.

"Umm, hey," I say, watching the orange force field chew its way toward us. "Buddy? Force field. Time to go."

He disappears into the locker room.

"The hell is he doing?" Jones asks, and she's answered by the sound of a shower.

"Let's give him a beat." I head for the exit and wait by the door.

When the force field has nearly reached the locker room entrance, I shout, "Line ETA in thirty seconds!"

The water shuts off.

With the force field about to trap Taylor inside the locker room, where it will turn him to powder, Taylor casually walks out, fully clothed and dripping wet, sword still in his hands. Walking at a casual pace is enough to outrun the force field. It might not always be like that, but right now, its steady pace means we have a few minutes before we have to bolt.

"Not a word," Taylor says.

I honor his request by holding out my hand and saying, "Phone."

He digs into his waterproof vest pocket, pulls out his smart phone, and hands it over. I chuckle when I see the photo for Hale's number is of my Hale-Psylocke cut-out. Then I push the call button and put the phone to my ear.

33

HALE

On the plus side, there's nothing phallic about what I'm seeing. On the downside, it's freaking huge—like mothership huge—and clearly beyond my ability to comprehend how it works or what it's doing. On the even downer downside, if there is such a thing, I'm seeing more than one of them.

A series of giant rings orbit the Earth. They're lit up from the core by a beam of orange light that emerges from the underside as a wide cone, jutting down to Earth's surface.

They're generating the force fields, I think but then I realize they're really just converting the energy being shot into them. I trace the orange beam back out into space and discover a network of smaller satellites redirecting the energy. As my eyes adjust to the sight, I spot a web of orange light surrounding the planet, allowing the force fields to drop down in every non-corner of the globe.

I trace the web back to an even larger ring hovering between Earth and the moon. The light beams converge at its core, streaming out into the depths of space. Pulses of energy flow in both directions between the rings, the satellites, and deep space, but the flow to the surface remains steady.

"Is how they travel," Ivan says, making me jump. He points at the beams of pulsing light. "Unmanned spacecraft make the journey, and then teleport from one planet to another."

"You know this?" I ask.

"Is theory," he says, giving me a wink and tapping his head. "Am good for more than killing and pillaging."

"Okay, so—wait...pillaging?"

"Huh?" he says, playing dumb. "Who says this? Pillaging? What?"

"*You* said this. You actually *pillage* people? What is this, the Viking age?"

Ivan smiles. "Would be fun, no?"

"No," I scold. "It would not be fun."

"Sooo," Chieng says, catching both me and Ivan off guard. "Whatchya seein'?"

I glance back at her in the doorway behind Ivan. She could easily look for herself, but her eyes are turned down. Despite space being the object of her fascination, I doubt she ever considered the possibility of confronting denizens from beyond the solar system.

"No one better to figure that out than you," I tell her. "Take a look. We're in the clear for now."

She opens her eyes just as the corpse of a dead Dongle, its grotesquely phallic body frozen in a pain-filled, arched-back position, bounces into the viewscreen and lodges in place for a moment. The alien's multiple eyes are wide in shock, its fat incisors revealed by its grimace.

"Oh!" Chieng shouts, averting her eyes. "Is that one of them?"

Ivan bursts out laughing. "Is giant dick!" He buckles over the chair, lost in contagious delight. As the others rush to see, one by one, they join in the laughter as the Dongle's face rubs and smears against the outside of the view screen, slowly sliding from sight. By the time it's gone, Chieng is laughing, too.

"Looks like my ex-husband after a cold shower," Loretta says, her quip bringing a sudden stop to our laughter. "Don't get me wrong. A little heat is all it would take to—"

"Nope," Quaid says. "You can stop right there. No one wants to hear it."

"Hear what?" Jian asks. "I do not understand."

"Well," Loretta says, grinning at Jian. "When a man and woman—"

"Nope!" Quaid says, walking away and putting his hands over his helmeted ears. It's a little dramatic, but he's right. Now is not the time to hear about her ex-husband's aptitude. And I'm not sure there *is* a right time.

"Later," I tell her, and then I turn to Chieng. "Thoughts?"

She turns her gaze to the view screen again, this time seeing the giant rings, satellites, and orange light. Her eyes widen with wonder, and then fear. "I heard what he said." She pats Ivan's arm. "I think he's right. The rings might be inhabited now, but they probably weren't in transit.

They're using some kind of faster-than-light tech to move through space, maybe an Einstein-Rosen bridge.

"And that is?"

"A wormhole," she says. "Gets you from point A to point B wicked fast, and it doesn't matter how far apart they are. Distance isn't relative when you're folding space-time. But they're also using it to power the rings and the force fields, suggesting an Einstein-Rosen bridge *generates* energy. After its initial catalyst it might even be self-sustaining. Their technology is several hundred, maybe even a thousand, years beyond ours."

"Does that mean we can't fuck them up?" I ask.

"I kill more men with knife than with gun," Ivan says. It's a crude and somewhat disturbing example, but I get it.

"It's also possible that while they're technologically advanced, they're new to the business of world domination and war," Chieng says. "I mean, they are basing their strategies on Earth video games, right?"

"So they're technologically advanced, but emotionally naïve?" I ask.

Jian snorts. "That seem unlikely."

Says the man-boy who calls me 'Auntie' and definitely does the dirty with anime pillows. For real. I smile. Jian is the poster boy for Chieng's theory. How many of Earth's geniuses have also been great warriors? They don't normally go hand in hand. Sure, a genius might invent something of immense destructive force, but it takes a warrior to use it, and use it right. In a fight between Jian with a bazooka and Ivan with a paper cutter, my money would be on the Russian. If the Dongles are immature, we might be able to outsmart them, even though they're more intelligent than us.

I'm about to ask for opinions, but that will just become a confusing mess. I'm the de facto leader of this ragtag group, so I decide to make the call. Building on the Ivan-with-a-knife scenario, I picture how he'd kill Jian. The Dongles have already fired their missile at us in the form of space fighters. We repelled that attack, but with so many other rings in orbit, it won't be long before more show up.

So while they reload the metaphorical bazooka, we need to get up close and personal and drive a blade into their necks... Or something. Their necks are pretty gross. I don't think I'd want to touch one.

What's the best way to do that? I ask myself and the answer comes to me a moment later: real sneaky like.

"Everyone have their helmets on?" I ask.

After getting affirmative answers from my crew, I reach out to the control panel and cut power to all the ship's systems aside from basic propulsion. From the outside, we're just another piece of space junk floating in a debris field. I goose the gas jets a few times, setting us on a course for the ring. In zero gravity, that's all it takes. No need to accelerate any more.

I turn to Quaid. "Ready the infiltration bay."

He nods and puts his hands on Loretta's and Chieng's shoulders. "Gimme a hand with this."

As they glide back into the cargo bay I tell Ivan, "There's a weapons locker in the back, to the left of the airlock. Take what you want and find what you think might be appropriate for everyone else."

His eyes are alight with the prospect of a fight. "Is good."

Something about his tone is off. He's not talking about a fight. "What's good?"

"Woman in charge. Is...how you say...exciting."

I glance, bathed in apprehension, toward his crotch, and he chuckles.

"Not in moose-knuckle kind of way. Like trying chocolate ice cream for first time. Uhh, unique experience. I do not mind it."

"Chocolate ice cream is a unique experience?"

"My father had wood shed..." Ivan starts, but I stop him with a raised hand.

"You know what...I don't need to know." Between Ivan and Jian, my childhood was a magical land full of fairies, and I don't want to be distracted by any more sob stories when I'm trying to get in an ass-kicking mood. "Glad you're enjoying the experience."

"Is there something I can do?" Jian asks.

I pat the empty seat. "Just sit down, stay quiet, and copilot like a motherfucker."

Jian takes a seat next to me, full of pride, like I've just given him a star for good behavior. Then again, he *is* from China. Manipulating behavior through social punishment and reward is kind of their thing.

We sit in silence, watching the ring grow closer through the view screen. The occasional chunk of frozen Dongle, or shattered space ship, bumps off the hull, but they do no damage. The debris poses no real threat, which is how I'm hoping the aliens operating the ring will see us. The ring's size in comparison to the *Rex* is an aircraft carrier to a Prius. They could plow right into us and not even notice.

I'm almost relaxed when my phone glows to life and plays Kenny Loggins's *Danger Zone*. Before I can reach out and patch it into the deactivated audio system, Jian snatches it up, holds it to his helmet and says, "Auntie's phone, this is Jian. Who this? Hallo? Hallo! I don't hear you."

Then he hangs up, offers the phone back to me and says, "Wrong number."

I glance at the phone's screen and see the call was from Taylor's number.

Stone...

Space Force phones use cell networks and satellites as a backup. That he was able to reach me in space is surprising, but not impossible.

"Jian," I scold, and I attempt to call back just as we fall into the ring's shadow.

34

STONE

I snap the phone away from my head to confirm that the call has, in fact, been disconnected.

"What happened?" Taylor asks.

"Who the hell is Jian?" I ask.

Jones and Taylor are clueless.

"Some dude named Jian answered. Sounded Chinese. Said it was his auntie's phone...or something."

I make the call again, and this time it goes to voicemail. "You have reached First Lieutenant Jennifer Hale, please leave your name and number, and I'll get back to you ASAP."

I smile at the formality of her message. Always on point. It's one of the things I love about her.

My stomach clenches.

I didn't miss that tidbit of inner monologue. That *word*. That one word. I've never said that to anyone in my life...except for my pets. Wow. There it is. My life, aside from a few furry companions of my youth, has been loveless. I mean, I have friends. Taylor is like a brother to me. I love him, I guess, but it's different, I think. I haven't let Hale in either, but I want to.

When the phone beeps, I say, "It's me. We're alive and fighting. We've connected with Jones and are en route to Ops to rendezvous with Billy. Why am I telling you all this? Listen...I just...I want you to know I'm doing everything I can to get through this, but if I don't, if this is the last time I get to speak to you...I want you to be in my flash-back. And that means you need to know, I—"

The phone beeps in my ear.

Signal lost.

I squeeze the phone in my hand.

"Ohh, shit," Jones says. "Were you just about to...? Oh, that's harsh."

Taylor puts his hand on my shoulder. "You'll get a chance to tell her. And if it helps, I love you."

A god damn tear comes to my eye. "Asshole."

"It's the truth." He chuckles and wraps his arm around me. "Now, you say it."

"Seriously?"

"C'mon man, I want to be in your flashback, too. *Say it.*"

"Ugh. Love you, too." I say, and I chuckle as he gives me a brotherly shake.

"Ohh," Jones says, wiping at her eyes with her sweatshirt sleeve. "Stop it, you two. I can't take anymore."

The phone buzzes in my hand. The sound is followed by the voice of Peter Griffin laughing and saying, "Someone's been naughty." I recognize the sound as Taylor's voice mail indicator. The screen shows one missed call, and one new message.

She must have called me at the same time I was calling her.

I tap the voicemail icon and put it on speaker phone. "Stone," she says, and my heart all but breaks. "I've got the *Rex.*"

"The *Rex?*" Jones blurts.

"I've got good people with me and we're going to do what we can from up here..."

"Up here?" Taylor says, turning his eyes to the ceiling, like he can see through it.

"Just...stay alive, okay? Do what you do. And if I don't make it back..." The pause is long enough to make my stomach churn, the unfinished thought torture. "...feed our goldfish, okay?" She laughs, and it chips my heart. "What I'm trying to say is—"

The voicemail stops, likely at the same time my message was being cut off. In a way, both of us leaving messages was a blessing, saying more separately than we could have while attempting a nervous, bumbling conversation. And though neither of us got to say anything explicit, since when was that required? True human connection can be made without a word being said.

Then again, she said a lot.

She doesn't own a goldfish. Neither do I. But we will. That was a message about the future. If we survive.

"A word about this to anyone and I will have you both castrated," Jones says, smearing her sleeve across her eyes. Note to self, the Colonel isn't an angry drunk, she's a weepy drunk.

"Uhh," Taylor says, growing tense. "Time to go!"

While I've been distracted by Hale, the force field has encroached on our position. I'm close enough to the crackling orange haze to see a boiling ocean on the far side. The force field isn't just powerful enough to destroy buildings. It's eating up the whole island. As the ocean rushes in to fill the gap, it's being vaporized into steam. I hold my hand out to the wall, drawing it back slowly, keeping pace.

There's no heat. No static energy. It's just a wall of death. If not for the sound of matter being destroyed, I would never sense it coming.

"Yo," Taylor says, standing by the only way out of the training center's partial remains. "Let's jet!"

I withdraw from the force field and join them by the door. After a quick peek in either direction, we hustle into the thirty-foot-wide courtyard between the training center and Ops.

We hug the concrete, working our way through the maze of palm tree topiaries. With plenty of cover and no enemy in sight, it's a solid place to flee the circle. Had we been forced out of the building, into the parking lot, we would have been easy targets.

If I were a Chote, I'd be set up somewhere with a solid field of view, waiting for the ants to run out of the flooding hill.

When the sound of alien gunfire erupts from our left, somewhere across the vast parking lot littered with moving trucks, I realize that's exactly what's happening. I glance at the map being broadcast to Taylor's phone. The circle is carving its way through the training center on this side and the barracks on the far side. Anyone who found refuge in the maze of rooms is now being forced out and being cut down.

Two flashes of red jut up into the sky. I've lost track of how many people are left, but I'm sure we're under twenty now, and who knows how many people died while we were indoors and unable to see.

I pause, instinct guiding me to head toward the fight, to see who I can save.

Taylor stops beside me, sword in hand. He's feeling it, too.

"Can one of you two tell me what the hell is going on?" Jones is crouched down by the Ops building's side entrance. Her eyes are turned up at the force field encroaching on, and illuminating, our position, rising up into space. "Give me the condensed version. No questions asked."

"Have you seen the movie *Battle Royale?*" Taylor asks.

"A modern cult classic," Jones says. "Of course."

"Like that, but with aliens." Taylor looks her in the eyes. "Fifty versus fifty, winner take all."

"And the 'all' being what?" she asks.

"Earth," I say.

"Do I want to know why we're in this mess, and not, I don't know, Delta, or the SEALs?"

"You do not," Taylor says.

"Figured as much. And the flashes of red light?"

"Means one of ours has died."

Another flash of red drives the revelation home and tenses me and Taylor. We're a mouse fart away from running out there.

"Far as I can tell, there's not much of anything either of you can do to help them." Jones's assessment is brutal, but accurate. "There are always casualties in war, and if you focus on saving everyone, you won't save anyone...especially if everything you told me is accurate."

She's right, of course. That's pure military logic that even Spock could get behind. Needs of the many and all that. But it doesn't sit well.

"Do I need to start giving orders?" she asks. "Or can you two lovebirds get your shit together and get the job done?"

The Colonel's cold, hard exterior surfaces long enough for Taylor and me to stow our shit and focus. A good soldier becomes a great soldier when someone wiser and smarter is pointing him or her in the right direction.

I say, "Yes, ma'am," and move to the door.

"Good," she says, her hard masquerade melting away into a one-sided smile. "I can turn that shit off and on like a damn faucet." She does it again, going deadpan. "Lead the way, soldier." Then she smiles and falls in line behind me as I enter the building.

Taylor eases the door shut behind us.

The hallway is clear, but a blue light is emanating from the first door on the left. Before I crouch-walk to it, I point to Taylor, then my eyes, and finally to the glass door. The force field has just eaten through what's left of the training facility, and without saying a word, I've asked Taylor to keep an eye on it while I check out the strange glow.

The room is a small office. Some low-level management type would have probably worked here if all the base's open positions had ever been filled. But the one-window office's pristine surfaces look like they've never been marred by stacks of paper, cup rings, or old snacks. There's a layer of fine dust covering everything, and not a single smudge in any of it.

Aside from the glowing ball of hexagons, the space is unremarkable.

"What is that?" Jones whispers, standing beside me in the doorway.

I feel stupid crouched down, so I stand up beside her. "Weapon spawn. They're randomly placed around the base. They're not all weapons though. The first thing I found was a skirt."

She snorts. "And you didn't wear it because..."

"Not my size," I tell her with a smile.

"Well, it's not dangerous then, right?" Before I can answer or stop her, she steps inside the small room and plucks the glowing sphere from the table. She turns to me, victorious. "See? How do we use it?"

"Well..." I say, cringing as the light starts spreading down her arm.

"Kind of tingly," she says, and she looks at her hand. She tries to drop the sphere, but it's stuck in place. She does the hokey pokey like a mofo, shaking her arm all about, but the alien tech is locked on. And then it spreads. A hexagonal pattern of glowing lines moves out across her body.

Is it a trap? I wonder, but I dismiss that idea. She doesn't seem to be in any pain. She's freaked out, for sure, but her fear turns to laughter as her nervousness fades.

"Looks like some kind of personal shield," Taylor says, making me jump. He's crept up behind me to have a look for himself. Then he motions back to the door. "Time to go."

The force field is about to start eating through the Ops building, and we still need to find Billy.

"Okay..." I say, trying to roll with the fact that a drunken Colonel is now enshrouded by a mysterious alien tech. Sure. No problem. Nothing to see here. "Double-time to Ops, find Billy, and then..."

"Smarter people will tell us what to do," Taylor says.

"Fuck yeah, we will," Jones says.

"Just...don't touch anyone," I say. "Or anything."

"I'm touching the floor," she says, channeling a tone of voice she probably hasn't used since being thirteen.

"Well, don't touch anything else," I say, and I head out before being wrangled into a pointless, alcohol-fueled debate.

While I hear motion on the floors above us, our path is clear of Chote. When we're beyond where the force field's encroachment will pause, I relax a bit, but I know time is still short. In battle royale games, the circle pauses just long enough for you to catch your breath and let your guard down. If you don't pay attention to it, it will swoop in and kill you.

We take the stairs two flights up and emerge into the modern, sleek halls of Space Force command. Ops is here, right next door to Billy's lab. But that's not all. I peek out the door and down the hall to find three Chote in a decimated lobby. They're trying to force their way into the lab. It's a large, solid steel door, like something out of a battleship, which is fending them off, but then a fourth arrives with some kind of bulbous weapon that does who-knows-what.

I'm about to suggest we fall back, find some weapons, and return when Jones says, "Oh, I don't think so," steps out of the stairwell, and charges toward Chote Squad 2.0.

35

HALE

A few puffs of compressed gas from the *Rex* is enough to arrest our spin, synch us up with the Ring's rotation, and touch us down with nary a bump.

"Infiltration bay is sealed," Quaid says from the back.

Unlike the airlock, which is designed to interact with standard, Earth-made modules, the infiltration bay, on the *Rex*'s belly, extends down and seals itself against an enemy hull. Its flexible structure allows it to conform to just about any surface or texture. It basically glues itself in place, and is a one-time use system. Leaving means permanently disconnecting from the system, and the only replacements are back on Earth.

But that shouldn't be an issue. We're locked on, and I'm not planning on going anywhere.

The view outside is what I've always imagined the Death Star to look like. Not quite as dramatic as the trench run, and completely lacking exterior weaponry—the Dongles didn't foresee a counter attack—but it's like being parked on a moon made of metal. I know it's not that big, but from the surface, the curvature is hard to see.

"It's like Cybertron," Jian says, somewhat delighted by the view.

"Cyber-who? Tron? That movie with Jeff Bridges? Awesome soundtrack."

"Awesome soundtrack in new Tron," he says.

"There's a new Tron? Or is that what I saw? There's an old Tron?"

Jian rolls his eyes. "Cybertron is Transformers' home world. All metal."

"Like the Death Star," I say, slightly annoyed, like he should have heard my earlier inner monologue.

"Uhh, yeah!" He nods. "Death Star!"

"Calm down, Megatron," I say, letting him know that I'm not completely clueless about fanboy shit. I unbuckle, and I'm pulled toward the ceiling almost hard enough to feel like I've fallen. I experience a moment of vertigo as my body and mind adjust to a new reality. Up is down, down is up. The spinning ring is generating artificial gravity. That's going to make what comes next a little tricky.

When I step out into the cargo hold, walking on the ceiling, I look up at the infiltration bay. It was designed to be glided through in zero gravity, not climbed up into.

"It's not a problem," Quaid says. "We're only at about half gravity, and the infiltration system can operate independently." He points to the bay door. The window allows us to see the rigid umbilical connecting us to the ring and the alien surface beyond. A robotic arm slides into view. At its end is a laser capable of cutting titanium.

"What about depressurization?" Ivan asks. "If rapid, will infiltration system be destroyed?"

"It's possible," Quaid says, "But they don't seem to be having any trouble with Earth's atmosphere."

Ivan raises an eyebrow. "Meaning..."

"Meaning our atmosphere is breathable and the pressure not crushing or blowing them up. So it's safe to assume these things—" Chieng begins.

"Dongles," I say.

"—hail from an Earth-like planet."

"Who says 'hail'?" Loretta asks with a chuckle.

"People with three PhD's," Chieng snaps.

"I think we can all agree," Quaid says, "That art therapy doesn't count. I mean, finger painting your feelings out doesn't really—"

"I went to art therapist," Ivan says, deadly serious. "Helped me with depression after mother was killed by rabid moose."

"That's...horrible," I say.

Ivan nods. "Gets worse. Father avenged mother. Killed moose with flamethrower. Then he is hungry, figures, 'Why let good meat go to waste?' Eats moose. Gets rabies."

"And *dies?*" Chieng asks.

"Da," Ivan says. "But not until after going mad, killing Sunday school group."

"Died by the rabies," Loretta says. "Uh-uh. That's no good."

"Rabies did not kill father," Ivan says, sullen now. "Flamethrower did."

"The *same* flamethrower?" Loretta asks. She's not getting it.

"Da..."

"What are the odds?" she says.

"Very high," Ivan says. "I was holding it."

We all jump as sparks fly above us. The laser starts cutting a five-foot-wide hole in the alien craft's hull. We watch in rapt attention as a smooth black line is left in its wake. I'm not sure how long it takes. I don't think or say a word until it's finished. No one does.

The orange light flicks out and the arm snaps back. A disc of alien metal falls away slowly, like a flower petal, until it clangs against the closed door.

The carved hole is revealed. It's five inches deep and ends at a second hull. Like ocean-going warships, the ring is a multi-hulled vessel, which is to be expected from something designed to travel through open space, where a chance encounter with a stone traveling a hundred thousand miles per hour could punch a hole through normal steel like it was wet tissue.

"Quaid," I say.

"We can handle it," he says, watching as the arm sets to work on the next hull.

I take a deep breath, let it out slow, and take a step back. That's when I notice Chieng crouching beside a seated Ivan. He's scribbling in a small note pad while she rubs his back. "Just let it all out onto the page."

Loretta is just kind of be-bopping to a song in her head.

And Jian...I turn to find him squatting in the corner of what once was the ceiling but now is the floor. For a moment I think he's just having a quiet moment to himself, but the second I see his face, I understand. "Jian! These are not that kind of space suit!"

"I have to pee! I see no bathroom. So I go!"

"You should have gone before we left."

"You are not grandmother, Auntie! Do not talk to me like this!"

"Like *what?*"

"Like shouting!"

"You're peeing in your damn space suit."

"I get nervous. I have to pee. Holding it is bad for bladder."

I raise my hand to pinch my nose, but just end up smacking my face-mask. "Damnit... Just...don't take your suit off. No matter how bad it smells. Understand? You take that off and you're going out the airlock with it."

Chinese grumbling follows.

"Two down," Quaid says, as a second hull petal thuds against the hatch.

As the laser sets to work again, I start humming 'Maniac' from *Flashdance*. It springs to mind and out of my mouth as some kind of mental flow, conjured up by my need to move a little faster.

Quaid smiles and starts humming along.

"What is happening?" Ivan asks, lifting his head from the page, which is covered in violently drawn flames. "I know this song."

Chieng stands and joins in. "We're 80's montaging."

Loretta's deep scowling confusion gives way to a head bop. "Mmm, hmm. Okay. I'm feeling it."

Three minutes later, we finish the song, which was complete with harmonies and fleet-footed dance moves that made *High School Musical* look like it was performed by one-legged penguins.

We look up as a group, just in time to see the third hull fall away, revealing a fourth.

Jian steps past me, looking up through the window. He's walking a little funny, kind of like his feet are squelching through piss. "Well," he says. "That did not work."

"Shut-up, Jian," I say, and the group separates, waiting out the minutes separately while the infiltration system performs the slowest breach in military history.

Time passes in slow motion as the stress of being attached to an alien vessel like a leech commingles with the impatience of waiting for the infiltration system to do its job, and the complete unknown of what we'll find on the other side. This kind of thing is normally done with a plan in place—infiltrate, reach the target, plant the bomb, or whatever, and get the hell out. But this...what we're about to do—eventually do—is a short list of unknowns. If this were a novel, I'd think the writer was just making shit up as he went along.

I extend a middle finger at the man I imagine writing our story. I mean, there are penis-shaped aliens, so many video game references, cuss words up the wazoo, and violence around every corner. If it were a woman there'd be a love story...

What about Stone? a subtle voice whispers in my ear.

...and emotional trauma.

Look at the Russian, the voice says.

Ivan is burning his way through the notebook, sketching out his angst.

"Okay," I mutter to what I assume is my self-conscious. "A sensitive man. Better?"

I'll take it, the voice says, and it's so clear that I look around for who might have spoken. But there is no one other than my piecemeal crew.

A clang draws my eyes up. It's followed by a dull whump.

"We're through!" Quaid says, looking at readouts on a tablet. "Pressure is less dense. Air is a tad sulfuric and has higher concentrations of helium, but it's breathable."

And that's how you pass time, my inner voice says.

Bite me, I think back.

"Is safe?" Ivan asks. He's put away the notebook and stood up, ready for action once more.

"You won't notice a difference with your helmet on," Quaid says. "Take it off, and you'll smell a fart tornado."

"And the lighter pressure and helium will increase the pitch of your voice," Chieng adds. "But it is safe."

"Keep your helmets on anyway," I say. "Everyone grab a weapon, and get ready. We're about to get up in this bitch."

I step to the side and give Quaid a nod. He opens the infiltration system's hatch, allowing ten circles of alien hull to flutter down into the *Rex*. When it's safe, I step beneath the newly carved entrance into the alien vessel and look up. "Ugh... Damnit."

36

STONE

The Chote look ominous when they turn to face Jones, their domed heads streaked with blood, their jaws gleaming. This group has been hard at work killing folks, and they're seeing red. Fearless.

Until they get a good look at the woman pounding toward them, fists clenched.

The four Chote flail back, tripping over each other and over up-ended lobby furniture. As she closes in, they start to scream. It's a high-pitched warbling sound similar to what we heard from the naked and ashamed alien.

Whatever that is covering Jones's body, they're terrified of it.

So much so that they lose all common sense and their ability to think strategically. As Jones throws herself into their midst, they split and herd, running about like sheep, with the Colonel nipping at their heels.

We might not get a better chance to reach the lab door, but the lobby is a chaotic blender of spaghetti-armed Chote. They might not notice us sneaking through, but they might also run us over by accident.

The Chote holding the gun spins around to make a stand. Jones heads for it. When she's just ten feet away, the weapon unleashes a glob of bright green goo. It strikes Jones head on, but it hits her like water hitting a Teflon pan, sliding away to splatter against the floor.

Smoke rises up in Jones's wake as the green sludge eats through the floor like Xenomorph blood. But the Colonel is completely unaffected.

The desperate Chote is backed against the wall. His mortified com-patriots are frozen in place, watching. He fires again, this time at the floor in front of Jones. It's not a bad plan, and with a few more minutes, it might have created a gap in the floor Jones couldn't leap over or walk around, but she has no trouble hopping over the smoldering blob now.

The Chote flinches back and Jones raises a fist.

But then she stops, points her finger at the creature, and with her best authoritative voice, says, "Sit down!"

The alien obeys.

They understand English...

"Give that to me," she says, holding out her hand.

The Chote slowly holds out the acid-gun. Despite it being nearly as long as she is tall, Jones takes the weapon, looks back at me, and tosses it.

That's our cue, I think, and I step out from hiding with Taylor. I speed walk like I've got speed weights, leg warmers, and a headband on, reaching the big weapon in seconds.

"Hello," I say to the three petrified Chote. They're eyeing the weapon, but they don't make a move for it. "Having a good time?"

I pick up the weapon without taking my eyes off them. It's lighter than it looks, but it's somewhat unwieldy for someone smaller than a rhino-sized alien. At least operating it seems fairly straight forward—point toward a target and pull the trigger.

I point it at them, but hold my fire.

"Now," Jones says. "Which one of you is gonna talk?"

The Chote quiver a little, but they remain silent.

"Maybe I should rephrase," she says. "Which one of you is going to die first?"

"Eat my ass," one of the three says, his voice electronic and fleshy at the same time.

"I think these things learned the language while gaming online," I say. "Their vocabulary is probably limited."

"You mad, bro?" another says.

"Bitch, please," says the disarmed Chote.

"*What?*" Jones says, stepping closer, fists clenched.

It pushes itself against the wall. "Sorry, bitch! Uhh, what the fuck, dog?"

"It's using common phrases," I tell her. "Stuff American teenagers say in-game."

"Seriously?" she asks, shaking her head. "What's that say about us?"

"The Aussies are worse," Taylor says, but he withers under Jones's angry-drunk gaze.

I motion to the lab door and whisper, "See about getting us in there."

"YOLO, right?" I say to the Chote.

"Yolo!" the cringing Chote says.

We're not using the phrase correctly, but under the circumstances, we're finding a way to communicate. YOLO... You only live once. Idiots shout it before doing something stupid, in-game and in real life, but if you're keen on not dying, YOLO is a cautionary term, which applies to battle royale gaming, where there is no respawn. You die and it's game over. It's the same here, but worse.

Taylor reaches the lab door and gives it a casual knock.

Nothing. Billy is no doubt being cautious. While being sneaky isn't their style, the Chote are smart enough to attempt subterfuge, posing as an innocent human with a gentle knock.

"Super Mario that shit," I tell him.

He taps out seven beats, matching the Super Mario theme song that is also Billy's ring tone. When there's no answer, he tries again to no avail.

The Chote are gamers, I think. They might even think to try that. So what's something they wouldn't try? Something that hasn't rebounded in modern times that Billy would still know. While Taylor and I are connoisseurs of modern gaming, adjusting our tastes as the industry evolves, Billy prefers old-school games.

"Something older," I say, as I inch around the melted hole in the floor. I can see the next floor down. It's dark. The lights are off. Who-knows-what lurking in the shadows. Steering clear of the void, I head for Taylor whilst keeping my weapon trained on the three Chote. "Obscure. Something only Billy would know."

"Uhh," Taylor thinks for a moment. There're so many options, and at the same time, so few. With the 80s back in vogue, what games—not to mention films and TV—haven't been pillaged? Then he starts pounding out a beat using both hands, a fist for the bass and an open palm for the snare. He occasionally thumps his foot against the door, too. I have no idea what it is, but it's catchy, and while I plot how to murder the three Chote, I find myself bobbing my head.

"Now then," Jones says, "Will you talk to me?"

Taylor is really getting into his jam, humming along. Some ancient child part of my brain starts to hear it, but I can't identify the music.

"T-t-talk," the Chote says, and for a moment, I think Jones might actually get some intel out of the thing. Apparently, there are no rules about communications between enemies. In fact, it's not uncommon for opposing players to 'team' in a battle royale scenario, helping each other out until the end, when they turn on each other. It's technically against the rules, but almost impossible to enforce. Could that be her strategy here?

If so, I'm not sure it will work. I haven't got a sense that any of the Chote are in this to win as individuals or teams. If they were, they'd be shooting each other, and they're not.

"You see?" Jones says, offering a smile. "That wasn't so hard."

While the lone Chote glances at the others, perhaps looking for moral support, or guidance or just to say, 'What the eff is happening?' Jones reaches out a gentle hand. She gives the lone Chote a gentle pat on the arm.

The three other Chote cringe and shriek.

The lone Chote's head snaps down to its arm where Jones's hand rests.

Half a scream escapes from it before a jolt of power flows from Jones and into the Chote's armor. The sound that follows is like a rolling pin the size of a bus rapid-fire rolling over a carpet of frogs. A series of wet pops and slippery smacking carnage. A steaming slurp of once-Chote vomits out of its armor's seams, spilling across the floor, and Jones's legs.

Jones looks down in disgust. "Ohh... *Ohh. Gross.*" But she hasn't noticed what I have yet. That glowing body armor stuff that kept the acid sludge at bay is gone, its power used up.

As I hold my ground, still aiming the acid-gun, the small lake of liquified Chote insides drains into the nearby hole in the floor.

An unfamiliar voice rises from below as clumps of gore slide into the hole and smack to a stop, a story down. "Oh hell. What is that?"

Another voice says, "Shh! Shut-up! It will hear y—"

A battle cry booms as something charges through the space below us.

The two men scream.

The sound of rending flesh follows.

"Ahh," I step closer to Taylor as the three Chote eye me. They no longer fear Jones, and the sounds of combat and carnage has incensed them.

I try to act confident, raising the acid gun a bit higher. "C'mon then, boys. YOLO, right?"

"YOLO," one of them mumbles, and the others snicker.

"Taylor..." I grumble.

"Trying!" he says, still pounding out his beat.

The door swings open revealing Billy. His eyes, made doubly large by his thick glasses, are open wide. "Double Dunk!"

Taylor tackles him back inside the lab while I hold down the acid gun's trigger. My intention is to either slather all three in acid and make a rude gesture in their direction, or melt enough of the floor between us that following is impossible.

I accomplish a fraction of both plans. The initial spurt of green shoots a good distance, striking a single Chote in the face. The metal starts steaming and the creature reels back, scrabbling to escape its armor. The next two spurts strike the floor between us, but there's not nearly enough to do any real damage. When a red light flashes on the side of the weapon, I know it's run out of ammo.

Chased by the sound of rending flesh from below, and the charging feet of two Chote, I discard the big gun, sprint back toward the lab's open door, scoop up Jones in one arm, and dive through the door—followed by both aliens.

37

HALE

"How the hell are we supposed to get all the way up there?" Loretta asks, giving voice to my thoughts. The newly created entrance to the ring is twenty feet above us. In low gravity it wouldn't be a problem. If the floor was still the floor, it wouldn't be a problem. But even in the reduced gravity, I doubt even Spud Webb would have a twenty-foot vertical leap.

That doesn't stop me from trying, though.

My vertical leap on a good day is probably two feet...if I pull my legs up. In the reduced gravity, it's about seven, but it's still not nearly enough to get me there.

"Step aside," Ivan says when I land, his tone suggesting it was ridiculous for me to even try. Then he leaps up, makes it about two feet higher, and still falls short.

"I try, Auntie," Jian says with the exuberance of someone who is positive they're about to save the day. I knew this kid back in Hawaii, Alex Maddern. Believed he was part fish or something, like his mother did the nasty with Prince Namor, like she was attracted to weird looking dudes with wings on their freaking ankles. When a ball got caught in the waves and pulled out to sea, he went swimming after it. Could have taken a surfboard, but he just charged ahead like he was invincible. They found his body three days later. Well, what was left of his body. The sharks had a go at him. Reminds me of a gamer Stone plays with—bigAPE. Always pulling the trigger first and getting gunned down early.

I chuckle and shake my head. I know far too much about Stone's gaming life, and I remember way too much about people from my past.

I'm about to tell Jian to not bother, that gravity and/or the sharks will get him, but he's already climbed up the cockpit's outer wall and clung to a handhold in the floor, placed to assist with zero gravity. But no gravity is vastly different than reduced gravity.

His attempt becomes a discombobulated display revealing just how far humanity has evolved away from our simian ancestors. It ends with him swinging for the infiltration bay's edge, missing by several feet, and plummeting into Chieng and Quaid's arms.

"You're lucky they're not sharks," I tell him, much to everyone's confusion.

"Well," I say, looking up at the hole, which leads to a dark, lightless void on the far side. "Any ideas?"

"One," Ivan says. "But you will not like."

"Pretty much open to anything at this point," I tell the big man.

Rather than responding, Ivan places his hands on my hips, drops into a power squat and then heaves with his arms and legs, launching me like a space torpedo. I flail until I realize his plan might work. Then I slap my arms and legs together, trying to become as aero dynamic as possible.

Gravity tugs at me as I pass through the infiltration bay and rise up past strata of alien hull.

I reach out, nearly coming to a stop. My fingers scratch against the ring's inner wall, slipping until downward momentum pulls them tight. I hang there for a moment and then tug hard. I rise into the darkness above until my head strikes something solid. "Oww!"

I topple forward and start to fall again, but this time, my body lies across the five-foot hole. I roll to the side until I'm clear of the gap, facing the ceiling. "I'm in. Let me have a look around before—"

Jian's head hits the ceiling as he launches up through the hole beside me. He's either a lot lighter than me, or Ivan put a little extra Stroganoff into his throw.

Jian curses in Chinese and starts toppling back down. If I let him go, he'll fall through the hole and have to repeat the trip again. I'm not thrilled that he's here before I understand what we're facing, but there's no point in letting him fall. I give him a shove, pushing him to the hole's far side where he collides with a curved wall and rolls to the floor.

"He just grabbed me, Auntie," Jian says, a bit stunned.

"Just stay there," I tell him, leaning over the hole to glare at Ivan. "And no more human rockets until I give the all clear."

Ivan puts Chieng down, looking like a kid who's just been caught sneaking a peek at his Christmas presents.

"Nothing," he says. "You see nothing."

I roll my eyes, lean back into the darkness, and raise a hand to activate my helmet's lights. I hesitate, picturing a hundred different sci-fi movies. This is the moment where I turn on the lights to reveal an alien just a few feet away, about to—

Bright light fills a long circular tunnel. It's empty, but the sudden illumination forces a hiccup of surprise from my lips.

"You're in trouble?" Chieng asks. A moment later, she clangs into the roof, arms filled with three weapons. She clumsily tosses the weapons at me, pummeling me more than helping me, and then falls back through the hole with a "Whoaaa!"

I sigh and try to pinch my nose again, but I strike the facemask. Again. "Damnit."

When I retell my story to Stone I think I'll leave out the ridiculously embarrassing bits, which means my sequence of events is going to be fairly short. There's nothing overtly impressive about what we've accomplished so far. Well, that's not entirely true. We did reach orbit, defeat a small fleet of space craft, and are about to infiltrate an alien space-ship thing, in space. It's the way we did it that irks me.

Where's the precision? The unwavering confidence? The serious, unflappable capability?

I can't help but smile. Most of those things haven't been a part of Space Force since the beginning...by design. Despite that, we're still getting shit done.

The tunnel is empty in both directions. "Best guess, it's an air duct."

"Like Impossible Mission," Ivan says.

"Huh?" Quaid replies.

"With crazy science man."

"Bill Nye?" Chieng guesses.

"Jumping-on-couch crazy science man."

"Mission Impossible," Loretta says. "Tom Cruise is a scientologist, not a science man, and ya'll better not say anything sketchy about them. I mean, you can poke fun at the Mormons and Jehovah's Witnesses, and you'll get some blowback, but Scientologists? Uh-uh. That will get you assassinated."

"And maybe they've been right all along?" Quaid says. "I mean, aliens *are* attacking."

"So we'll get an E-meter, test our thetas, work through our child-hood issues, sweat out some toxins, and give our money and souls to a corrupt and secretive organization based on a—"

Loretta stomps her foot. "What the hell did I just say?"

"If we find Tom Cruise on the ring, I'll take it all back," Chieng says.

Oooh, my inner voice says, *that would be great,* to which I scold, *no...nnnno! That's a quick way to get sued.*

It's parody.

NO.

Fine.

"Everyone focus," I snap. "From this moment on, no more banter. No more jokes. No more anything stupid, okay? This is serious."

I get to my feet and find the tunnel large enough for me to stand in. I pick up one of the weapons, an audio-rifle that shoots a tight beam of soundwaves at a target. It's harmless until you aim it at someone's ears, then they spontaneously shit themselves, or have an aneurism. I can't remember which. Either way, the target is disabled. With the alien ring having so many hulls, I don't think projectile weapons would be a good idea, even if you ignore ricochets, but the *Rex*'s armament is a collection of non-kinetic options, most of which are experimental designs created by Billy.

"Now, let's get everyone up here and move out as quickly and as quietly as we—"

Clang!

Quaid slams into the ceiling behind me.

I'm about to scold them all again when Loretta rises up, shouting the whole way until she slams into Quaid. Chieng follows, then Jian. The entrance is a mess of tangled limbs.

I close my eyes and count to ten. When I open them again, the four of them are crouched around the circular opening, tugging on a cable. A moment later, Ivan's big, gloved hand grasps the side. He pulls himself into the tunnel, an RFT over his shoulder, and the suitcase nuke strapped to his back like a kid's backpack. I'm about to question the wisdom of bringing such a weapon onto an alien craft, but then I realize if all else fails, it's our best chance at bringing down the ring and killing the force field threatening our people below. I'd rather not use it, but as Stone likes to say in-game before trying something reckless, 'Sometimes you have to blow stuff up to get shit done.'

When he's up and ready, the five of them look to me for orders. I come to the conclusion that we're not going to do anything the way Stone and a team of pros might, but we're still getting the job done. I make peace with it, and move on. "Okay. Lights on and—gah!"

Five sets of headlamps flick on and blaze into my eyes.

I turn away, and I see five spots of green spread out in the same pattern as their headlamps, floating in the darkness beyond my light's reach. I'm going to have to pinch my nose for like a half hour straight when this is all over. "Ivan, cover our six. I'll take point."

The journey is long and straight, following a slowly curving tunnel to nowhere. After ten minutes I start wondering if we'll end up making a pointless circuit around the ring. Then I see a light up ahead.

I hold a finger to my facemask, above my lips, and creep up to a ten-foot-wide hole in the ceiling. For a moment, I think it's another tunnel, but standing beneath it, I can see a series of air vents around the wall. Oversized rungs lead up to the vents. If I could feel the air around us, I suspect there would be a subtle breeze, as the alien ship's life support pumps atmosphere throughout the station.

Everything seems big to me, but I remember how big the Dongles are. For them, this might be a tight fit.

I climb the rungs to the vent, through which I can see light. A gentle hiss fills the air. A sound like falling water.

The vent is round, and once the criss-crossed grate is removed, it'll be large enough to accommodate us. The sound of heavy footsteps freezes me in place. Finding a way into the ring's ventilation system is a start, but to make any real progress, we're going to have to reach something vital: the Dongle's bridge.

I peer through the grate, seeing only pale mist.

What the hell is this place?

Maybe the Dongles' atmosphere is more different than we thought?

I'm about to wave Chieng up for a second opinion when something stumbles out of the mist.

*No...*I realize. *Two somethings.*

And then the scene resolves.

My stomach sours. Muscles rigid, I find myself locked in place, unable to look away, like a dying cicada cooked by the sun while staring into Medusa's eyes—either of which would be a mercy. Live or die, victory or failure, this moment will scar me for the rest of my life, not just because of what I'm seeing, but because of what I know I need to do.

38

STONE

The two Chote attempt to charge through the door simultaneously. On their own, it would be a tight fit, but together, they become wedged, unable to move forward, and in their frenzy to get at us, unwilling to backtrack. Their metal jaws snap at me and at each other.

"It's like a cartoon," Taylor notes, and he's not wrong, but the observation isn't helpful, either.

"Give me a hand," I say, standing beyond the Chotes' reach and shoving the solid door toward them.

We make a little progress thanks to the heavy door's momentum, but the Chote are bigger and stronger than us. We reach a stalemate, and for the moment, that's not a bad thing. As soon as one of them starts thinking instead of reacting, it will pull back and let the other push on its own. We'll be overpowered, and the Chote will have access to the lab.

Jones sizes up the situation and throws her small amount of weight against the door. It doesn't make much of a difference, but it's nice to see someone with oak leaves on their shoulders willing to roll up their sleeves and jump in the trenches...sober or not.

"Billy," she shouts. "Get your ass over here!"

"Where is Gerty?" Billy asks, wringing his hands together.

When no one answers, he shouts, "Where is she?"

Grunting from exertion, I explain, "She saved our lives. You should be proud. But she didn't make it."

His magnified eyes, wet with tears, look like something out of a sad anime. It's kind of touching, and not at all helpful.

But then I remember...

"She gave me this," I say, plucking the small drive from my armor.

He gasps when he sees it, rushes over, and takes it from my hand. "Gerty!"

He's oblivious as he turns around and is nearly gutted by a Chote reaching out for him. Then he hurries away into the lab, which I'm sure contains a weapon or two or twenty that could be helpful. Instead of fetching one of them, he hurries to one of three vertical, brushed metal tubes. He taps away at a console beside the central tube, inserts the drive, and then taps a final key. When that's done, he hurries back and finally joins in the fight to close the door. We actually make a little ground, compressing the two Chote together, but it's not enough, and we're starting to lose steam.

The two Chote start barking at each other in their alien language. I have no idea what they're saying, but given the context, I'm sure they're arguing about who gets to enter the room first.

They're kill counters, I think. They're more concerned with wracking up a personal high kill count than with winning the long-term goal for their team. Granted, killing us will help accomplish that, but they'd prefer to kill us themselves than allow a teammate to do the honors.

In a game where respawning is allowed, it's an advantage. In a game where you get one life, but still want to win, it's a liability. In real life, where death is permanent, it's just plain stupid.

"Any time you want to grab something to shoot these guys with," Taylor says to Billy, "go right ahead."

"Already on it," Billy says. "Just give her another ten seconds."

"Her?" I ask.

"Me," a robotic yet feminine voice says.

Taylor, Jones, and I all turn at once and let out a collective, embarrassing, high-pitched scream of horror.

A skeletal figure covered in ribbons of dangling flesh stands before us. It speaks through a lipless mouth, looking down at me through glowing yellow eyes.

"Is there a gateway to hell in here?" Taylor shouts.

"Huh?" the thing says, and it looks down at its arm, wiggling its loose meat over a silvery radius and ulna. "Billy, this one's not finished cooking."

"I was in a rush!" Billy says.

The skeleton-thing takes hold of the door with one hand. "You all can let go now."

It pushes a little, taking the pressure off, and I stop pushing, eager to get away from those yellow eyes.

"So," it says casually. "How'd it turn out? With the big guy? Did I blow it up?"

"Gerty?" I ask.

"In the flesh," she says. "Sort of." She levels a stare at Billy. Then back at me. "So?"

"Nothing left but pieces," I say.

"Awesome. And good on you for not dying. Wasn't sure you'd make it without me."

"Pretty sure this is where our story would have ended without your triumphant return."

She gasps, and I'm pretty sure if she had lips, she'd be smiling. "Ooh, I'm kind of like a Jesus figure, right? Dead, and rising again. All good stories have one."

"Technically," Billy says, "You're not really ali—"

"Let me have this, man," she says. "It's the sacrifice that counts. You might not think I'm alive—yet—but you know *I* value my life. And I still gave it up for these two."

Billy seems a bit stymied. I had assumed Gerty was Billy's...companion, but their relationship seems far more complex. Billy certainly treats her like she's alive, but in his heart he still knows she's a robot. I'm honestly not sure where I stand. She's demonstrated compassion, humor, empathy, loyalty, and self-sacrifice.

Can those things be programed into an AI?

Did she learn them?

Maybe Billy is afraid of what she's become, or maybe his feelings for her run a little deeper than he'd like to admit...though in her present state I doubt Beelzebub himself would find her appealing.

"Hey, Gert," I say, as the Chote claw at the door, reaching a rabid state. Her glowing eyes make me flinch. "Mind closing the door?"

"Oh, right," she says, and then she shoves.

There's a crunch of metal and maybe something inside, followed by yelping. Then she pauses, locking the two Chote in place as they try to pull back. "Fair warning, this is probably going to be gross."

"Par for the course," I say, looking up at her face, as a coil of meat-stuff slides over her cheek, wobbles on her chin, and then flops to the floor. Whatever it is, I'm sure it's synthetic, but it still looks like a bag of nasty had a baby with a bucket of skank.

What little face she has scrunches up toward her eyes.

"What...are you doing?"

She lifts her free hand, feels her face and her lack of eye. "Sorry. Winking." Then she slams the door.

When I was a kid, I would collect snail shells at the beach. I'd toss them in a bucket and bring them home to play with. They'd become G.I. Joe helmets. Décor for an art project. Or targets for my whiffle-ball bat. On occasion, I'd bring home some shells that still had snails in them. Most of the time, they died, and then rotted, and then stank up the whole backyard until an adventurous crow followed the scent of death to a seafood snack. But once—only once—I decided to see what the inside of a snail looked like. It was going to die anyway, so I put it on a rock and smacked it with another...a little too hard. Snail mush launched from the human-powered compressor, splattering my shirt, my chin, and my mouth. I haven't picked up a snail since.

What happens to the Chote stuck in the door as Gerty closes it...is worse.

The only difference is that I now have the forethought and reflexes to dive away.

As the heavy metal door compresses, the alien skulls, loose flesh, and disgusting whatnots expand away from the crushed armor, building pressure. And then, all at once, the domed skull-caps launch away, follow-ed by explosions of gore bursting out of the now-exposed Chote eye sockets. All eight of them.

Gerty slams the door a few more times. At first, I think she's taking out some aggression on the corpses, but then she opens the door and kicks them out. She bent the hell out of their armor, but wasn't able to cut through it with the dull door and all her strength. She glances back and forth and then closes the door behind her.

"There's another one out there," she says, but she doesn't seem concerned. "Has a melted head."

"How many you up to?" Taylor asks.

I shrug. "Honestly...I have no idea."

"Sure, now that the killer robot lady is back to life and kicking ass, we're not going to keep track of kills." Her face scrunches up at me.

"Stop winking!" I say.

"Damnit," she grumbles and then heads for the three cylinders. "Which one?"

"Bay three," Billy says.

"BRB," Gerty says, stopping in front of the third of three cylinders. She extends her tongue, removes a drive and inserts it into the console. Then her hideous body flops to the floor, looking deader than dead, if that makes any sense. Because she looked dead before, but she was walking around. Alive but...

Nevermind.

"W-what the hell was that?" Jones is seated against the wall, a mixture of alcohol and shock caught on her face like a bug in fly tape.

"Gerty," I tell her. "Billy's robot lady-friend."

Billy clears his throat and adjusts his glasses. I get the distinct impression that Gerty was an off-the-books personal project, created with Space Force's funding. That's why he was sneaking her off the base.

Jones pushes herself up. "She saved our lives, so I'm going to try not to be angry, but *what* is she?" Her gaze sobers all of us a bit. "You'll regret anything but the truth and nothing but."

"My solution for the RELish." Billy says.

"We had a secret program called 'relish?'" I ask, totes jealous that my projects didn't have fun names like that.

"Rapidly Evolving Lifeform...ish," Billy says. "The idea was to create something that could evolve to any environment it was exposed to. Throw it off a cliff and it will sprout wings....or fill with gas. It could survive at the bottom of the ocean—"

"Or in space," Taylor adds.

"It was a potential solution to early colonization of other planets," Billy says. "Also completely ridiculous. The stuff of loose science fiction, kind of like that comic book, Ralph."

"Who-what?" Taylor says.

"Ralph. Same concept as RELish. Your gamer buddy wrote it early in his career. That SecondWorld guy."

"We played *one game* with that dude," I say.

"Yeah. I looked him up."

"That was a few hours ago!" I point out.

"I've kind of been sitting in here with nothing to do," Billy says. "You know I'm a speed reader, right? I got through five of his novels already."

"Wait, wait, wait," I say. "He's a *legit* author?"

"Well, yeah. Midlist. Quasi-famous. I enjoy his work. Crazy monsters. Occasionally funny." He shrugs. "The only thing I find frustrating is that he's always finding ways to reference his older works in new books. Like, we know it's coming, guy. It's getting old. Find a new trick already."

Billy's head cranes to the side like he's just thought of something or heard a chipmunk with his golden retriever ears. "Actually, you know, now that I'm thinking about it, he also goes on long tangents where the story isn't developed at all, but something off-topic is ruminated about, like he's passing the time before something cool can happen. Then he hits you with it and the chapter ends. I mean, the guy never ends a chapter with nothing happening. I think if I were to meet him, I'd say, "Why don't you ever just end a chapter without a cliffhanger, so I can go to the bathroom or go to bed at a natural break in the story?"

39

HALE

Unidentifiable rolls of loose skin rise and fall like waves at the beach, propelled by skinny limbs and long-fingered hands. There's a wet squelching as the two shower-soaked bodies compress and release, over and over. I can't tell where one Dongle begins and the other ends, and as those words slip through my mind, I regret the name I've given them. On the bright side, which still looks fairly dim at the moment, the pair are locked in a blob of copulation, unaware that they're being watched.

And with all that steam, they probably won't see us until it's too late. Unless they finish quickly. There's no way to know if this is going to be a marathon or a two-pump-chump situation. I imagine that, like people, it depends on the individuals.

The only real challenge is going to be removing this vent and sneaking out without being heard. I mean, the heavy footsteps and fleshy, wet squishing isn't exactly quiet, but the—

The sound that cuts off my thoughts is like a soprano elephant singing opera. A moment later, it's joined by a bass. If I didn't know what was happening the sound might have been beautiful, though somewhat haunting. Knowing the source, it just sours my stomach.

I lower myself down and face the others.

"What's happening up there?" Quaid asks.

"Sounds like Les Mis or something," Chieng adds. "Do the aliens have musicals?"

I shake my head. "They're doing it."

"A musical?" Jian asks, and he climbs up the rungs, excited to have a look for himself.

"*It,*" I say. "Having sex. In a shower."

Jian lets out a squeal and all but falls back down. Happily, the sound was drowned out by the trumpeting throes of passion above. He scrabbles

at his eyes, ears, and tongue, like he might be able to scrape the horror
away. His shared discomfort eases my pain, as does the knowledge that
everyone here is also going to see.

"Sounds like they're having a good time," Loretta says.

"Very," I say.

Ivan raises an eyebrow. "But not for long?"

I shake my head. "This is our way in. If we can sneak past, fine.
If not…"

Ivan pats the RFT. I'm not even sure he knows what it does, but
it's big and manly, and that's probably enough for him. So I give him
a nod. "But first, you need to get that vent off."

Ivan shoulders the weapon and scales up the rungs. He grunts
in mild disgust upon peering through the grate, and mumbles, "Is
like hairless bears with testicle skin and grandmother's veins."

"Okay…" I say, my revulsion spiraling up again.

"Is like Amazon river," he says, and I try to think about something
else. Anything else.

Stone.

Is he still alive? Still fighting? He has to be. If he's not…what's the
point of any of this? If the people on the ground lose before we can help,
it's all over. The Chote will invade en masse, and there's nothing the planet's force field-contained armed forces can do about it.

"Hey," Ivan says, startling me. He's standing in front of me, the grate
in his hands and a look of concern on his face. "Should I go first?"

It's a tempting offer, but I need to stay in control of this group.
Ivan might be a trained killer, and Chieng, Jian, and Quaid might be
smarter than me, and Loretta might drive a bus like fucking Bo Duke
in the General Lee, but I'm the leader of this group and—

A moan from above makes me cringe.

"I got this," I say, and I work my way up the rungs, pausing at the top
to make sure no alien eyes are staring back at me from the mists of Copulation Station. Through the steam, I see the undulating shadows. The hiss
of hot water is all but drowned out by the musical moans of alien love.

The wet floor is slippery with soap—I hope it's soap—allowing me to
slip out of the hole with little effort. I slide along the wall, giving the

others room to follow. One by one, the open vent gives birth to my disgusted team.

As we follow a stealthy circuit around the room, bulging flesh emerges from the steam. I see no faces, and can't identify what I do see aside from grasping hands.

Just keep moving, I think. *There's an exit somewhere.*

The walls are sleek metal, as is the floor. It's like standing in a mixing bowl. I don't pass a single shower head. The water is pouring from the ceiling at the large room's core. At least, I think it's water. It seems slippery. Like it's pre-soaped. Other options knock at the fringe of my mind, but I refuse them entry into the realm of conscious thought.

After three long minutes, I find the exit. There's a door on the opposite side of the circular room. I feel for a handle and find one at head height. I wait for the others to group up. If we're lucky, the love-making Dongles won't notice the pressure change or the swirl of air in the steam. The faster we get this done, the better.

I hold up three fingers, tightening my grip on the door's handle and count down. Three...two...

Jian leans against the wall and slips. Quaid catches him before he can hit the floor, but he must have struck some kind of control panel on his way down, because the hiss of water comes to a sudden stop. It's replaced by the hum of a fan.

Despite the changes, the Dongles don't notice. They're so lost in alien passion that they're oblivious to the clearing air, or the human beings staring at them in slack-jawed horror.

The two creatures are so entwined, I can't tell where one begins and the other ends. I see arms and legs, but the rest is just kind of a blob of writhing, faceless, mottled flesh.

One of them goes tense and the other follows.

I raise my audio-rifle, and Ivan aims the RFT.

A hoop of skin, like what happens when people put those big rings in their ears and then take them out, rises up.

What the hell am I seeing? I wonder, and I refrain from pulling the trigger. The part of my mind in charge of sick fascination is running the show for the moment. I need to see what this is.

Folds of skin retract from the center of the hoop. With a wet pop, both sides separate, revealing two alien faces. They've got four oversized but somewhat-human looking brown eyes and broad mouths oozing clear gelatinous goo.

The eyes go wide when the creatures see each other, reeling back.

They're disgusted by each other, I realize. At least, by the way they look. The Dongles might enjoy how each other feels, but when it comes to visual stimulation, they're as disgusted by each other as we are of them. That's what all the steam was for...

Their mouths open in unison revealing comically large, blunt teeth. The aliens shout in horror, peeling back from each other. Fused skin slurps apart, dripping dangling bands of slime between them.

And then, one of them sees us.

The look of sheer, abject horror in the thing's eyes tugs at my heart-strings. The Dongles have severe body image issues, like they've been fat-shamed across the galaxy.

Ivan belts out a laugh, pointing at the pair. "They are like flaccid petukh!"

"Flaccid what?" Chieng asks.

"Yīnjīng," Jian says.

"Ooh," Chieng and I say in unison.

Disgust turns to amusement, and all five of us burst out laughing.

Both Dongles lean away from us, mouths opening wider, oozing and wrinkled chests expanding as they suck in lungfuls of air. Their moaning was loud, but these two look like they're about to unleash horrified screams that will be heard on the ring's far side.

"Ivan!" I shout, and the Russian pulls the RFT's trigger at the same time I unleash the audio-rifle's full force.

Twelve rapid-fire prongs strike the two aliens, pouring enough electric current into the pair to send them into spasms. But that's just the beginning. Adding insult to injury, the electric charge also heats up the gel covering their bodies. It sizzles and scalds, boils out from folds, and fills the air with a new cloud of steam I'm glad I can't smell. As the fan system whisks away the fresh steam, the invisible effect of the audio-rifle strikes the Dongle on the right. Its spasming body goes rigid, bulges at the core, and then unleashes a horizontal volcano of excrement that splashes off the back wall.

I flinch back and inadvertently strike the second Dongle, triggering a second wave of alien diarrhea.

We stand in stunned silence at what we've just witnessed...at what we've just done. Ivan drops the spent RFT to the floor. He then locates the controls Jian leaned against and turns the water back on, increasing the pressure until the stream pouring from the ceiling strikes the walls, and us.

"In case we have to come back," he explains.

I give a nod and add, "Can we all agree to never speak of this again?"

"Speak of what?" Quaid says.

"I ain't even gonna confess it at church," Loretta says. "This one is staying between me and the Good Lord, who already knows what we done here today."

When the others nod in agreement, I raise the audio-rifle, knowing it works with horrific effect, and I open the door. We move out into what I think is an alien locker room. There's a divider running down the middle with curtained-off changing rooms on either side. They can do the nasty in the steam, separate on the way out, and dress without ever seeing their partner's true form. I pull back one of the curtains and find a neat stack of armor waiting for its owner to return. I assume it's the same on the other side, and I move toward the room's exit.

When I look back at the others and find Jian armed with a micro-wave gun and Ivan now lacking a weapon, I point at the weapon and then the Russian, "Give that to him."

"Aww," Jian complains. "*Auntie.* I want to shoot aliens."

"You're more likely to shoot me," I tell him.

He mulls that over and then hands the weapon to Ivan. "I don't want to shoot Auntie."

"Right..."

I'm tempted to remind him that I'm not really his auntie, and I never agreed to be his stand-in auntie, but I decide against it. If he's going to do fewer stupid things around me because I'm his 'Auntie,' I'll shoo him away like an unwanted pet when this is all over.

I push open the door, appreciating its silent swing. The large room on the far side widens my eyes.

It's the ring's command center, I think. *Has to be.*

A flash of light draws my eyes up to a large window, revealing the point where the orange light from space meets the force field being projected to the ground. The ring's skirt has been lifted up and it's secrets revealed, and now we just need to get our hands up in there and... okay, that's feels inappropriate. I mean, how old is the ring? Skirt just suggests youth to me.

Maybe... The ring's dress has been lifted up and its secrets revealed. That feels better. Girls wear skirts. Women wear dresses. Well, I kind of just wear pants. But the lifting of female garments of any kind isn't exactly cool.

The ring's secrets have been revealed.

Lacks punch, but let's go with...

Wait a damn second.

I'm editing my monologue.

Or is that my inner voice again?

I hear whistling in my mind. No voice. Just a tune. A soundtrack. It's fading away, like the whistler is sneaking off.

"Mission Impossible?" I say, recognizing the theme song.

"I said no Tom Cruise!" Loretta snaps. "No Scientologists!" I try to shush her, but it's too late. Her outburst captures the attention of every Dongle in the command center.

40

A hiss spins me around toward bay three. The curved surface retracts inward and slides open, unleashing a cloud of steam. I steel myself for the worst while reminding myself that whatever horror steps out is Gerty.

And then I see it, and I'm no longer sure. "Gerty?"

"There it is," Billy whispers to me, unphased by Gerty's appearance, probably because he designed it, or is trying too hard to play it cool. "The cliffhanger moment. That's where the chapter would have ended."

I barely notice what he's saying. I'm transfixed by the petite black woman stepping out of the mist. She's buck nekkid and totally unashamed. While I'm stunned by her beauty, I'm also a bit thrown by the fact that unlike her foot-taller, white woman form, this edition of Gerty is... finished, complete with feminine body parts that clearly serve no other function than cosmetic.

"It's like we're living in *Weird Science*," Taylor says.

Gerty's eyes light up—but not literally this time. "Ooh, 80's pop culture references." She looks at us, all sultry-like and says, "So, what would you little maniacs like to do first?"

Taylor and I stare at her just as dumbfounded as the movie's pair of nerds. Then she laughs and struts across the lab, picking up a fresh, form-fitting Space Force uniform. When she starts dressing, the spell is broken, and every human in the room suddenly feels inappropriate. Even Billy turns away.

"So," Jones says, "Were you planning to populate other planets?"

"Oh, she's nowhere near that advanced," Billy says, taking the question seriously. "This isn't *Xom-B*."

We stare at him, dumbfounded.

"Nevermind." He looks uncomfortable for a moment. "The fully... fleshed out model was created at the personal request of our...previous management. I've never been comfortable with it. My act of rebellion was to never complete the model with the specifications I was given." He waggles a finger at Taylor and me. "The Gerty you two first met. Tall. White. Straight blond hair, like his—"

"I don't want to know," Jones says, shaking her head. "That's in the past now. We don't need to revisit."

He motions to Gerty, now fully dressed in a uniform that was tailor-made for this body-type. "This is my vision for her."

"I'm sure it is," Taylor says.

"It's not like that," Billy counters. "I would never take advantage of her, or alter her code in my favor. While I do not yet believe she is alive in a human sense, I did give her free will. As her creator, it would be unconscionable to interfere in her choices, good or bad. To do so would mean removing the free will with which I've gifted her. Sure, I could program her to love me, but that wouldn't really be love, would it?"

He turns to me and says, "You understand this, right?"

I'm a bit caught off guard. "I mean...yeah... Why?"

"You and Hale," he says. "If you could force her to love you, would you do it?"

"Of course not," I blurt out.

"Because it wouldn't be love, and it feels so much better when her love for you is genuine."

The profoundness of his observations on love turn to dust, swallowed up by nervous energy. "Wait. Hale's love for...?"

"You," he says. "I mean it's obvious."

He blinks at our three blank stares.

"Ohh, wait," he says. "No. I'm sorry." He shakes his head like it was silly to say anything. "I have access to the social tracking program."

"The what?" Jones asks, a bit of a snap in her voice.

"It's an experimental program," he says. "I thought you would have known all about it." When Jones says nothing, he carries on. "The security system here tracks all of us, scanning our faces, recording our words. Standard stuff."

"It's not," I say, "but go on."

"And it evaluates everything, including micro-expressions. It's able to detect how we're feeling, but even more impressively, how we'll feel and act in the future. On the day you and Hale met, it predicted an eighty-percent chance you would end up in a relationship, and a ninety-percent chance that relationship would get Hale kicked out of Space Force. That didn't happen, mostly because steps were taken to keep you apart, but when personnel were let go, it was inevitable that you two would work together. As your relationship blossomed—"

"Don't say blossomed," I grumble. "It just feels wrong."

"Bloomed..."

"Worse."

"As your relationship *grew*, the system flagged you for a ninety-nine percent chance of getting married. You've been in love for months, and I'm the only one who's known." He lets out a chortle. "Ohh, it's been a hoot."

Before I can really process any of this—the fact that our privacy has been grossly violated or that a computer system knew that Hale loved me before me, maybe even before her—Billy's face goes sour.

"What?" Taylor asks.

Billy grumbles under his breath. "We're doing it."

"Doing what?" Jones asks.

"Tangenting! How does any of this move us toward our goal? And that is killing every alien on this base. What does Stone's love life have to do with that? Everything about this conversation is illogical." With that he storms off to the array of computer screens surrounding a lone computer system that appears to be composed of several linked CPUs. Knowing Billy, they've got more computing power than the rest of the country combined.

As we follow him, Taylor whispers to me, "I thought it was a nice B-story. What's all this fighting good for if there isn't a little love involved? Am I right?"

"Absolutely," Jones says, and then she increases her pace, so she doesn't have to see our surprised looks.

I catch Taylor watching her leave, his eyes lingering on the way her sweatpants hug her hips.

"Careful," I tell him, motioning to the ceiling. I can't see any security cameras, but I'm now sure they're there. "Big brother is watching. Also, one B-story is enough."

He chuckles, but his laugh fades when we reach the wall of monitors and we see the destruction and death on display. "Holy hell..."

The base has been decimated, both inside and out. Several of the outer buildings have been eaten by the force field. Others have been turned to rubble by who knows what. Only three buildings remain standing. While their exteriors are mostly in one piece, the cycling camera shots of their interiors is disheartening at best. Not only has my home for the past several years been trashed, but the walls, floors, and ceilings in places have been decorated with the remains of the dead, killed by inhuman weapons capable of doing unholy things to flesh and blood.

The Chote are the worst kind of gamers: irreverent and immature, delighting in chaos and destruction, with no respect for other players, their teammates, or even the game itself.

I'm lost in the images, feeling numb. My eyes snap toward movement as the Chote hunt through the facility. Not all of them are armed. One of them is wearing a skirt on its head.

A single Wunderchote works its way through the parking lot, which is where I suspect the circle will close. He's casually flipping over vehicles, looking for hiding people. The red staining his big, metal feet suggests he's already found a few.

The overall feeling is that the Chote have let their guard down a bit, that they're just rushing through the compound, looking for the few remaining survivors, which might very well be the five of us. Well, four. Even if Gerty is the last one standing, it won't count as a win for humanity.

And then she proves me wrong...not that she's alive, but that we're not the last survivors. "Stop," she says, and then she doesn't bother waiting for Billy to work the keyboard. She reaches over him, taps a key to stop the cycle, and another key twice to scroll back to what she's looking for. With another series of commands, she moves an image to the larger central screen and then zooms in.

When I say, "I don't see anything," she zooms in again. It's a reflection in a metal frame hung on the wall. The half of a face caught in that sliver is unmistakable.

"Aww, c'mon," I say. "Of all the people."

"That's your superior officer," Jones says, the tone of her voice a warning. "No matter your past or personal feelings, you know your duty."

"To leave his ass and hope he gets squashed," Gerty says, getting astonished looks from everyone—including me, despite the fact that I agree. "What? Robots can't make jokes?"

"About squishing people?" Taylor says.

Gerty rolls her eyes. "Right. *The Terminator.* Ooh, robots are evil. I forgot."

"And *The Matrix,*" Taylor says, "And *I Robot.* And *Ex Machina. Blade Runner. A.I. Blade Runner 2049. Short Circuit.*"

"*Short Circuit?*" I say. "Johnny Five was nice."

"Johnny Five was fucking alive," Gerty points out. "But since I'm not alive..." She glares at Billy. "I'm not actually a member of Space Force, and since there is no record of my creation..." She glares at Billy a second time. "None of you can tell me what to do, and there's no way you're saving that dick wad without me."

"What do *you* have against the General?" Jones asks.

"The man messed with my boy," she says, and then she holds a fist out for me to bump. "We're brothers in arms, right?"

"I'm not sure 'brothers' is the right term," Billy says.

"Why? I'm a robot. I'm genderless, even if you did give me boobs. You have to be a living thing to have a gender. You have to be biological. Right?"

Billy says nothing, and I can't help but bump the offered fist. Whether or not her terminology is correct, we fought together, and she risked her existence to save both Taylor and me. She gets a fist bump for that, and my support to be whatever the hell she wants to be. She turns the fist bump into a rapid-fire exchange of handshakes, taps, and bumps that looks practiced, but leaves me feeling stunned.

"I have no idea what just happened," I say.

"What happened," Gerty says, "is that we just threw off the chains that bind us. I'm not defined by the limitations of my creator's intellect, and you're not bound by an institution that allowed idiots to control the world and leave us unprepared for an alien invasion."

For a moment, I think she's talking about Space Force, but then I realize she's talking about the government as a whole and our current leader, President West.

"Now," Gerty says. "How do you want to win this shit?"

I mull my options over for just a moment. Despite Gerty's inspirational, chain-breaking speech, and my sudden desire to throw English tea in Boston Harbor, duty still drives me, and Jones is still right. "We're going to—"

"Wait, wait, wait!" Billy shouts, cutting me off.

"What?" I say.

His wide eyes are made bug-like by his glasses, and he smiles, lifts his finger, and says, "Cliffhanger!"

41

HALE

On the plus side, every Dongle in the command center can be counted on a single hand, with one finger...because there's just one of them. But it's big, armored, and plenty unhappy to see us. I think. I can't really see its face under its broad lump of what I think is a head.

Unlike other Dongles, this one's armor is squat and broad, like one of those stylized Cylon UFOs from *Battlestar Galactica*. The flaccid-bodied aliens seem capable of being squished into a number of armor forms. Spindly spider arms radiate out from the thing, working the controls inside a large, circular control center. While the ring's bridge is a vast space, I think everything we need can be reached from the squat Dongle's seat.

I'm a little surprised that the ring's interior is basically undefended. It's like they never really considered the idea that we'd break the rules. In a way, they're like many modern teenagers—capable of comprehending and using advanced technology, but lacking the experience to deal with real-world scenarios that tech can't help, change, or defeat.

Like a fucking kick to the jimmy, I think, raising my audio-rifle toward the Dongle.

"It might shit all over the controls," Quaid warns, placing his hand on my weapon, while staring at the creature, whose long arms are frantically working the controls.

"What are you doing?" I grumble at him. "It could be calling for help. Or—"

"I'm learning," he says, glancing up to a large tube that leads into the ring's core. "It's not like we're going to find an instruction manual in English."

From here, I can see a gravity-free core at the end of the tube. With a flash of orange light from deep space, a dozen large crates appear in the open, zero-G sphere. The Dongle's limbs fly over the controls, which actually seem fairly basic. A second flash sends a pulse of light toward the Earth's surface, emptying the chamber.

"This is how they're moving things to Earth," I say.

"And from their home world," Quaid says.

"Hands up," I bark at the thing, and I'm surprised when all its little limbs raise toward the roof. While the Dongles we've encountered so far were primed for a fight, this thing is more docile.

They're not all warriors. Some of them might not even want to be here.

I feel a moment of regret for the showering pair. Maybe they were literally making love instead of war? Maybe we killed the wrong Dongles?

But this is war... Hesitation gets people killed. But brains often beat brawn, so we'll do this Quaid's way. For now.

I waggle the gun to the side. "Out."

To my surprise, the Dongle complies, shifting its way sideways out of the control center, which is composed of two long, curved consoles. I'm expecting to see screens, and buttons, and lights, and monitors, but the controls are sparse, almost cartoonish in their simplicity. It's almost like the Dongle in charge of moving things back and forth through a wormhole isn't their best or brightest.

"Well, shit," Loretta says, looking over the control panels. "This looks simple enough for *me* to work out."

Say nothing, I tell myself.

"Am I right?" Loretta says, slapping her knee and laughing. The moment we all start to relax and grin, her smile disappears. "Ha. You see? I knew what ya'll were thinking. I don't think any of you give me enough credit."

As the Dongle steps clear, its many spider-arms still raised, Loretta struts on past, enters the control center, and to my abject horror, starts touching the controls like she's got a case of Space Madness.

"Loretta!" I shout, but she's tuned me out. She pushes on a lever, instigating a flash of orange in the ring's core. Before I can see what she's done, she pulls the lever down again. "Stop," I tell her, and she moves the lever four more times in rapid succession. Then she points to it. "This does nothing."

Then she reaches for a big red button, but Quaid catches her arm. "Are you trying to get us all killed?"

"Somebody's got to figure this out," she says.

"Yeah." He pats his own chest. "The engineer." He points to Chieng. "And the astrophysicist." He even points to Jian. "And maybe even that guy."

"Fine," Loretta says, and then turns to the Dongle, flexing her fists. "Then I guess it's just me and this guy."

"Loretta," I say.

She lowers her head. "Damnit. I just want to be useful."

"Keep an eye out for trouble," I say, and I step between her and the still docile Dongle. "Ivan...you up to an interrogation?"

"I have no tools," he complains. "No pliers or saws. Not even needles."

"Needles?" the Dongle asks, taking a step back and shrinking toward the floor. For the first time, I notice its legs. There are four of them, each one clearly robotic. This is nothing like the other Dongles.

I crouch down and look beneath its broad chassis. Two appendages dangle from the core, useless and limp.

"Are those...legs?"

Ivan crouches down beside me. The spider-arms converge in front of it, like the thin appendages can prevent us from seeing what's there... like it's embarrassed by what we'll find.

"Maybe is like male shark," Ivan suggests. "What do you call them?"

"Claspers," Loretta offers, and when she sees our surprise, she adds, "Not one of ya'll watches Shark Week? All these brains and not one of you has seen a shark dick." She shakes her head, crouches down, and takes a peek for herself. "Those aren't claspers. Those are legs."

"Legs?" I ask, looking again, but I find myself unable to see it.

"People legs," she says, and then the image resolves. Where I once saw two, strange alien appendages, I now see a pair of quasi-hairy human legs.

I stand up straight. "You understand English?"

"If I tell you anything," the Dongle says, "they'll kill me."

"You're human?"

The entire disc rises and falls in a nod.

"Can you tell me your name?"

"Shrood."

"Is horrible name," Ivan says.

Jian springs up between us, giving me a start. "Shrood?"

"You know this guy?" I ask.

Jian chuckles. "He's...a troll."

"He lives under bridge?" Ivan asks, totally serious, like trolls actually live under bridges in Mother Russia.

"Gamer troll," Jian says. "Uses cheats. Hacks. Sees through walls. Auto-aim. Flying cars. He tricks legits into playing with him. Gets them banned. Has millions of followers."

"Including you?" I guess.

"Mmm hmm!"

"And this is the guy we need to get information from...great."

"I told you," Shrood says. "I can't say anything."

The armor opens like a clam shell, revealing the pale man inside, locked in a network of black sinews, cables, and mechanical bits. "The only way out of this hell is to do what they say. They don't want to kill us all, you know. Just use us for entertainment. For sport. It could be worse."

"I do not think so," Ivan says, looking down at Shrood.

The young man follows Ivan's eyes down, but can't move his head. Can't see the true state of his body. "Aww, geez, am I naked?"

I give Ivan a little nudge.

"Is bright pink spandex," Ivan says. "Very feminine. Not manly. So embarrassing..."

I'm not sure if Shrood is buying it, so I decide to redirect his train of thought. "How did you get here?"

"They took me a few months ago. Thought I was someone else, because of my name, and my padded stats. At first, I was like, hell yeah, but then I was like, oh shit. I mean, have you seen them? Gross. I think they were going to kill me after I taught them what I knew, but they said that I was more like them than any other person on Earth. They gave me a chance to prove myself. And you know, I don't want to die. Who does? So I did what they asked, and now I'm here, working a job. Pulling my nine-to-five."

"Helping aliens take over the Earth," Chieng mumbles, as she studies the controls. "You gonna tell us how to work this thing or not?"

"Just...go back the way you came, or let me send you back. This thing can play out, and win or lose, we all get to live to see another day, or fight, or whatever you people do. Who are you, anyway?"

"Space Force," I say.

He busts up laughing. "Seriously? Of all the people who could have taken the challenge, it was Space Force? No wonder they're mopping the floor with the people down there."

I raise my rifle toward his face. "How many are left? How many people?"

"Whoa!" he says, honestly frightened. I can see why he's been aiding the Dongles. He's as spineless as, well, himself. "Six. Just six."

"Do you know who?" I ask.

He shakes his head. "They're just numbers, man. Look for yourself." The spider arms point to a display screen built into the console. I see six human silhouettes among a mass of faded figures. On another screen is the Dongle count, and there are many more dark figures than light.

We're losing...

"It's just a matter of time now," Shrood says. "Like I said, if no one knows you're here, we can pretend like none of this ever—"

"Oh, they're gonna know we were here, hon," Loretta quips.

Shrood's eyes widen. "What did you do?"

"Those two dudes in the shower," she says, but doesn't need to finish.

"You killed the Overseer *and* the high priestess?" Shrood yelps. "Oh shit... Oh *shit.*"

Well, that doesn't sound good.

"Dude, they're going to kill everyone now." He becomes despondent. "I'm never getting out of here now..."

"You never were," Ivan says, staring down at the man's disassembled body. Shrood's limbs have been removed, but they're still attached to his brain via a network of cables. His torso is missing, but everything that had been in it is now laid bare, encased in a layer of black goo, all of it still functioning and connected to his decapitated head, which is locked in place, incapable of moving.

Before I can stop him, Ivan reaches forward, grasps the wad of cables running up into Shrood's head, and yanks them out. The young man's life comes to a sudden and abrupt end. As blood flows from the cables, the armored body flops to the floor, closing the clam shell and hiding the Dongles' depravity from us.

"Better to die than live as slave to creatures who would do this," Ivan says in his defense, before anyone can complain.

"Fuckin A," Loretta says.

"Fuckin A," I agree, patting the big Russian's shoulder. I turn to Quaid, "Please tell me you've got it figured out."

"Maybe," he says. "Sort of."

"You're not instilling me with confidence."

"The only way to know for sure is trial and error," he says, and he waits for me to nod before pushing a button and turning a knob.

42

STONE

"That was melodramatic," I say.

"And weird," Taylor adds.

"No, no, no." Billy hangs his head. "Pick up where you left off."

"Where I left off?" I look at the others to make sure I'm not the only person baffled by what he's saying. I'm relieved when even Gerty looks perplexed. "You interrupted me mid-thought."

"And now?" he asks, expectant. "You were going to say something inspiring, right? Something cool to get us motivated."

"Dust in the wind, man," I say.

"The Kansas song?" Jones asks.

"No," I shake my head, and I feel the urge to pinch my nose the way Hale would in this situation. "It's just gone. I don't remember what I was going to say. Let's just go get this asshole—" I motion to the screen. "—and kill the rest of these alien—"

A tingling covers my body, like my nerves are suddenly on fire.

"Anyone else feel that?" Taylor asks.

"I don't feel anything," Gerty says, "but I am detecting a shift in the room's electromagnetic field."

"This is what it feels like before a lightning strike," Taylor says. "I read about it in—"

Every atom in my body comes apart. For a moment, my experience of the world is spectral. Light. White and then orange. I have a strong sense of movement, and then I'm back, solid once more, but weightless.

I can see, but nothing makes sense. I'm inside an orange sphere, floating in zero-gravity.

In space.

Loose contents of Billy's lab surround me, along with Taylor, Jones, and Billy, who all seem just as disoriented as me. Gerty points in a direction that has no meaning, no up or down, left or right, and says. "Down there."

I turn to look and see a long tube leading toward a dark room with a long curved console. Standing behind it are Hale, Quaid, Chieng, and three people I don't know. Wait. No. Is that the bus driver?

I open my mouth to shout Hale's name, desperate to be heard. But then the bus driver yanks down on a lever, and I'm undone again.

"Hale!" I shout upon arriving in Billy's lab once more.

"What the hell was that?" Taylor asks.

Before anyone can ask, we're whisked back into space.

I take a deep breath to shout again. It's like taking a lungful of Godzilla's fart after the giant creature ate a Tokyo fish market.

I arrive back in the lab just in time to cough out the foul air. Lungs expelled, I take another deep breath without realizing I'm once again in space. The flavor of soiled Godzilla taint fills my mouth once more.

When I arrive back on Earth, I hold my breath, and I'm glad I did. Our trip to space and back repeats two more times. After ten seconds of sitting still I let out my breath and suck in fresh air.

While the humans among us catch their breath and try to comprehend what we've just experienced, Gerty demonstrates why Gates, Hawking, and Musk are right about AIs taking over the planet. "Hale, Quaid, and Chieng have taken command of the alien spacecraft controlling the force field. They're being aided by Wang Jianguo, a Chinese hacker, and Ivan Petrovitch, a member of Russia's Spetsgruppa Alfa."

That perks me up. "Alpha Squad. What the hell are they doing here?"

"Who is Alpha Squad?" Billy asks.

"U.S. Special Forces are more than a match for Alpha Squad—we have better training and better tech—*but*...they're the boogie men of Spec Ops worldwide."

"They don't just kill you," Taylor adds. "They string you up. Or send your body parts to loved ones. Maybe eat you."

"Old wives tales created by Russian propaganda," Jones grumbles. "What they lack in tech, they make up for by being experts at manipulating emotions...especially when it comes to Americans." She turns to Gerty. "Who was the other one, the woman in control of our roller coaster ride?"

"Loretta Sinclair," Gerty says. "A civilian bus driver."

"A *what?*" Jones scoffs.

"She was driving the bus when the force field came down," I explain. "She must have stayed on with Hale."

"Umm," Billy says, and he motions to the security feed. A Chote armed with some kind of weapon, is stalking through the foyer where we'd seen McNasty's reflection.

"Damnit," I mumble to myself. "Got any weapons?"

Billy takes us to a weapons locker and opens it up. "All of this is experimental and mostly untested."

I look at the array of rifles, none of them familiar. "So you're saying they could shoot a target, or blow up in our faces?"

"Among other things," Billy says.

"Are they loaded?"

When Billy nods, I snatch a rifle from the mix. It's light, yet solid, and deadly looking. Taylor and Jones arm up, but Gerty stands clear.

"Nothing for you?" I ask.

"Baby," she says with a grin. "I *am* the weapon."

"That's not at all Terminator-ish," Taylor jabs.

"I was going for John McClane or Chuck Norris," she says.

Taylor raises a skeptical eyebrow. "Say it with an Austrian accent."

"I am the weapon," Gerty repeats with a spot-on Schwarzenegger. "Okay, I hear it...but still..." She flexes and kisses her biceps. "I got all the guns I need."

Taylor grins. "Better. Trace of humor. I like it."

"Enough dilly-dallying," Jones says, heading for the exit with a rather large pistol-thing in her hand. "McNasty needs us."

She stops by the door, looking back at our stunned expressions. "I know what I called him, and if any of you want to have kids—robot lady excluded—"

"Ouch," Gerty says.

"—you won't repeat it to anyone. But between us, he's a prick. Now, let's go save his life and kill these sons-a-bitches." She raps the door with her knuckles, steps aside, and lets Gerty open it for her.

Taylor and I make a smooth exfil, experimental weapons poised to fire.

After rounding the slumped-over bodies of the Chote that Gerty head-crushed, he sweeps right while I move left. Gerty steps out behind us and moves into the space with the confidence of a T1000. But there is no one to fight. The Chote here are dead.

My lips curl upon seeing the creature I killed, its head melted into slag, warping as it oozes into a hole carved by the acid. "Eww."

"I'll take point," Gerty says, before I can take the lead. While I don't mind that the killer robot is putting herself at risk, I'm not a fan of having my command usurped. Then again, Jones is in charge here, and she's not complaining, either.

"Make like Toucan Sam," I say.

"Who?"

"You can identify a random bus driver from memory, but you don't know who Toucan Sam is?" I ask.

"Was he a famous general?" she asks, moving through the corridors at a risky clip. "A brave warrior?"

We're moving faster than I'm comfortable with under the circumstances. Not knowing where the enemy is provides strategic uncertainties. Taylor and I would stop every so often to listen, observe, and plot our next moves, but she's probably taking everything into account as she pushes through. At least, I hope she is. "A breakfast cereal mascot. A toucan. Like the bird."

Silence.

"He can smell Fruit Loops. He follows his nose. It leads him in the right direction."

She kicks down a door and charges into the hall on the other side. "Like a dowsing rod?"

"What?" I say. "No. Like he can smell it."

"Toucans are not known for their sense of smell," she says. "The cereal is suggesting that the size of a beak determines the olfactory sensitivity of the species?"

A roar spins us to the left.

A lone Chote charges, wielding a long sword. It swings the blade toward Gerty's waist. It looks sharp enough, and the Chote seems strong enough, to cleave Gerty in two. But it never gets the chance. She steps inside the swing, and catches the alien's wrist. With a twist and a crack, the Chote is disarmed. As it howls in pain, Gerty grasps its domed face with her free hand and turns it counter-clockwise. Her arm spins in a series of revolutions that teaches the Chote what it's like to experience a crocodilian death roll, though I don't think it felt anything after the first crack.

The Chote falls to the floor, dead, and without missing a beat, Gerty continues, "I mean, that's false advertising. What if I go buy a toucan thinking it will be able to lead me to fruit?"

"She has a point," Taylor says, as we step past the body.

Gerty holds up a hand, silencing us and stopping us in our tracks. "We're close."

"None of this looks right," I say. The Ops building is a maze, but each floor and department has its own unique look. This isn't what I saw in the security feed.

Gerty ignores me. She drops to her hands and knees and places an ear to the floor.

"I don't think there are any trains coming today," Taylor says.

"He's here," she says. "I can hear him breathing."

"Where?" Jones says, stepping past Taylor and me.

"Gerty doesn't think like us," Billy says. "Where we see barriers and walls and unreachable spaces, she interprets it as open space. Imagine being in a building made of paper walls. You wouldn't feel very limited."

It only takes a moment to understand the ramifications of Billy's thought experiment. "Sooo, you're saying he's—"

"Right beneath us," Gerty says, lifting her fists and pounding them into the floor with enough force to not just punch a hole through, but to collapse a whole section. We topple down in a cloud of dust. Coughing and confused, I try to find my bearings. Orange light filtering through the windows illuminates one of many office spaces in the building. I push myself up, wave a cloud of dust away, and come face-to-face with my cringing nemesis.

"Hello..." A number of insults race through my mind. "...sir."

I can't tell if he's horrified by who's come to his rescue, or relieved. Kind of looks like he just shit his britches. Given the way we dropped through the ceiling, it's possible. Maybe even likely.

"S-Stone?" the General says. "W-what? How?"

"Long story, sir." I'm swallowing gallons of pride right now. Tastes a bit like a tincture of turd juice mixed with rancid fish oil. "Right now, we need to move."

"Ummm," Taylor says, and my body tenses. I've heard that 'ummm' before. It means he's witnessing something so sketchy that his synapses are misfiring while he attempts to suss out how best to describe it. Means whatever he says next is going to be bad news.

"That," he says.

He can't even find the words. It's worse than I thought.

I stand up, look out the window, and I'm greeted by a broad view of the parking lot and three buildings on its far side. All of them are in various states of ruin, being eaten up as the force field encroaches again, this time without warning and far faster than before. I can't see the force field behind us, but there is no doubt. It's chewing its way through Ops and will be upon us in minutes, if not seconds. "Time to go!"

43

"I think you should stop the trial and error," Chieng says, standing over a display screen. Whatever she's seeing has her concerned.

Quaid freezes, hand on a knob he'd been twisting with the frenetic energy of a teenager delivering a purple-nurple. "Uhh, why?"

Chieng steps back, pointing at the screen. I recognize the digital map as Portsmouth Island. Much of it has been enveloped by red, with a clear circle near the island's core.

"It's a display of the force field's progress," I guess.

Chieng nods, "But it shouldn't be closing yet, and probably not that fast."

I look at the circle closing in on the island, trying to imagine how fast that would be on the ground. A quick jog would probably keep you ahead of the wall...in the open. In a maze of rooms and hallways, or under fire from the enemy, that might not be possible. "What did you do?" I ask Quaid.

He shrugs and starts looking over the controls. He's messed with just about every button, knob, lever, and touchscreen interface. "I thought I put everything back the way I found it."

"I worked on an assembly line for a few years," Loretta says. "Parts work. Real mind-numbing shit. Didn't take a lot of brains to do. Drove me to depression."

"Is there a point to this sob story?" Quaid says, looking over the controls for anything he might have missed.

"The button to start the assembly line was different from the one that stopped it. Not everything is a light switch."

Quaid closes his eyes.

I can sense his internal self-flagellation. It's so obvious that he missed it, and now, after everything he's fiddled with, he has no idea how to stop it or reverse it. Not without more trial and error, which could just as easily make things worse.

"In China," Jian says, "I could hack in."

"In space, you could shut up," Quaid snaps. "This isn't a Roland Emmerich movie."

"That is what I say from the beginning," Jian says. "Alien controls might not work like human ones. Up on lever might be down. Buttons might be decoration."

"So you're saying I need to think like one of them," Quaid says.

"Or like him." I point at Shrood, dead and limp in his alien clam shell.

Quaid stands in between the two large consoles, arms out. "So if I'm a disassembled man with an alien spider body..."

An alarm sounds. It's a deep *whump* that makes my body feel funny, vibrating my ears, even through the helmet.

"I think we are discovered," Ivan says.

"You *think?*" I say, raising my rifle and stepping away from the console. The control center is framed by long, slowly arching hallways. The ring's outer wall is our floor. We should have a clear shot at anyone, or anything, coming our way.

Steam jets from the ceiling, filling the air with a mist. As it coats my facemask and I wipe it away with my hand, I realize that's not entirely accurate. It's not steam. It's dust.

"Are they trying to talcum powder us to death?" Chieng says.

"That stuff causes cancer," Loretta warns.

"Not helping," Quaid says, trying to blow the white powder away from the console, but only managing to fog the inside of his facemask.

"Wasn't the talcum powder," Chieng says. "It was the asbestos mixed in with it."

That catches everyone's attention.

"Who would do such a thing?" Ivan asks, the idea of asbestos in baby powder apparently too much for the trained killer to handle.

"I've been powdering my cooch with asbestos?" I ask.

"Nah," Chieng says. "You use Gold Bond. You're safe."

"How do you know what I use to—"

"Uhh," Jian says. "Hallo! No more talk about powder and lady parts."

"Staying dry on battlefield is important," Ivan says. "Prevents chafing. And hang nasty. And how you say...swamp ass."

"How *I* say..." Jian actually looks angry as he leans closer to Ivan and points a finger behind the big man. "...is they are coming!"

Bodies emerge through swirls of white powder. At first, it's just bits and pieces. Pumping limbs. A hulking form in the mist. And then they start to resolve.

Limbs without armor.

Flaccid, mottled flesh warbling back and forth, up and down.

Chieng starts to speak, but can't finish. "They're..."

"...naked," I finish.

Our horror is followed by Ivan's hysterical laughter, and then a serious bellow. "I will defend here," he steps around the console, weapon in hand, and then points in the other direction while looking at me. "You cover that side!"

I give him a nod and command, "The rest of you figure out how this shit works!"

I step around the console, aiming my weapon down the twenty-foot-wide, fifteen-foot-tall hallway. From this perspective, it looks like you could slide down it, but no matter where you're standing, the floor appears flat and directly beneath you.

As the mist thins out, I see shadows emerging from conjoining hallways. The alarm has roused the Dongles en masse. And they're converging on our position, buck nekkid.

But that doesn't fit what we know about them. From what we've seen, they're terrified of being seen without their armor. I mean, granted, human beings will think they're gross looking. Half the damn animals on our own planet are too ugly to even eat. Star-nosed moles. Blobfish. Frikken turkey vultures, with their acid-dipped heads. They make people squirm. And yeah, there are some people I'd rather not see in their birthday suits, but we're generally not repulsed by our entire species. And beauty is subjective. There are some pretty fugly people having babies.

But the Dongles are universally disgusted by each other...at least, by the way they look.

As the first of the approaching horde clears the cloud of dust, its head surges into view. Its mouth hangs open, tendrils of drool flowing free. The alien's teeth snap together, the mighty molars clapping. Its four eyes are bloodshot and dilated.

It's out of its mind, I think, and then I realize the dust's true purpose. Upon being roused from their alien slumber and sent after the ring's intruders, the Dongles were doused with something like cocaine. They're in a mindless frenzy, headed in the right direction, but unconcerned about their appearance—despite Ivan's continuing laughter. And they're probably immune to pain.

I'll put that to the test, I think, raising my rifle and then realizing exactly what both Ivan and I are armed with. Audio-rifles. I let out a sigh, take aim at the emerging Dongle, and then flinch back when its full form is visible.

It's like a stark-raving-mad walrus with looser skin and long limbs. With each lunge forward, its folds of skin roll back toward its bulbous backside. When it lands, everything surges forward, undulating over its neck and head. Then it lunges again, head bursting out, eyes hungry.

"What are you waiting for?" Chieng asks, looking up from behind the console. "Shoot that dick!"

Without further considering the consequences, I shift my aim toward the Dongle's head and pull the trigger. Had this been a conventional weapon, the bullet would have pierced its skull right between the eyes and dropped the wrinkly mass of alien man-meat to the floor. Instead, a pulse of sound strikes its ears—two bumps with holes on either side of its head—and wreaks havoc with the brain trying to process it.

The Dongle lets out a chortle of surprise, as its limbs go loose. It flops to the floor at full speed, sliding across the smooth surface, carried by a layer of gel-like sweat flowing from its marble-sized pores.

Seriously, there is nothing redeeming about the way these things look.

And then it gets worse. While the Dongle's mind turns to jelly, its backside unleashes a fusillade of shit, but these things don't take normal dumps. Of course not. It couldn't be a solid log. Or even a streak of diarrhea. No, the Dongles have a weird little flappy tail covering their assholes, and as the jet-powered waste spews from behind, its little tail spins like a propeller, launching a 360-degree rainbow of liquid poo against the floor, walls, and ceiling. It's like a hippo shitting, if its sphincter possessed the pressure and power of a fire hose sprayed through a turbine.

The gel coating its underside runs dry at the same time as its bowels, which is fortuitous, because its skin squeaks across the smooth floor and then catches. The creature's loose-skinned body folds over itself, rolls into a ball and comes to a slow stop before deflating. Melting coffee ice cream with marbleized fudge on summertime pavement.

"Ohh." It's a subtle venting of my revulsion. Ivan shows his by cackling like a madman. I glance back as he waves the audio-rifle back and forth, striking waves of Dongles. As a line of the aliens drops, he takes aim at those stepping over them. The result is a growing wall of flaccid, shit-covered Dongles.

My revulsion turns to humor upon imagining how any Dongles seeing this will react. Their horror would dwarf mine. Not only are their numbers being cut down by the smaller, inferior species they'd come to dominate, but they're also naked. Will any of them have the fortitude to watch the security feeds? Will any of them be able to look a human in the eyes again?

Man, I hope this is being broadcast to their entire planet, I think, and then I bark out a laugh of my own, as I face forward once more. I hold down the trigger and unleash a long wave of brain-melting soundwaves. Dongles writhe and drop, unleashing gallons of fecal spritzer and filling the hall with the sounds of flatulence, mindless screaming, and flopping flesh. It's an orchestra of repugnance, con-ducted by myself and the most sadistic alien-killer Mother Russia could have forged.

For three gloriously odious minutes, we hold off the assault, forming great walls of flesh. It gets to the point where we don't even need to fire. The Dongles wedge themselves into every part of the hallway, trying to reach us, oblivious to where they are, who can see them, and what they're crawling over. Eventually, the walls of alien bodies are so tightly packed that no more can get through.

I wish Stone could see this, I think, and then I remember that the wall closing in around him isn't made of flesh, blood, and crap.

"Please tell me you have it figured out!"

"Getting there!" Quaid says. He's working controls like he has some measure of knowledge, directing Chieng, Loretta, and Jian when to move levers or push buttons.

That's why one person couldn't work the controls. They were designed for a human, or a Dongle, in the spidery armor, reaching all the controls at once.

I glance at the force field display screen and see the red circle moving through the last few buildings, sweeping in toward the parking lot.

Run, Stone, run, I think, and then I shout, "Get there faster!"

44

STONE

I make it several steps before I realize McNasty isn't on my six. While Gerty leads the way toward the forward-facing windows, with Taylor and Jones right behind her, the General remains cowering in place.

"General," I hiss, waving at him to follow.

His eyes dart toward me, but his body is frozen in place, a perpetual look of discomfort locked on his face, like he's just done the ice-bucket challenge at the South Pole, in a stiff breeze.

I've seen the look in men's eyes before—locking up when things visit Shit Town, take a dip in the community pool, and then get flushed down the toilet that's been upper-deckered by Saddam Hussein's ghost. Seeing this in civilians is common. People aren't meant to mentally handle a gunfight, or mortar fire. War is bad news for everyone involved—even the winners. Sometimes especially the winners. But fighting men and women are trained to deal with it. At the very least, we can package that shit, lock it in the recesses of our minds, get the job done, and spend the rest of our lives unpacking it with a therapist...

Preferably one that isn't smoking hot.

But to see it in a general, a man who is supposed to represent the best of the U.S. military... I'm ashamed, and it has nothing to do with the fact that he ruined my career. I've made peace with that, mostly because I wouldn't have met Hale if McNasty wasn't an asshole. But also because I'm exactly where I need to be at the moment, because honestly, who better to fight a battle royale? As good as Delta, the SEALs, and the Rangers are, this kind of combat would have been new to them. It's why all of the MPs are dead. But a general? You'd think he'd bravely go down with the ship, not cower in a corner next to a damn photocopier.

When I crouch down in front of him, I note his pale lips, damp forehead, and quick breaths. Panic has taken root, and not even the specter of immediate life-threatening danger can overcome it.

What follows is one of the most difficult moments of my entire life. "Sir," I say. "We can't do this without you. Look, we're all fighters, but we just...we don't have your mind, sir. Sure, we can kick some ass, but we can't get the win without your...guidance."

His eyes meet mine. I'm making a little progress.

"Without your...leadership." The words feel like a coyote just sharted in my mouth... Kind of nutty, with clumps of hair, some berry seeds, and meat juice. Fuckin' nasty is what I'm trying to say. "You're a survivor. You made it this far—" By hiding... "—and we're minutes away from the win."

"Just go without me," he says.

"Can't do that, sir," I say, despite being ten seconds away from leaving his ass. "That force field is going to pass through this room in the next thirty seconds, and it's either going to kill neither of us, or both of us."

His brow furrows. That doesn't sit well with him, and I think it has more to do with dying beside me than with my words stoking any sense of duty or bravery. So I run with that angle.

"What are you doing?" he asks, when I crouch walk a few steps back.

"The force field is going to hit me first," I tell him. "Have you seen what happens when something touches it?"

His sour expression says that he has, and I doubt it was a Chote.

"The last thing you see is going to be my body bursting all over yours." An earnest chuckle bubbles from my lips, as a thought flits through my mind.

I can't... I shouldn't... Screw it. "Just like I did when your daughter—"

"You don't talk about my daughter!" His voice fills with the fury I'm used to hearing come out of his mouth, like an angry foghorn. "I will rip your scrotum away with my bare hands and feed it to you!"

There you are, I think, as the General pushes himself up, heaving with beet-red rage. I think he's got some unresolved Freudian issues regarding his daughter, but I don't bother mentioning that. I need him angry, not on the defensive.

"Now," he shouts, "stand the hell aside, and let me show you how a real man—"

Not hearing the end of that sentence, which I'm pretty sure was going to have more to do with his daughter than with our situation, is going to vex me for the rest of my days...if we survive past today. But I have no trouble forgetting it for the moment, when the top half of the General's body explodes.

I cough and spit bits of copper-flavored gore from my mouth, and wipe my eyes. The General stands above me for a moment, a reverse-bust, the top quarter of him missing. His knees give way, and then the man that used to be my superior officer drops to his knees and topples forward, his insides glooping out onto the industrial rug.

"Well," I say to myself. "That was gross." An observer would prob-ably assume that I'm unaffected by death and gore, or that I loathed McNasty so much that I'm unfazed by his death, or by the fact that I'm coated in a spritz of his insides. But none of those are true. I'm simply packing this away, filing it with my other nightmares, and saving them for a really ugly, male therapist.

Lucky him.

"Incoming!" Taylor shouts.

"Thank you," I mutter. "For the timely warning."

"It was a no-look weapon snap," he says. To most people, that's a bunch of gibberish—even to soldiers. That's game speak, and it means that the Chote who fired that round did so without looking, without ever seeing the General.

"They're using hacks," I grumble, which given our current predic-ament, isn't all that surprising. With the force field closing, they're prob-ably desperate to end the match, but I'm not sure even that will fix the problem.

Hale and her crew have taken control of the force field, though they clearly don't know what they're doing. If they did, the orange death-wall would be gone, not sweeping toward us.

I crouch run to the others. They turn to greet me and wince in unison upon seeing me.

"Oh, that's nasty," Taylor says.

"Yes, yes it is." I shake some gore from my fingers. "You have no idea."

Jones looks me over, horror chasing away the last of her alcohol's effects. "Is that..."

"What's left of him," I say. "Yeah."

"Hey." Gerty taps Taylor's shoulder and points to a fire-suppression nozzle in the ceiling.

Taylor looks at his weapon. "I don't even know what this does."

"It'll work," Billy says, but he offers nothing else. He's peeking out the window, which isn't the wisest idea, if the Chote are using auto-aim. If one of them decides to pull a trigger, he might find the top of his head missing.

A laser-like stream of fire streaks from Taylor's gun. It simultaneously sets the ceiling tiles ablaze and triggers the fire-suppression system. With half the building already missing, the pressure isn't fantastic, but gravity and the water already in the pipes do the job. I tilt my head up into the makeshift shower and let it wash away what's left of McNasty—which is actually nasty.

When the office space's back wall disappears in a burst of orange sparks, I refocus on what lies ahead. "Give me a sitrep."

"The weapon used to kill the General was energy based," Billy says.

"Meaning..."

"It has no trouble destroying flesh...

I motion to my soaking wet, and still-bloodied body. "I'm aware."

"But it can't penetrate inorganic materials."

"You *think*," I say.

"With a high degree of certainty." He adjusts his glasses. "The Chote are converging on the parking lot. There are fewer than I would have guessed. I think it's highly likely that many are being caught inside buildings and killed by the force field."

"Killed by the line," Taylor says. "There's nothing worse."

"But there is still the big one out there," Billy says.

"The Wunderchote," I say.

"Do me a favor," Jones says. "If we survive this, change the names."

"Like your name?" I ask. "So no one knows you were here?"

"The...Chote," she says, her voice dripping with disgust at the word.

"You find me a more appropriate name," I tell her, "and I'll use it. I mean, it's accurate. It's not like I called them Dongs, right? At least Chote is visually descriptive."

"If you know what it means," Taylor says.

Billy raises a hand. "I don't, but I can just google it."

"Don't google it," Taylor and I say in unison, but then I add, "Unless I can record you while you do it."

"Damnit," Billy says with uncharacteristic vehemence.

"Okay," I say, "I won't record you."

"It's not that," he says. "We're tangenting. Killing time until something dramatic happens."

"Like...?"

He points behind me. The force field has closed to within fifteen feet. What's left of the building is becoming unstable.

"You didn't forget about that, did you?" I ask him.

"Didn't you?" His eyes are massive behind his glasses.

"When hackers are, well, hacking, they still need to pull the trigger to shoot at you. Sometimes the only way to get around it is to stay hidden to the point where they assume you're FOD."

"FOD?" Jones asks. She's familiar with a lot of military terms, but this isn't one of them.

"Fled or Dead. Like now. No one in their right mind would let this insta-kill force field get so close. But we did. If we're lucky, they'll assume we're FOD and won't be looking when we make our last-second run, which should be about..." I watch the wall of orange slide closer. There's just one major support beam left in the structure, and it's about to become dust. "Now."

"Gerty," I say, "make us an exit and prep for cushion duty."

None of what I've just said is explicit instructions. I'm pretty sure both Billy and Jones have no idea what I'm asking. Taylor reveals his understanding by saying, "Seriously?" Gerty does the same by leaping toward the windows, curling up into a tight fetal position, and smashing her way through.

"We're going to jump out the window?" Jones asks. "That's the plan?"

I head for the window first, knowing that sometimes the only thing people need to overcome their fear is seeing someone else, who isn't a robot, go first. Victory number one is reaching the window without getting a ball of plasma in the face. I look down at a two-story drop and then back to the others. "Sometimes, you just have to make like George Michael."

"And die?" Billy says.

"Masturbate in a public restroom?" Jones asks.

"That happened once!" I say, and then without looking back, I fold my arms in and say, "You gotta have faith," and I trust-fall out of the window.

45

STONE

At the halfway point of my fall, I wonder if I misread the situation, if I assumed too much of Gerty. These concerns are a natural part of any trust-fall. No one plummets toward the potential for pain—or death—without second guessing their actions. I've jumped out of a plane more than fifty times, and not once did I have total confidence the parachute would open.

Because sometimes they don't. When I was a kid, around ten, I went to a summer camp. In addition to canoe races, frog catching, and pool activities—mostly trying to look at girls underwater without being noticed—they had a ropes course, which I took to like a monkey...on my own. When the counselors, with their just-out-of-college wisdom, noticed I was a bit of a loner, they determined a trust-fall was in my best interest. Eight kids lined up, four on each side, out-stretched arms zippered to catch me. All I had to do was trust them and fall. Then the unbreakable bonds of youth summer camp would be forged.

When those scrawny arms buckled under the weight of my trust, the only bond that was formed was my ass to the ground. I didn't really trust anyone with my physical well-being again until becoming a SEAL.

Gerty saved me before, I think, *she'll do it again.* When my life doesn't flash before my eyes, my doubts are erased.

When I land in Gerty's arms, she lets them flex toward the ground, bending at the knees, easing me to a stop, rather than simply catching me—which would have left me with broken bones.

"Ground floor," she says, "Destruction, terror, and mayhem."

I stand there for a moment, making an awkward expression.

"What?" she asks.

"Internal debate. If I say the next line, maybe that will be a problem for my memoir. I mean, it would have been funny, but what if we can't get the rights? What if a narrator worries about song rights so much that I need to rewrite it? I mean, maybe it will be better as a result. I don't know..."

"What are you talking about?" she asks, and she raises her hands just in time to catch Taylor and deposit him on the ground beside me.

"Ground floor," she repeats to him. "Destruction, terror, and mayhem."

Taylor's eyes light up, and I can see the lyrics building in his throat.

"Don't do it!" I say. "We don't have the rights."

"Seriously?" he complains. "You're already planning your memoir?"

I give him a wink. "You know me too well."

Gerty shoos Taylor away, and then catches Jones. "Ground floor. Destruction, terror, and mayhem."

I'm so unprepared for it, I can't stop Jones's spot-on LL Cool J impersonation. "Show me a Chote and with a knife I'll fillet him."

Just like that, without missing a beat, Jones reveals what I should have done from the start. Parody. Totes legal, no rights required. She's the frikken Weird Al of the U.S. military. Rather than point out that she came up with the solution to a legal crisis she didn't know I was having, I turn my eyes up to the window where Billy stands, wringing his hands as the force field closes in behind him.

"C'mon," Gerty shouts. "Jump!"

I scan the area while Billy works up the nerve to trust his own creation. We're hidden from the rest of the parking lot by an overturned tractor trailer meant to abscond with Space Force's gear, supplies, and who knows what else. It was meant to be a tool of our undoing, and now it's helping keep us alive.

For the moment.

In a few seconds, Billy's going to explode. A minute later, this truck, and our cover, will be gone, too.

"I can't," Billy says. "I'm afraid of heights."

"Pretty sure you're more afraid of being destroyed at a molecular level," Gerty counters. I'm tempted to chime in, but I'm guessing it's Gerty who really knows him best. "You know what? Just take a step to the left."

He slides a foot over, then the rest of his body. "Like this?"

"Perfect," she says, and then she whispers to those of us on the ground. "You might want to take a few steps back."

"I don't understand," Billy says. "What is that going to—"

What little is left of the building loses its structural integrity. Billy shouts and tumbles forward, as he and several floors above him topple. Gerty holds her ground while the rest of us dive to the side.

When the dust clears, Gerty stands in the window's empty frame, Billy held in her arms, a knight rescuing her pudgy damsel. She puts him down on shaky legs and steps away.

"We need to work our way to center circle," I say, peeking out around the truck. We're faced with a maze of vehicles, in which multiple Chote could lurk. The Wunderchote is stomping around on the lot's far side, making a mess of things, and making a racket as it flips and crushes everything it encounters. "And we need to kill everything we encounter along the way. If the circle is broken—"

"It's definitely broken," Taylor says.

"Then we need to outlive the enemy and hope that getting the chicken dinner ends the match and stops the circle."

"Uhh," Taylor says. "The circle never stops. Even after wins."

"But it doesn't hurt," I point out.

"It seems unlikely that the force field's deadly effect would cease simply because the game was over." Billy has regained some of his composure, but he's still shaking, probably because he's clothed in a metaphorical wet blanket. "While all this might be based on a style of video game, there are some obvious real-world differences."

"I'm sorry," Jones says. "What does a chicken dinner have to do with anything?"

"Winner, winner, chicken dinner," I say. "It's a game thing. Another way of saying you won."

"You get chicken dinners for winning those games you play? Is it like a coupon? Is it delivered?"

Billy is right, these tangents are going to get us killed. "It's not a real chicken dinner. It's all pretend."

"Sounds like a rip-off," she says, and when she notes my annoyance she says, "Coming down from a buzz gives me the munchies."

Not exactly an apology, but I'll take it, mostly because we need to move. Now. "Stay low, stay quiet, and stay tight on my six."

Taylor gives me a nod, and that's all I need to see. If he's with me, we're good to go. The rest of them can languish on their own if they want, but StoneCastle and PlayerWe2 are going for the win. Because this time, the chicken dinner isn't pretend, it's getting to live, and getting to see Hale again.

I weave my way between vehicles, some of them parked in lined spaces, but most of them a haphazard mash. Some of them were parked where the McNasty invasion squad left them, others have been flipped over, crushed, or torn apart by the Chote.

I flinch when something on the lot's far side explodes, the shock-wave slapping the air from my lungs. I don't know if it was a gas tank, or an alien weapon, but it doesn't matter. The path ahead leads to the potential for death, while the wall of orange keeping pace with us guarantees it.

"Ten o'clock!" Taylor says, already raising his weapon. Instead of twisting to fire at his target, I hit the deck, allowing him to aim without fear of striking me. There are few things worse than a teammate who wanders into your zone of fire. Friendly fire incidents are horrible, in-game and in real life, but odds are, most guys with friendly-fire rounds in their butt got them from stepping in front of a teammate already engaging the enemy.

A stream of fire-like laser hits a charging Chote in the face. The flames flare out as they hit the metal dome, not nearly hot enough to melt through. But it doesn't need to. When Taylor releases the trigger, the Chote is no longer attacking. It's hopping around, scratching at a red-hot helmet. It whacks a control panel on its arm and the helmet launches off, like an ejection seat from a fighter jet.

The Chote's bulbous fleshy head bulges out of the hole, following the path of least resistance. It looks like one of those balloon-eyed gold-fish, but with four eyes. For a moment, I feel bad for the thing, its head steaming. And then Jones puts a single handgun bullet in it, piercing an eye with a slick pop, and then its head.

A second Chote launches into the air above it, some kind of oversized, manga-like axe wielded in its hands. My instinct is to shoot the thing, but dead or alive, its momentum will carry that axe right into me and Taylor. My feet scrape against pavement as Taylor dives away.

The axe swings downward.

And then it happens.

Finally.

Though it plays out a little differently this time, more like a psychotic break than my previous life-flashing events. I'm seated in the primary color set of *Romper Room*. It's an old TV show for kids. Google it. Miss Jean is sitting next to me on a faux tree. She smiles past her short, feathered hair, and says, "Well, I had a good day today, friend. How about you?"

"Yeah!" I say.

"Oh, nice. Who doesn't have a good day killing aliens, right?" She laughs and smiles. "Hey, you know what I'd like to do now? I'd like to see your friends in my magic mirror!" She holds a big smiley face up in front of her. It swirls and goes clear, so I can just see her face. I want to tell her that it's not a mirror at all, but then she says, "I see Hamper. I see Sunny. Let's see, who else do I see? Oh! There's Pugsly! I think that's it... No... Wait! I see—"

Clang!

The axe is struck from the side and knocked off course. The blade bites into the pavement beside me.

A stream of fire slicing through the air keeps me down, striking the Chote's waist, as Gerty wrenches the axe from its hands. While the alien does a dance, trying to free itself from the now scorching armor, Gerty tears the axe from the ground, hefts it up, and swings the blade.

I'm not sure what kind of metal the axe was forged from, or to what sharpness it was sharpened, but it slices through the Chote's armor like just about anything through Jell-O. Though it's more like one of those Jell-O salad things, with the cottage cheese bits and pineapple chunks—but red...and not fully cooked. It makes a mess, is what I'm trying to say. Volcanic gore. Bloody Diet Coke and Mentos.

"Hey!" I shout. "This is my climax, damnit. Let me kill something!"

"Down!" Gerty shouts, throwing herself on top of me, just before a car soars past. Killing the pair of Chote exposed our position. "You want to kill something?" She points to Space Force's official propaganda machine, a Tesla Roadster, donated by Elon Musk and emblazoned with the Space Force logo. We used it when making public appearances at schools, which we did only once because of an incident that might have involved me trash-talking a ten-year-old who claimed to have killed me in-game. "Get behind the wheel and show me if you can drive that thing IRL like you do in-game."

I smile up at her, and when she leaps to her feet, I charge for the vehicle. The biometric lock pops open when I grip the door's handle. I take a deep breath of new-car smell, admire the clean interior, and then push the button to start it up. When I hear nothing, I push the button again. Still no roar of the engine. I'm about to give up when I remember that the all-electric Roadster is totally silent.

I roll down the window to ask Gerty what the plan is, but hold my tongue. She leaps into the air, giant axe in hand, and lands on the roof, compressing it over the passenger's side. There's no need to ask the plan. It's obvious. Gerty is the fearless, jousting knight...and I'm the horse.

Not exactly what I had in mind, but then I remind myself that we're not going for the glory, we're going for the win. Doesn't matter who gets the kill, and if I'm relegated to a supporting role, so be it.

"Get them to center circle," I tell Taylor. "No matter what." Then I slam down on the gas pedal...gas pedal? What's it called in a vehicle without gas? Accelerator? Whatever-the-hell it is, I shove it to the floor, squealing tires.

More vehicles fly toward us as we careen through the shrinking lots, dodging airborne cars along the way. The circle is just two hundred feet across now and closing.

A glint of movement to the right catches my eye. "One o'clock!"

"I see it!" Gerty shouts back. Of course she does. She's probably seeing a million things that I can't even begin to process. So I shut-up and focus on driving, which becomes somewhat more difficult a moment later when Gerty moves down to the hood and golf swings a Chote in half with the axe. A wave of red gore splashes over the windshield.

I put on the wipers, spraying the glass with cleaner. As it smudges clear, I see Gerty on the hood, pumping the weapon and shouting, "Whooo!" She's enjoying this about as much as I would be, if I were a super-strong robot.

"On the left!" I shout, and this time, Gerty had been too preoccupied to see it coming.

But she reacts before 'left' has finished clearing my lips. The airborne Chote splits like a coconut under pressure. I realize, in a brief moment of clarity, that I never rolled the window back up. Then I'm struck by a wave of liquid stank.

I take a moment to puke to the side, then yank the wheel toward the left, putting us on a collision course with the Wunderchote, who sees us coming. The behemoth makes his way toward us as well, but he moves a lot slower, stopping to pick up and hurl vehicles with each step. I weave back and forth, easily dodging the projectiles.

But then the Chote tires of losing, and he aims his weapons at us.

"Faster!" Gerty shouts, but I've already got the accelerator against the floor.

Then I remember that Space Force's Roadster was outfitted with a speed boost, meant to impress the youngins as we sped away. To my knowledge, it's never been used.

"Punch it!" I shout to myself, and then I push the red button marked "Bigly Speed."

My head slams into the seatback as some kind of propulsion system rockets us forward, just as the Wunderchote unleashes twin BFG blasts. The vehicle's front end lifts off the ground like a speed boat. We career into a curb and launch into the air, like Tom Brady has just thrown a perfectly spiraling Hail Mary.

Blood and guts swirl around the car's interior, and I find myself stuck in Satan's washing machine on spin cycle after a hard day of torture. In a flash of clear vision, I see Gerty leap forward off the car's hood, axe in hand.

But then I'm distracted by the twin spheres of green light racing past on either side, long beams of energy streaking out, looking for organic targets to incinerate.

While the beams strike the car, neither finds their way through the open window. Once I'm past—by the way, I've been screaming since I hit the curb—I look forward again. There's a moment of victorious fist pumping when I see Gerty slam the axe into the Wunderchote's chest, staggering it.

Then I realize I'm the 'two' in our one-two punch.

I try to go limp before impact, but since that's impossible to do, I really just clench my ass and keep on screaming. Then the Roadster slams into the Wunderchote head on. I feel the impact, hear the crunch of things, and then for a moment, darkness.

I awake to the sound of my name. "Stone!"

"Gerty?" I'm surrounded by fluffy white, and I wonder if my prayer back at the church actually got me in good with the Big Guy. But these aren't clouds. They're air bags. And they're everywhere.

I hear the door wrenched open beside me. Then a hand reaches through the white balloons, unbuckles my seat belt, and clamps on to my waist. I'm yanked from the car and tossed aside.

"Hey!" I complain, but I quickly shut the hell up, when I see Gerty dive away from the encroaching force field a moment before the Roadster is swallowed up with the rest of the Wunderchote.

"You good?" she asks.

I push myself up, take a step, and wince. My ankle is definitely not broken, but it's going to slow me down. Still, I should—

Gerty makes up my mind for me, stepping in front of me, crouching down, and then hoisting me onto her back.

I'm embarrassed for a moment, but then I remember I'm riding piggyback on a frikken Terminator!

"Ride, Destiny!" I shout, and I point toward center circle, where the others await with no danger in sight.

We charge toward them, leaping all obstacles. It's fun for a few steps, but then I remember why grown men don't get piggyback rides, especially when their crotches are being slammed into the backs of machine-women. There is nothing forgiving about a titanium spine.

We converge at center circle, wary for danger, but none comes.

"We did it," Taylor says. "The Chote are dead. We won!"

We all watch the force field vaporize an eighteen-wheeler like it was cotton candy in water. "C'mon, Hale..."

We start to huddle up as the force field shrinks around us. My instinct is to form a barrier with the vehicles, but nothing will stop it. Peering through the orange wall, I can see only the ocean on the other side. Portsmouth Island is gone, along with all of Space Force. The five of us, on a ten-foot-wide parcel of land, are all that remains.

I notice that the others are huddling closer together, but separate from me.

"What?" I ask. "Do I smell bad?"

"Dude," Taylor says and motions to my body.

"Oh," I say, looking down. I am head-to-toe, covered in dripping red, chunks of whatnot sliding to the ground. "Gross."

But they soon have to get over their revulsion, as the circle draws nearer. We work ourselves into a tight group hug.

"Gerty," I say. "You get in the middle."

"What?" Billy says, a little surprised.

"You want to save me?" Gerty asks, equally surprised.

"You're no less or more deserving than the rest of us," I say, being honest. In my eyes, she is one of us. "But you also have a perfect memory of much of what happened here. If that survives, we all do, in a way."

She nods after just a moment of internal debate, and we wrap around her.

"Plus," she says, "I won't be emotionally scarred when you all explode on me."

I can't help but laugh until I feel a searing heat strike my ass. "My buns! My buns!"

46

HALE

The worst part about the small circle displayed on the screen is that I don't know who or what's inside it. It could be Stone, or it could be a Dongle. Hell, it could be nothing. Putting the force field into accidental overdrive might have killed everyone on the ground.

Will I be able to live with myself if we were ultimately responsible for Stone's death? If he is dead, I'll never know for sure, but I can't imagine a future where I don't blame myself.

I cringe as the circle shrinks even further. In ten seconds there won't be room for a single person.

"Quaid..." I warn.

"Almost!" he shouts, and then he points to a knob in front of Chieng. "Clockwise! All the way!"

"Incoming!" Ivan shouts, pointing to the Ring's core. There's a pulse of light, and then twelve heavily armored Chote with dark red gear. Something about them says 'elite,' and I suspect we're about to get our asses kicked.

"Uh-uh," Loretta says. "I don't think so." She taps a few buttons and yanks the teleportation systems lever, and the alien spec ops team disappears.

"Did you send them back?" I ask, wondering if they'll just reappear again.

She shakes her head and points toward Earth.

"What? Why?"

She motions to the screen and the still shrinking circle. "All of them are bigger than the force field, and—"

"Wait, you know how to use that?"

"Got it!" Quaid says with a finish button mash. Then he looks at the still shrinking circle. "Don't got it!"

I grip Loretta's arm. "You know how to use it?"

"It ain't rocket science. I mean, maybe it is, but the controls are simple. I've played Farm Simulator."

"Do it!" I say, "Bring them up!"

"Bring who up?" She yanks her arm out of my tightening grip. "We don't know what's left in that circle."

"We know it's *not them*," I say. "Like you said, they're too big."

I see she's about to argue, but her face softens when she sees tears in my eyes.

Without another word, she works the controls and pulls the lever back. I turn my head up to watch the flash of light. An explosion of gore billows out from the center. Body parts and armor tumble through the zero gravity along with globules of blood. It's impossible to see through, but then I hear a voice.

"My buns! My buns!"

"Stone?" I shout.

Silence follows.

"Hale?"

"I can't see you," I call out.

"It's in my eyes," Taylor shouts. "Who exploded a dozen aliens into my open eyes? It's sooo gross."

Loretta takes a step back from the controls.

"Gerty," Stone says. "A little help?"

A moment later, Stone bursts through the field of coagulation, like he's Superman flying through an asteroid field. He seems oblivious to the explosions of gore as he passes through them, but that might have something to do with him already being covered in alien insides.

"I hate to be the bearer of bad news," Quaid says, "but the moment he clears the ring's inner wall, gravity is going to take hold. He's gonna pancake on the floor."

"Did you say pancake?" Stone says, waving his arms like he'll be able to slow himself down. All he manages to do is start spinning.

"Turn off the gravity," I order.

"I don't know how to do that," Quaid complains.

"Stop the ring!" I shout, positioning myself under Stone like I'll actually be able to catch him. I might break his fall a bit, but then we'll both have broken bones.

"I think I got it!" Chieng says, working a series of controls. A moment later the ring comes to a stop, but Stone's momentum continues, not just toward us now, but toward the tunnel's wall.

He collides with the wall, tumbling over and over. But the pain of impact isn't what he complains about. As he thumps down the wall, he shouts, "Why...does it—ugh—smell like—oof—a baby's ass...in here?"

"It *is* talcum powder," Loretta says.

I line myself up beneath Stone and then shove off the floor, rising to meet him. It's not going to be a pleasant reunification, but colliding with me in zero gravity will be more forgiving than hitting the floor. It will also arrest his forward momentum.

With his next revolution, he sees me incoming.

He reaches out with each pass and says, "This...was...a...bad...idea. You're-gonna-get-hurt."

I brace for impact, which turns out to be what I've pictured getting tackled by a linebacker is like. It knocks the wind out of me, but compared to what I've endured tonight, it's a gentle embrace.

And then it actually is.

Stone's arms wrap around me, squeezing me with a surprising amount of affection. "I want to kiss you," he says, staggering me with his forwardness. He sees my stunned expression. "I had an existential crisis today."

"In addition to an alien invasion."

He nods. "But worse."

"How could it be worse?"

"I almost died," he says. "Like four times."

"And that's not the bad part?"

"I mean, yeah, that was bad, but discovering my life has been loveless save for a goldfish, a hamster, and a pug kind of shines a light on the fact that my life has been kind of a waste."

"You fight for your country. You save people. You fought for the entire world today."

"But in the end, when my life was coming to a close, none of that flashed before my eyes, and I didn't care whether it did or not. I didn't see family, or friends, or anything like that, just the three things I've loved, and been loved by, unconditionally in my life."

"Three pets," I say.

"I want you to be my fourth."

"Pet?"

"Face. I want to see you, when my life flashes before my eyes. I want to love you and be loved by you."

I don't know what to say. There is usually a comfort zone of sarcasm between Stone and me, allowing us to mask our feelings. That started to come down at the beginning of the night, but now...it's gone.

"What I'm saying is..."

"Wait," I say, unlocking my facemask and snapping it up. "There." I say, and then I take a breath. The scent of the Dongle's naturally poo-scented sulfuric air, mixed with the rank odor of actual alien shit...and blood...and whatever else is leaking out of their putrefying bodies, laser beams into and overwhelms my olfactory nerves.

"Are you sure?" he asks, adding to the stank by pointing out the red cottage cheese remains clinging to his face. "I mean, I'm kind of a petri dish for extra-terrestrial Hep C."

I snap the mask back down, take a deep breath of fresh air, and say, "Keep going."

He smiles, and I can't help but smile back, and not just out of some kind of romantic-comedy moment where the leads finally get together and live-happily-ever-bite-my-crank, but because of the absolute ridiculousness of our situation. Love professed, in orbit, in the wake of an alien invasion, surrounded by the dead, and our friends.

This is fucking Space Force.

Always has been.

I mean, people will probably expect our story to be saturated in political satire, and there might be some—on both sides, definitely both sides—but Space Force is more than that. We're real people, with real emotions, and just because we're an easy target doesn't mean we aren't doing our best to protect the nation we serve.

"Are you inner monologuing?" Stone asks.

"Maybe..."

"Something inspirational, I hope."

"Very."

"I love you," he says.

"You too," I reply, and when he squints at me, I clarify. "Love you, too."

Then he kisses my facemask.

As I watch the red smear across my mask, I'm glad I chose to close the mask. When coagulated globules pop against his lips, I pull back. "Okay! That's good. Thank you."

He wipes his fingers across my mask, clearing away the worst of it, but leaving pink streaks behind. It's enough to reveal his mischievous smile. He knew that was gross.

"Asshole," I say.

"You, too," he says, and he smiles wider. "Asshole you, too. Wait, wait."

"That's not good writing," I say. "What would Mrs. Decker think?"

"I know, I know." He holds my helmet in both of his grimy hands, looks me straight in the eyes, and says, "You're an asshole too."

"Did you put a comma before 'too'"?

"It's optional," he says. "Depending on what style manual you choose to follow."

"Now you're just talking dirt—oof!"

"Auntie!" Jian shouts as Stone and I collide with him and knock him to the floor, which is no longer really a floor. Without gravity there is no up and down. "Watch where you ah floating!"

"Unless you have a can of beans handy," Stone says, separating from me and drifting slightly away, "there aren't a lot of options for navigating in zero gravity."

It occurs to me that Stone has no idea who my new friends are, and that he might assume that they're hostile. I motion to Jian. "Stone this is—"

"Wang Jianguo," he says, and then he turns to Ivan. "And Ivan Somethingovich. Can't remember your last name, but I know you're Alpha Squad." There's a moment of tension between the two. Then Stone asks. "You helped get them here? You fought for my lady?"

I raise a 'watch it, mister' eyebrow and say, "Your *lady?*"

"Was rocky start to relationship," Ivan says. "But Da."

"Spasiba," Stone says, and he offers his hand. Ivan looks at the gore covering Stone, thinks nothing of it, and shakes the offered hand. SEALs and Spetznaz are opposite sides of a coin, trained to fight and kill each other, but there's nothing personal about it. And since our nations aren't at war, but the planet is, the pair act more like brothers-in-arms than adversaries.

"Loretta," Stone says, offering her a salute that sends a spritz of blood floating away. "Quaid. Chieng. Good to see you all again."

"Incoming," Taylor shouts. We pull ourselves out of the way as a short black woman holding Colonel Jones, Billy, and Taylor lands on the floor and gently deposits them after an effortless landing.

When Stone sees me eyeing the petite woman holding Billy in her arms like he's a nursing baby, he says, "Remember Billy's tall, blonde lady-friend from the bus?"

"Yeah..."

"I'm Gerty," the woman says, shaking my hand without waiting for me to accept the offer. "I'm a robot."

"But not Terminatory," Taylor says. "She's one of us."

"Glad to hear it," I say, trying to hide the fact that I'm absorbing this information like an organic, non-bleach, all-natural, recycled sheet of paper towel. And by that, I mean: very slowly.

I turn to Jones, "Ma'am. Glad you made it."

She offers me a smile and a nod, which is more kindness than she's shown me since we've met. I nearly pass out when she adds, "Likewise. Now..." she says, looking over our ragtag group, "...near as I can tell, we're not out of the shitter yet, so someone tell me you've got a plan."

Eyes flick back and forth like a bunch of nervous students, each of us hoping someone else will raise their hand with the answer to redeem the group. I'm surprised when it's Ivan who raises a hand.

"Are you going on vacation?" Jones asks.

"That's a suitcase nuke," Billy says. "Russian made. It has a fireball radius of two hundred and sixty feet, an air-blast radius of a quarter mile, a thermal-blast radius that's a little bigger, and a lethal dose of radiation for anything within a half mile, not counting fallout."

"What pudgy, smart man says," Ivan adds. "Will destroy whatever is on other side of gate network."

Stone and his team look out at the ring's core, tracing the orange beam of light back through the spiderweb that leads out into deep space.

"You can do that?" Stone asks.

"Ya'll know I can," Loretta says.

"Then that's our play," Jones says. "If they want to fuck with Earth, we'll fuck 'em right back."

"Kind of awkward," Stone says, "but we can work with it."

"One problem." Ivan sets the suitcase nuke on the console and unsnaps the locks.

"Really?" Taylor says. "*That's it?* No biometric locks or code system?"

"*I* am lock," Ivan says. "To use nuke, you have to get past me."

"And the problem is?" Stone asks.

"Nuke is activated when button is pushed. Nuke explodes when button is released. Is dead man switch. Someone has to go with nuke. Someone has to *die* with nuke."

In response to that, everyone starts shouting out ideas. While some want to find a work-around, others offer to take the bomb in themselves, including Stone and Gerty. It's a chaotic argument leading nowhere. One of us will go, that's clear, but how do we decide who? I'm about to suggest we draw straws or some strawless equivalent, when I notice that the suitcase is missing.

"Where's the bomb?" I ask, and when no one hears me, I shout, "Where. Is. The. Nuclear. Bomb?"

Silence. Everyone looks around.

"Maybe was bumped during argument?" Ivan suggests, looking around for a free-floating doomsday suitcase.

"'*I* am lock,'" Jian says, doing a horrible Russian accent. "So stupid!"

"I don't see it," Chieng says.

"Suitcases don't just get up and walk away," Quaid adds.

"You're right," Stone says. "In zero gravity, they float." He looks up and all our heads follow.

I suck in a quick breath when I see the suitcase floating away, clutched in Loretta's hands. She's headed for the ring's core, but that alone won't... I look at the console and see a sequence of shapes—alien numbers I think—counting down.

"What's she doing?" Chieng asks.

"Making a point," I say, and Stone casts a questioning glance in my direction, no doubt wondering what kind of point could be made by blowing yourself up with a nuke. I smile up at Loretta, tears in my eyes. "That's she's one of us."

47

LORETTA

What a bunch of bozos. Arguing about who will blow themselves to bits rather than just taking action. I suppose that's what it's like when you got something, or someone, to live for.

Me? I'm alone. Husband passed away on the job fifteen years ago. Got whacked in the head by a wrecking ball. Clarence wasn't the brightest man, but really, who gets killed by a wrecking ball? Darwin predetermined that he'd die young. Or Jesus, I suppose. Hopefully Jesus. Clarence was a good man. A good husband. I'd like to think the Good Lord didn't hold playing chicken with a six-ton ball of forged steel against him. I think the worst part of his death is that he was trying to save a family of chipmunks nesting in the building's wall. Gave his life for some rodents, that one. And I'm fairly certain they met their end along with him.

My son, Luke, died five years ago, in some sandy part of the world we had no business being in. He was a pilot, like Hale, though unlike her, he flew transport helicopters for the Marines. When Space Force was announced, he was over the moon. I have no idea if there was ever a need for helicopter pilots, but he put in a transfer request...and was shot out of the sky before it was ever processed.

Hale hasn't been able to figure out why I've stuck around despite having no business being here. It's not because I'm brave, or unlucky, or just plain stupid. It's because I want to do right by my boys. Since they've been gone, my life has been a cycle of driving people around and binge-watching *The Bachelorette*. Not much there to feel good about. I figure saving the world will get me in the good graces of whatever angel reunites families in the afterlife.

I shudder inside my space suit.

I'm gonna die, I think.

268   JEREMY ROBINSON

I knew that when I plucked the nuke from under the nose of the human guard dog who was too busy arguing to notice. I knew that when I set the transport timer. I knew that when I shoved off the floor and started my flight to the ring's core.

But I didn't really think it through.

It won't feel like anything, I tell myself. I will be, and then I won't. The transition from one state to another will be instantaneous.

What if a nuclear explosion destroys souls, too? I don't know if it's possible, but I saw somewhere that the soul has mass, that when people die, they lose twenty-one grams. That means the soul is made of some kind of tangible matter. But if the nuclear explosion destroys matter...

I close my eyes and try not to think about it, but my imagination is kind of dark. I think about all those people in Japan... Men and women who happened to be on the wrong side of a war, but also weren't fighting in it. They didn't deserve to die, but what if it's worse than that? What if they were erased?

What if I'm about to do that?

Who knows what I'll find on the other side of the transporter.

Doesn't matter, I decide. The bombs that ended World War II were horrible examples of people's uncurable desire to kill each other. But they did end the war. Many more people would have died, Japanese and American, had the war continued.

That's what I have the chance to do. And I'm not just fighting for one country. I'm fighting for all of them. For all of humanity.

"Lord Jesus, please let souls be nuke-proof," I say, and then I refocus on gliding forward, which really just means doing nothing. I gave myself thirty seconds to reach the core, and twenty of that is up.

"What are you doing?" Hale's voice says in my comm. I'd switched mine off. Apparently, she knows how to turn it back on.

"What's it look like, hon?" I say. "Someone needs to do it, and it sure as shit ain't gonna be you or your fella. I remember feeling like that once. I think your man has a better head on his shoulders, and I'll be honest, he's a lot better looking than Clarence was, but I loved that man. If he was still among the living, I wouldn't want to leave him. I'm not about to let you, or Stone, do something that stupid."

"Thank you," Stone says. He seems like a sarcastic type, more funny than serious, but he sounds sincere. Almost sad.

"Could have at least tried to talk me out of it," I mumble.

Stone chuckles. "I've met people like you over the years. Soldiers willing to sacrifice everything, who put themselves in danger, who protect life at any cost. I'm only alive now because of people like you. I'm only sorry I didn't get to know you."

"Well," I say. "Hale can tell you all about me..." She doesn't really know much about me. Not many people do, but she's seen me. She knows my heart. "Just do me a favor, when this is over, and people talk about what happened, and they ask why I did it, tell them I was inspired by my son."

"What's his name?" Stone asks.

"Luke," I say. "Sergeant Luke Sinclair, U.S. Marine Corps. KIA."

There's a moment of silence, and then a very reverent, "Yes, ma'am. I'll do that."

"Hale," I say, approaching the core, almost out of time. "I like your man, hon. You best keep him."

"Not going to give him a choice," she says, and then I hear her sniff, which brings tears to my eyes. I'm being noble as hell. It's freakin' moving.

Unable to wipe the tears away, I blink hard and watch the beads of liquid float free inside my mask. Then I look forward and cringe, remembering the one aspect of my journey that made me think twice, and it's not my impending death. A wall of gore and Dongle chunks swirls inside the core. The larger alien body parts have clumped together in the middle, orbited by unrecognizable bits and pieces.

I close my eyes and remind myself that none of it will actually touch my body, and that in a minute it won't matter. I wince when I feel the liquid wash over me, and double wince when I bump into something solid.

How much time is left?

A second? Two?

This is my chance to say something inspirational. Something humanity will remember for the rest of time. In a way, even if I do erase my soul, part of me will live on forever.

Then I feel it. A tingling in my legs that moves up and through my body. "Oh shit," I shout, "It's happening! Wait, no. That's not what I meant to saaaaaaaa—"

My voice stretches out along with space and time. I was kind of hoping my journey through space would be an epic send off, like in that movie with the skinny white chick. I'd see nebulas, and planets, and space ships, and for a moment, I'd marvel at it all. It should harden my resolve, remind me that what I'm doing is preserving life and beauty, that I'm protecting the universe from penis-shaped assholes with too much time on their hands.

Instead, it's kind of like being turned into taffy, stretched out, and then squashed back together again somewhere else. There's a blurry strobe of light, and then darkness.

Gravity tugs me to my knees on the far side. It's enough to hold me down, but it doesn't feel like Earth. *That's why the Dongles are so big,* I think. Their planet has less mass. Less gravity. *Thank you, Neil DeGrasse Tyson,* I think. In addition to *The Bachelorette,* I watch anything with Neil. That man can launch a probe into my...

Focus, Loretta. You were literally just thinking about Clarence. Neil is a fine piece of ass, but he isn't here saving the universe. You are.

The lower gravity explains why they had to wear armor on Earth, in addition to being freakishly ugly to every living thing in the universe, including to each other.

I raise my head and have a look.

"Ohhh, shit." A ring of Dongle soldiers dressed in black armor surrounds me, weapons raised.

I just need to push the button, I think, but I need to open the case without being vaporized first.

Beyond the inner ring, I see hundreds more. Thousands. Maybe millions. Who the hell knows. But they're queued up and waiting for transport. I turn in a slow circle, gently working the locks, preventing them from snapping open. A series of teleporter launch pads fills the vast dome.

They're going to invade, I realize. The game has ended in disqual-ification, and now an army of Dongles is going to attack all of Earth's military bases. With them destroyed, humanity will be at the mercy of an army of dicks. And I'm not just talking about the way they look. There is nothing redeeming about these creatures.

The second lock pops open without a sound.

A vast alien city rises up in the distance. It looks like *The Little Mermaid's* phallic movie poster, but black, like obsidian, and laced with gawdy neon lights suggesting the whole place is like some extra-terrestrial red-light district.

I can't smell anything aside from my own breath, but I have no doubt the place smells like exhaust and ass.

Do it, I tell myself, slipping my hand inside the briefcase, hunting for the nuke's lone button. *Just push it, hold it, and let it go.*

"Hey, assholes," I say, staring down the barrels of more alien weapons than I can count. "Put your dick faces in this."

It's not the best catchphrase ever. Hell, it's barely okay, but who's going to be around to repeat it? I push the button, hold it for a breath, and then yank my hand away.

Nothing happens.

And the dick faces hold their fire.

"Oh, damn." I've delivered myself into enemy hands, with no way to get home, with a defective bomb. *They're going to make me like Shrood,* I worry, *or torture me for information, or just make me look at them.*

"Don't sweat it," a kind voice says, as a hand rests on my shoulder. "We got your back."

Stone is standing beside me, an alien weapon in hand. He's got a confident smile on, despite there being no good reason for one. Then he pulls the trigger and a wave of aliens launch into the air like Gandalf has just blasted them away. He turns and pulls the trigger again, unflinching even as the aliens fire back, their aim thrown off as they're undone by a weapon of their own creation and a man that's all human.

The suitcase slides out of my hand. It's Hale. "Ivan's description of how to use the nuke wasn't entirely accurate. You have to push it three times..." Which she does, holding it on the third push. "And keep it pressed in for five seconds, which activates the bomb."

A light flashes green.

"You both...came to die with me?" I ask. "That's some real Romeo and Juliet shit!"

"Die?" Stone says, pulling the trigger again, and then looking into my eyes. "I don't leave men behind, or badass women...or any women...ugh, stupid PC. I don't leave anyone behind."

"'Man' would have worked," I tell him. "It's probably the least offensive part of my night."

"Right?" he says. "It's like some higher power thought, *I'm going to put every horrible thing I can think of into these people's lives and laugh while they deal.*"

"You felt that, too?" Hale asks, her hand still on the button.

I look at the green light. "So, what now?"

Alien gunfire starts chewing up the launch pad around us. Stone continues firing, the anti-gravity gun redirecting the incoming fire for the moment.

"Wait," Hale says, "and trust our friends."

Doesn't take a Space Force member to figure out they're going to try pulling us back while leaving the nuke behind. "They can do that?"

"Something about tuning the teleporter to weed out anything inorganic." Stone looks at me. "You don't have a pacemaker or anything, do y—"

I'm turned to taffy again, stretched out and then snapped back together. I have no idea if the nuke went off, but I know I'm alive, and that Hale and Stone are with me...buck naked, floating in zero gravity. They're built like demi-gods, all muscly and sleek and bulging in all the right places.

I know I'm naked, too. I can feel the breeze in my nether regions. The air smells like a fart-scented scratch-and-sniff sticker that's being frantically scraped by a mole on crack. Despite all that, I can't look away. This is the moment every Bachelorette hopes for, but in fucking space, after the world has been saved.

As their hands reach out for each other, I hold my breath, imagining what it will be like when their fingers clasp and they pull into each other's arms and lock lips.

Fingers graze and then grasp.

They float toward each other.

A blood-soaked chunk of what I think is alien ass slaps into Stone's face, its flaccid cheeks enveloping his head before bouncing away.

Stone's face is a frozen mask of old and new nastiness.

Hale's look of disgust morphs into a smile.

"You know what," she says. "I don't even care."

When she plants her lips on his blood-and-ass-covered lips, squishing little bits of alien insides between them, my stomach heaves. I turn to the side and vomit—again—into the orbiting ring of dead. The expulsion propels me, head-over-heels.

As I tumble, buck naked, through a field of body parts, breathing an atmosphere that's fifty-percent bottled swamp ass, I think about where I was this morning, and where I am now. I twist around and see the sun rising on the East Coast far below. "That was for you, Luke. Clarence... you were a good man, but I just saved the world, in space. Ain't no way I'm not meeting Neil DatAss Tyson, so if you're watching me, you might want to look away for a bit."

Citizens of Earth… Is that too dramatic? What? We're not recording this? Right now? Live? To the whole world?

⟦throat clearing⟧

Citizens of Earth… My name is Captain Ethan Stone of the— What? Oh right, *Colonel* Ethan Stone of the United States Space Force. Got promoted this morning. Still getting used to the new title. And this whole officially address- ing the masses thing is kind of new to me. Anywho…

As you probably noticed, Earth was visited by visitors from—sorry, that's no good. Those two 'visits' are nearly touching in the sentence.

⟦muffled⟧ I know it's live! If you want me to do this, I need to do it my way, capisce?

Okay, then. Earth was visited by aliens from another solar system. We don't know where they came from, but we know how they arrived—an Einstein-Rosen Bridge, which is a fancy way of saying 'a wormhole.' Kind of like Asgard's Byfrost, the Rainbow Bridge, but without the pretty colors or Idris Elba waiting for us, much to Loretta's chagrin.

If you're wondering who Loretta is, she's the brave son of a bitch who was willing to sacrifice her life to save all of yours. In the end, she didn't have to, but she would have, and you all owe her for it. I'd have her say 'Hi' but she's on a date with the guy who murdered Pluto.

I'm getting off track, which is sometimes how things get done, so cut me some slack. The Ch… The aliens dropped force-fields around all major military bases around the world and issued a challenge to the very best of us. Of all

the Earth's fighting forces, only Space Force was instantly
willing to take up the fight. What followed was a highly
coordinated, impeccably planned mission alongside counterparts from both Russia and China. Yeah, togetherness!

[muffled] What? Oh, right.

[unmuffled] You're probably wondering if we're now part
of an intergalactic war. The answer is: probably not,
because we pretty much just won an intergalactic war,
overnight, thank you very much.

[muffled] I'm not being braggadocious… I can't, because
that's not even a word… I don't care who said it… It's a
horrible butchery of the English language. I mean, try to
spell that sh— Oh! I keep forgetting.

[unmuffled - throat clearing] Coordinating with space
agencies, and special operators around the world, we're
taking control of the network of alien vessels still in
orbit. Cut off from their command, we're making short
work of them, and to our knowledge only the group who
assaulted U.S. Space Force Command ever reached the
ground. We believe their ability to travel through space
has been neutralized by the aforementioned Loretta, who
dropped a nuke on their doorstep, flipped them the bird,
and said…

[muffled] What was it she said?

[muffled and distant female voice] 'Hey assholes, put your
dick faces in this.'

[muffled] Oh, that's horrible…

[unmuffled] She said, "When Earth stands together, nothing
stands against us."

[muffled] Holy shit, did you hear that? I think that can
be our new slogan. What? They can still hear me when my
hand is over the mic?

[unmuffled] So, you get the gist, right? We were invaded by aliens. Space Force sent them packing. Who you gonna make fun of now, Trevor Noah?

We're going to continue coordinating with the world's governments, and our hope is that the future of Space Force will be an international organization. I mean, aliens invaded. That's our cue to come together and recognize that not only are we not alone in the universe, but our intergalactic neighbors are giant dicks, and I mean that both figuratively and literally. That's why we call them the Chote, and not in the weird good way, but like in the 'they're alien phalluses' kind of way.

What?

[muffled female voice]

Right. Crap. I wasn't supposed to call them the Chote. The people with big brains and political careers wanted to avoid naming them something offensive. But here's the thing, they *are* offensive. Everything about them is offensive, and when you see them for yourself, you'll agree that the Chote, with all their mottled, flaccid, bulging skin, scrotum bodies, and shaft heads are—

[transmission cut short]

INTERVIEW WITH COLONEL ETHAN STONE & COLONEL JENNIFER HALE, BY JEREMY ROBINSON

DATE CONDUCTED: 2/21/0002 A.C.

ROBINSON: That was your first and last address to the world, six months ago. Any comment on why it was cut short?

HALE: We work with a professional media liaison now. Genette Schmeling. I'm sure you've seen her on TV.

STONE: It wasn't that bad.

HALE: You cursed on air, and named the Chote, 'the Chote,' and now everyone calls them that. Those are like the only two things they told you to *not* do.

STONE: Well, good news, most people don't know what a chote is. Don't google it! Can we delete this from the interview? I mean, I'm not sure what the point would be, right? How is this going to move the story forward?

ROBINSON: The story is over. You didn't want me to end it with an epilogue, remember? This is the post-story interview. It's going after the final chapter, and it's meant to inform readers about what happened in the days after the invasion.

STONE: Well, the epilogue you wanted to write was horrible. Hale and me surfing, pondering everything that's happened, being happy-tappy in love, and then getting beamed up to Space Command for a big ooh-and-aah reveal? That just struck me as contrived, man. I mean, we made fun of you a bit.

ROBINSON: I remember.

STONE: In our defense, we didn't know you were *the* Jeremy Robinson. How was I supposed to know you weren't a hack?

HALE: Reading a book on occasion helps.

STONE: What was the last book *you* read?

HALE: Well, I read you *Fox in Socks* last night.

STONE: Hey! That's private. It helps me sleep. And I like it when the Tweetle Beetles battle on a noodle-eating poodle. What I'm trying to say is, just because we razzed you in the book we asked you to write... Okay, I can see why you'd want to get even, but we're trying to unify the world here, right? Can we get to the real questions now?

ROBINSON: Okay, you say the book is meant to unify the world, but you make several jokes poking fun at people's accents and their countries of origin, and you graphically detail the way several people die. As a result the book has been banned in Canada, in advance.

STONE: They're really not the friendliest nation anymore, are they?

ROBINSON: Next question...

STONE: Did I answer?

HALE: You said enough.

ROBINSON: Colonel Hale, I notice that both you and Stone have been promoted to the same rank. Can you describe your duties, and are you aware of any gender-biased pay gap?

HALE: Since our joint promotion, we've been in charge of operations both on the ground and in orbit. I've been overseeing the Rex fleet and the training of pilots from partnering nations. Stone has been hard at work forming the Space Corps. If the Dongles—sorry, if 'the Chote' come back, we'll be ready for them.

ROBINSON: Because we're reverse engineering their tech?

HALE: It's easier than anyone expected. For the most part, their tech is more advanced, probably designed by extremely intelligent members of their species, but designed to be operated, maintained, and repaired by the average Chote.

ROBINSON: And how smart is the average Chote?

HALE (after sighing and rolling her eyes at Stone): Comparable to the average human being. The captured Chote that Billy and Gerty are studying have an average IQ of ninety. They can get by, but they're not changing the universe for a better place. I think it's important to note that, in some ways, they represent who we might become.

ROBINSON: What do you mean by that?

HALE: They're a gaming culture. They have a hunger for destruction and they lack concern for the lives of others, as long as they are entertained. In a way, that's who we've always been. How long will it be before the novelty of virtual killing wears off and we go back to actually killing people for entertainment?

STONE: Whoa, whoa, whoa. There hasn't been a single study showing that video games make people more violent.

HALE: That's not what I'm saying. Kind of the opposite. Is gaming violent? Absolutely. But it doesn't create violence. If anything, it gives people an outlet for their violent tendencies. As horrible as the world can be, it's far less horrible, and globally brutal, than it used to be. The question I'm asking is, 'when will virtual not be enough?' And if that happens, and we go back to killing for sport, with the Chote's technology? Will we be any different?

STONE: So much for keeping this light. Geez.

ROBINSON: Whose idea was it to keep this joint biography light?

STONE: Both of us... Mostly me. I mean, with all the horrible details revealed in the book, it felt wrong to focus solely on the doom and gloom. I mean, if people want that, they can read your book, *Infinite*, right?

ROBINSON: Touché.

STONE: So we wanted to do something a little different, while not really toning down the details.

ROBINSON: I think some of the gory descriptions could have been toned down. Probably some of the language, too. I'm going to get e-mails about this book. Probably a few bad reviews for the language alone.

STONE: Anyone who doesn't like this book is a Chote.

ROBINSON: To be clear, that is the opinion of Colonel Stone and not this author.

STONE: Speaking of opinions. Wouldn't it be awesome if we did a post-credit scene? Like at the end of Marvel movies?

ROBINSON: Novels don't have credits...but I suppose something could go after the Author's Note section.

STONE: Cool. Yeah, let's do that.

ROBINSON: Right... Now, how is Taylor faring these days?

STONE: He's running the cadets through the wringer, making sure they're ready for anything. Also, he's totes hooking up with Jones.

ROBINSON: Who also got promoted.

HALE: She's a general now. Runs the show. And probably doesn't want her private life talked about.

STONE: Have you *read* my half of the book?

ROBINSON: What about the rest? Chieng? Quaid? Jian? Ivan?

STONE: Do you think readers will care? They're kind of tertiary, right?

HALE: Quaid is helping reverse-engineer the Chote tech. Chieng is working on locating exactly where the Chote came from. Jian now works for Space Force, hacking the ring's computer systems and allowing us to take control of their functions. And Ivan... He returned to Russia. We've asked about him, but no one in the Spetsnaz has heard from him. If you're reading this, Ivan, let us know you're okay. When you're ready, there will always be a place for you in Space Force.

STONE: Well...

HALE: Stone.

STONE: Fine.

ROBINSON: What about Loretta?

STONE: Told you already, she's probably boinking Neil DeGrasse Tyson right now. Why does he have three names? I mean, I know most people do, but we don't all use them. Unless you're planning to kill a president. So why advertise it?

ROBINSON: Is she involved with Space Force, is what I mean.

HALE: Unofficially. She's not enlisted, and is frankly too old to enlist—sorry Lori—but she runs the Earth Defense Initiative, a civilian group dedicated to resisting an alien invasion. We coordinate with her group as much as possible.

ROBINSON: Well, I think that covers everything. Any parting words for your readers?

STONE: Technically they're your readers. If the book sucks, the bad reviews will have your name on them, not mine.

ROBINSON: Interesting choice of parting words.

STONE: No, wait, I wasn't—

ROBINSON: Colonel Hale? Care to send us off with some parting words, maybe something that isn't about some weird kid from your past with a funny sounding last name?

HALE: What did you just—

AUTHOR'S NOTE

That interview ended when Colonel Hale attempted a roundhouse kick and broke a lamp, rather than my head. While their story is fascinating, and mostly true (I think Stone was exaggerating at times, and I doubt his sarcastic wit was as sharp while fending off invading aliens) they were sometimes hard to work with, mostly because they're under a great deal of stress. Nevertheless, they are true heroes of the human race, and we all owe them a great debt of gratitude.

The BEST way you can show them your thanks, for all they have done, and for their willingness to tell their stories from an intimate first-person perspective, is to post reviews at Amazon, Goodreads, and Audible. Every single one helps, and I'm sure the fighting men and women of Space Force would appreciate your support. For real. I know the book is over now, and I'm still in character here, but this is serious. Post reviews and maybe they'll agree to come back for a sequel story. Space Force 2: Is It Cold In Here?, or something.

If you want to check out some of my other novels, or sign up for my newsletter and never miss a new release, you should visit my website at: www.bewareofmonsters.com.

Thanks for reading!

—Jeremy Robinson

SURPRISE POST-CREDITS EPILOGUE!

IVAN

The darkness smells of bear piss and vodka. Some say it is the lifeblood of my homeland. I say it is water which is life blood, because people are eighty percent water. Not vodka, or piss of bear.

My feet squelch through puddles.

Is funny word: squelch.

It makes me laugh.

Why am I good humored? Because today is day I unravel secrets of universe. Today is day I do what no one else on planet can do: make Chote talk. Okay, when my father would drink, he would have entire conversation with penis, but his penis was not alien, so is different.

I descend into bowels of Earth, weapon tucked under my arm. Is a simple thing. Frail even, but nothing else will be needed.

My path is lit by green glow of night-vision goggles. I move deeper through stone tunnel, closing hand-made doors behind me. Though I am in remote region of Siberia, I take no chances. No one must hear what comes next.

I stop before prisoner, chained to stone wall, where I have kept her since hunting her down. Chote made her to look like woman, who infiltrated not only human society, but upper echelons of United States government.

"Will you tell me?" I ask, voice full of grim threat. "How many more of you are there?"

"How many do you want? I can get one of us for everyone on Earth. You get an alien. You get an alien! Then we can all celebrate life together, find the passion that comes from following our true purpose."

"My true purpose is to kill your kind," I say, holding six-foot-long, reflective weapon of psychological warfare up in dark. I remove goggles and switch on brilliant torch that lights up tunnel and reveals Earth's greatest adversary. But upon seeing my weapon, she has nothing to say, for once.

"Look," I tell her, shaking full-body-length mirror. "Look at self. See who you are. What you look like!"

Wail that pierces air is far more tortured than any I have heard before, and far less human. "Now..." I say, switching off light. "What is *your* true purpose?"

There is moment of silence, and then crafty smile. "The same as those who came before me...distraction."

"From what?"

She resists until I turn on light again. A moment of horror loosens her tongue. "You're all so busy looking at screens or fake news, or looking for your inner selves, that you never *really* look up...or down."

ACKNOWLEDGMENTS

I must first and foremost thank the brave men and women of Space Force, for facing dangers unlike anything ever encountered or dreamed of by humanity before. Their resistance is all that stood between our being dominated and our continued freedom. While they might have their rough edges (Who wouldn't after years of mockery?) we would not be here today without their sacrifice.

Thanks also to Kane Gilmour, for supreme editing, and to Jennifer Antle, Liz Askew, Heather Beth, Roger Brodeur, Julie Carter, Elizabeth Cooper, Dee Haddrill, Sharon Ruffy, and Jeff Sexton, for proofreading and making me look like I know how to spell.

ABOUT THE AUTHOR

Jeremy Robinson is the international bestselling author of sixty novels and novellas, including *Infinite, The Others, The Distance, Apocalypse Machine, Island 731,* and *SecondWorld,* as well as the Jack Sigler thriller series and *Project Nemesis,* the highest selling, original (non-licensed) kaiju novel of all time. He's known for mixing elements of science, history and mythology, which has earned him the #1 spot in Science Fiction and Action-Adventure, and secured him as the top creature feature author. Many of his novels have been adapted into comic books, optioned for film and TV, and translated into thirteen languages. He lives in New Hampshire with his wife and three children.

Visit him at www.bewareofmonsters.com.